A
Model
Summer

A Model Summer

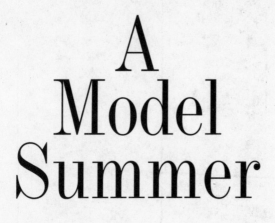

Paulina Porizkova

HYPERION

NEW YORK

Original hardcover ISBN: 978-1-4013-0326-6
Paperback ISBN: 978-1-4013-0936-7

Hyperion books are available for special promotions and premiums.
For details contact Michael Rentas, Proprietary Markets,
Hyperion, 77 West 66th Street, 12th floor, New York,
New York 10023, or call 212-456-0133.

Design by Karen Minster

FIRST PAPERBACK EDITION

10 9 8 7 6 5 4 3 2 1

For Monique Pillard,
my Momo

In youth and beauty wisdom is but rare.

—Alexander Pope

A
Model
Summer

I

June 1980.

t's not as if I'm scared to fly.

Even after the divorce, my mother usually scraped together enough money to take us on a reduced-fare vacation each year. But this trip is different. My mother, her ever-changing boyfriends, and my little sister Kristynka are still snugly ensconced in our small apartment back in Lund, while I am on my way to Paris, alone.

Well, alone except for Britta, whom I met less than an hour ago here at the airport. After introducing ourselves, we immediately sized each other up. Britta, with her long golden hair, dark eyes, and soft curves is nearly my exact physical opposite. I have straight brown hair cut in a bob, pale green eyes, and am as tall and flat-chested as the guys in my ninth-grade class. That I got selected for the high-fashion world of models not only confused my classmates, but also made me suspect I was the target of some elaborate joke. I still half expect someone to pop up from behind a hidden camera and laugh in my face, like on that American TV show.

"Flight 343, final boarding call," a female voice announces over the loudspeakers.

I look over at Britta. She is standing with her mom near the security gate, hugging tearful good-byes as I wait on the other side. My own mother had full confidence in my ability to make it to the airport by myself, though the trip entailed three buses, a ferry to Denmark, and an additional bus ride to the terminal. "If you can't get to the airport on your own," she said, "how are you going to model in Paris all by yourself?"

"WHAT WOULD YOU LADIES like to drink?" the stewardess asks with the kind of smile all flight attendants seem to spray on before starting their shifts. "We have a nice red Jacques Dubois, Beaujolais Village, and a crisp white Burgundy."

My jaw drops to the vicinity of my knees. This is the first time anyone has taken me for a grown-up. I nudge Britta. She may be my modeling competition, but right now, she is also my only potential friend. What better way to break the ice than to share in the bounty of a stewardess who has mistaken us for alcohol-worthy adults? But Britta looks as though she's fallen asleep.

"What?" she moans, and opens her eyes.

"Drinks," I tell her, wide-eyed, nodding toward the wine bottles held up for our inspection.

The stewardess, seeing my expression, retracts the bottle and her grin, and grabs a can of Coke. "A soft drink, perhaps?"

We each get a Coke, Britta completely unaware of our missed opportunity.

She sits up and rubs her eyes. "Sorry, I must have dozed off—I had a late night with Lars yesterday." She sighs. "He's worried I'm gonna forget about him or something, you know, being around all those gorgeous French male models and stuff. But I told him—'Look,' I said—'I'm sixteen and you're twenty; if we find somebody else, then it just wasn't meant to be, right?'"

I nod understandingly, as if I ever had a real boyfriend. Bengt hardly counts.

She pops her can open and pours the Coke into her plastic cup. "So, how do you pronounce your name, anyway? My mom and I couldn't figure it out from the spelling."

"*Yee-ree-na*," I tell her, mangling my actual name, Jirina, in the familiar Swedish way. The correct pronunciation, *Yee-r-shi-nah*, I hear only at home. My name has always been a sore spot for me. Why my parents cursed me to navigate a world of Anikas and Gunillas with a name that so clearly indicates an immigrant background (a communist background at that), was, and still is, incomprehensible to me. To top it off, there is also my last name: Radovanovicova. It's a mouthful even in my parents' native language.

"Wow, is that, like, Russian?" Britta says. I think I can detect a slight wrinkling of her nose, a common reaction to my "communist" roots.

"No, Czechoslovakian." Not that that's much better. "My parents are from there. But I was born in Sweden," I quickly clarify, "so I am Swedish."

Britta looks at me with raised eyebrows and I'm immediately afraid she doesn't believe me.

"You want to see my passport?" I offer.

But she just shrugs. "I believe you," she says, and takes a gulp of her drink. "So, how did you get discovered?"

Relieved, I babble on about my best friend, Hatty, to whom I owe this outing in the clouds. It was her obsession with fashion and makeup that led her to find an ad in the local paper for a modeling seminar, run by a "famed modeling scout to the most exclusive modeling agencies in the world," whose only requirement was a fee of twenty-five kronas. Hatty seized this as an opportunity to offer her services as a makeup artist to a bunch of model wannabes and convinced me to tag along to keep her company. The class was held in the living room of the famed scout, and we turned out to be her only clients.

Malin, an older woman with dyed-red hair set in waves, pale, papery skin, and arched, black, stenciled-on eyebrows, looked like a nineteen fifties glamour shot that had been crumpled into a ball and smoothed out. Her living room was a mess of photos, many of which were old modeling shots of herself. They consisted of hand and foot ads from ancient newspapers. She removed her brown sneakers to let us admire her famous feet and I noted with a touch of horror that her toenails were long, filed pointy, and the same dried-blood color as her fingernails. Malin fluttered her hands about her as she went through stacks of magazines, clicking her nails against glossy pages. "Did you know Mia is missing a finger? No, you wouldn't because of the way she has learned to hold her hands. Do you see this smile? How real and inviting it looks? That's because this girl is really smiling, inside. Do you understand? You have to feel the smile on the inside." For three hours, we sat on her couch, nodding politely as she shuffled through page after page of models with perfect teeth, abundant hair, and never-ending smooth legs, while she pointed out their poses and expressions with a steady torrent of words, of which I retained about a third. How to merge this information with my life remained a mystery. At the end of the so-called seminar, Malin nodded at me and announced I had definite possibilities. She didn't specify, and as Hatty and I walked home, she was convinced Malin was talking about modeling. Yeah, right. Only a few days before, my classmate Pelle had whacked me over the head with his history book to "kill the lice," though my hair was, as always, spotlessly clean.

I don't tell Britta this part. Instead I describe my meeting with Jean-Pierre—the owner of Sirens agency in Paris—which Malin had set up right before my fifteenth birthday. The meeting took place on a bench in a mall and lasted all of five minutes. Jean-Pierre complimented me on my pretty skin, told me he appreciated conservatively dressed girls, and asked me if I wanted to model in Paris over the summer. As if I'd say no. Britta finishes her Coke and orders another.

"Hey, are you gonna eat those nuts?" She eyes my pack of peanuts. I put them on her tray. I haven't the slightest hint of an appetite.

"How about you?" I say. "How did you get here?"

"Well, I was shopping at the mall with my mom and they had this contest thing. So my mom signed me up, they took a Polaroid of me, and I won the contest. The prize was meeting Jean-Pierre, to see if I would fit in his agency." She pops a handful of nuts into her mouth and chews with relish, her mouth open. My mother would slap me if I ate like that. "What did you think of Jean-Pierre?" Britta asks, munching away.

"Uh, he was nice. I didn't really hang out with him," I say and try to ignore the squelching sound of nuts and saliva.

"I think he's hot. My mom said he looks like Alain Delon."

I compare my impression of Jean-Pierre's cow eyes and overbite to the dashing French actor. "They both have dark hair," I concede. "But isn't Jean-Pierre kind of old—like thirty or something?"

"I like older men," Britta says with a wink. "My mom thinks it's because my dad died when I was a baby."

My Coke burns my throat. "I'm so sorry!" I'm suddenly no longer resentful of her loud chewing. At least I have a father, even though his presence in my life is as intangible as the Holy Ghost.

"It's okay," she says and pats my arm. "I don't remember him at all."

She shakes the last morsel into her mouth and pulls out her Walkman.

It's the new model, bright yellow and waterproof. If I had the money for one, I'd definitely get the smaller metal one.

Britta puts her headphones on, shutting me out. I take my book out of my backpack: Kafka's *The Castle*. My father's only comment about my summer plans was to voice his fear that my IQ would shrink to my bra size. He handed me the paperback before I left, making me swear I'd write a twenty-page book report to hand him upon my return. The cover of my book shows an ominous silhouette of a castle set against a deep red background. I open it, but after the first paragraph, I space out. My hopes and anxieties are as high as my current altitude. I lean my head against the window, which is warmed by the high sun and vibrates like a purring cat. I'm on my way to Paris! Me, the girl with an unpronounceable name, second-hand clothes, and a smile that reveals wide-spaced front teeth. When Hatty informed everyone at our school of my summer plans, it was greeted with the same disbelief as if she had just announced I was a secret love child of King Carl Gustaf. I stood at my locker where someone had scribbled in black magic marker, "Hot chick NO, hot chicken YES," a few months back. Despite my vigorous attempts to remove it, it remained imbedded in the orange paint; a clear, if somewhat faded statement of who I was. But now, I was someone different. I was someone to be envied. I straightened my back for the first time in nine years, and felt the unaccustomed warmth of self-confidence. That is, until Kristel slammed her locker next to me and, with a toss of her hair in my direction, exclaimed, "Well, if *that* can be a model, then even Fatty Hatty stands a chance."

Hatty, to whom I owe this outing in the clouds. Of course, her name is not really Fatty, or Hatty for that matter. Her Egyptian mother named her after Queen Hatshepsut, which forever condemns Hatty to people "sneezing" her full name and shouting, "bless you!" I must admit she's a bit on the pudgy side, although she has the most beautiful, black, almond-shaped eyes. We bonded immediately on our first day of school, since I had the dubious honor of bearing the other unpronounceable name and questionable background.

The engines of the plane suddenly switch from an even purr to a heavy rumble. My ears pop. I know this signals a landing and my stomach twists into knots. With a sweaty palm, I shake Britta.

"Wake up, we are about to land."

She opens her eyes and, for a fleeting moment, I think I detect in them a hint of panic mirroring my own. She removes her headphones and leans over my lap to look out the window. We are floating through dark rain clouds. Drops of water streak the window. The noise intensifies and I yawn to unclog my ears. "Are you scared?" I shout to Britta, who has resumed her position.

"Gosh no, what is there to be scared of?"

BRITTA HAS A NICE, sleek suitcase with polished metal locks, but it hits the luggage carousel at the very end along with my lumpy orange duffel. So much for my theory that nice luggage travels faster.

We get in line for a taxi and inhale French air, which seems mostly composed of cigarette smoke and diesel fumes. It's a little past noon and the flat, leaden sky threatens rain. My stomach lurches uncomfortably. At this point I'm not sure if it's due to hunger or nerves.

By the time we get into a taxi, sharp raindrops tap the windshield. The car also smells of cigarettes, but if I roll the window down I get wet. Windows up—I can't breathe. So I alternate between the two as I watch Paris approach.

At first, the city is an indistinct mass on the horizon. Soon, we leave the billboard-littered plains behind and enter upon avenues lined with trees and the elegant, haughty buildings of the city. Magazine stands grow from cement like pointy green mushrooms. A red blur of a woman walks her poodle. In outdoor cafés customers peruse newspapers under burgundy awnings. A man with a beret huddles against a wall, trying to light a cigarette. A stone wall drips with blooming lilacs. Short women in perfect shoes clutch thin baguettes under their arms. Eventually, the avenues become small twisted lanes overflowing with boutiques, gourmet shops, and bakeries.

Our taxi comes to a stop and we get out in front of a large green door. It leads into a courtyard, set with cobblestones, where a brass plaque hangs on the smoky glass doors of a carriage house. The engraved letters, darkened by time, announce SIRENS.

I wonder if anyone would notice if I puked into the nearby potted palm. I fall back a little, so Britta walks in first. The people who gather around us in the square white room are at first indistinct, but then I recognize Jean-Pierre. True, his eyes are large and rich brown, shaded by lashes any woman would kill for, but Alain Delon he's not. I smile at everyone with my lips closed, so as to not reveal my teeth, though pretending I'm mute doesn't seem a viable long-term option.

A pretty brunette with a pug nose eyes me suspiciously; a blond woman with very short hair and an Asian guy both wave hello. "Bienvenues" and "Bonjours" are exchanged.

My stomachache has intensified; I am in immediate need of a bathroom. It's located behind an L-shaped white Formica desk with four chairs. From within, I overhear the smatter of rapid-fire French and realize that if I hear them, they certainly hear me. I flush obsessively, unsure of which is worse, the explosive sound of troubled intestines or the repeated rumble of someone trying to cover it.

When I finally exit—closing the door firmly behind so no offensive odor escapes—Britta is being shown around the office. In truth, there is not much to see. The desk takes up most of the room and the white walls are lined with black-and-white checkered posters of passport-size heads, which on closer inspection don't bear much resemblance to actual passport pictures, since every person exhibited is too gorgeous for real life. I glimpse a few faces familiar from magazines and Hatty's sermons: Evalinda, the blond Swedish goddess; redheaded Mia who, according to Malin, is missing a finger.

We are shown the intricacies of the desk, where the three people I've just met, "bookers," sit all day, taking and making phone calls, booking jobs. When they get a call for a girl, they fish around for her chart from a deep round bin set in the tabletop, a sort of Rolodex set on its side. The charts have a month's calendar printed on them with cryptic words scribbled in ink or pencil across the days: *Confirmed*, *On Hold*, *Second Hold*, *Booked Out*.

Our charts are pulled out, blank and clean.

But my name is there!

All conversation is conducted in English, which is a relief. I, like everyone else, have had English classes from third grade on, and am by now perfectly comfortable with the language. My French, started in grade six, is still on par with a three-year-old's. I understand the small exclamations that litter the booker's English, the "ah bon's," the "ça va's," and the "comprends," but unless they ask me for a yellow pencil that just so happens to be on the table, I will be out of my depth.

The pug-nosed brunette introduces herself as Anne, and pulls out a tape measure.

"We must now see your sizes, so we can write them on the chart and also on your composites," she says.

I have no idea what a composite is, but there is no time to ask.

Anne winds the red-and-white strip around Britta's chest, waist, and hips with a slight frown. "Dis donc," she says. "You are a little fat. Have you gained some weight since Jean-Pierre saw you last?"

I'm shocked. Britta has a perfect hourglass body.

Britta blushes. "My mom hasn't had the time to cook lately, so I've been eating a lot of pizza."

Jean-Pierre sidles over to her and puts an arm over her shoulders. "The pizza no more. Tu comprends? Only the healthy French food now and you will be fine."

Britta laughs with obvious relief. Her measurements, thirty-six, twenty-five, thirty-five, are noted, as is her height, five-eight; hair color, blond; and eye color, brown. This does not in any way do her justice. Why not describe her hair as gold with hints of champagne, and her eyes as chocolate?

The bookers scrutinize her perfectly manicured hands at close range, debating whether she merits an "Extraordinaire" under the heading of "Special Qualities," and decide against it. Britta doesn't look too crestfallen. She sits on the countertop, kicking her legs and chatting with the short-haired woman, whose name is Odile, I think.

Anne slides the tape around my sweating body. "Thirty-four, twenty-two, thirty-three," she says, and smiles. "Perfect."

This is a word I have never heard in regard to myself. I flame up in gratitude.

"You are"—Anne pauses, pencil hovering above paper—"what? Sixteen, yes?"

"Fifteen," I correct her.

She looks at me with momentary surprise. "Mon Dieu, si jeune," she mutters. This I understand from my school French. *My God, so young.* I hold my breath. Is that bad? Should I have lied?

"Listen, we will say you are sixteen, for purposes of, um, taxes. Okay?"

I nod my head frantically. Right now I'd agree to have both my arms amputated if it meant staying in Paris. The thought of going back home—to drizzling skies over windswept fields, our cement apartment block, and, worst of all, my mother, smug in her knowledge she was right—that no one else wants me either—is as pleasant as a slow death from mushroom poisoning.

"I finished ninth grade," I tell Anne. "You see, I started school a year early, so I've always been in class with kids a year older anyway."

"Ah bon." She nods, seemingly satisfied. "So let us then keep it our little secret." She jots down my height, five-ten; my eyes, green; and stops at my hair color.

"Dis donc," she says, "what color would you say your hair is?"

The first thing that flashes through my mind is "poop brown," a term Kristel and Anika came up with. Greetings of "poop head" and "frog eyes" were liberally thrown my way whenever they passed me in the hallways.

I shrug uncomfortably. "Brown?"

Anne laughs. "Mais oui, brown. But it is like the brown of this small animal, I cannot think of the name—"

Mouse? Rat? Embarrassment for showing up with the hair color of "a small animal" stabs through me. Come to think of it, nearly all models I've seen in magazines are blondes.

"It will come to me." She waves her hand and writes down "brown."

Then she asks me for my photos and waits patiently as I free them from my underwear in my duffel.

There are three of them, printed on eight-by-ten glossy paper, all from my one and only photo session to date. The first photograph is of my face in muted pastel colors and soft focus. My eyes are staring at some invisible spot behind the camera, which was in fact the photographer's balding pate. He was a soft-spoken Indian man who ran a pizza parlor by day and did test photos for Malin as a hobby. The other two are black-and-white prints of me sitting in a window, dressed in a lace camisole and a frilly skirt. It was an attempt at copying Brooke Shields in *Pretty Baby*, which fails in part, I think, because of the clearly visible toggle from the drawn-up blinds that hangs next to my left ear.

Anne hands them around, and everyone comments on them too quickly in French for me to fully understand—something about beautiful eyes, and something else "ça va pas," which I know means "is not good." I break out in new sweat. Is it my teeth? So far, nobody has mentioned them and I've been feeling as though I've gotten away with a naughty prank. Will they be my undoing now? I remember Mother once mentioning to an

Uncle that I would be quite pretty if it weren't for my teeth, and I've tried to smile with my mouth shut ever since. I anxiously glance around at the bookers, but they have moved on. Shoji, the Asian guy, brings out a water-blue portfolio embossed with a gold Siren logo, and slides the photos under transparent plastic. Anne hands me the portfolio and adds two books with the same covers. "This little book contains all the information you need, plus addresses and phone numbers to all the photographers and studios," she says as she waves the thinner one. "And here," she says, opening the first page of a diary, "are your appointments for tomorrow." Britta comes up behind me and looks over my shoulder. "How do we get to them?" she asks Anne. "Does someone drive us?"

Anne laughs. "Ah non. This you must learn by yourselves, you will have many to go to." She tells us to get a Plan de Paris and leave plenty of time before the appointments—which are called go-and-sees—"in case you get lost."

We scoop up our bags, books, and portfolios, and lug them outside. The rain hasn't let up. But somehow, rain in Paris, rather than being depressing and cold, seems mysterious and romantic, like a thin gray veil over a beautiful woman's face. Jean-Pierre pulls up in his car. Britta eyes it with obvious admiration, which seems to please Jean-Pierre. "Not many people in France have a Rolls Royce," he says proudly. I can't help but think it looks rather like a white refrigerator on wheels. Jean-Pierre helps Britta with her suitcase and opens the front passenger door for her while I struggle to heave myself and my bag into the backseat. Jean-Pierre steps on the gas and we speed off to settle into our home for the summer: his apartment.

CHAPTER 2

After the magnificent turn-of-the-century façade, the sweeping circular staircase, and the intricately wrought iron elevator, the apartment is a disappointment.

A narrow dark hallway with high ceilings opens into a living room where an enormous aquarium presides over the entire back wall. It effectively blocks both windows and turns all available sunlight watery blue, which spills over a hodgepodge of black leather couches and rickety coffee tables that are topped with overflowing ashtrays. Jean-Pierre sets down Britta's suitcase and rings his keys like a bell.

"Cherie, on viens d'arrive!"

His cherie shuffles to greet us from the depths of the murky hallway like some creature from an Edgar Allan Poe story. Jean-Pierre introduces her as Marina.

"Bonjour," she says in a raspy whisper, revealing the large yellowed teeth of an old piano. She's a good foot taller than her husband, and in the rippled, watery light—with her stringy blond hair and unfocused pale eyes—she looks like a mermaid gone to seed. Jean-Pierre pecks her on the cheek, murmuring something in French, and heads back out the door. "I'll see you for dinner," he says.

The three of us stand in silence, uncertain of protocol.

"Hi, I'm Jirina, it's a pleasure to meet you." I reach out and shake Marina's hand, which is appropriately damp and limp.

Britta introduces herself and then Marina sticks her hands in the pockets of her dingy blue satin robe and fishes out a small cigarette and a lighter. She lights up and a sweet aroma of burning hay covers the reek of old cigarettes and fresh toilet bowls. Marina inhales and keeps the smoke inside her lungs for what seems an eternity. Britta and I stand, waiting for her to exhale. My lungs start to burn and I realize I've been holding my breath along with Marina. Finally she blows out a cloud of smoke.

"Vennez," she says.

She rushes us through a tour of the apartment. There is only one bathroom we are all to share, tiled in dark blue and lit with fluorescent lights. "Keep it clean," Marina says and flicks cigarette ashes into the bathtub. She shows me the toilet—housed by itself with a stack of out-of-date magazines in a claustrophobic closet accessible only from the hallway—while Britta reapplies her lip gloss in the bathroom. From here, the hallway veers a sharp right, leading into complete darkness. "Our bedroom is that way," Marina points. "There is no need for you to ever go there." She pivots on her heel and loses a slipper. "Goddamn fucking motherfucking piece of shit." She kicks it with her bare foot, takes three steps to the left, and opens the door to the kitchen.

My ears still burn with Marina's vulgarity as sunlight temporarily blinds me. I blink. A big wooden table sits in the middle of the room, a large stainless steel range looms against the right wall, and white glass-fronted cabinets exhibit stacks of dishes. It's bright and cheerful and as incongruous in this apartment as coconut palm trees on a Swedish beach. A faded red vinyl high chair with an empty bowl on the tray stands by one of the French windows.

"You have children?" I say, with more than a little surprise.

"One," Marina replies with the tone of someone recounting cancerous tumors.

Nonetheless, it cheers me enormously. I already miss Kristynka with the same sharp pangs as hunger.

She was born after my father left us, the year I turned seven. At first I had no idea why my mother suddenly swelled up and turned even more irritable than usual. I figured it was somehow my fault, like so many other things: the unwashed dishes in the sink, my father leaving, the crack in the kitchen wall, my bad grades in math, the disappearance of the scissors, and my audacity for physically resembling my father when he became the person most hated on my mother's list.

But from the moment my mother brought Kristynka home, all peeling, furiously red and bald like a baby vulture, my loneliness dissipated. Here, finally, was someone who needed me. I fed her formula, burped her, learned to change her diapers, and, as soon as mother had trained me, gave her baths so mother could go to her night classes. I used to sleep on the floor by the crib when Kristynka had colic, and the next day I would be walking around in a blurred stupor in school. My grades suffered, which infuriated mother on the odd night she was home. But Kristynka became my real live doll; my baby. When she first said "ma-ma," it was to me.

I wish I had brought her picture to put on my bedside nightstand, like Britta's photo of her mom. The room Marina dubs ours is painted a muted green, but saved from the Twenty Thousand Leagues Under the Sea decor by a large floor-to-ceiling window and a cheerful, if somewhat dirty, floral carpet. Britta has claimed the twin bed on the left wall.

"I have to call Mom and tell her I've arrived," she says and readjusts her picture so it faces her bed.

Of course she's arrived. What else could she do? I begin to unpack my things and put them into a large wooden chest of drawers at the foot of Britta's bed.

She pulls the phone from the fireplace mantel to the floor, sits down cross-legged, and picks up the receiver.

"Mommy! I'm here—Yes, I miss you too already!" Her voice is suddenly high-pitched and babylike. I can't fathom speaking to my mother like that.

"Um, Britta, which drawers do you want?"

"I don't care." She shifts her body so her back faces me, and she cradles the phone. "The top ones, I guess."

I remove my things from the top drawers.

HATTY PICKS UP on the second ring. "Are you there? How is it? What did they say?"

I describe my trip, while Britta repeatedly slams the drawers in the background.

"What's she like?" Hatty says. For a moment, I'm discombobulated, and then I remember. Once Hatty found out I was to travel with another girl, she made me swear I wouldn't like the new girl more than I liked her.

"Okay, I guess," I say, and realize this is the wrong answer. But Britta has unpacked, and sits on her bed watching me, so what am I supposed to say?

"Okay?" Hatty's voice is shrill. "How okay?"

"How is Claudius?" I quickly insert our code for "I can't talk, person is in the room," which we came up with after watching every episode of *I, Claudius*.

"Oh, got it," she says. "Call me soon when she's out so we can dish some dirt."

I hang up, slightly annoyed. Britta is my only safety from utter loneliness, and I like her, I think. I glance at her, sitting on her bed with her big brown eyes staring at me.

"Was that your mom?" she says.

I shake my head. "No, my friend Hatty."

"Your mom not home?"

"I don't know. My mother doesn't expect to hear from me until the weekend."

Britta cocks her head in surprise.

"It's cheaper that way." I shrug. No need to add that my father doesn't expect to hear from me until the summer's end. I think he was relieved he no longer has to drive the fifty kilometers from Malmö, where he lives with his new wife, to pick me up for the monthly weekend.

Kristynka is a different story. She hardly ever sees my father, in part because father doesn't like small children, but mostly because he suspects Kristynka is not his child anyway.

I pull out *The Castle*, and set it down on my nightstand next to *Anna Karenina* and my well-worn copy of *The Wild Ass' Skin*. Britta hops over to browse through my reading selection, and wrinkles her nose. "Don't you have any magazines?"

MARINA STANDS BY the stove when we enter the kitchen, stirring the contents of a large pot. A cigarette bobs in her mouth and gently deposits ash into what, I presume, is our dinner. Britta sits down next to Jean-Pierre and I take a seat on the opposite side of the table. Jean-Pierre pours every-one red wine and lifts his glass in a toast. "A vôtre bienvenue."

"He just poured us wine," Britta says to me in Swedish with an unut-terably goofy expression, and gulps the contents in one go. Jean-Pierre watches her with an amused smile. "You Swedish girls, such big drinkers, always, eh?"

"This is how we drink in Sweden." Britta shrugs.

"Yes, alcohol and sex, the most popular Swedish pastimes," Marina mumbles from the stove.

Britta lets Jean-Pierre refill her glass. "Sex is a very healthy pastime," she says and giggles.

I'm immediately reminded of my own shameful little secret: still a vir-gin at fifteen. Since I have nothing to add to this conversation, I sip my wine. It's kind of bitter; I thought it'd be more like grape juice.

"Oh yes." Jean-Pierre nods. "I very much like the Swedish approach to the human body."

Marina snorts and burbles something that sounds like "Yeah, you would."

"It is something perfectly natural," Britta carries on, oblivious to Marina's frown.

"One shouldn't be ashamed of one's body and its need for happiness. Sex is like—like having a really good dessert, minus the calories!"

This sends Jean-Pierre into a cavalcade of baritone laughter. Marina re-moves the pot and slams it on the table before us. The room goes quiet. My grandma used to say that an angel flew over the table when dinner conver-sation came to a halt. A whole horde of angels must be flying over now.

The pasta proves to be better than expected—though it remains un-certain whether it's because we are now so famished that jellied ants would be a treat, or because cigarette ash is a tasty food additive. Marina sits down next to me with a few lone noodles, which she twirls with her fork on her plate, and continues to smoke. The only sounds are the rasp of cutlery on plates and muted traffic outside.

"So, where is your daughter?" I say and feel my words fall into the silence with the subtlety of a hand grenade.

Jean-Pierre looks to Marina for confirmation of their child's where-abouts and she takes a deep drag. "Olympe? With the nanny, bien sur." She has twirled her noodles into a neat spiral.

"At least she knows her kid's name," Britta says to me in Swedish.

I feel my ears burn. *"We shouldn't speak Swedish in front of them, it's impolite,"* I say. I take a gulp of my wine, trying to shake the feeling I'm acting like some prissy fifty-year-old.

"Oh, what the hell, they don't understand," Britta says.

As if to confirm, Jean-Pierre calmly pours her yet another glass, without remarking on our exchange. She drinks it up and ends with a slight burp.

"Oopsie." She bursts into giggles again and playfully slaps Jean-Pierre on the chest. "Are you trying to get me drunk?"

Marina parks her cigarette in the noodle spiral on her plate and stands up. I have a sudden vision of her walking around the table to punch them. But she turns away and heads for a drawer by the stove and emerges with a chocolate bar, which she nibbles between puffs of her cigarette, while keeping a cold eye on Jean-Pierre's arm across Britta's shoulder.

Britta falls asleep in her clothes without even brushing her teeth. I pull on my pajamas and crawl under sheets that don't exactly smell freshly laundered and open the Sirens book. It has three sections: model's memo, pratique, and addresses. The first section is written in English and French, but the other two are in French only. I guess "pratique"—with what appears to be emergency telephone numbers, obligatory vaccination for residents of France, and five pages of small print that I think may be something to do with the law and the rights of models—is exclusive to French models since there is no translation. I skim through the first section. Go-and-sees, bookings, the voucher where I find out a "composite" is a model's calling card, and it is "*essential* to leave one with every client." When I get to: *Tarif 6. For a three hour booking, the sum on the voucher in 1980 should be F.1 386,00 H.T.*, I feel as though I'm reading Chinese and nearly give up. Numbers and math have never been my strong suit.

One page, however, gives me pause. Page ten, *List of Necessary Accessories,* tells me I must have a complete makeup kit containing: *makeup remover, skin toner, light foundation, dark foundation, loose powder, compact powder* . . . it goes on and on listing beautifying equipment, half of which I've never heard of. I'm also told I need "*different shades of panty hose, flesh-colored lingerie, slips, scarves, and jewelry,*" and that I needn't be reminded that my lingerie and myself should be impeccably clean *for my own image*. I glance over at Britta, who's splayed out and gently snoring. Does she have all those things? How the hell am I supposed to acquire them with a hundred francs? And where?

These thoughts may keep me up all night. That, and Britta puking into the wastebasket. She's obviously not as used to alcohol as she is to sex.

By two A.M. she finally falls asleep, leaving me perfectly awake after the endless runs to the kitchen for another glass of water. Not that I mind. I know that because of my ministrations, she can't just dismiss me now. With each kind act, I barter her precious friendship. Eventually I drift off to an uneasy sleep and dream of trying to purchase makeup in a French hardware store.

AFTER A QUICK BREAKFAST, Britta and I hit the streets. We study the Plan de Paris on a bench close to the newsstand where we purchased our copies. It is a small book, with a map of the subway on the inside front cover and then maps of the city divided by arrondissements, from one to twenty.

Our go-and-sees are different from each other's, meaning Britta and I will have to figure out how to get around the city for ourselves. But it also means we aren't competing for jobs, today at least.

My first go-and-see is in Port de Clignancourt, at the very end of a yellow subway line. "It's in the boondocks," according to Britta.

"Yeah, but it's for *Elle* magazine," I say and watch her face drop a little.

We descend into the Metro together and buy a carnet de ticket, ten small yellow tickets stapled together.

"Break a leg," I shout to Britta over the din of trains and French babble that echoes in the white-tiled tunnels.

"Kick ass!" she yells back.

The doors of the Metro car swallow me with a hiss. I sit down on an orange plastic seat and marvel at the darkness rushing by outside. I've never been on a subway before. After a while, the novelty of being underground wears off and my eyes refocus to my reflection in the window glass. This other me, floating in the windowpane, has hollowed eyes and cheeks, and looks very young and scared.

Port de Clignancourt is full of small pastry shops, dusty drugstores, and cars parked haphazardly on the narrow sidewalks. I negotiate through them with my portfolio under one arm, my diary, address book, and Plan de Paris in a plastic shopping bag in the other, while keeping a busy eye on storefronts for any signs of cosmetics sales.

I find a heavy burgundy door with the corresponding number, and push my way into a long white hallway lined with poster-size *Elle* covers. A receptionist with sunglasses doesn't smile back, and points me in the direction of a small room crammed with racks of clothing where a sparrow of a woman emerges from the folds of fabric.

"Buh-jooh," she says and narrows her dark eyes into slits. Her cigarette is somehow glued to her bottom lip, impeding her speech. She extends a leathery brown hand adorned with a trillion thin silver bracelets, which tinkle like bells when I shake it.

"Bonjour." I smile at her and pump away so energetically I nearly break a sweat. Her face remains impassive and when my arm finally gets tired and drops to my side, her hand remains outstretched. So I grab it again and shake some more, but this time with less vigor. "Bonjour," I repeat.

She shakes her head. "Your book."

"I am sorry?" Does she want to know what I'm reading? Good thing it's Kafka, because that sounds pretty intellectual.

"Your *book*. Your portfolio."

Ah! I fumble with my portfolio and place it into her hand. She opens it to the first page and studies the picture. Then looks at me. Then looks back at the picture. Then looks at me again. My cheeks are trembling in a fixed, lip-locked smile.

She turns to the other two photos but doesn't linger over them, and flips through the rest of the blank pages.

"C'est ça? Is this all?"

I nod and feel horribly inadequate.

"Can you take off the pants?" she says.

Is this a joke? I smile uncertainly.

"I am waiting," she says.

"Oh. Like, now?"

She puts her hands on her hips and scowls. "I do not have the time to wait until tomorrow, non?"

I kick off my Converse and unbutton my jeans, excruciatingly aware of my tattered undies and the smell of my socks. I wore them yesterday, a fact I now sorely regret.

She looks at me, her frown never changing. "Merci," she says and lights another cigarette off the stump of its predecessor.

Is this it?

I don't dare to ask, so I pull my jeans back on and leave.

The streets have suddenly lost some of their charm. I squeeze between two cars parked on the sidewalk and hit my knee. Why can't the French park like normal people? A tickle of tears nestles in my sinuses. What now? Will the woman call the agency and tell them to fire me? I imagine them all sharing a chuckle over "the poor, dirty commie cow" who thinks she can be a model.

My next appointment in Les Halles is diagonally across the city, according to my Plan de Paris subway map. I distract myself by studying the huge posters in every station, ads for panty hose, yogurt, car tires, perfume, and sometimes pictures that are flat-out puzzling, like the giant billboard of a girl clothed in a white bikini standing in front of a turquoise ocean, her back facing us, and the text, *"La semaine prochaine j'enleverai le haut."* As far as I can tell, it means she will remove something next week. Why, and what I'm supposed to buy, remains unanswered.

The train arrives at my stop and the first thing that hits me is a godawful smell when the train doors open. Les Halles appears to have a sewage problem, because the dank air smells strongly of rotten eggs. I look around me, but no one else seems to mind or to notice, so I breathe through my mouth as I climb a steep staircase into the street.

After a quick consultation with my map, I head for rue St. Denis. Lined with tourist shops selling T-shirts, and leather goods stores, the street is long, narrow, and intersects with a pedestrian square, where a fountain squirts merrily in front of a Fiorucci store. Here are clothes I've only seen in magazines. I glance longingly at the neon wares displayed in the windows: pink ruffled mini skirts, lime-green tube tops, cotton candy–pink leg warmers on mannequins with electric-blue hair. Further down the street, I enter a cobblestoned courtyard filled with rusty bicycles, and finally find an unmarked door behind an old, mint-colored Vespa.

My footsteps echo in a cavernous white space. The photographer stands before a giant roll of gray paper, pulled down like toilet paper between two support poles, where a small object propped on a table seems to be the focus. He waves at me without turning around, intent on his task. Four lights with metal bonnets and spindly, long legs are directed at the thing on the table, which upon closer inspection turns out to be a box of tampons. Instantly, I blush. How I envied girls sneaking a tampon into their jeans' pocket from their locker. In school, tampons are a sort of badge: If you use them, everyone figures you have had sex, and if you've had sex, you are obviously good-looking enough to be desired by boys. By ninth grade, it appeared only Hatty, myself, and Monika—a tall, hunched A-plus student in the other class—were the only ones left "on the rag," literally speaking. I still wince when I remember the most shameful incident of my life: Someone had stuck a soiled sanitary napkin to the back of my brand new winter coat, and I walked around school for God knows how long, pleased at the smiles I mistakenly attributed to looking great in my new coat. And I wasn't on my period.

The photographer straightens up from behind the camera. His hair is graying at the temples and he is wearing a tweed jacket and jeans. He reaches out for my portfolio and flips through it at the speed of light, like one of those cartoons you make move by flipping the pages.

"Merci," he says, handing it back to me without ever looking at my face. At least he didn't see me blush.

The invitation to Paris had seemed like Cinderella's invitation to the ball. Just being asked, or even considered, was so out of the ordinary I had somehow assumed that once there, I'd immediately be someone else, someone better, more worthy. It seems I was wrong.

My last go-and-see is on a quiet street on the left bank. I exit the Metro and walk down Quai St. Michel. On my right, a setting sun bounces fiery sparks off of windshields and side mirrors of dusty cars seemingly intent on driving through a red stoplight, on my left, it colors the buildings Byzantine gold and turns the river into a gleaming snake. Small wooden bookstands that are really just boxes with a few shelves line the walkway, exhibiting old paperbacks, maps, postcards, and photographs of Paris. I look upward, to the cloudless sky and silvery roofs. The twin towers of Notre Dame are saturated with an orange glow and shaded in violet blues. Without the hordes of people littering the sidewalks, and the endless smoke-burping Peugeots, Paris hits me. *The* Paris. The city of Balzac, Victor Hugo, George Sand, and Chopin, candlelit dinners sparkling with literary conversations and cascading piano notes in salons hung with brocade, the city of refined manners and tastes, the city of wild, crazy nights in smoky cafés with flirtatious Picasso, drunk Hemingway, and penniless

Fitzgerald. The city of romance, of lights, of unsurpassed beauty. I have a sudden urge to open my arms wide and shout "Je suis arrivée!" I am here!

Although, maybe not for much longer.

Rue de la Seine is twisted and narrow, already sunk in shadows when I ring the bell. I enter a room overflowing with clothes hanging on metal racks and strewn on every available surface. A small balding man and a wispy-haired woman take my portfolio. They study the first picture intently.

"There is something interesting going on here," the man says. For a moment I marvel at the enormous improvement of my French, until it dawns on me he's speaking English. Still, I'm heartened they are actually paying attention.

"Thank you." I attempt a light, bantering tone. "Mr. Vishnu, who did these photos, is a huge fan of—"

The woman swats her hand at me as if I'm an annoying insect. "Her jaw is a bit angular, isn't it?" she says.

I quickly clench my teeth so my chin isn't as pronounced, but they are still not looking at me. The man flips to the next pages.

"Ooh, an homage to David Hamilton," he smirks.

I rise a little. They noticed the effect my tiny Indian photographer tried so hard to get.

"How cheesy," the woman says.

I'm not quite certain what "cheesy" means. Fat-laden? Good with bread? Smelly?

I blush again. Remarkable how many times today my body has sent extra blood to my head.

The man closes the portfolio and glances at my name written on the spine. "And this name . . ." he says. "How do you pronounce this?"

I open my mouth to answer, but the woman is faster. "*Zhee-rree—Zhee-rree-na?*" she says to the man.

"*Yee-ree-nah*," I say and hope she won't take offense that I'm correcting her. But they don't appear to have heard me anyway.

"Quel nom," the man snorts. "C'est un disastre."

I understand my name has been judged a disaster.

They finally narrow their gazes at me, under which I melt into a puddle of self-consciousness.

"How old do you think she is?" the man asks.

The woman shrugs.

"Fif—sixteen," I volunteer.

The woman shakes her head. "That would account for the gawky posture." She hands the book back without looking at me.

I have the unnerving impression I don't exist but on the printed page. My voice and body simply don't register. I whisper a tentative good-bye and thank you, and am further confirmed in my suspicion, as nobody acknowledges it.

A dreamy twilight stains the air when I walk out, adding to the strange sense of unreality, as if I were trapped in a bad dream. I double-check my reflection in the storefronts. Yes, still here. But even my reflection is dim, on the edge of dissolving. My old fear, from the days before my sister was born, squeezes my throat. But I will not cry. Crying in front of others is a weakness my father abhors. Only my mother cried, and when she did, her loss of control embarrassed me. Couldn't she see how easily my father won an argument when she was reduced to tears?

I swallow repeatedly. They don't want me. I'm no good. I'm ugly. Nobody wants me. The pressure builds, but I will not cry.

My vague dreams of Veni, Vidi, Vici, are rolling away from me like a beautiful countryside out a train window. What did I expect? To simply arrive and be clasped to the renowned bosom of *Vogue*?

The only thing I'm sure about is that this go-and-see stuff really blows.

CHAPTER 3

Britta is on the phone, huddled on the floor in near dark, her shape outlined by the streetlights outside.

"It was awful—miss you . . ." Her voice is thin and high.

I clear my throat and she jumps.

"I'm sorry, I didn't know you were home," I say.

She turns to me and cups the receiver with her hand. "I've got to go, call you later. I love you," she says softly into the mouthpiece and hangs up.

"Lars?" I ask, tossing my stuff on the bed.

"No, my mom."

This still floors me. Saying I love you to my mother is as inconceivable as her saying it to me.

"Are you okay?" I say.

"Yeah, great!" She passes her hand across her face. "So, how was your day?"

"Uh, can I switch on the light?" I say and turn on the lamp on my bed-side table. The room is immediately brightened and Britta looks caught in the headlights. She stands up and moves to her bed. "You want to go out and have dinner?" she says.

"Sure, let me just find a sweater, it's getting cold out." I walk to the dresser and rummage for the lavender acrylic sweater I bought with money made from the tobacco store last summer. The shop was owned by a then-current Uncle and I made enough money over three months to also purchase my other prized possessions: a pair of baggy jeans, a black-and-white-checkered T-shirt, and a red military-style belt. That particular Uncle was a favorite; he would give me and Kristynka candy from the store when Mother wasn't looking. Unfortunately, he lost his spot shortly after that summer. The recent Uncle, Ingmar, studies law and is ten years younger than my mother. At twenty-one, he is really closer to my age. It doesn't matter, for he is obviously on his way out too; before I left for Paris, Mother had been instructing me to tell him she was not home when he called.

Suddenly, the door opens and nearly hits Britta in the face.

Marina stands in the doorway. Her robe is open almost all the way, affording a glimpse of pale pubic hair and long, bony legs the color of a fish belly. I'm directly in her line of sight; Britta is hidden by the door.

"Which—one—of—you—shit—in—the—bidet?"

I glance at Britta, who has turned a vivid red. My ears start to burn in symbiotic shame.

"I, um—" I stumble for words.

Marina considers me for a moment while I feel my blood rise to the occasion. "I—it wasn't—"

She lunges out and grabs my arm. I have no time to react. She drags me behind her as though I am a wayward child, and shoves me into the bathroom, where the offense lies on blue porcelain like a sausage on a plate.

"This is the bidet," she hisses through her teeth. She pulls me into the hallway and throws open the door to the toilet. "And this—is the toilet. Now, clean it." She ambles back into the depths of the forbidden hallway, her slippers whispering on the bare wood floors.

This is really not that different from a diaper of a three-year-old. I breathe in through my mouth as I scoop. Marina hasn't given me any cleaning products, so I make several trips with loaded toilet paper, and end up rinsing the bidet with Joy body wash I find on the bathtub rim; touted as the most expensive fragrance in the world, it's not likely Britta's.

When I come back to our room, Britta sits on her bed, in tears.

"Come on, let's go," I say and pick up my sweater.

"I didn't know"—she sobs with her face in her hands—"that it wasn't a toilet, you know? I mean, how is one to know? It kinda looks the same."

"It's no big deal. Let's go, I'm starving."

She looks up at me with red swollen eyes. "Did you—I mean—you didn't—"

"It's okay, I took care of it."

Her eyebrows fly up. "You did?" She wipes her cheeks and stands up. "Thank you. Thank you so much, for doing that and you know—for not telling on me. You are a true friend."

I smile, feeling a rush of pleasure.

AN ELECTRIC-BLUE NIGHT has fallen over the streets, polka-dotted with the yellow of street lamps. Britta slips her arm through the crook of my elbow as we walk: Swedish for "best friends." It seems to mean something else in French, however, for every passerby on foot or wheels whistles relentlessly at us.

"Isn't it weird, that it's dark but warm?" Britta says. "I keep thinking it's winter."

I'm used to dark summer nights from my trips to Czechoslovakia, but I still agree there is something unsettling about the combination of a black sky and warm air. Back home, the nights in the summer never get darker than tarnished silver.

We finally settle ourselves at an outdoor café and order Sandwich Jambon Fromage from a surly waiter with a handlebar mustache. Our new bond feels sweet but thin, like sugar crust.

"So, I found where we can buy the makeup," Britta says. "There's this store, Prisunic, close to the agency, and they have loads of things, and cheap, too. We should go sometime, between appointments."

I agree, but can't summon much enthusiasm. If today was any indication, I may never need all that makeup.

We sit in silence for a moment. Britta traces the marble veins in the table with her finger. "You know, when you came in? I was just telling Mom about my day." She pauses, searching my face as if to decide whether to tell me the rest, and then sighs. "I don't think it went very well."

I know how much this admission costs her. Five minutes ago I would have rather had rabies shots than admit the same truth. But now we are treading on the sugar crust, and she's reaching for my hand, which I offer with only the smallest pang. What if her bad day was still better than mine?

"Mine wasn't good either."

"Really?"

Her eagerness decides it for me. "Yeah. Mostly they didn't even look at me, or they spoke about me as if I were deaf," I say.

Britta's face grows brighter. "This one guy asked me out for dinner, and when I told him I was busy, he told me I would never make it in this business."

That stops me. Being asked out for dinner sounds like a good thing. Why did no one want to take *me* out?

"Yeah, that sucks," I say without conviction.

The waiter sets two Oranginas before us and pours them into glasses. We take a few sips and lapse into silence again.

"Do you think we'll make it here?" Britta finally says.

"I'm sure you will."

"No, I think you will."

"No way. You're way prettier," I insist.

Alarmingly, this is where she drops this conversation. She mixes her drink with her straw.

"I just want to do this over the summer, you know, to make some of my own money. I've applied to the nature sciences line for fall." She puts her index finger over the hole in the straw and lifts it to her lips, moving the finger away to let the liquid pour into her mouth.

"Yeah, I'm just doing this for the summer too," I say and gulp my drink to cover the insincerity oozing from my eyeballs. As if my whole life wasn't riding on this summer. As if I wouldn't sell my soul to stay in Paris forever.

"What line did you apply to?"

"Humanities," I say, and look down at my half-eaten sandwich.

"Do you know if you got in yet?"

Unfortunately, I do know. I didn't get in.

"You know, I think our school system is seriously messed up," I say. "I mean, what if you're great at languages and apply to humanities, and don't get in because your grade point average is compromised by a D in math? What does math have to do with languages? Or say, in your case, you're great at science and math, but get a bad grade in art or music, so you can't get into nature sciences. That's messed up, right?"

"I already got my acceptance letter," she says.

Thankfully, the waiter interrupts with our desserts.

"So, tell me about Lars. How long have you been going out?" I say quickly.

Between mouthfuls of ice cream, Britta divulges her romantic history. It may not be the most fascinating tale ever told—it's composed mainly of drinking beers and having sex in her room—but still, I'm thrilled at her easy confidences. Aside from Hatty, I can barely remember a time when a peer treated me as an equal. What I do remember, however, is the incident that began my nine years of school hell.

My father was offered the position of principal in Lund's technical gymnasium, which of course meant we had to move from Malmö. (The move was conducted during the summer break, while I was in Czechoslovakia with grandmother.) Two days before I was to start first grade, my mother and I went into the town center to buy school supplies. While we waited for our bus, I spied an apple-cheeked blond girl holding onto her mother's sweater. We played a sort of peekaboo from behind our mothers, giggling, until I tugged at my mother's purse too hard and broke the shoulder strap. Her purse went flying, scattering its contents over the pavement. My mother extended her hand and brought it full across my face in a resounding slap. I didn't even have a chance to duck. My new friend and her mother looked at us in wide-eyed alarm. I smiled to show them I was fine, but got no smile in return. Instead, the girl's mother stepped up to mine, who was on the pavement trying to collect her things, and in none-too-gentle tones explained that she had a good mind to call the authorities, for "we don't hit children in our country." My mother snapped some obscenity, and the woman pulled her daughter—my former new friend—as far away from us as she could.

That night, when Mother slapped me because I didn't tidy up my books, I turned to her with a brave "children shouldn't be hit in this country, you know," and got smacked for talking back, thus quickly squelching my newfound rebellion.

Two days later, I met Kristel again, this time at school. When I offered her a cookie from my lunch box, she made herself perfectly clear. "I don't take cookies from dirty immigrants," she said loudly, so everyone could hear. I had to look up "immigrant" in the dictionary at home.

No matter how often I tried to explain that I was born in Sweden, it stuck. No matter how hard I tried to insinuate myself with my new classmates—running errands, giving up my pencils, handing out Ahlgrens bilar jelly-fish candy—I was labeled the official immigrant, the outcast, the communist bastard. It didn't help matters that the teacher couldn't pronounce my name at roll call, but this was when Hatshepsut Nilsson looked up from her desk and recognized a kindred soul.

"So, how many do *you* have?" Britta brings me back with a start.

"Uh," I say. "How many—?"

"Orgasms? How many?"

The word nearly makes me choke on my last sip of Orangina. I do an instant calculation on a scale from one to ten. "Like—five," I say.

"Five?" Britta's eyes threaten to pop out of her head.

Did I over- or under-do it?

"Are they, like, multiples?" she says.

What in God's name are multiples? "Yeah, I guess."

"Ah." Britta nods with an unreadable expression.

KRISTYNKA! I HEAR HER voice, indistinct, crying. She needs me. I have to wake up, make her breakfast, and take her to school.

I open my eyes to an unfamiliar room. The window pours white sunlight across a black carpet dotted with white flowers and a tangle of mint-green leaves.

Kristynka's cries continue.

It takes me a moment to realize it can't be her. I'm in Paris; the other bed is occupied by a sleeping Britta. I jump out of bed and open my door to the twilight of the apartment.

A little girl, maybe two years old, stands naked in front of the aquarium and cries. Her hair is pale like her mother's, her eyes the chocolate brown of Jean-Pierre's. She stops crying and looks at me with a streaked face and snot dripping from her nose. A quick glance reveals she is alone and I run up to her.

"Hello, what's the matter?"

Her chin starts to tremble. She looks at me with big, scared eyes that creep up over my shoulder and howls, "Maman!"

We both look around, but Marina is nowhere in sight. I crouch down to her level and stroke her goose-pimpled arm with my fingers. "It's okay, Mommy will be back soon." How do I say this in French?

She flinches at my touch. Mucus has dribbled down her nose, past her mouth, and hangs in strands from her chin.

"Je m'appelle Jirina." I point to myself. "Toi, Olympe?"

She doesn't respond. Her eyes bore into mine; she inhales and on the exhale lets out an ear-piercing shriek.

"It's okay, Mommy will be right back," I tell her in English but her screams continue. "Maman, viens, maman viens," I try in French, hoping it's true.

I pick her up and she sobs staccato into my shoulder. "Shh, shh, everything is fine, tout va bien." I rock her back and forth and her small cold body finally gives in to mine.

"Mais qu'est ce que tu fait?" Marina's rasp comes up from behind me. I duck from habit. Marina's face registers mild surprise before settling into her habitual vacant gaze.

"I don't usually hit girls," she says. Her mouth turns up at one corner. "Only if they mess with my husband."

I'm stunned into silence and Olympe suddenly turns into an eel. "Maman!" She clambers from my arms as if I were doing terrible things to her. It's worse than a slap.

Marina holds her awkwardly. "Goddamn fucking nanny's day off," she mutters. "Can you watch her a minute longer?" She holds out the child to me, while Olympe struggles to stay with her mother. "Non, maman. Je veux maman!"

"I'll get her a bottle," Marina says and stomps off.

Olympe goes stiff in my arms again and I struggle to get a better hold on her. "Look. Look at the fish, le poisson jaune—il est—" What's the word for funny-looking? I suck in my cheeks and bulge out my eyes. A fish face. "Comme ça."

I have her attention now. A hesitant smile creeps across her face. Relief washes over me; I haven't lost my touch yet.

"Jirina, are you here?" Britta's tousled head peeks out from our room.

"Here, in the living room." I rock Olympe back and forth on my hip. She's getting heavy. "Look, this is Olympe. Isn't she cute?"

Britta rubs sleep from her eyes. "Yeah, cute," she says, but barely looks. "Do you have something for a headache? My first go-and-see is in an hour."

"Yeah, so is mine." I enter our room with Olympe and set her down on my bed while I go through my bag in search of Panadol. I hand it to Britta, and she shakes out four little pills.

"Um, you only need two," I say.

"Not for this headache," she says and gulps them down without water. "So where's Marina? We've got to get ready."

"She went to the kitchen to get a bottle," I say. "But that was like fifteen minutes ago."

"I'll get her. Need to get some coffee anyway," Britta says and clomps off. I entertain Olympe with a game of peekaboo under my blanket, until Britta comes in holding a cup. "She's not there."

I'm puzzled. "Where did she go?"

Olympe throws the blanket away and shouts, "Boo!"

"I walked to her bedroom. She's asleep." Britta strips to her underwear and rummages through her drawers.

I'm momentarily floored by her nerve. "You went to the forbidden part?"

She pulls a T-shirt over her head, and as her face pops out of the neck hole, she exclaims, "Jirina, she is asleep!"

"So, what do I do?"

"You get dressed. Let's go."

"But what about Olympe?"

Britta, fully dressed now, faces me with her hands on her hips. "Did you come here to be a model or an au-pair?"

I'm wracked with indecision. Fragments of vivid scenes featuring me getting fired for both offenses—for *not* babysitting, and for babysitting instead of going to the go-and-sees—play out in my head.

"I can't just leave," I repeat.

"Jesus!" Britta shakes her head. "Here, I'll do it." She picks Olympe up off the bed and is out the door with her before I can even react.

CHAPTER 4

I'm tired, dusty, and very hungry when I finally get back to Jean-Pierre's apartment building, and bump right into Britta on the doorstep. She's carrying her portfolio under her arm just like me, but sports a nice leather handbag slung over her shoulder. She already looks like a model, like she belongs here, throwing my own inadequacies into stark relief. I need to upgrade my plastic shopping bag at some point.

"How was today?" I ask once we step into the elevator.

She grins. "Better."

That gives me pause. How *much* better?

A pounding, like a heartbeat, radiates through the hallway when we get out of the elevator. Britta presses the doorbell and moments later Jean-Pierre opens it. The heartbeat intensifies to music, the bass drum kicking away at top volume. Jean-Pierre looks to be in high spirits, and behind him is a crowd of people.

"Ah, mes belles petite Suédoise," he says. "Come and join the party."

Everyone looks expectantly as we enter, but seeing only us, they go back to circulating the room and smoking. There must be about fifty people in here, no one is familiar and everyone looks old. The guys are dressed in brightly colored silk shirts, unbuttoned so one can admire the gold chains resting on their hairy chests. I guess they didn't get the "Disco's Dead" memo. The women are glossier and haughtier versions of the girls in Fiorucci. They sit on floors, recline on couches, and rest against the none-too-steady side tables. Cigarette smoke mingles with scented candles and the stereo belts out an electronic pop song with a deadpan vocal in oddly accented English. Something about seeing someone on the cover of a maaagazine. It must be about a model.

Marina sits cross-legged before the aquarium. She is dressed for once, in black leggings and a tunic, belted with a wide blue sash. She smiles and waves at us. "Did you girls have a nice day?"

I resist looking behind me for the girls.

"Yeah, it was great," Britta shouts back and promptly blushes when Jean-Pierre sidles up to her and hands her a glass of wine. I just smile and shrug. My four go-and-sees today hardly restored my shredded ego. I wonder if I'll ever get used to being talked about as if I am deaf, or not present, or if everyone simply hates me, and how long it will take the agency to discover I'm a dud.

"Would you also like a glass?" Jean-Pierre asks and presses one into my hand without waiting for an answer. He looks relaxed and cheerful and bounces around his guests, tapping backs, pinching bottoms, and laughing out loud. Olympe's toys have been cleared away, there's nary a trace of her. I hope she can sleep with this racket.

Britta fluffs her hair with her fingers. She leans in closer to me. "*I'm feeling a little underdressed*," she whispers in Swedish.

"*Yeah, me too. And my feet are killing me.*"

Someone taps me on the shoulder and I turn to see Anne's bright smile. She has added a bright-purple liner around her eyes and her freckles are nearly invisible.

"Jirina, Britta! I wondered where you girls were." She double airkisses us and her eyes veer from us into the crowd. She waves.

"Have you met Didier?" she says and leans in closer to us, continuing in a hush. "He's a photographer; he does a lot of work for *Les Mariages*, you girls would be perfect for it—Didier, ça va toi?" Her head flies up to greet him. Didier is a beefy, florid man with an obvious comb-over who is rather neglectful with personal space; he practically glues himself onto Anne.

"Have you met our new girls?" she says, and steps away a touch.

"Non, I haven't had the pleasure," he says, licking his lips and eyeing me as though I am a delicious morsel. There is a moment of creepy pleasure in this. I can't recall a time in my life when I had such an effect on anyone.

"This is Jirina," Anne introduces me, pronouncing my name in the French way, *Zheerreenah*. Unfortunately, it sounds even worse than the Swedish version.

"Bonsoir, Zheerreenah," he says and brings my hand to his lips, all the while studying me intently. "Dis donc," he says, letting his arm drop but keeping my hand in his. "Elle a l'air tellement de la Birkin, n'est ce pas?"

Anne squints at me, and then smiles. "Ah oui, t'as raison!"

I understand Didier said I look a lot like someone or something named "labirkin," and that Anne absolutely agrees. But who or what this labirkin is, or what it looks like, is completely beyond me. I can only hope it's not a small brown animal.

"Do you like the wedding dress?" he says, his moist little eyes studying me up and down. I stare back in alarm. Is this some kind of a proposal?

"I love wedding dresses!" Britta jumps in.

Anne introduces Britta and Didier kisses her hand. He lingers a moment longer over hers.

"I look at wedding magazines all the time," she continues. "Not that I'm anywhere near getting married," she says, laughing, "but the pictures are so beautiful, so romantic, you know?"

I'm such an idiot. *Les Mariages* means "weddings." He does photographs for a wedding magazine. I quickly smile at him, lips firmly closed.

Didier inspects us both with a clinical eye, like a doctor. "J'ai un boulot Mercredi," he says to Anne. "Et, j'ai besoin de sang nouveau."

I understand he says he needs new blood, for something on Wednesday.

"I love wedding magazines, too," I quip. I don't need the nudge from Britta's elbow to tell me I sound like a complete sycophant.

I am spared further embarrassment by the arrival of a tall brunette with sharp collarbones and a glittery tube top.

"You want some?" she says. She's holding out one of Marina's small cigarettes that's burning down to a stump. Britta smiles. "No, thank you, I don't smoke cigarettes."

"But it isn't"—the brunette giggles—"a cigarette."

"Ça va, Lauren," Anne says with a frown. *That's enough, Lauren.*

Didier puts a flabby arm around the brunette's shoulders and with his other pulls her hand close to his mouth, inhaling the smoke as though she is his human cigarette holder.

"It is much better than a cigarette," he says, coughs, and winks at Britta.

"Well, in that case"—Britta says and steps in closer to them—"let me have a puff." Didier eases the cigarette from Lauren's fingers and passes it to Britta. She holds it between her thumb and her index finger and inhales. "Good stuff," she says, coughing, and passes it to me. There is not much left of it; the tiny cylinder almost burns my fingers. It won't even fit between my lips: If I try to have a drag, I'll probably swallow it whole. Anne comes to my rescue. She snatches it from me, shoots Lauren and Didier a dirty look, and walks away.

"Mesdemoiselles, c'était un plaisir, we will meet very soon." Didier gives us a small bow.

"So, what *was* that?" I ask Britta when Didier and his human cigarette holder are out of earshot.

"What, you don't know?" she says. "You've never smoked marijuana?" I shake my head. I have no idea what that is, but it sounds illegal.

"Geez, what rock have you been living under?" Britta laughs.

I should have taken a puff.

Jean-Pierre approaches us. He's holding a photograph and waves it back and forth like a fan.

"Oh. What's that, can I see?" Britta squeals and pinches the photo out of Jean-Pierre's grasp. She studies it and then laughs uncomfortably, as if something is stuck in her throat.

"C'est la vague, non?" Jean-Pierre says.

"May I look?" I ask. Britta hands it over. It's a black-and-white Polaroid. Jean-Pierre's face is in the left corner, with his tongue stuck out in a slightly obscene way. Something large and white fills most of the frame. I can't quite make it out. It looks like a blurry moon with a cleft on the bottom. I turn the picture upside down, sideways—and still can't figure it out.

"Let me just go and clean up. I'll be right back," Britta says to me as much as to Jean-Pierre. She sets off at a brisk pace through the crowd. That leaves Jean-Pierre and me in awkward silence. I take a gulp of my wine and glance back at the photo. Suddenly the amorphous white blob takes shape. A large, naked—presumably female—bottom. Marina's, it dawns on me. My wine spurts out my nose.

"Ça va?" Jean-Pierre comes to my rescue, slapping me on the back.

"Fine, fine," I cough. His hands on my back feel indecent, dirty somehow.

"Let me get you a tissue," he says and runs off.

I set the picture down on a nearby table, but the image won't go away. I wipe my nose with my sleeve. In this world, I'm judged an adult. One that can be shown pornographic images, offered marijuana and glasses of wine as casually as if they were candy. I'm not sure if I ought to be flattered or disgusted. My head reels. I feel slightly nauseous, but it could be the alcohol. I take another sip and pretend I'm fascinated by the liquid in my glass. Out of the corner of my eye, I notice a tall man with broad shoulders standing by the fireplace. He's dressed far more casually than the rest of the crowd, in black jeans and a faded denim shirt. His hair is longish and wavy, an indeterminate color somewhere between brown and blond. I watch his back and wonder what the front looks like. If it's anywhere near as good as the back, he's gorgeous. He's in a conversation with Didier, who is now sweating so profusely, droplets spray every time he nods or shakes his head.

For the first time I see the appeal of a cigarette. Hold one and you can stand anywhere looking like you're doing something. "What, me alone? No way, I'm busy—smoking!"

Marina spots me standing alone and weaves her way over. I realize for the first time that she's actually not bad looking; her pale eyes rimmed with black are nearly translucent and her hair is clean and shiny, hugging her head like sleek fur. Shoji is on her heels, holding the small noncigarette in one hand, a glass in the other.

"It seems you impressed Didier," Marina says with a nod toward him, and parks her butt on an armrest closest to me. Her white bottom. I blush.

"Um." I have trouble meeting her eyes, and instead cast glances at the owner of the handsome back who still hasn't turned. "I don't know about impressed," I mumble, "but he seemed very nice."

"He asked Anne to put her on hold," Shoji says to Marina and takes a deep drag of the cigarette, doing that weird holding-his-breath thing.

Put me on hold? I know this is the step before "confirmed." Anne explained it briefly at the agency: If a client is interested in a girl but not ready to commit, he puts her "on hold," so no one else can book her the same day. I try, and fail, to hide what feels like a conceited smile: It's not like I have been confirmed.

"Just her or both of them?" Marina says while Shoji passes her the burning stump. My smugness instantly evaporates. I look to Shoji for confirmation, but he's shaking his head and waving his arms, intent on not breathing. I'm impressed; it looks painful.

Marina shrugs and inhales. "If there's a choice, he'll pick this one," she croaks, pointing her cigarette at me.

I look at her wide-eyed. Where did *this* Marina come from?

Suddenly, the man of the handsome back turns to wave good-bye to someone and I finally see his face. With sparkling black eyes under an unruly fringe, sharp-cut cheekbones, tanned skin, and a dangerous looking white grin, he looks like a pirate from a Barbara Cartland novel.

Our eyes meet for a brief second across the room. He smiles. I turn purple.

An overly tanned man leans out of the chair on which Marina perches. "Who will be our next star?" he says. "I overheard."

"Ah, Claude, meet Jirina," Marina says.

Claude's face breaks into a hundred little creases with his smile.

"Oh, the girl with the funny name," he says. "Who didn't know the use of the bidet!"

Shame rushes over me so hotly I feel like I have been set on fire. Did everyone hear that? Or maybe Marina has already told them all, a fun little anecdote about her idiot guest to get the party started. I dare not look around, so as not to see the smiles, the smiles that are probably once again pointed at me like weapons.

THE DOOR TO THE bathroom is closed and the hallway is mercifully dark and empty. I lean my head against the wall and feel humiliation continue to prickle my skin. A strange sound comes down from the forbidden part of the hallway. A mewl, like a cat singing on a roof.

A sliver of light creeps across my face as Britta steps out of our room. She has put on makeup and changed into a blue tank top. She sees me and jumps. "Hey there, you scared me. You okay?"

"Fine, fine." I squint into the light. "Just need to use the bathroom."

She hesitates. "You don't need to puke or anything—"

"No, no, really, I'm fine." I jerk the door open and step into the bathroom where I startle a blond woman in front of the mirror.

"Oh, sorry, didn't know anyone was in here," I say. The woman spins around to face me and I feel the air dip, like turbulence in a plane. Evalinda.

The Evalinda stands but two feet away. Her long legs are sheathed in faded blue jeans so tight they look like panty hose and her cleavage is shown to the greatest advantage by a plunging V-neck sweater. With a small oval face set on a long thin neck, she looks like a young racehorse. She smiles.

"I came in . . . to wash my hands," I say.

"Go right ahead," she says. Her hair is a startling platinum shade, nearly pearlescent under the light. She rummages through Britta's makeup bag that sits on the shelf below the mirror. She pulls out a lip gloss and smears the wand on her full lips. "Black eyeliner and pale lips, that's the shit," she says, dropping the lip gloss back in favor of a kohl pencil. "Don't you think?"

"Oh yes." I nod eagerly. My every move seems exaggerated: the way I walk to the sink, how my stupid head nods and bobs like one of those Hawaiian hula girls stuck on dashboards. I can feel her eyes on me as I quickly wash my hands and do a quick calculation: She mustn't have heard about the bidet or she wouldn't be talking to me.

"Here," she says, handing me the pencil. "You could use some."

I fight with black grease inside my eye while she leisurely strolls to examine the bottles on top of the tub.

"Timotei!" she exclaims and holds up a bottle of Britta's shampoo. "Who's Swedish here?"

"I am Swedish. And so is my friend Britta," I say in Swedish.

"Yeah, Skåne," she says. *"Your accent is impossible to miss."*

I smile, although I'm perturbed at this slight cut. I know my accent immediately confines me to being from the Skåne region and it smacks of farmers, fields, and manure, but affecting the more "cultured" accent of Stockholm—although easily enough done—makes me feel like a fast-food waitress in a ball gown.

"Hmm," she says and holds up Joy body wash. "Marina's, I bet." She untwists the top and dabs a little behind her ears.

"That's soap," I point out.

She glances at the text on the bottle. "Yep, so it says," she says indifferently. "What kind of perfume do you like?"

I throw out the first name that comes to mind. "La Grande Passion," I say, although I've never smelled it.

She smiles. "Cool. I'll get you some." She has been the face of La Grande Passion for two years.

"Really? That would be so nice of you!"

"I *am* nice," she says.

"Oh, yes, of course," I agree quickly.

She has run out of things to open and examine, and with a falling heart I realize she will leave soon.

"I read an article about you recently, in *Woman's Weekly,* and it said something about you being an actress now?" I toss out uncertainly.

This seems to be the magic that holds onto her a little longer. She brightens and sits down on the rim of the tub to tell me about the movie she was in, a convoluted plot of drug dealing, the Arab mafia, and prostitution, financed by an Italian movie studio. I nod so eagerly my neck threatens to snap.

"I play this prostitute who gets killed while she's going down on her client," she says, sliding her hair between her fingers and examining the ends.

There it is again, the mewl from the hallway.

I manage a "wow" and wonder what it means to go down on a client.

"Yeah, it was intense," she says. The sound from the hallway intensifies.

Evalinda pulls out a cigarette and crosses her legs. "This director called me, 'cause he saw me on the cover of *Madame Figaro,* and—"

"Hang on just a sec?" I stick my head out the door to listen. The party's noise level is high, but yes, there is that sound, woven in between the laughter and the music.

Olympe! There is breathiness, a hoarse quality to her shrieks. She must have been crying for a long time. I glance back at my new friend. Evalinda is here, talking to me, confiding in me. How cool is that? Everyone back home would be dying of jealousy if they knew.

Another shriek pierces right through me. Now that I'm aware of Olympe, I have trouble focusing.

Evalinda smiles. "He sent me the script, and—"

I stand up. "You know what? Can you just hold that thought for a second, I need to attend to something. It will only take a minute."

"Well, all right, I need to take a piss anyway," she says. She stands up and starts unbuttoning her jeans.

"Um. That's the bidet," I say. "The toilet is next door."

She laughs. "As if I don't know."

"I'll be right back," I say, and run out.

Marina still sits on the armrest where I left her. "Olympe is awake and crying," I tell her. I cast a quick glance around the room and note the pirate is gone.

"So? She'll go back to sleep soon."

"But she's been crying for a long time," I insist. She looks at me with glazed eyes and giggles.

"Then she'll be exhausted and sleep better."

I run back to the bathroom. I put my hand on the door handle but the sad, ragged cry of a baby that's too tired to call for help stops me. I stand, twitching like a horse at the starting gate.

I hope Evalinda will pee for a while.

I make my way down the forbidden dark hallway, letting Olympe's voice guide me to her room. Hopefully Marina won't mind what she won't know.

Olympe stands in her crib, soaking wet from tears and her leaking diaper. Scant moonlight filters through the window. Her face is distorted from the exertion.

"Ça va, ma petite," I tell her. "It's me, Gigi." I pick her up and she quiets to whispery sobs.

I change her quickly in the dark, while fervently praying Evalinda is still waiting for me. I set Olympe down in the crib, retrieve her pacifier and stick it in her mouth. There, I'm free. But the moment I turn away, she starts screaming again. The pacifier falls out. I bend back down to find it.

"It's okay, ça va," I repeat, but Olympe grabs a hold of my neck. Gently I pry her little fingers off and sit down on the floor next to the crib, holding her hand through the bars to reassure her.

"I'm here, je suis ici," I mumble, and stroke her hair. Go to sleep. Please go to sleep. I think of Evalinda waiting in the bathroom. My hands shake with impatience.

She finally sits down and I continue to stroke her until she falls over like a puppy wanting to have its stomach tickled. I listen to her breathing as it steadies. This dark musty bedroom with diaper odor feels like a grave in which my newly acquired touch of importance is laid to rest along with the child. The music is a barely audible rhythmic thump in the distance, pierced with the occasional loud laughter of happy people having fun. My eyelids are so heavy I need to close them, just for a minute.

.　　.　　.

A GUST OF AIR and the blaring of car horns wake me in my own bed. Britta stands by the open window facing the room. Her hair catches the breeze and glows gold in the backlight. I have a quick, sharp pain, a physical manifestation of jealousy as the image sinks in. She looks impossibly beautiful: *Venus* by Botticelli. All she needs are stenciled letters above her head—*Vogue, Elle, L'Officiel*. I cringe under my blanket at a sudden, horrible wish that she'd step just a little too far backward, out the window, out of my way. My remorse is instant and equally painful. This is a wonderful opportunity for God to smite evil, wicked me. *Please God; I'm sorry. Let* her *get the wedding job next week.*

Grandma had long ago instilled in me a fear of God. For everyday misdemeanors, there was always my mother to dole out punishments (my father on the odd weekends). But during the long hot days of vacation, the responsibility was Grandma's. And God's. I spent every summer of my life (until Kristynka was born) getting shuffled off to my father's mother, learning Czech, and soaking up an accidental religious education. Two months of Grandma and me, while I fumbled my pronunciation and the impossible, soft "*R*" sound, eating dumplings, pork, and farmer cheese to put some meat on my bones, spending lazy days in the garden reading, mushroom hunting in dark fairy-tale forests, being hugged and kissed and slapped and fed and lectured and prayed for and tucked in and held at night. God was an overwhelming presence at Grandma's house, he was frequently consulted, cajoled, and appeased and—I learned—watched my every move and heard my every thought. "God knows everything," Grandma warned me on the odd occasion I'd try to fib. Maybe that's why I am a clinically incompetent liar.

"Get up, lazy," Britta shouts across the room and turns to close the window. The curtains fall back into place and the sunlight is gone.

OUR STREET IS EMPTY but for a few harried Asian women who push strollers, while gusts of air whip up papers from garbage cans and deposit them on the babies. The Metro is, in contrast, all exhale-breath warm and smells metallically of train brakes. It's a straight blue line from Porte de Maillot to the Palais Royal-Louvre station in our Plan de Paris.

Finally, I get to gaze at the *Mona Lisa*. Unfortunately, it's from fifty feet away through a mob of German tourists and a glass pane with a solid reflection of the spotlights above it. All I can make out is her left shoulder. A girl with bangs teased so high and flat she looks like someone pressed her between the pages of a book steps in and blocks my view.

Britta nudges me. "All right, done?"

I sigh. We've only been here for five minutes, but she wants to go shopping. I will have to come back on my own some other time.

We walk out and make a right on rue de Rivoli, which eventually leads us to rue St. Denis.

"Are you sure this is the right street?" Britta asks after we pass yet another woman dressed in dirty lingerie, stilettos, and a feather boa, leaning on a door frame, a cigarette dangling from her lips. "These are prostitutes, you know," she whispers loudly.

I nod as if I were perfectly aware of this, but my perception of a French prostitute, like Zola's *Nana*, takes a serious beating.

We finally find the pedestrian square with the fountain and the flaming pink sign announcing Fiorucci. The scent of butter and burned sugar waft through the air from a cart selling paper-thin crepes soaked in jam or butter, sprinkled with powdered sugar. I buy one and Britta wolfs down three while we sit on a bench and watch people. Some have caught on to the Adam and the Ants bandwagon: The guys are sporting old-fashioned vests over T-shirts, studded belts, tiny braids, and the occasional long earring; the girls' hair is teased into palm trees; they wear leg-warmers over high heels and scarves around their hips. A few punks huddle by the back of the fountain, pale, pierced, and mean-looking with their spikes and black lips. But the overwhelming majority is dressed in jeans and motorcycle jackets, a sort of middle of the road between the two extremes. Britta points out a young guy who leans on the side of the fountain strumming a guitar while his friends recline on the stone lip. "He's kinda cute, isn't he?" she says. With a mop of dark curls and faded jeans, he looks like a younger version of Jean-Pierre.

"Hmm, in a French way," I say with a shrug.

We enter the cavernous Fiorucci store to the beat of a mournful rock song in which the singer sounds as though he has a bad cold. I can only make out the words in the chorus, *London calling*. Fashion here is different from the way it is back home; everything is brighter, shinier, and a lot more expensive. My hundred francs will buy me a T-shirt, but since it's all the money I have in the world, I resist temptation and instead make a long mental list of all the things I would buy if I could. Britta buys a pair of fuchsia hot pants so tight she has to lie down in the fitting room to zip them up. She spends the equivalent of my monthly salary at the tobacco store.

When we exit, Jean-Pierre Jr. and his friends at the fountain whistle at Britta. I fall back a little, feeling like a Victorian spinster escort.

"Bonjour Mesdemoiselles, ça va?" Jean-Pierre Jr. says and unfolds to his full height—our waists.

Britta smiles. "Je ne parle pas Francais."

"It is okay, I speak the English good," he says proudly. "You want to go to the movie this night with me?"

"Oh yeah, now *that's* good English," I whisper to Britta. She shrugs me off, but her smile is a little surprised. Back home, it's usually the girls who ask for dates. One of his friends steps up to us. He's slightly pudgy with a potato nose. Jean Pierre Jr. and he exchange a few words, casting quick glances at us.

"Eh, you can take your skinny friend with you," Jean Pierre Jr. says to Britta, indicating me with a casual wave.

I've never felt quite this much like the ugly stepsister. With Hatty, at least neither one of us got any attention.

Jean-Pierre Jr. gives Britta his phone number and she tucks it into her pocket.

"You call me, I give you a good time," he shouts after us.

BY THE TIME we reach Prisunic, the store is closed. I swallow my annoyance at Britta; it was her idea to walk around until dusk. She wants to go and have dinner, but I need to call Mother, so we split up at the Metro.

Mother greets me with, "So, are they sending you back yet?"

"No," I retort, my voice sounding a bit more defensive than I'd like. "In fact"—I know I shouldn't jinx it, but I can't stop—"I might even have a job next week."

There is a slight pause.

"You *might*?" Mother says coolly. "I wouldn't count the money made off the eggs from the chickens you haven't bought yet." It's one of her mangled Czech proverbs she uses when she doesn't quite know what to say. At least this one is pretty comprehensible, unlike: "He is as quick as though he's shitting and painting," which means someone is dawdling, and "It's on the sack," which mean something is useless. I'm sure they make perfect sense in Czech, but in my mother's heavily accented Swedish they make her sound quaint, if not downright incoherent.

"So, how is Kristynka?" I change the subject. "Did she finish the antibiotics?" I dare not say, "Did you remember to give them?" but she picks up on it anyway.

"Don't be ridiculous. I'm her mother." Her tone has something uncertain about it, and I'm not sure whether it is because she did forget the medication, or because she is unsure of her maternity.

"Can I speak to her?"

"Uh, she's playing outside with Ingmar."

"Please."

I hear the drop of the receiver, and her voice from far away shouting Kristynka's name. Footsteps, door slams, and my little sister's breathing precedes her on the line.

"*Eena!*" she exclaims, out of breath. It's what she's called me since she discovered my name wasn't Mama.

"Hi, my little Green-bean."

"When are you coming home?"

"Not for a while. After you're out of camp."

"I can't go to camp. Mommy said we don't have enough money because you went to Paris, France." I'm not sure what hurts more, her suddenly calling Mother "Mommy" or my mother's outright lie. My ticket was paid by the agency, and the hundred kronas I was handed shouldn't have made a significant dent.

"Listen, Green-bean, I think I'll have a job next week, and I will send the money right away. So you can go to camp. Tell Mom, all right?"

"Okay," she says, sounding doubtful. Then her tone changes. "Eena, guess what, I got a diamond necklace in a plastic egg. Mommy bought it for me from the supermarket!"

We conclude our conversation with a thousand kisses, but she is distracted, anxious to go back out and play.

I hang up consumed by frustration. Mother has clearly been "mothering" in my absence, and though I know I should be happy on Kristynka's account, I can't help feeling shoved aside, by both of them. I'm no longer important. I'm no longer needed. And to top if off, I'm positive I've now completely jinxed any chance of a possible job.

Through the open door I glimpse Olympe in the dark living room, seemingly on her own, playing with something on the floor. It takes me a beat to realize she's taking out cigarette butts from an ashtray and sticking them in the pocket of her dress. I run over to her. Her face and hands are smeared with ashes, but she gives me a dazzling smile. "Gigi!"

I pick her up. She smells of cigarettes and poop. This child sorely needs a bath. Only now do I notice a small Asian lady, fast asleep on one of the leather chairs. This must be her nanny. And what a good one, I think ruefully. I take Olympe to the bathroom and fill the bathtub with water. While I bathe her, I try to convince her to call me Eena. She repeats it a few times and laughs. The nanny stumbles in with sleep-swollen eyes as I'm getting a towel ready to get Olympe out. She's clutching her hand to her chest, and when she sees us, obvious relief washes over her face. I try to explain, but her French seems worse than mine and she rips the towel from my hands and holds it out to the child.

Olympe frowns and shakes her head. "No, Gigi. Je veux Gigi."

So much for Eena. But still, a wave of warmth washes over me. She wants *me*. I look to the nanny and indicate by pointing to the towel and at myself that I'll get the child out. She hands me the towel and backs away to perch on the rim of the bidet. Olympe reaches her chubby little arms to me and I envelop her in the towel and pick her up. Maybe if this modeling thing doesn't work out, I could be Olympe's nanny? The thought flashes in and out, but I quickly rewind it to fully savor it. Why not? That would be a way to stay in Paris.

I CALL THE AGENCY first thing Monday morning as we've been instructed. Britta is by the mirror, making a production out of brushing her hair, but I know she's listening.

Anne's voice over the phone sounds excited. "I have some good news for you."

My heart adds a beat.

"You have a job on Wednesday!" she says. "For *Les Mariages*."

Happiness unfurls inside me like an umbrella. "Really?"

"Yes, you have been confirmed," Anne laughs. She goes on to give me the list of today's go-and-sees and asks to speak to Britta.

My happiness snaps shut. Oh no, what about Britta? Will this be the end of our friendship?

I hand her the receiver and begin making my bed while I watch her out of the corner of my eye. She turns red at whatever it is that Anne relays to her.

"Cool," she says into the mouthpiece and throws a quick glance at me. "Great, I will." She hangs up and we face each other in silence.

"So what did she tell you?" I ask. How will I tell her I got the job?

She breaks out in a huge grin. "I got a job for *Les Mariages* on Wednesday!"

She did? We *both* did? My disillusionment is immediate. I'm not special.

I fluff my pillow and set it down. "Guess what. I did too."

For a brief moment, something like disappointment flickers across her face. The air between us goes thin and crackly. I'm suddenly in an old-fashioned cowboy shoot-out, facing my friend, guns loaded and pointed at each other.

I decide to lower mine first. "Isn't it wonderful?" I say. "We both got the job."

"Great," she says, and looks as unhappy as I feel.

CHAPTER 5

When at last the sun illuminates the fronts of the buildings across the street, we board a dusty red van helmed by a young man named Jean Marie.

Out the window, a tangle of highways gives way to foam-green wheat fields and huddled gray villages. About an hour later, and just as I start to wonder if we have been kidnapped for white slavery, we arrive at the photographer's country estate: a small stone house surrounded by vast lawns and flowerbeds in bloom. It's the most perfectly romantic setting one could conjure. Inside, however, the house is furnished with—gasp—black leather couches and cheap side tables, which leaves me to ponder if there was some sort of a giant sale on office furniture recently, or whether it's a natural French inclination toward home furnishings, like naming all males Jean-something.

Didier, the sweaty photographer we met at the party, greets us inside a kitchen with a fireplace large enough to roast a whole cow, where an array of fresh fruit, coffee, and croissants is spread on the table.

A group of people stands about and we are introduced to Emanuel, the makeup artist, and Hank, an Australian hairdresser with no hair.

Emanuel looks like a caffeine-loaded squirrel, all teeth and nervous energy. He's tiny, and his mop of mahogany hair sticks up all over his head in spiral curls. It's impossible to guess his age: He could be a very worn twenty, or a well-preserved forty. Britta wastes no time and loads up a plate with croissants. I follow suit, spearing fresh strawberries with my fork next to some guy. Our forks collide over slices of cantaloupe.

"Oh, sorry," I say and turn to face him. Black curls frame his pale face: limpid amber eyes stare into mine. He's dressed in black, but radiates coolness like an open refrigerator door. I immediately go through my thin catalogue of things to say to gorgeous men and come up with, "Hi."

He looks at me. I look at his hands. They are long-fingered and delicate, his nails clean and shell-pink-smooth.

"Bonjour, I'm Frederic," he says.

"Do you play the piano?" I blurt.

He eyes me with momentary surprise. "How do you know?"

"Uh. Frederic. Like Chopin?"

He smiles. "Call me Freddy." His teeth are long and uneven, which lends his poet features a slightly decadent air. "I will be your husband today."

I have a flash of inspiration. "My name is *Yee-ree-nah*," I say. "But you can call me George."

He looks puzzled. "That is a strange name for a woman."

Emanuel interrupts my fumbled flirtation and whisks me off to the shade of a tree where he has set up his makeup station. He asks me how to pronounce my name while nudging me into a tall chair. I spell it out for him in Czech, Swedish, and French as he pins the hair off my face and begins to apply a cool liquid foundation.

"What pleasure," he says, "to have such beautiful skin."

I've never given my skin much thought, in fact, I would have gladly traded it for a casual case of acne any day if it also came with big boobs, curvy hips, blond hair, and a respectable height of five-two.

Emanuel's words don't have the soft guttural roll of a French accent. Instead, he speaks with a singsong, lisping lilt. "So many girls, they don't have good skin, and you know, it is very hard to make good skin on pictures."

Suddenly, I'm quite proud to be the owner of unblemished skin.

"Even some of the top models don't have good skin. Can you imagine? It costs the magazines a fortune to do retouching."

"What's that?"

"Oh, you are new," he laughs. "Why do you think all the girls look so perfect on the magazines? It is not because they were all born that way, honey. Oh no. Half of it is me." He points the sponge at his chest. "The other half is retouching. You see, they take the photo, and they paint away all the nasty stuff before it is printed. Pimples: gone. The red eyes: poof. They can even change the color of the eyes: but only for the covers or beauty spreads, because it is expensive. Comprende?"

I try to nod my head, but he holds my face still with his hands and exclaims, "No, no, don't move!"

"So which of the top models have you worked with?" I ask, while his fingers sweep across my face.

"Oh honey, most of them. Janice, she's *craaazy* but so much fun, Evalinda, Kelly, Josephine, you name them—I have done them."

I'm so impressed I nearly break a sweat. These hands—that push, press, smudge, and rub my face—have touched the faces of angels. Doing my face must seem, in comparison, akin to Picasso painting his kitchen wall.

"What is Evalinda like?" I try to sound casual about my almost friend.

"Oh she? She is *craaazy*. But not in such a good way, you understand? No, no, don't nod."

Every time he leans over me, I have the unnerving impression he is about to kiss me.

"And now I am putting on the eyeliner so no talk from you, okay honey?"

I close my eyes to the cold lick above my lashes and Emanuel's scent of cinnamon with a slight garlic undertone.

My grandma put garlic in everything she cooked. Her breakfast consisted of black coffee with a half cup of sugar, and toast spread with raw garlic. Every time I hugged her large, bony frame, I'd get a comforting whiff. Unfortunately, back home garlic is a dirty word. How I suffered on those days my mother decided in economical fury to cook garlic soup. Made with nothing more than hot water, a little egg, and heaps of garlic, it effectively stretched my mother's budget, as well as the tolerance of my classmates who withdrew even further away from me, calling me "stinky" besides the old reliable "communist bastard" or "communist cow."

I am acutely aware of my own breath and make sure to breathe only through my nose. Emanuel hovers above me and asks me to "look up, look down, sideways to the right, upper left." I catch a glimpse of Britta on a chair nearby where Hank twists her hair up in strange knobs. I can't help but rejoice in the depths of my miserable soul that the style makes her look like a demented sheep.

A black car pulls into the driveway and an impossibly beautiful creature gets out. Everyone abandons their posts and runs to greet her.

"Hello, girlfriend," Emanuel shouts and waves to her. "You excuse me for a moment," he says to me. "I have to go and kiss Lorna."

Lorna totters across the lawn toward us in very spiky heels, clutching a tiny bag under her arm. Her hair is a black cloud framing a face the color of milk and the orange eyes of a Persian cat. This girl is so exquisite, so far above me, that my jealous fangs remain withdrawn in shock inside my open mouth.

Emanuel sprints to her and leaps into her arms like a monkey. "Oh, honey, it's been a long time! Where have you been?"

With their arms entwined and chatting happily, they make their way to me.

"Do you mind?" Emanuel asks me and tilts my chair so I slide off. "The clients asked me to do her first."

I sit down on the grass next to Lorna's feet and memorize her gestures, admire her casualness, envy the ease with which she informs us of her vacation, her abortion, and the old Arab that stalks her, offering her diamond rings the size of ostrich eggs for the pleasure of a single night.

It takes Hank an hour to finish my hair, and when I look in the mirror it looks exactly the same: a straight brown bob parted in the middle. My face is pale and even, and my eyes are bruised with blue and pink eye shadow. It's still me, and really not any better.

I go back to Emanuel for the finishing touches. He applies blush all the way to my temples, and then outlines my lips with a pencil.

"You know, you remind me of someone," he says, unscrewing a lipstick and dipping a small brush into the pink cylinder. "No, don't speak. It will come to me in a moment."

That leaves me sitting in tense silence, while he painstakingly dabs at my lips.

LORNA MAKES IT LOOK so easy. She sits on a bench under a mound of blooming roses, the skirt of her wedding dress spread around her, her hand in Frederic's. Her hair is swept up in a chignon at the nape of her neck where a single white rose glows against her black hair. Jean Marie runs out in front of her and holds a small black box by her nose. Then he scurries to the camera, adjusting something, and Didier bends over the tripod. Lorna turns her face slightly this way, then that, with a small smile on her glossy lips as the camera whirs and clicks in approval.

I'm chomping at the bit. Let me out there; let me show you how well I can sit and look besotted by Frederic.

"You, viens avec moi." The stylist taps me on the shoulder. My stomach leaps sideways. Suddenly, I'm not so sure I can do it.

We walk to the house, passing Britta on the way. She's in the makeup chair, her face coated with a smooth layer of powder. But no amount of makeup is going to improve those silly knobs on her head. I'm awful. I know.

One of the upstairs bedrooms has been converted into a temporary dressing room and we have to sidestep racks of foamy white fabric. I imagine myself in a princess dress, nipped at the waist, maybe a long veil and a diamond tiara?

The stylist throws me a bundle of blue-white textile and I take it to the bathroom. It has a high neck with some sort of a lace bib attached to it and it shines like an oilcloth—which is exactly what it feels like when I put it on. There must be some mistake. The dress is huge. I walk out of the bathroom.

"I'm sorry, it doesn't seem to fit," I say, and start to remove it, but the stylist whips me around to face the mirror and grabs a firm hold of the excess fabric from behind. Yes, that's better, but before I have the time to contemplate how I can do a picture with a stylist attached to my back, she fastens the dress with giant industrial clamps. Hank sticks a floral headband in my hair and I take a look in the mirror. I look like—me. Hot chick NO, hot chicken, YES. There is nothing remotely inspiring about my test-tube-shaped body in a cheap polyester wedding dress and scraggly white flowers perched on my head. How would Lorna look in this? What would she do? The clamps on my back clink against each other with my every step.

Hank leads me to the rear of the garden, where Frederic waits under a tree. We pass Britta, whose head is suddenly full of the most perfect ringlets. So that's what those knobs were for! Envy edges under my skin. Why couldn't Hank have done that to my hair?

Frederic looks bored. With one hand he leans on a small table with a bowl of cherries, with the other he leisurely pops the cherries into his mouth and spits the pits over his shoulder. Didier indicates my spot with a casual wave and I clomp over to Frederic. Jean Marie holds the black box in front of my nose and I get a whiff of sweaty hands. He clicks a button on the side a few times and, satisfied, returns to Didier.

Now what? Panic sets in. How can I pretend to be someone else? How can I look like Lorna's swan when all I see is a scrawny pigeon?

The stylist stands behind Didier, with a hand shading her eyes. I rewind to Lorna's doe-eyed smile, and attempt the same.

"Attention! C'est pas bien, ça!" Didier exclaims.

It takes me a moment to realize that by turning sideways, I've just revealed my disfigured backside. So I turn full on to the camera. Is this good? Apparently, no. Didier straightens out from behind the tripod. "Do not be so stiff. Do something!"

I rearrange my bouquet. Is this better? Nope. Didier is still standing up, and now looks impatient. Sweat trickles under my arms and the knowledge I will return the dress sopping wet only increases the output.

Didier turns to Emanuel. "Tu veux mettre la musique?"

I understand Emanuel has just been asked to put on the music. I lean on the table while Emanuel disappears inside the house. Frederic keeps eating the cherries. I offer him a smile, but realize he's not looking at me. My smile feels as pathetic as an outstretched hand blindly waving about, so I cast my eyes down, pretending I'm smiling at some amusing inner thought.

The sound comes blasting out from corners of the house: first a plucked bass in traditional rock-and-roll chords, then it stops, and an organ spins out notes that sound familiar, like I may have heard it at weddings. Emanuel hops out, arms open wide, and twirls around like a dervish, exclaiming, "Je t'aime, ah oui, je t'aime," along with the voice of a little girl that hurls out from hidden speakers in the garden.

"Alors, on y va." Didier claps his hands and bends over the tripod.

The little girl is answered by a velvety masculine voice as the organ spins the same familiar notes over and over. Hidden outside speakers. What sophistication. I put a hand on my hip—a gesture that seems to work in a million magazines—and clutch the flowers with my other hand while I gaze at the horizon.

"Mais non, trop posée, too much posed," Didier exclaims. "Be natural!"

The music isn't helping. Instead, it conspires to make me feel as though I'm onstage under a spotlight, the orchestra playing and the audience holding their breath for my performance to begin. If only I knew what the performance was! I let my arms fall to my side. They have unexpectedly grown heavier and longer; I sag under their weight. Gorilla in a wedding dress. Is this natural enough? I throw a hopeful glance at the camera. Didier stands straight, hands on hips, and shakes his head. I guess not. On the soundtrack, the little girl warbles "*Je t'aime*" and the male voice insists "*Moi non plus,*" which I think means "me neither." It doesn't make any sense. Nothing makes sense. I am a big dumb beast, glaring around in fright, reduced to a moo when I'm expected to tap dance.

"You want?" Frederic offers me the bowl of cherries. I take one out and hold it in my fingertips. Now what? To eat it is out of the question. The little girl moans as if she's in pain. Frederic's face is very close. He winks at me and parts his lips. Am I to kiss him? What in the name of God am I supposed to do?

In utter panic I gag him with the cherry.

There is a momentary surprise in his eyes, and then his lips enclose the fruit. My finger brushes his lip, which is soft and dry. His eyes narrow, wrinkling at the corners. The little girl sighs and moans, but it doesn't seem like pain anymore.

"C'est bien! Do it more!" Didier exclaims.

I become aware of the clicking camera. I dip my fingers back into the bowl and pull out another cherry. I hold it out to him and then, as he's about to take a bite, I withdraw it. Pleasant flutters run up and down my arm as his lips make contact with my skin. The real music recedes to melodic sighs, and the whir of the camera motor takes on the main beat like a drumroll. *Ladies and gentlemen, heeere's Jirina, a model in the making!* I hold out the cherry again. His teeth sink into the flesh and juice stains my fingers. He pulls the fruit out of my grasp. My outstretched fingers hover emptily by his face and he licks the juice from my finger. He licked my finger! *Eeew.* Do it again! The lick leaves an imprint on my flesh, a small spot of lingering warmth. I have to resist the urge to look for a physical mark.

"Done," Didier says, and straightens up from behind the camera. The music is gone. I feel as though I've woken up from a dream. I look at Frederic for smile, a confirmation of the special moment we've just shared. He spits a loogie over his shoulder.

Okay. But he *is* good-looking.

. . .

MY PUMPKIN COACH has turned into a red van, my ball gown reverted to jeans and T-shirt, and the prince asked Lorna for her number.

Darkness whizzes by the rear window and the drone of the engine is both comforting and oppressive. The inky sky on the horizon is split by a scar of dying sunlight. Britta sits next to Jean Marie in the front with her head resting on the glass. We've barely spoken to each other throughout the day, her silence more pronounced with every dress I got to wear and she didn't. Lorna, of course, trumped us both, but that was to be expected.

I feel Britta's resentment like a physical force, a negative magnet pushing me away. I want to apologize, make her feel better, but how? "Sorry I got to wear three dresses and you only one," doesn't have quite the right ring to it. Nor does "I couldn't refuse, the gowns fit me better."

"You looked so beautiful in your shot," I say out loud to the silhouette of her shoulder. "You should have seen yourself. You looked like an angel."

She clears her throat as if she is about to say something, but then remains silent.

I WAIT UNTIL BRITTA has left the bathroom before I enter to take off my makeup. I stare into the mirror above the sink to see how my face, the same face I'm presented with every single day, has suddenly changed. How is it possible to go from a communist cow to beautiful in a mere week?

All right, my skin is good and my eyes look large. Eyes the color of frogs, Anika and Kristel said. But maybe, eyes the color of spring leaves? The color of sea glass?

The nose is my mother's, small and perky with a little flip at the end. A tiny skier could be launched off the tip. My lips that still bear traces of lipstick are evenly shaped but a little too wide, too full. Big enough to close over my wide-spaced front teeth. My dentist promised they would grow together, but for now, I could still floss with a broomstick.

I tilt my face up to the lights and let shadows carve my cheekbones and jaw. This is a rather nice angle, vaguely reminiscent of old movie-star photos. I part my lips and my teeth peek out like white mice.

. . .

WE WAKE UP and pour our morning coffee in silence. The warmth of our kindling friendship is gone. Instead, there is a chill, gusty breeze, the kind that makes for small choppy waves on water.

The fridge is nearly empty; no milk and nothing to eat. I wonder where Olympe is.

"What's on your schedule today?" I say.

Britta shrugs. "Don't know," she mumbles.

"You want me to run out and get some milk and a croissant?"

"I don't need anything," she snaps. She's wearing pajamas with shorts. I've never noticed before, but she is a little plump—as models go. She stands up, puts her cup in the sink, and leaves the kitchen. I walk back to our empty room; Britta must have gone to the bathroom. I pull out a drawer and search for something clean and it dawns on me I have no idea how I will wash my things once I run out of clean clothes. I take out a white T-shirt as Britta bursts through the door, shaking her bottle of Timotei at me. "Did you use my shampoo?"

"What?"

Her face is mottled and the rims of her eyes are red. Has she been crying?

"It's gone. All gone." Her voice is rising. "And I had a full bottle when we got here!" She flings the empty bottle on her bed.

"You are welcome to use mine."

"My hair only looks good with Timotei," she cries. "I bought a big bottle of it and now it's gone. Gone!" Her voice is full of accusation.

"It wasn't me, I swear."

She puts her hands on her hips. "Yeah, then why is it empty?"

"Britta," I say reasonably, "Timotei is for blondes, so it obviously wasn't me."

"So who was it?"

"I don't know. Marina? But listen, my shampoo is pretty decent, and if you don't want to use it, I can go and buy you a new bottle—"

"They don't sell Timotei in France. That's why I brought a big bottle," she hisses at me, every syllable clipped and precise.

Red sparks of anger flicker through me, but I breathe through them to remain calm. I cannot afford to lose the only friend I have here.

"Britta, please tell me what I can do to help you. I don't know who used your shampoo and I don't know how to get you a new bottle, but please, don't be mad at me, because I didn't do anything wrong."

"Right, you never do anything wrong, do you?" She turns away and adds, "Little Miss Perfect," under her breath.

This is the second time "perfect" has been used to describe me. And this time it hurts. I pick up my sweater and bag, and let the door fall closed behind me, before the sparks have time to flame.

CHAPTER 6

Shoji is talking on two phones at the same time, Odile is chewing on a cigarette while also on the phone, and Anne waves at me through the haze of cigarette smoke.

"Jirina! How was *Les Mariages* yesterday? Sorry, she's confirmed for Friday, how about Lauren?" she says into the receiver.

"It was fine. Great, actually," I say, but Anne has no time for my bragging.

"We have some new girls, maybe you would like to see them?" she says into the phone. To me she says, "Sorry, it's a madhouse in here right now, June is always a really busy month, for September, you know." She spins the bin, pulls out a chart, and makes a few notes.

I don't see what June has to do with September, but don't dare to ask. "Would it be all right to speak to Jean-Pierre, if he's here, that is—"

"In his office," she says, pointing her pen at the door next to the bathroom.

Jean-Pierre sits behind an enormous desk that takes up the entire cubicle. A huge poster of a beautiful woman's face is hung up on the wall, directly above his head. The face looks familiar. A large-toothed smile, sharp cheekbones, and icy blue eyes—the symmetry of Marina's face dawns on me for the first time. There is a certain amount of gruesomeness in seeing her face so youthful and blemish-free, when I know how the years will press their bitter lines into her smooth skin, cast a watery film over her eyes, and yellow the freshness of her smile. The picture of Dorian Gray, only reversed.

"How can I help you?" Jean-Pierre says. He indicates a folding chair opposite his desk.

I sit down. "I was wondering, well, I never got paid for *Les Mariages*, nor did Britta—I would love to send some money to my mother, if that's possible—"

"Ah, oui, no problem. Give me your voucher, please."

Uh-oh. "I'm sorry, I was a little overwhelmed by the language and the legal terms—"

He pulls out a rectangular booklet from his desk. "Anne gave you this with your portfolio, manual, and diary, n'est-ce pas?"

I nod.

"After every job, you fill out a voucher and have the client sign it. At the end of each week, you can come to me, give me your vouchers, and I will advance you the money."

I had assumed they would hand me the money at the end of the day like my Uncle at the tobacco store.

"The clients, they don't pay right away, sometimes not for many weeks," he says. "So we give you advance, and then they pay us. Only clients from other countries will pay you cash."

He shows me how to fill out the voucher. My name on top, followed by the client's name, the name of the company or magazine, and the rate, Tarif 3, which works out to be four hundred francs for one day. I'm floored. That's two months' salary at the tobacco store, and I've made it in *one day*!

"This one, we do not need the client's signature, for we work with them all the time, so I sign and, voilà, your money." He sticks his hand in a drawer and fishes out a wad of bills. "Would you like for us to send the money straight to your mother?"

"That would be great."

"Now, this is a higher than average rate, for the wedding magazines are not as prestigious as others."

My face is probably a huge question mark, and after a quick glance at me, he continues in a steady monotone that sounds like he's said this very thing a million times. "C'est comme ça. Editorials usually only pay Tarif 1, which is one hundred francs, no matter which magazine it is, because from the magazines, you get seen, and also you get the printed page, called a 'tear sheet,' for your book."

I nod my head seriously to show him I'm paying attention. "If I may ask, how much for something like *Vogue*?"

He looks slightly annoyed. "I just told you, Tarif 1, one hundred francs, it doesn't matter which magazine, how many pages, or even if you have the cover. The magazine rates are always Tarif 1, which is one hundred francs per day." I am momentarily stunned. Wait till Hatty hears this.

"Now, how much shall I send to your mother?" Jean-Pierre says, and rummages through his drawer.

I calculate quickly. "Three hundred," I say. "And can I have the remaining hundred? I need to buy some makeup for my kit." My kit—what a joke. I only have a dried out mascara and a Bonne Bell lip gloss.

He gives me a crisp hundred-franc note; I thank him and head for the door, when his voice stops me. "And one more thing," he says. "We need to talk about your teeth sometime."

The floor dips under me. Since nobody brought it up yet, I had stupidly hoped they didn't notice.

"Yeah, sure," I say over my shoulder, and launch myself out the door. I have a notion that if I make it out quickly enough, it will be as if it was never mentioned.

I sprint to the couch to pick up my portfolio. My teeth. My stupid teeth. Is this it?

"Jirina, wait," Anne shouts. I hold my breath. "Did Shoji tell you about Olivieri?"

I shake my head. Who is Olivieri?

"You have a go-and-see for him," Anne says to me. "He called expressly to see you." It seems like good news. I breathe out. "That's nice." I smile with my lips closed.

"Nice?" Shoji exclaims. "Olivieri wants to see her and it's *nice*?" He shakes his head, the coils from the phones undulating like snakes.

OLIVIERI'S STUDIO IS A large, white, L-shaped room, where light pours in through enormous skylights and erases all shadows. A girl with long black hair sits on a red couch by the entrance. She looks familiar, and I think I must recognize her from a magazine until she lifts her head. It's Lorna.

"Hi!" I say. She stares back blankly.

"It's me, Jirina, we worked on *Les Mariages* together the day before yesterday."

"Yeah." She continues to suck on her cigarette.

"Are you working with Olivieri?"

She shrugs.

I keep grinning, waiting for her to tell me more. But she just keeps smoking.

"So, what are you doing here?" I say blithely. She shoots me a dirty look.

A thickset man rounds the corner with heavy steps. His pudgy face is unshaven and the hair from the top of his head seems to have migrated to his chest, nostrils, and ears. With his dirty wife-beater and soiled loose jeans, he looks like a farmer who's walked in by mistake. But Lorna shoots up like a spring with the brightest of smiles.

"Ciao, Olivieri, come stai?" she exclaims.

I'm confused. This is Olivieri?

"Eh, bene, bene," he says and holds out his hand into which she puts her thick portfolio. My eyeballs are probably popping out of their sockets. Lorna is here on a go-and-see? Lorna, who must have enough tear sheets to wallpaper an apartment? I thought go-and-sees were only for beginners. I watch her toss her hair and smile at Olivieri, her desperation to please rising from her like heat waves off asphalt.

Olivieri flips through the portfolio halfheartedly, nodding, as if he knows all the pictures in there already. "How long you were away?" he asks.

"Three months," she says, blushing.

"Long time," Olivieri says. "You are feeling better?"

Lorna nods eagerly. "Oh yes. Much better."

There is a moment of awkwardness in which the two stare at each other; Lorna with a hungry, pleading look, and Olivieri with a slight indecisive frown.

Olivieri snaps the portfolio closed and hands it back to her. "Thank you." She takes it with downcast eyes and storms out.

The minute the door closes behind her, Olivieri turns his attention to me. "She disappear for long time, I think in hospital," he says, without a hint of pity.

Poor Lorna! She hadn't mentioned anything about being sick. And three months is a long time.

"She has the problem with the drugs a little bit," he says and lifts his finger to his nose, pinching one nostril shut and sniffing vigorously. "Capisce?" He laughs.

I have no idea, but I nod.

"Eh, bene, let me see what you have here." Olivieri reaches for my portfolio. "Not much," he chuckles. "But Emanuel say you will be the next big star."

An electronic switchboard makes the connections in my brain. Emanuel, the makeup artist—Olivieri—thank you, Emanuel.

Olivieri closes my book and stares at me, while I struggle with a smile that hopefully indicates my easy, pleasant nature while keeping my pearly whites out of sight.

"I will see you soon," he says, and taps my back with the delicacy of a moose.

He didn't say that to Lorna.

MY LAST GO-AND-SEE of the day is only a few steps from Jardin du Luxembourg. On my map, the park is a flat green blob with a blue oval in the middle, but is, in fact, a perfectly manicured large garden fronted by a palace of golden stone where tightly clipped green lawns surround flower beds bursting with color. The blue oval is a reflecting pool: People sit on plastic chairs reading while children run around floating toy boats on the glassy surface. A small girl sits next to her mother, rocking a baby doll in her arms with a very mature scowl, while her mother is completely engrossed in a magazine. Kristynka would love it here.

Rue Malebranche is already in shadows when I find the black front door. It squeals when I push my shoulder into it. Behind it, an open-air hallway, cool and damp, leads to a small cottage in the back. Interesting, how all these buildings in Paris, their haughty facades like grand old dames, spring little surprises once entered. It's like finding a little child hidden underneath the skirt of a duchess.

A handwritten sign, STUDIO ROB RYAN, is taped to the cottage door. That gives me a start. Rob Ryan. Hatty had an Italian *Vogue* spread taped to her wall, photographed by a man with this name. In the pictures, moody girls with sleepy eyes and pouty lips sucked on cigarettes while slouching across crumbling, wisteria-smothered gravestones.

"Now *this* is cool," Hatty announced importantly. "You gotta work with *this* guy."

I take a moment to compose myself, and push the door open. An empty, cavernous room spreads before me, but a thin ribbon of light spills from a half-closed door on the left. I peek in to what is obviously the makeup room: a tiny cubicle whose back wall is a large mirror surrounded by bright yellow spheres of light. A long trestle table and three director's chairs stand before it. Everything looks a bit shabby, but like well-worn slippers, it holds a measure of comfort. I imagine Mr. Ryan looking like his studio: old and unassuming, but maybe with a kind twinkle in his smile. I pull out a chair. I may be a bit early.

"Ahem," someone says behind me. I look up into the mirror.

And there he is. *The Pirate from the party*.

My blood drains out my feet and pours back in through my head in a great, gushing swell. My reflection turns bright red.

"Hi, I'm Rob," he says.

Rob Ryan? *This* is Rob Ryan?

"Sorry to keep you waiting, ran out to get myself something to eat," he says, shaking a paper bag. His English has a funny sound to it, a rolling wave that doesn't sound quite British or American. "You want some?" He walks to the table and sets the bag down.

"No, thank you," I squeak. Inside me, sirens wail, alarms ring, teapots whistle, dogs bark, and babies cry, but, unfortunately, not loud enough to drown out the memory of the last time I saw him: Did he hear about the bidet? I dare not look straight at him. Instead, I watch us through the mirror, where he looks like Apollo, and I'm a dorky girl with flaming cheeks in a shapeless lilac sweater. I'm not likely to entice him with looks alone. Please God, let me think of something witty, something memorable.

"Uh, you are Rob . . . Ryan?" Now that's wit about as sharp as a cudgel.

"As far as I know," he says with a grin. "And you are . . ."

My brain goes into overdrive trying to sort out all the possible pronunciations of my name. I choose the English-Swedish version, *Yee-ree-nah*, because it sounds the least "Czech."

"That's a lovely name. Where you from, then, Jirina?" The way he says it suddenly lends my name an unexpected flair.

"Sweden," I mumble.

"Really?" he says. I can feel him studying me. "I'd thought with your name, and those cheekbones—something more exotic, like one of the Eastern countries, maybe."

It's exotic to be Czech? "My parents are Czech," I admit. "But I was born in Sweden."

"I knew it," he says with a victorious smile. "It's those cheekbones, they give it dead away."

I think that was a compliment. A moment of silence passes, thick with tension. His eyes are so dark they are nearly black and there is faint stubble across his chin. The intensity of his gaze makes me all trembly and wanting; *I want him to pull me in, grab my hair, and kiss me hard—*

"Well, Jirina, may I see your book?" He looks amused.

I flinch. My thoughts feel like they are broadcast over a loudspeaker. Can he see the effect he has on me? I practically throw the book at him. He catches it easily enough and laughs again. "That thing is a weapon in your hands!"

"Just give me a blunt object and I'm danger personified," I say, and punctuate my wit with a little laugh. My white mice are suddenly displayed in their full glory and I quickly snap my mouth shut.

He tilts his head. "A beautiful girl with a sense of humor is dangerous indeed."

I'm almost certain this is a compliment. I blush so furiously I'm afraid I'll combust. He studies my three paltry pictures and I study him. He's wearing a clean white T-shirt and baggy shorts; his exposed limbs are tanned and muscular.

"Where are *you* from?" I say in a moment of boldness.

"Sydney, Australia." He pronounces it *au-stra-ya*. I'm certain I've never heard anything so sexy. "The Land Down Under." He grins. "Ever been?"

"No."

He closes my book and hands it to me. "Thank you."

I desperately want to say one thing, just one more thing, but I'm as blank as most of the pages in my portfolio. I thank him back and walk out into the courtyard.

I stroll down the street, making a left onto a wide avenue where linden trees are in full bloom, and analyze his every word, his every sigh, his every glance. A sweet, dull ache fills me like hunger. Or a craving: a taste for something very specific. Him.

But I already know this will be a one-sided affair. What could he possibly see in me? Bengt, my first and only boyfriend if one can even call him that, was the only male who ever showed any interest in me. He was twenty years old, which was a plus in a whole lot of minuses: His red, raw face bubbled new pustules every week; his round eyes were set in a round face, fronting a rather flat skull that was revealed all too well by shorn, dirty-blond stubble. We met at a disco to which Hatty and I gained admittance by applying thick layers of makeup in the hopes of looking eighteen—not a mean feat considering Hatty had just turned fifteen and I was a year younger. Though I was anxious to get rid of my virginity, I wasn't desperate enough to do so with Bengt. I kept our occasional sweaty tryst at his apartment to myself, and waited for my fifteenth birthday. Then, if nothing else came along, I'd do it even with him. An ugly boyfriend was better than none.

One week before my birthday, Malin called. One month later, I am in Paris. And still a virgin. What a certain turnoff for a guy—no, *man*—like Rob.

The strains of "La Vie en Rose" drift from an old-fashioned organ on a corner, propelled by the hand-cranking of a tall redheaded woman in full Gypsy gear. This is the Paris I wanted, the Paris I imagined. The street lamps come on, making puddles of gold on the blue street. *"Quand il me prends dans ses bras, il me parlez tout bas, je voir la vie en rose,"* the woman sings in a high tremulous voice.

If he took me in his arms and whispered to me, I'd see the world in pink, too.

AFTER BRITTA LEAVES for the day, I decide to call Hatty. My first go-and-see isn't until noon, and it's already been a week since I last called her.

"Guess what? I met Rob Ryan," I tell her as soon as we get past the initial "how-are-you's."

"Great," she says. "So, when are you working with him?"

I go into an explanation of the modeling business—go-and-sees, tear sheets, vouchers, the editorial rates—and somehow, my passionate feelings for said photographer get completely lost in the process. Only when I mention Evalinda does Hatty change the subject—rather abruptly—to Rob. I describe him only briefly in minute physical detail, and give her a blow-by-blow account of our dialogue And she still wants to know what job I went for.

"I don't think it was a specific job per se," I say with an exasperated sigh. "You see, the way the go-and-sees work—" I trail off, because I've already explained how the stupid go-and-sees work. Hatty is either not listening, or our communication is getting scrambled. We end rather awkwardly with "call you next week—miss you." It's as if I tried to relate my story in a foreign language in which Hatty had only a tourist's vocabulary.

I go to the bathroom to wash my panties in the sink. Olympe is in the bathtub, pouring out *my* bottle of shampoo into the bathwater, while her nanny squats by the side of the tub. I instantly imagine Britta's remorse at having wronged me, and the gloom of my day lifts.

I spend my morning in the company of Olympe and her nanny, whose name is Swong or Suong. We feed Olympe and take her to the park, and on the way back home, I stop in a drugstore to buy a bottle of shampoo for Britta. It has a chamomile flower printed on the label like Timotei, but the bottle is glass and much smaller and costs me twenty precious francs. There are some makeup items, powders and lipsticks, displayed on the counter, but they are much too expensive. Maybe now that I've bought Britta a new bottle of shampoo, she will finally go shopping with me as promised.

MY LAST GO-AND-SEE of the day is on Ile St. Louis. I never knew Paris had two islands, anchored smack in the middle of the Seine. The larger one, Ile de la Cité, is where I exit the Metro. I pass Notre Dame on my way to Pont St. Louis: a small bridge connecting the two islands. The bridge itself is already coated in shadows but the last of the sunlight pounds down in full glory on Quai de Bourbon up ahead. The river full of molten gold flows on my right and buildings fashioned from meringue and vanilla ice cream stand fast on the left. Glittering windows are open to the summer breeze, where sheer white curtains dance behind pots of brightly colored flowers, the plaintive notes of a Chopin nocturne mingling with the smell of frying onions. I don't need any further incentives to know with absolute certainty that this is where I want to live. I picture a small apartment, its windows thrown open to the breath of sun, a record player filled with Chopin, Schumann, and Edith Piaf, and a bed with white sheets. I don't need anything else in life but that.

And Rob.

"You have an urgent message from Anne," Marina says through our open door. It's four o'clock, and I've taken my shoes off to lie on the bed with Kafka. Damn, I was almost getting into it. Britta is still out on her go-and-sees, her new bottle of shampoo twinkling on her pillow. I call the agency, but Shoji tells me Anne has already left for the day.

"Oh, and you have a booking tomorrow," he says.

"What?" I'm not sure I'm hearing him right. A booking? Another job?

"It's for *Linea Italiana*, and your plane leaves at seven thirty."

"Tomorrow?" Oh my God, I have to go to Italy *tomorrow?*

"No, today," Shoji says matter-of-factly. "The ticket is at the counter in the airport." He gives me an address for the studio in Milan. "You better hurry. Traffic is not so good this time of the day."

I hang up and take a deep breath. I can do this. I'm a resourceful young woman. The agency obviously thinks so, or they wouldn't be sending me. I got a job. I'm going to Italy. Holy cow, I'm going to Italy—now!

In the taxi, it dawns on me that Shoji didn't mention who the photographer is. As I watch Paris disappear through the taxi window, I try to contain the most fervent wish of my life: that it is Rob.

THE AIRPORT IS BUZZING with travelers and the sound of crackling feedback preceding possibly important announcements with the clarity of a deaf mute shouting into a tin can at a soccer match. Filled with purpose, I march up to the Alitalia counter and demand my ticket in my best school French.

"Votre passpoor s'il vous plâit," the woman says without looking up.

My newly acquired maturity dribbles away. Oh, that. *That* I never thought to bring. I calmly explain to her I forgot my passport at home and she—with equal calm—explains I will not be let aboard an international flight without one.

With mounting concern, I ask for the next flight out and she informs me that it will be tomorrow.

Nobody picks up the phone at the agency and I try not to panic. It's already seven according to the electronic numbers on the announcement board. Over the top of the phone-booth wall, I watch airplanes glide into the skies, filled with lucky, passport-bearing people. I dial the number to our apartment with faint hopes of getting Britta to the airport with my passport within the next twenty-five minutes, but it's Marina who picks up on the fourth ring. I tell her my situation as succinctly as possible while I wipe sweat off my upper lip.

"You models," she snorts, "not the brightest bulbs." Her words are followed by a click, a padded silence, and then a dial tone. She just hung up on me!

I mustn't panic. Everywhere I look, people, so many people, are going about their business with expectant faces and swollen bags—but I am not one of them.

I will be fired. I will be sent back home. I will have to go to the economy line, learning about the intricacies of small business without one iota of interest, or any talent for numbers. My mother will rejoice at having been proven right—with my father's looks I'm not beautiful enough, with my father's mannerisms I am not likable or charming enough, and with my father's bookish interests, not interesting enough for this glamorous world. My father will take it as a definite prophecy that I should be nurturing my brain and writing literary critiques for fun, instead of gallivanting half-naked before smelly Frenchmen. And Hatty? Her fragile web of dreams—each delicate strand woven over long evenings sipping lingonberry cordials—will be torn to shreds. No more Jirina and Hatty living in a cozy attic somewhere in Paris—Jirina as a successful model and Hatty, the equally successful photographer or makeup artist.

There must be other ways to get to Italy. I do a quick mental scan of public transportation. If not a plane, a bus? A boat? A train?

YES, THERE IS A TRAIN to Milan, departing from Gare de Lyon at 8:30 P.M. that arrives at 6 A.M. in plenty of time for me to get to my booking. With passport in hand and pumped with my newfound resourcefulness, I purchase the cheapest ticket. How clever of me to think of a train. So what if I have no seat assignment and must cower in the corner by the bathroom for close to ten hours—once I find myself standing on the platform in Milan, my lack of sleep or cleanliness are secondary to my accomplishment. I've made it.

The taxi driver leaves me by a tall glass building in the middle of a field, far from anything that resembles a city. I walk around it, testing a few locked doors, and desperation nudges in. I have no money left. And even if I did, there are no taxi stations here, no bus stops, not even any people—

just a close hovering metal sky under which fields are drained of color, and an equally colorless parking lot with a few deserted cars. I stand with the crumpled address in my sweaty palm. It's seven o'clock on the dot; I'm where I thought I ought to be, on time, professional, self-sufficient.

I will not cry.

A small man in a suit walks out of the building.

"Excuse me!" I practically throw myself at him. "Is this the correct address?" I smooth out the paper with the address and hold it out. He looks at it, frowns, and shakes his head. "No, no, questa adressa sei in Milano."

It was already pretty clear to me that one building does not a city make. I'm left with stating the obvious. "This is not Milano?"

"No," he smiles and points a finger at the fog-obscured horizon. "Milano."

"Taxi?" I ask and have to do some serious gulping to keep the tears back.

He shrugs. "No taxi questo."

I run my hand across my face in a desperate attempt to remain in control. I can feel him watching me.

"You—Milano?" he says, his tone a little gentler.

"Yes! Si."

"Venne," he says and waves at me to follow him. We walk a few feet to a green car and he opens the door for me. I hesitate. What if he takes me for a ride and rapes me in some deserted area? I look around and realize this *is* a deserted area, so I get in.

To be on the safe side, I keep my hand on the door handle. If he gets weird on me, I can always rip the door open and jump out. But he is a perfect gentleman, if a somewhat questionable driver. By the time he deposits me before a dirty beige row of town houses, I'm seriously carsick. I wave good-bye to him and take a couple of deep breaths. I wish I could go to the bathroom and brush my teeth before seeing Rob, but I'm already an hour late.

I push the door open to a large white room, where two people huddle and smoke in a corner by the makeup station. Olivieri turns his big, beefy head to me.

I should be thrilled.

CHAPTER 7

"**O**kay bambina, be sexy," Olivieri says from behind his camera.

Francesca, the stylist with the snouty face of a baboon and a black bob, grinds out her cigarette under her spike heel and sniffles with obvious displeasure. I'm standing on a white paper background in a polyester dress sprinkled with loud geometrics, shoes a size too small, and my face painted a shade too dark with Francesca's makeup. Not only was I late and a bit dirty, I also didn't bring my makeup. The fact I had the wherewithal to take a train overnight impressed no one: Instead, Francesca only murmured something about dumb models always getting lost.

Hmm, sexy. I search my memory for sexy looks in magazines. Half-open lips? No, that won't work with my teeth. Narrowed eyes? I park both hands on my waist and squint at Olivieri.

"You have something in the eye?" he asks.

"No, no, I'm fine." I feel sweat beading my upper lip. Why is it that when you look at models in magazines, they seem to just sit or stand there so effortlessly? Like they've been captured in a moment of simply looking good. Malin's words come back to me: *You see this smile? How inviting and real it looks? That's because the girl is really smiling, on the inside.* I probably should try to feel sexy, on the inside. But what does "feeling sexy" on the inside mean? And how does one do it on command? I scoot up my dress to reveal a little leg.

Olivieri sighs and brings his camera to his face again. "The position is okay now, so give me a look."

I give him a look.

"No, no, no. Not like a dog I tell sit! Look at me," he says, trailing off, scratching his armpit in thought and then smiles. "Like I am your lover."

Eeew.

"You give me the look like you want me to come."

I struggle for composure. Come? Come from where?

"Si, si, bambina," he continues, his voice sinking to a low rumble. "Imagine me between your legs, I am licking you in the soft spot, your juices they are all over my face . . . Aah, merda!" he exclaims, puts his camera down, and sticks his hand down the front of his pants to rearrange something. "I have the big hard-on for you, bambina," he laughs.

Fire ants of embarrassment gnaw at my skin. Francesca snorts back a laugh, walks up to Olivieri, and slaps him on the shoulder, saying something in Italian while looking sharply at me. Probably that I'm obviously a virgin, and that I obviously don't get it. My ears burn with shame. Her attention is fortunately drawn away from me by new arrivals at the door. Olivieri looks through his camera again. I take a deep breath, scoot up my dress a little higher on my thigh, and pout my lips.

"No, this is not working," he says and sets the camera down on a plastic roll-cart next to him. He comes up to the edge of the paper and wiggles his finger at me to come closer.

"Look, bambina," he says, not unkindly. "You try too much. Is not good to photograph. You are beautiful girl, you open the eyes, think of the nice things, yes? And presto—we will have photo. Capisce?"

Yes, I understand. But understanding what I'm supposed to do does not necessarily translate into being able to do it. How do I think "sexy" when I'm close to tears?

"We go again," Olivieri says and picks up his camera.

THIRTY ROLLS LATER, I'm a shaky, sweaty mess, and still no closer to pleasing Olivieri.

"Eh, bene," he grunts. "You can take the break now."

I stagger off the set like a condemned man whose death sentence has been put off for a little while. The three new arrivals now sit in the makeup corner, and with a yelp of joy I recognize Emanuel's mahogany curls.

"Well hello there, honey," he exclaims and opens his arms for a hug.

He introduces me to Simon the hairdresser, a thin, pale guy with blue hair, and a girl whom I take to be an assistant, until she plops herself in the makeup chair. With her flat cheeks, big round eyes, and thick lips, she's decidedly on the homely side. A small spark of hope ignites in me: I may be unprofessional, but next to her, I'm not that bad looking.

"Hi, I'm Lisa," she says in an American drawl.

"Jirina," I say.

"That's a fucked-up name," she giggles. "How do you pronounce it again? *Yee-ree-na*?"

"Yeah, sure."

"No, no, it's *Yee-r-shee-na*," Emanuel corrects her. I have to laugh. His pronunciation, although closer to the original, is still miles off.

"You can just call me *Yee-ree-na*. I'm used to it," I say.

"Well, *Yeereenah*, come and have a sit for me, luv," Simon says. I slide into the shorter chair, and he runs his hands through my hair. "Didn't have the time to wash?" he says.

I wince. Do I smell?

"I like dirty hair," he continues. "Easier to work with, you know?" He loads up his hands with gel, and massages my scalp. "*Yeereenah*," he sort of sighs. "Lovely name. Hard to learn, but once learned, hard to forget. Don't ever change it."

I smile at him gratefully. "I like your name too."

"Common enough in Britain, luv."

"Really? I've never met a Simon before," I say. "You're my first." I immediately realize this came out not the way it was intended.

"Ooh, I'd like to be your first." He grins at me in the mirror reflection. I blush. His teeth are uneven and gray, but in spite of it, or maybe because of it, I find him cute. He reminds me of one of those guys that sings about London calling.

After Simon twirls my hair into a messy bun and Emanuel (horrified at my own attempt with Francesca's products) loads my face with makeup, Francesca totters over to me.

"You," she points a long-nailed finger at me, "are not very professional.

You are late, you have no makeup, and you are molto—come si dice—rigido."

"Stiff," Simon translates for me.

"Eh, what kind of model are you?" She sucks in smoke and holds it as if it will help her decide.

A bad model, obviously. An impostor. A desperate little communist-cow model wannabe. The model of what a model shouldn't be. I hang my head and prepare for the ax to fall.

BY THE TIME we finish for the day, it's six o'clock and we step out on the street where a delicate sprinkle of rain mists our faces. I never got to do any additional shots; Lisa did all the remaining five outfits.

Emanuel, Simon, Lisa, and I all walk back to the hotel together since it's within walking distance. The mercury-colored sky above us is webbed by black strands of electrical wires which, along with the uniformly gray buildings that line street, conspire to an effect of a long-ago-abandoned factory. So far, Italy is nothing but a complete disappointment.

I intentionally fall behind a little to prepare for my farewells. I'm sure to have a message waiting to tell me I'm fired.

"Why so quiet, girlfriend?" Emanuel slows down to let me catch up with him.

My words spill out like pebbles from a sack with a hole. "I'm so sorry to let you down, I know it was you who recommended me to Olivieri—"

Emanuel stops walking and grabs my hand. "Tomorrow will be better, don't you worry."

"If I'm still here."

"Pfft." He waves his hand. "Tomorrow I will make you look like a million bucks, and I happen to know all the good clothes are coming, and you, honey, will blow them away."

He doesn't contradict me on how poorly I did today. Nonetheless, I'm slightly comforted.

We stop before a shabby town house, wedged between equally dismal residences, where an old neon sign on a metal pole blinks PENSIONE ASA BLANCA. I think it's meant to be Casa Blanca, but the "C" is broken. In any case, the name is completely inappropriate, as the only "white" in the hotel comes from cigarette butts on the brown linoleum floor inside the lobby. Brown corduroy couches are amassed in a corner by the window where a mustard-colored curtain shields the view from the street. A dying potted plant tilts on the side, its imminent death precipitated by its use as an ashtray by a group of dark-haired men smoking as if their cigarettes were life-support systems. They stare at us as we walk in. Behind them is a series of wooden cubbyholes, some with keys hanging in front of them on tiny hooks that seem too anemic to hold the bulbous appendages. The clerk hands me a pink paper folded in half. "A message for signorina."

My blood congeals. The ax has fallen. I unfold it. *Lobby, 7 A.M.* it says. I glance around in confusion. Emanuel has the same pink slip, as do Lisa and Simon.

"Ah, bloody hell," Simon says with his funny accent. "It's so bloody early."

I am still in!

MY ROOM IS SMALL and narrow, with an old-fashioned wooden bed on the right, an armoire on the left, and a single window, before which stands a small desk and a chair. The ceiling light is overly bright; a wall sconce over the headboard, when lit alone, plunges the rest of the room into dark shadows. The bathroom is decrepit and turquoise. But it's mine, all mine. I've never had a room to myself before. The freedom is at once exulting and unnerving. I set my bag on the bed and sit down next to it. Now what? I pick up the phone to call Lisa and dial one and the room number as per the instructions taped to the phone. It rings interminably. I hang up. My feeling of isolation intensifies. With sweating hands, I try Emanuel's room. He doesn't answer either. I sit down on the bed and look around my room with despair. I think of the term "the walls are pressing in," one I've read countless times in different books, and now come to find they actually do just that. The room seems to get smaller, as if it were inhaling. Maybe I should try to sleep. I stretch out on top of the lumpy pink bedspread and close my eyes. In the silence, the pumping of my blood and each breath takes on the volume and significance of a particularly noisy last movement of a symphony—Wagner? Beethoven? I get up.

I walk to the window and push aside the dusty drapes to a facade of another gray building. I sit down on the windowsill, uncomfortably jammed by the desk. This is all too eerily reminiscent of my life before Kristynka was born: days of loneliness, a ticking clock in the kitchen, books spread on the floor around me, and a gnawing anxiety that I've been forgotten. I remember thinking then that maybe I existed only in my own mind. Sometimes I'd sit in the open window to catch a fleeting glance or smile of a passerby. Sometimes I'd pinch myself for the reality of pain, until my mother caught me and told me if I kept doing it, I'd be carted off to the loony bin.

Cautiously, I pinch the inside of my arm. The pain is briefly gratifying but pinching myself *is* crazy. I pick up Kafka, and decide pinching was more fun. I stare at the phone, willing it to ring even if it's just a wrong number. I go to the bathroom and wipe the garish color off my eyelids. The phone rings just as I decide to draw a bath. I sprint out to get it, my relief so overwhelming Emanuel is taken aback by my joyous "hello."

"Were you waiting for someone important?" he says with a laugh.

"No, no, you're just the person I wanted to talk to."

"Oh? I hope it's because you want to go to dinner with me then."

We agree to meet in ten minutes, and I hang up with a smile. I have just enough time to change to a pair of cleaner jeans and T-shirt.

WITH A SPARKLY SCARF, wild reddish-brown curls, and super-tight black leather pants, Emanuel looks far more glamorous than I. We walk past the scruffy men, who are now in the middle of a card game, and they all look up. I catch the eye of a rotund one with balding greasy hair. He purses his lips in the semblance of a kiss and murmurs, "Bella bambina" as we pass. I know I probably shouldn't, but I can't help but smile at him. He starts getting out of his chair but Emanuel quickly steps in front of me. "Why thank you, honey," he says with a toss of his hair. The man quickly sinks back into the couch to the laughter of his friends. Still, it adds a swivel to my hips as we walk across the lobby.

We stroll a few blocks to a trattoria, where we order minestrone soup and pasta.

"Today was an absolute disaster." I sigh over my glass of red wine. "I was sure they were going to send me home."

"You know, I worked with Josephine on her very first job for *Elle* and the poor girl was sent home without doing a single photo," Emanuel says. "So the shit happens, and it happens to the best, too."

"How do I do better tomorrow? What can I do to improve?"

He smiles uncertainly. "Well, honey, this is not like a sports event, you cannot train for it."

That's exactly what I'm afraid of. "Nothing? I can do nothing?"

"The only thing you can do," he says, and pauses in thought, "is not be afraid, I guess. Or sleep with the photographer."

"Emanuel!" I exclaim, shocked.

"Oh come on, honey, how do you think girls like Lisa get work?"

"She is—she's not—"

"Oh yes she is. Or at least she *was*."

"With Olivieri?" With his looks and age, I thought he was permanently single, or maybe in the market for a heavyset, mustachioed woman similar to himself.

"Certainly not with *me*," Emanuel laughs. "Trips, you know," he continues more seriously, "are like the perfect date. The photographer books a girl he likes, she is completely dependent on him and can't leave. So much better than asking a girl to a movie, no? This way, they get paid, flirt, and fuck."

"Do they all do that?" I ask and think, *not my Rob*.

"Only the straight ones," he says.

Another puzzling detail. How can a photographer be upstanding *and* a sleaze?

"Of course, there are a few who don't have to book girls to get them in bed," Emanuel says, and his eyes take on a dreamy glaze. "Have you met Rob Ryan yet?"

The pasta sticks in my throat. I nod.

"He's divine, isn't he? I worked with him recently, him and his girlfriend Mia."

Girlfriend? My heart plummets to my toes.

"She was a bit of a surprise, I must say, not up to his usual physical standards—"

"Mia, the Swedish one?" I interrupt.

"Big smile, too many freckles—so hard to cover, you know."

"Oh yeah, her." Her? Rob, *my* Rob, is going out with her? The cripple? I quickly admonish myself for this uncharitable thought.

"You know what would be genius?" Emanuel widens his eyes, puts his hand on my arm, and leans in closer. "Working with him—and you! I mean, Mia is the nicest girl, you know, but not a great beauty like you."

I gape. Me—a great beauty? I must have misheard.

I wouldn't mind pursuing this topic a little closer, but Emanuel chooses this moment to excuse himself to go to the bathroom. I take a huge mouthful of pasta just as someone taps me on the shoulder.

"Buona sera, signorina."

I look over my shoulder to face a tall, thin-haired man in a suit and sunglasses, his arm outstretched in greeting. "Giancarlo Spetza," he introduces himself. "I own the best model agency in Italy, Prima." The shoulders of his shiny silver jacket are so enormously padded that his head seems two sizes too small.

I swallow. "That's nice," I say, at a loss for something more interesting.

"May I?" He points to Emanuel's chair and sits down before I have a chance to tell him someone is sitting there already.

"So, bella signorina," he says and slides his sunglasses down on his nose, revealing tired blue eyes. "What agency are you with?"

"Sirens."

He frowns and shakes his head. "Ah, Jean-Pierre. Poor man. He has not been doing so good of late. All this trouble with the Swedish models—not so good with the business." He pauses dramatically and fingers Emanuel's wineglass. "Where are you from?"

"Sweden," I mumble. What does he mean about trouble with Swedish models?

"Aah." His voice sinks empathically, as if I just told him I was from Biafra. "Paura bambina." He sucks his cheeks in and shakes his head again in concern.

"Why? What is wrong with Jean-Pierre and Swedish models?" I say.

"Oh, I cannot spread the rumors about my rivals." He waves his hand. "No, I can only tell you, you are not safe with that agency and you will never get your money on time, and also the big, important clients, they do not like Jean-Pierre, they do not trust him. Listen to me good, bambina. I have the number-one agency in Milan, Prima, and I extend to you an offer to come with me."

I'm stunned. He seemingly takes my silence for disapproval, for he continues quickly: "And I will give you contract for one million lire. Your money if you work, or not work."

A million? That sounds like some sort of a joke.

"Ciao, Giancarlo, what are you doing in my seat?" Emanuel has returned.

"Eh, ciao, Emanuel," the man says. "This magnifico creature is your friend?"

"Oh, lay off it, Giancarlo." Emanuel laughs. "Jirina is much too smart for you."

Giancarlo doesn't seem at all offended. He pulls out a card embossed with silver print and pushes it into my hand. "You call me. I will make you a star." He turns to Emanuel with a good-natured wave and leaves us.

"What was all that about?" I ask as soon as he's out of earshot.

"Only the first one of many," Emanuel says and sinks into his seat. "Stay away from the Italians, girlfriend. They are like ants on a sugar cake. They all promise to make you a star and give you millions, only they forget to tell you they mean a star in their bed and a million lire is worth maybe fifty francs."

"He said something about Jean-Pierre being in trouble with—" I say, but Emanuel interrupts.

"Honey, all the straight boys in this biz are in trouble all of the time. The men that get into this business are like gynecologists—they do it because they hate women or love them."

Still, Giancarlo's attention warms me on the way back to the hotel more effectively than my sweater. But it could be the wine, making my fears fuzzy and small, like dust bunnies. I can brush them under my bed along with the real ones without losing sleep.

OLIVIERI HAS SET a timer. Each time it rings I must come up with a new position. I am contorting myself into frantic poses, my clothes are too small, they are strangling me, the timer rings, change, change, Kristynka is crying but it could be Olympe, my scarf is wound too tight around my neck, the timer, change, I'm sweating, the timer, change, I can't think of what else to do—I open my eyes but I'm surrounded by darkness. I've gone blind!

But no—I'm in my room. The phone is ringing. I reach out to pick it up.

"Hello?"

Heavy breathing precedes a raspy male voice. "It's Franco. Come downstairs."

"Excuse me?"

"It's me, Franco. I want to take you for a drink, yes?"

"I'm sorry. You must have the wrong room."

I hang up. The sheets are twisted around my body and damp with sweat. I turn on the light over the bed and notice the pounding of my heart doesn't decelerate. I sit up and lean against the headboard, willing it to slow down. Please God, not now. Not again. Not here! But God isn't paying attention. My heart keeps hammering away and I'm running out of air. Fear sinks its acid fangs into my stomach. My room is a padded cell. No one will hear me cry for help. No one will care. I gasp for breath. Purple globs pop before my eyes. It's been at least a year since this happened last. I thought I had outgrown it.

I stumble out of bed and crawl to the bathroom. The floor is a boat deck in a storm. The bathroom floor is mercifully cold. I stretch out under the sink and let the tiles cool my cheeks.

My heart condition is back. Although I'm not quite sure when it went away, I'll never forget when it first struck.

I was twelve. Kristynka was asleep. I had tucked her in and read her a story, then, to study for my geography test, I went into the bathroom so I wouldn't wake her. On the way back to our room, I passed mother's bedroom. The door was slightly ajar, and the warm flicker of candles gave away my mother being with an Uncle. Used to gasps and heavy breathing, it was the silence that stopped me. That and the utterance of my name. I crept closer to the wall and held my breath.

"I am at my wit's end with her." I heard my mother sigh. "It's not as if I don't try, you know. Last month I took her to my book club, thinking since she is so into books this could be something the two of us could share, and she just sat there, with that expression on her face—just like Jan—without a word."

"She'll be okay, don't worry so much about her," Uncle Olle said. "She's a pretty little thing, and smart—she'll do all right."

For a moment, I was floored. Uncle Olle had called me pretty. My mother sighed again. "I just don't know how to get through to her, you know?"

She wanted to get through to *me*? I suddenly had an urge to throw myself into her arms. *Mommy, I want to get through to you too!* But my mother continued.

"She's just like her father with that attitude; the two of them with all their books and literary references—she makes me feel—I don't know. Stupid."

I don't think you're stupid, Mommy, I cried silently. Daddy might, but not me, not me!

"Like I'm a bad mother," Mother's voice continued. "I know I have too little time for her, I mean, between my classes and work, how am I supposed to do it all? Jan doesn't do shit. And Kristynka, she is so much easier to deal with, you know? She is so easygoing, more like me, I guess. That's why I asked Jan if Jirina could live with him."

Anguish stabbed through me, so sharp it almost made me cry out. But it was the ensuing words that finished me off.

"And?"

"He doesn't want her either."

I crept back to my room and got into my bunk. For once, Kristynka's peaceful breathing held no comfort. I already knew I was flawed somehow. "The devil's spawn," Mother called me in moments of frustration, which happened frequently and for reasons I couldn't anticipate. But until this moment, I didn't know they wanted to get rid of me. How come I tried so hard to please and yet I was bad? I cried myself to sleep. And when I woke up, my heart pumped as if I had been running, my breathing constricted into short gasps, and my muscles cramped with imaginary cold. My teeth chattered. I dared not call for help; I was already undesirable enough. I crawled to the bathroom on all fours. Mother's bedroom door was closed. I sprawled on the bathroom floor, gasped, heaved, and shook for what seemed like hours, until I was so exhausted I could barely get back into bed.

I figured I was dying. My mother's words had somehow damaged my actual heart. Each night, after tucking Kristynka in, I said silent, tear-filled good-byes to her while I held her and breathed in the scent of her strawberry shampoo. I doubled my efforts to be good and useful to Mother and prayed that if she couldn't understand me or love me, that she would at least appreciate my usefulness, and not separate me from my little sister before my imminent death.

I got to know the bathroom floor in great detail before the "dying attacks" got fewer and farther between. I never told anyone. Sometimes, when mother hit me or yelled at me, I even got some measure of comfort from imagining her regrets when I died.

The nausea is subsiding, and I focus on breathing in and out. Thank God, I'm starting to feel better. But a sliver of anxiety remains. My heart condition didn't go away. It's back, as bad as ever. I peel myself off the floor and make my way back to the bed. I turn the pillow over, straighten out the sheets, and crawl in. I probably should go to see a doctor about this at some point. But where? And how?

A knock sounds on the door, just as I'm drifting into sleep. I look at my watch on the bedside table. It's one o'clock.

"Yes?" I say. Nothing. Then another knock.

I get out of bed. Maybe it's Emanuel. Or Lisa. "Yes?" I repeat. "Who is it?"

"It is me," a male voice says, muffled by the door.

I make my way to the door. "Me—who?"

"It is me," the unfamiliar voice insists. "Open the door."

"Who? Who are you?"

"Franco. You see me downstairs and you smile at me. I call you for a drink."

Oh. Him. My rotund admirer. What does he want? "Thank you so much for your invitation, that's very nice of you," I say to the door, "but you see, I have to go to sleep because I'm working very early tomorrow—um, today actually, so if you wouldn't mind—"

"But you smile at me."

"Yes, I did," I say, and trail off. How do I explain I didn't mean anything by it?

"Ah, come, bambina, you know you want me." His tone is jovial but his words are slurred.

I lean my head on the doorpost. "I'm sure you are a very nice man, but I need to go to sleep, I have to work tomorrow."

"You bitch, you leading me on!" It sounds like he's saying "beach." You beach. He pounds the door. "Let me in!"

This is no longer fun. "I'm sorry, I can't do that."

"Let me in, you horny bitch," he shouts and hammers away. The door, although made of heavy wood, shakes and rattles under his fists. I take a few steps to the phone and dial the lobby.

"I'm sorry to bother you so late, but there is a man trying to break down my door," I say, trying to keep the panic out of my voice.

The pounding and shouting outside continues.

"Non capisco, no understand."

"A man, un homo?" No, that's not right. "Un uomo?" I try. "He bang bang on my door."

"Ah, capisco, a man he want to come in, yes?"

The thuds take on a sharper tone, as if he's kicking the door.

"Yes."

"You no want him?" There is real surprise in his voice.

"No, I no want him." A giggle escapes me. Maybe it's a sob.

"Eh, I no can do nothing, you are bella signorina, and man, he like you."

"But I no like him!"

But he has already hung up. I stare at the phone. I desperately want to call Emanuel, but it's 1:26 A.M. And what would I say? Sorry to get you up in the middle of the night, but remember the guy downstairs I smiled at? Now I need your help to get rid of him. It's overwhelmingly clear that I got myself into this situation and it's my fault. Even the receptionist thinks so.

I get back into bed and pick up Kafka. My hands shake.

My admirer continues to hammer away, as if done long enough or loud enough, it'll persuade me into his arms. Suddenly, being desired or desirable doesn't seem like such a good thing. BANG . . . *it vexed him to recognize already* . . . BANG . . . *in these qualms the obvious effects of that degradation* . . . BANG . . . *to an inferior status which he had feared* . . .

When the pounding finally subsides, I breathe out. The door held. I clutch Kafka to my chest like a shield and drift off.

CHAPTER 8

At seven A.M. I'm the first one in the lobby, my hair still wet from the shower. Within a half hour, the rest of the crew trickles down, seemingly unconcerned about being late. We walk to the studio, Simon complaining about the lack of a bathroom in his room.

"You can always use mine," I offer. Simon gives me a funny look. "I may take you up on that," he says.

In the studio, Olivieri's assistant is setting bamboo poles into rectangular containers so they form an impromptu forest on the fawn-colored paper background. I keep my eyes on Lisa and Olivieri for signs of togetherness, but they both act like they barely know each other. Maybe Emanuel is wrong. In any case, it's almost impossible to imagine lanky Lisa in the arms of that bear.

I sit to have my makeup done. Simon keeps glancing at me while he blow-dries Lisa's hair. "You know, you remind me of someone," he shouts over the hair dryer.

"Oh, she does, doesn't she?" Emanuel shouts back. "A young Jane Birkin. We all thought that the first time we worked together."

Jane Birkin, not Labirkin. A person, not an animal or thing. That's a relief.

"Who's that?" Lisa voices my question and gets to look stupid instead of me.

"Only the most gorgeous creature to ever come out of England."

Emanuel sniffs. I cast a doubtful look in the mirror. Gorgeous creature?

Simon holds the hair dryer in the air, squinting at me. "Oh, yeah, she does, now that you mention it. But that's not who I thought of at first. Remember Maartje?" He switches the hair dryer off.

"Maartje? She was divine," Emanuel purrs. "But I don't see the resemblance."

"Around the cheekbones? And the nose?" Simon says and starts to tease Lisa's hair. All these comparisons to other people are slightly disturbing. Are they compliments or insults?

"Of course, Maartje was blond—sit still for me luv, like that, yes." He tilts Lisa's chin up. "What ever happened to her, anyway? One year she was on the cover of everything, and then, poof, gone."

Emanuel dips a thin brush in black powder. "Close, honey," he says to me. I close my eyes and feel the brush prickle my eyelid. "What happened to her? I think she got pregnant. With some musician or something. Probably back in Holland now with lots of little babies. Remember how she used to bake those little pastries and bring them to jobs for everyone? Lovely girl."

"Yeah, a shame," Simon says.

"You poor girls, not much, how do you say—long life?" Emanuel says, and gives himself a pat of powder.

"Longevity," Simon corrects him.

"That's why I never became a model," Emanuel sighs dramatically and we crack up.

LISA IS UP FIRST. She wears white shorts and a white blouse and she takes her position in front of the bamboo poles. The assistant crouches down at the edge of the paper and turns on an industrial-strength fan, pointing it right at her face. Her hair is blown off her face, her eyes water, and she squints helplessly into the gale-force wind.

"Come on, open the eyes," Olivieri shouts.

"I can't. My eyes are really sensitive to the wind," she moans.

I resolve to keep my eyes open no matter what.

Olivieri bends over the camera, clicks a few dispirited frames, and straightens up.

"No, this is not going. Turn the wind off," he instructs his assistant.

Emanuel rushes in to touch up the tears, Simon fixes up the hair, and Olivieri bends over the camera again.

Lisa stands still, hands on hips, and pouts at the lens.

"You look as exciting as dead rat," Olivieri says to her. "Come on, give me a look." Not a very nice way to speak to his girlfriend.

Lisa adjusts her hips, parts her lips, and throws her head back and Olivieri dips behind the camera. The whir of the motor is painfully uneven. I watch and suffer with her: This was me yesterday. Emanuel wasn't kidding about not being able to train for this. Yesterday, everything Lisa did slid onto the film effortlessly, while my efforts were like staccato bullets. Dare I hope today the situation may be reversed?

I get out of my chair to look at myself closer. What I see is so unlike plain old Jirina, my breath catches. My eyes, outlined with black and smudged with iridescent copper shadow to intensify the green of my irises, look like traffic lights; my skin is bronzed to a light caramel and my lips have been filled with gold gloss, pale and delicate.

"Oh, Emanuel, thank you!"

He smiles. "You like?"

"I like! I love!" I exclaim. He looks pleased.

Then it's Simon's turn with me. He douses my hair with sweet-smelling setting lotion and rubs it into my scalp. He makes me flip my head upside down to give it a blast of the hair dryer, and when I toss it back up, my hair stands around my face like a lion's mane. He teases it and sprays it solid. While Lisa struggles on the set, I go back behind the makeup station and Francesca hands me a leopard-print tunic, silky and short. The neck is wide and keeps slipping off my shoulder in a most becoming way, I decide, after checking myself in the floor length mirror. My feet are vastly uncomfortable in four-inch strappy sandals a size too small, but they make my legs look endless. One last look confirms that the communist cow has taken a side seat elsewhere.

Olivieri is changing film in the camera while I slink in behind the poles and grab their woody stalks. The assistant takes this as a sign that I'm ready and turns on the fan. The impact lifts my hair and plasters the dress against my body. It's truly impossible to keep my eyes fully open; I squint at the blast and Olivieri looks up at the same moment.

"Hold it, don't move," he shouts and begins clicking away furiously. "Bella, bellisima, more, more!"

I gyrate my hips, toss my hair, tilt my chin down, and squint at the camera.

"Yeah, sexy baby!"

I can't see his face, only the top of his balding head, but the black box with the sparkly eye winks at me like a friend with every click. The wind is a cold second breath, a mouth-to-mouth; it awakens me and makes me shiver. I am filled with magic stardust, which shoots out of my eyes, my lips, my every pore. My body no longer belongs to me. It has a muscle memory of its own, as if I've done this a million times. My limbs are warm, my heart pumps away, and images of girls in magazines flicker behind my eyes like a slide show: Gia's pout and a red dress, Kim with her kitten eyes and crooked smile, Josephine wild and windblown on a beach.

I try out every image and approximate their expressions, borrow their poses, use their confidence. Olivieri keeps shouting and sweating behind his camera, Emanuel jumps up and down clapping, and Simon winks every time I meet his eye. Lisa sits on the couch eating an apple. The assistant cranks up the volume to the music, and I let Donna Summer possess me, move me, speak through me; *I want some hot stuff baby this evening; I want some hot stuff baby tonight.*

There is deliciousness in using this body, this face that's not mine but that belongs to all those girls I've studied on glossy pages. It's like slipping into someone you envy and then finding it's as good as you thought, and you never want to leave.

The music ends, Olivieri applauds, and the wind dies. Sound comes back, a cavernous, empty *whoosh*, marred by voices that register like annoying electronic blips.

"Brava bambina," he says, and comes up and hugs me around the waist. "You are a delicious little morsel." He kisses my neck. I throw a quick glance at Lisa and push him off. "You won't get much meat off this," I pinch my thigh. "I'd make a poor dinner."

"A wife should be fat to keep you warm, a girlfriend skinny to cool you down," Olivieri says and guffaws at his joke. "Now, you go and get the next one."

Lisa keeps eating apples and pretending to read fashion magazines on the couch, but I can practically see anxiety saturate the air around her.

"Bloody hell, that was gorgeous," Simon says when I sit in his chair to get my hair changed. "You looked, well, dangerous out there."

"Dangerous?" I laugh. "Dangerous how? Like a psycho?" I bulge my eyes and grin in an approximation of someone unhinged.

He laughs too. "Not quite. More like—dangerous like a panther."

"In a leopard print?"

"Ouch. See, I was right. You *are* dangerous, you just hurt my feelings."

The world is a wonderful place, filled with lovely people.

Simon pulls my hair up and purses his lips to blow on my damp neck.

"You know what's so great about you? You are so intense when you're out there, but the minute you're off the set, you become just a regular girl," he murmurs.

"Is that a compliment?" I say with a fake pout.

"Yeah, it is," he says and meets my eyes in the mirror.

His are cornflower blue, like his hair.

IN THE HOTEL LOBBY, Olivieri nudges me aside and asks if I can come to his room and wake him up from his nap before we all go to dinner. I assure him with my friendliest smile it would be my pleasure. I have about an hour of loneliness, so I decide to take a bath again to kill time. I run the water and move to the mirror. My work makeup is still on and it makes me look like a different Jirina. The new and improved Jirina. Maybe I have changed—at least a tiny bit—on the inside as well?

I get into the lukewarm water and lay back carefully so my hair doesn't get wet. The thrill of the day still hums in my veins. I run my hands over my body. Maybe it's not so coltish after all. My legs in high heels didn't look so unlike legs I've seen advertising panty hose and shoes; Francesca kept handing me all the short skirts and shorts. My breasts are small but, compared to Lisa's, they are high and firm. I brush my hands over them and imagine Rob doing it. A pleasant shiver runs through me.

Maybe I should try to masturbate? I never have. I always figured sex, masturbation, and orgasms were a part of being adult and had nothing to do with me. What Bengt and I did on his bed was just play; I never let him go lower that my waistband. But now I'm old enough to be in a different country, in my own hotel room, and I think I have a responsibility to take on this sex thing. Plus, it will kill time. I close my eyes and draw up an image of Rob, the same one I've been feeding on since our meeting. *He's riding a white horse across a meadow in pouring rain, and sees me cowering under a tree. He dismounts and offers me his cloak. He draws it around my shoulders and our faces come close, so close I can feel his breath. I tremble and he holds me tighter. Our lips meet.* This is usually as far as I go. But not today. *He slides his hands over my breasts,* like this. Warmth spreads through my body. *He undoes the buttons of my dress and lowers his head to my nipples.* I pinch them lightly and the heat goes straight between my legs. *His hand travels beneath my skirts, pulling the fabric up, and his fingers slide over me, like this.* I stroke my own finger over that sensitive spot, igniting an unfamiliar hunger. *He pulls up my skirts, and presses up against me*—I slip a finger in.

It's hard to imagine what it actually looks like, what it feels like. I've only seen men's penises in snippets of late night porn movies on TV I wasn't supposed to watch. Two fingers? I try two, but now this is all very clinical. My sexy Rob has evaporated and left me with a hot itch between my thighs in cooling bathwater. Where does this end, anyway? Suppose I get so horny I attack any man I see, just to put an end to it? I flash on throwing myself at my admirer of last night, and recoil when I realize that I almost wouldn't mind. I better stop now. Masturbation could be dangerous. I could do things I will regret.

FAINT MUSIC AND VOICES linger in the hallways as I climb the stairs to the third floor. I knock on his door. No answer. I knock harder and press my ear to the door. Nothing. I squeeze my mouth into the door crack. "Mr. Olivieri?"

The door opens so suddenly, I fall into his chest. His hairy, naked chest.

I shrink back. He wears nothing but a smile.

"I'm—s-s-sorry," I stutter.

"Come in, bambina," he says and casually turns to go to the big bed in the middle of the room. The room is much larger than mine, with three windows and floral wallpaper. He sits down on the bed.

I really try not to see the hanging skin-flap in the thick hair between his legs, but he sits with them spread apart so it's unavoidable.

Am I being punished for my attempt at self-pleasure? What am I to do now? I'm stuck and bewildered between the hallway and the room.

"Come here," he says jovially and pats the bed next to him as if he only wants to read me a bedtime story.

I can't move. I'm paralyzed.

He raises his eyebrows and smiles. "Well?"

"No, thank you," I say. The words come out pleadingly.

"Eh, bene." He shrugs and stands up. "You wait, I put the clothes on."

I glance over my shoulder to the empty hallway. "I'll just wait downstairs, then," I say.

"No, no, aspetta, I am almost finished."

I don't want to be impolite. He struggles into his pants and pulls a sweater over his head. "Okay, let us go," he says as if nothing happened. I dart out into the hallway and wait for him to lock the door behind us, then we walk down in silence.

Everyone is already gathered in the lobby, and we divide into two groups for the taxi ride. Olivieri acts perfectly normal, even ruffles my hair like a benevolent father while we wait for the taxis to arrive. An understanding starts to creep over me: He paid me a compliment. I really should be grateful.

Still, I stick with Simon and Emanuel.

THE TAXI DROPS US off in front of a large open square, where an enormous Gothic church looms in the backdrop; its spires of calcified lace reach for an endless star-scattered sky and pigeons bob on the cobblestones like foam on waves.

"It's beautiful," I sigh. Finally, Italy as I imagined it.

"This is Piazza Duomo," Emanuel says. "And there is this cool Galleria, over that way"—he points to the left where a large dome sits like a translucent hat atop a roof—"with a glass ceiling, where all the shops are."

Olivieri walks ahead of us across the Piazza, to a restaurant with a red awning. It's crammed with people; some spill out onto the cobblestones where they talk and smoke.

A friendly waiter escorts us to our table by the wall. I take a seat between Emanuel and Simon, facing the restaurant, and Olivieri sits between Lisa and Francesca. All the red-checked tablecloths are crammed with food, wine, ashtrays, dripping candles, glasses, and elbows of patrons who lean in and over to make their points in loud exclamations and animated hand gestures. The men all look like Giancarlo, "the owner of the best agency in Milan"; the women are all tanned and have fried fluffy hair, and the girls are all tall, skinny, and draped in Lycra. The waiter brings bottles of wine while Francesca and Olivieri get into a heated debate about God-knows-what in Italian. I spot a man with outrageously padded shoulders cradling a tiny head: Giancarlo himself. He sits at a table by the other wall, surrounded by girls, and waves at me, raising his glass in a silent toast. I wave back.

Olivieri good-naturedly smiles at me across the table and I grin back. Everything is okay. More than okay. I sit up straighter, feeling as if people are looking at me, and for the first time in my life, they aren't looking because there is something wrong with me.

They look at me because I am—pretty?

Lisa takes a mouthful of her wine and, after pensively swirling the liquid around her glass, looks at us.

"Did you know wine is made out of grapes?" she says, pronouncing each word with profound earnestness.

The rest of us gape at this conversational brick, but Simon is quick on the uptake.

"You don't say, luv," he says. "Grapes? Is that a fact?" Emanuel and I giggle.

"Yeah," she says wide-eyed. "I found out yesterday, because this Italian guy called me up and invited me for drinks. He was really sweet, and he told me all about it." She looks at Olivieri with a sharp little side smile. "And after the bar, he invited me to come to his house to have some, but since I had to get up early, I had to take a rain check."

Olivieri watches her, amused. "Ah, you looking for a boyfriend, bambina?"

"I guess. Since I don't have one," Lisa says, sitting up straighter, with a defiant expression.

"I no work with girls who has the boyfriends," Olivieri says, wagging his finger at her. "Nothing but the troubles with the boyfriends."

Lisa snorts with scorn or amusement.

I put my glass down. "The guy last night, his name wasn't Franco by any chance?" I ask her.

She ponders this for a moment. "No, I don't think so. I think his name was Nikolai or Nick or something like that." Another pointed glance at Olivieri. "He happened to sit in the lobby when we walked by, and then searched the entire hotel for me. Isn't that sweet?"

Olivieri utters a disgusted *tsk* and Emanuel laughs. "Is this your first time in Milan, honey?"

Lisa shrugs. "Yeah, why?"

"Because, those guys down in the lobby? They sit there all day waiting for the models. We call them 'modelfuckers.' They usually have rich parents and expensive cars, and nothing else to do." He turns to me. "I'm surprised you didn't also have a call."

"Oh, but I did." I'm suddenly happy about losing sleep. I describe the door pounding and my phone call to the reception. Lisa looks almost jealous. Emanuel laughs, but Simon turns to me with a scowl. "Tell you what, luv, if the wanker tries it again, just call me and I'll send him packin'." I flash him a grateful smile just as Emanuel exclaims, "Ooh, look who we have here!"

I look up. Evalinda!

Clad in a black miniskirt and a silver halter top, tousle-haired and bright-eyed, she puts a finger to her lips as she approaches our table. She tiptoes up behind Olivieri's back and puts her hands across his eyes. "Guess who?"

Olivieri doesn't even flinch. He must be used to girls' hands periodically obliterating his field of vision. He grabs her wrists and, in one quick move, yanks her hands away and turns to her.

"Bella bambina, you surprise me!" He laughs and pulls her into his lap. She kisses him on the lips and turns to me.

"Jirina, what are you doing here?"

I'm floored she even remembers my name. "Working with Olivieri."

Olivieri interrupts me. "I will make her a star bigger than you, you ungrateful little bitch," he says, and slaps her on the bottom. "I try to book you"—he turns to us and rolls his eyes—"but no, she has booking for *Bazaar*, she no do *Linea Italiana* no more."

Evalinda giggles and pinches his cheek. "You will always have a special place in my heart."

"But I want the special place in the bed!" Olivieri exclaims. Lisa's frown deepens.

"You can have that too." Evalinda laughs. "At the very bottom, to warm my feet. Like the bearskin rug you are."

Lisa empties her wine and slams the glass down on the table, but no one pays her any attention.

Olivieri buries his face in Evalinda's cleavage, which she completely ignores and turns her attention on me. "You never came back!" she says.

I'm so flattered I can barely speak. "I'm so sorry, I meant to but—"

"Oh, whatever, don't sweat it. Now we are both here, so we have to hang out, okay?" She flashes me a perfect, guileless grin and then spots Emanuel. "Emanuel, you're here too!" She jumps off Olivieri's lap and hurls herself at Emanuel. "I haven't seen you in months!" She air-kisses him four times and plops down in his lap. "Where are you guys staying?"

"Pensione asa Blanca," Emanuel, Simon, and I exclaim jointly.

"They still haven't fixed that sign?" she says with a laugh. "I'm not far from you, we're staying at the Venetia Grande."

Olivieri snorts. "Overpriced piece of shit."

"At least the shower works," Evalinda says and springs up from Emanuel's lap. "You need to go to the ladies'?" she says to me.

"Uh, no," I say, confused.

"Yes, you do," she says and walks around the table, firmly grasping my hand and pulling me to stand. We make our way through the smoke and the smiles.

"Ciao, bella." Giancarlo stops us right before the hallway that leads to the restrooms.

"Ciao, Giancarlo," Evalinda says, and bats her lashes.

"When are you going to come to my agency, eh?" he says.

"When I'm desperate," she laughs.

He takes my hand and brings it to his lips. "Ah, la bellisima Jirina. Are you surprised I know your name?" He plants a wet kiss on it. "I have everyone in Milan saying your name, for I will make you a big star. What Giancarlo promises, he makes." Evalinda tugs at me so hard I nearly lose my balance.

"You come to my agency tomorrow, we will sign a deal and I will—" he yells after us as Evalinda pulls me to the bathroom.

"Make you a millionaire," Evalinda concludes for him. "In lire. What a joke."

"I take it he's not very reputable," I say when the bathroom door closes behind us.

"What, Giancarlo? He owns the biggest agency in Italy," Evalinda says.

I'm bewildered. This is how a reputable agent behaves?

"So, how have you been?" Evalinda says, heading for the sink. She turns the water on, looks at herself in the mirror, and sighs. "I've had a hell of a time." She runs her hands under the faucet. "Antoine is driving me up a wall. He sent three hundred roses to my room yesterday, begging me to come back to him." Her voice echoes in the white-tiled space and a little scuffle and cough come from one of the stalls. We are not alone in here, but it's no matter since our Swedish keeps this private.

"I didn't know you guys broke up," I say.

"He wants to get married and have kids. As if," she sniffs and runs her wet hands through her hair. "He also sent me this." She holds out her arm so I can see a very sparkly bracelet around her tanned wrist.

"Pretty," I say.

"It's Cartier," she says.

"Oh, *Cartier*," I repeat as if it means something to me. "So, what are you going to do?"

"I'm not going back to him, that's for sure. You see"—she spins around to face me—"I've fallen in love. With someone else." She pauses, looking at me for a reaction. I screw my face up into an expectant smile.

"Oh God, he's gorgeous," she sighs. "You know how you feel when you can't think of anything else?"

I nod. This I know.

"It's completely different than before." She turns back to the mirror and musses up her hair. "I mean, I thought I was in love with Jean-Francois, and Jacques, and Claude and all, but when it really happens, you don't *think* you're in love, you *know*."

I keep nodding and try not to beam with happiness. Here I am yet again, in the bathroom with Evalinda, *the* Evalinda, who's divulging her romantic escapades to me. Me! Although it would be nice to eventually move out of toilets.

"So, where is he?" I ask, and lean against the sink. She obviously wants to talk about him and she couldn't have found a more willing set of ears.

A deep rumble of flushing water, and a woman exits the stall. She's wearing a pink dress, which stretches at the seams as she leans in to wash her hands. Evalinda casts her a diminishing glance, and the woman scurries past us to the door.

"He's here."

"In Milan?"

"Yep."

The overly bright lights above the mirror make us both look a little tired.

"Is he Italian?"

"Good Lord, no. I hate Italians." She raises her arm and sniffs her armpit. "Ugh, I'm sweating like a pig," she says and turns the faucet back on, dips her hands in, and rinses her underarms.

I'd never have the nerve to do that in front of someone else.

"So, what's his name?" I ask.

She walks to the hand dryer, pushes the nozzle up, and blasts her armpits with air.

"I can't tell you. It's a bit of a secret. It so happens he is still involved with someone else, so I can't go spouting his name, you understand," she shouts over the dryer. The air stops. "But he is going to break it off as soon as we get back." She lowers her voice, and then punches the button again to blow her face and hair.

"Okay, done," she says and casts a final glance at herself in the mirror. "Let's go."

She drops me off at our table and sways her perfect hips across the room to her own, which appears to be in an uproar of hilarity. Our table, for that matter, has also improved in spirits; Francesca's cheeks burn with high color and she laughs at something Olivieri is doing to her under the table. When he comes up for air, he's holding her red lacquered pump victoriously above his head. Emanuel, Simon, and Lisa applaud. Olivieri fills the shoe with champagne, disregarding Francesca's protests, and then drinks from it. "Champagne with a taste of foot, cosí delizioso!" he exclaims and passes the shoe on to Emanuel, who passes it on to me. Francesca is screeching with glee, trying to snatch her shoe back, but we keep passing it around although it's really only Olivieri who drinks from it. Simon holds it up and sniffs it.

"Give it back," Francesca squeals.

"Sorry, milady," he says. "This Holy Grail belongs to the people." His accent makes everything sound like a Monty Python skit.

Francesca tries to lunge across the table to grab it, but Simon holds her shoe up so she can't reach it. She falls back into her chair, red from laughter. Simon passes the shoe to Lisa, unaware of Francesca, who's loading up her fork with food. She bends the tines back and lets the contents fly straight at Simon. It hits him squarely between the eyes. He wipes his face, fills his own spoon with brown gooey stuff, and aims it back at her. Unfortunately, it hits Lisa, who wastes no time and throws a sausage at him, which ends up in my lap. Olivieri digs his fingers into his pasta, stands up, and hurls it at Francesca. The pasta flies through the air in an arc like a tomato-splattered wig, snags Francesca's shoulder, and smacks into the back of a man at the table next to us. Our table goes quiet. The man stands up and turns around very slowly. We are so intent on his probable wrath that none of us notices the plate of fettuccini con funghi in his hands until it hits Emanuel in the chest. This launches a full-out war between our two tables that within minutes carries to the whole restaurant. The waiters barely have time to duck between serving, clearing, and begging the patrons to stop. I catch a glimpse of Evalinda riding the lap of someone, someone with hair the color of sunshine streaking shade.

My heart stalls.

She's tossing well-aimed pats of butter at people near her, and then she takes cover behind the broad-shouldered back and the tanned muscular arms.

Please, let it not be him.

The impact of the bread roll on my forehead is barely noticeable. The man has just turned in profile; I'd recognize the sharp, straight cut of that nose anywhere.

Of course.

I slide down in my chair and empty the contents of my wineglass. *Rob and Evalinda.* I pour myself another and climb under the table to drink it. Evalinda and Rob. Perfect couple. I'm surrounded by darkness. Above me is the clamor of hyperactive children let loose in a toy shop. *He's still involved with someone else*, rings in my ears. *But he will break it off as soon as we get back.* Poor Mia. I bet she has no idea. Poor Mia.

Given a chance, I would screw her over just the same.

CHAPTER 9

The world is a kaleidoscope. I lie on my bed and let it twirl. The sound of gushing water rolls like a waterfall in the distance. Too much motion. Must set my foot on the floor. But the floor is spinning, too. I'm boat sick.

"Your bath is ready, my lady," someone says. Am I to take one? I forgot. So I laugh. Simon is picking me up off the bed. It's very wobbly, which is funny, too. I'm Scarlett; he's the butler—no Rhett Butler, this Simon. No, my Rhett prefers blondes. Oh, the pain of it.

The lukewarm water hits me with the shock of bullets. I go under and come up spluttering. My limbs are heavy; it takes me a moment to understand what's going on.

Simon put me in with my clothes on, which bloat up around me in the water, and stick coldly to my shoulders where the water is absent.

"Wait. Weren't you the one who was to take a bath?" I say. The dizziness is dissipating.

"Am about to," he says and climbs into the bath with me, still fully dressed. We sit in silence, one on each end like bookends, our legs intertwined. His hair sticks up at odd angles, stiff with food, and his black T-shirt clings to his thin chest. He leans over his knees and reaches for me, pulling me in close. He tastes of toothpaste. He must have used mine. I hope he didn't use my toothbrush.

His hand withdraws from my neck and ever so gently crawls to my breast. Heat goes straight down between my legs. He gets up on his knees and pulls my T-shirt over my head. It's cold. With both hands he cups my breasts, and lowers his head to my nipples. Um, that's tickly, in a good way. His desire fires my own. If he finds me attractive, then maybe I am. And an attractive mature young woman would go all the way.

I unbuckle Simon's belt, unzip his jeans, and let his penis fall into my open hands. I caress it; it's hard and very smooth. He stands up suddenly, water splashing over turquoise tile, and removes his shirt. The sight of his erection poking out of his fly, his thin pale body balancing on one leg as he tries to take off his pants, is hardly lust-inspiring. But I follow and remove the rest of my own clothes. My teeth chatter. He gets out of the bath to reach for a towel, but slips on the wet tile floor. His legs splay comically from corner to corner, as if he were about to do a split, but he catches himself with one hand on the sink. Unfortunately, slapstick is not sexy.

Lying down face to face in my bed, we go back to kissing. I wait for that heat to return, but his mouth is cold, his tongue slimy like a snail. I offer him my neck. His penis is pressed up against my leg, I find it and stroke it with an open palm, much like one would a child's hair. His breathing gets faster and, in one quick move, he puts an arm over and heaves his full weight on top of me. He pulls our towels aside; it's body to naked body. His face above me sags into an old man. I close my eyes and change it to the face I want. I feel him pushing in, and—there, it's in. No pain. Must have been the two years of horseback-riding lessons. I'm not a virgin anymore! Simon thrusts in and out a few times, and just as I'm finding a rhythm, he shudders and collapses on me.

"Are you okay?" I whisper.

"Perfect," he sighs. I take it that sex has been concluded, and wait for him to roll off, but he stays on top of me, and after a few silent minutes in which he grows heavier and heavier, I feel him harden again. Back in, back out. This time I count. Five thrusts before it's over. I'm beginning to feel like a mattress with a convenient hole. And it doesn't stop. A few minutes of rest, a few seconds of thrusting and collapse. This sex thing is truly overrated; even Kafka would be more entertaining right now. I wonder if Simon would be offended if I read while he's at it. I grow sleepy and very tired before he finally rolls off me and I get to draw a deep satisfying breath.

"I'd better get going," Simon says, and kisses me. "It would be odd if someone saw us coming down together in the morning. Too much explaining, you know . . ."

That's fine with me. In fact, I wish he could now simply disintegrate. I'm grateful I'm no longer a virgin, but I'm not sure I will like the sight of him tomorrow. A clammy wetness leaks from between my legs and pools coldly under my butt. I close my eyes and don't even hear him leave.

I WAKE UP WITH a queasy stomach. What seemed perfectly normal last night now seems pornographic and gross. My relief at no longer being a virgin takes second place to a nagging, sickly feeling of regret, especially when I picture Simon.

It's already warm outside and our gray street has transformed to sand beige, but is no prettier for it. I'm the first person in the van besides Olivieri's assistant, who's tapping his fingers against the steering wheel in a most annoying way. A brief mental picture of him naked, penis erect, flashes before me and I shake my head to clear it. There is an achy feeling behind my temples; I hope I am not coming down with the flu. I rest my head on the seat. Next thing I know, everyone is piling in. Olivieri's bulk skews the van and he groans as he heaves himself in next to his assistant, but doesn't say a word to anyone. The same quick image of Olivieri, naked and erect, flitters by. Good God, am I going to be assaulted by these images of every single person I know?

Simon sits next to me and pats my thigh. "Morning, luv."

His hand is small, almost girlish, the fingers delicate. Kind of like his penis. My insides are churning with memories of last night. "I feel so baad," Emanuel moans from the back. It's somehow hard to imagine him with a hard-on; it's like picturing a teddy bear with a cock. Cock. I cringe. What a strange word. More vulgar than penis. But sexier? Simon has a penis, I decide. Olivieri has a cock. I better stop thinking about this. But not before I flash on Rob, who definitely has a cock, and that thought is not unpleasant at all.

"We all had a bit much to drink, didn't we?" Simon says and Lisa moans in agreement from her spot next to Emanuel. I picture her with her legs spread apart.

"You shouldn't have had all that rum," Emanuel tells her. "It makes terrible hangovers. Vodka is better, especially for the day after."

"Now you tell me," she whines.

My own physical symptoms recede slightly with the knowledge they are shared by the rest of the crew. But the penises and cocks and vaginas and cunts—another cringe-worthy word—keep on rolling inside my head. By the time we reach our destination, I've pictured everyone I know having sex, including my parents, and my nausea is back. For the first time, I relate all those thumps, sighs, and groans in my mother's bedroom to a sensory image. And although I've always known she was having sex with Uncles, it was an abstract knowledge, one I took for granted. Now I wince in disgust. We park in front of a series of white marble columns. A large open square with a statue in the middle unfolds behind them, ending with a squat white church that huddles like a mother hen, surrounded by brown outbuildings as if she were nesting in egg cartons. Vaulted stone arches form the entrance to the church, where another photo shoot is about to begin—a black-clad girl with pink hair is bent over a tripod, pulling out Polaroids with smooth, forceful tugs that flex her arm muscles.

"Va fan culo," Olivieri exclaims and gets out of his seat, slamming the door behind him in disgust. He heads straight for the girl, presumably to eliminate her from our territory. He gets into a heated discussion with her, gesturing wildly, while Emanuel begins to lay out his makeup on the seat next to him. Lisa sits down on a camera suitcase outside while Simon starts doing her hair.

The pink-haired girl looks impatiently at Olivieri's tirade, and repeatedly points in the direction in front of us, where a large bus is parked, looking more like a little house on wheels, windows with curtains and all.

Inside our van, Emanuel leans across the back of his seat and I lean forward in mine, so he can reach my face.

"Honey, those bags under your eyes are big enough to hire porters," he says. "And your eyes are red." He rifles through his bag. "Where did I put those eyedrops?"

"I'm sorry. Didn't get much sleep."

"Really? I would have never guessed," he laughs. "You were *craaazy* last night."

Outside, Olivieri clomps angrily across the square to the bus and pounds on the door. After a few seconds, the door opens and Olivieri is swallowed whole.

"Good thing you're sixteen. That skin can take a lot of abuse. Look up, honey." He holds my eyelid open while pouring a searing liquid on my eyeball. "Blink and inhale," he instructs me, "so the eyedrops don't drip."

I sniffle while he pulls out a tube of cover-up and squeezes some on his fingertip. The quick sniffs really work; my eyes dry instantly, although now I can taste the eyedrops in the back of my throat.

"So?" He dabs away. "Look up, honey, that's good—so did we have a friend in our room last night?"

"What room?" I'm instantly covered in heat.

"I think the question is, what friend," Emanuel giggles. "It seems a certain someone was carried back to her room in the arms of someone else, someone we all know—"

"Oh God," I moan. "Who saw it?"

"Only me, since we shared a taxi. Don't you remember?"

I shrug. A foggy image of Simon kissing me in the taxi bubbles to the surface, but I can't remember a thing about Emanuel being there as well.

"So?" His voice is gentle, as are his fingers. His eyelashes are so long and black he could be wearing mascara.

Shame and victory battle inside me. After all, I'm no longer a virgin! "So—okay, yes."

"Hah—I knew it," Emanuel says. "So, how was it? Details honey, details. You must not spare a friend."

I blurt the only thing worth mentioning. "Well, we did it, like, six times."

"Six times?" Emanuel's eyes bulge and he stops dabbing. "Six? The man"—he looks out the window at Simon—"is my new hero!" He shakes his head while picking up a bottle of foundation. "Six," he mumbles under his breath and shakes the bottle.

"Well, you can have him," I mumble and promptly freeze. My words could be easily misconstrued, as though I'm accusing him of being a homosexual.

"Just between us girls," Emanuel says, laughing, "he's not really my type. I'm into the blond Nordic sailor kind, if you know what I mean."

Oh. My. God.

He *is* a homosexual.

I glance at his face, which is scrunched up in concentration. It is mascara that lengthens his lashes, and come to think of it, he may even be wearing foundation, for his skin is remarkably even.

As he continues to touch my face, I can't rid my brain of images of those very same hands caressing penises of blond sailors.

LISA IS HAVING TROUBLE keeping her eyes open in the sunlight, so I'm given her outfit, a pink angora sweater with pink jeans that conspire to make me look like a hairy lollipop.

I lean on a column, slide my hands into my pockets, and discover the sunlight is indeed way too bright for any human being. But I also find—while Olivieri pushes his tripod around to get the best angle—that if I rest my eyes on something dark, like his black jeans, I can open my eyes for a few seconds at a time. Olivieri clicks a few frames and stops. "I'm gonna make a tight crop." He moves his camera in closer and his assistant cranks up the tripod so it's level with my face. The nearness of the shining lens is disconcerting, like staring down the barrel of a shotgun. A cooling breeze pushes the hair off my face. *Click, click click.*

I rest my eyes on his jeans and look up quickly at the camera.

"Bella bambina!"

It makes me smile, for real, on the inside. Olivieri exclaims familiar words "bella—stay there—do that again—" each one a gust of oxygen to feed my insecure little flame.

Simon steps in to fix a flyaway. He licks his finger and flattens it out. "You look beautiful," he whispers. A shiver of disgust runs through me. His saliva on my hair feels toxic. Olivieri takes a few more frames, then pronounces the picture done and sends me to change.

As I walk to our van, the door of the house-bus slams open and Evalinda steps out. She is swathed in a blue satin dress with matching shoes, her hair is twirled up in a sexy 'do, and long sparkly diamond earrings and bracelets catch the sunlight and scatter it over her smooth skin.

"Hey, Jirina!" She waves at me. I stop to wave back. She's so beautiful it hurts. There is no competition here; that would be like competing with God. I want to be her, yet the obvious futility of the thought makes me wish she didn't exist. Except, I also want her as my best friend so some of that magic can rub off on me, so Rob will notice me, which he never will as long as I'm near her.

Mercifully, Olivieri shouts at me to hurry up, so I shrug apologetically and point to our setup. "I'm sorry, I have to run."

"Listen, why don't you meet me at my hotel after work?" she shouts.

"I'd love to," I shout back.

"See you there." She waves to me, just as the doors to her bus fly open and Rob walks out.

She is here with him. I wobble away as fast as my three-inch-heel leather boots will carry me.

HOTEL VENETIA GRANDE is that and more. The opulent lobby swims in marble and gold; I feel like vermin that's crept in by accident. My lilac sweater still wears the battle scars from last night's dinner, despite my energetic attempts to clean it with soap and water. After the uniformed clerk tells me the room number, I take an elevator to the twelfth floor, where a calm hallway stretches out for miles. I'm equal parts terrified and excited to see Rob, and hope to God it won't be just the three of us, so I don't have to be alone with my raw pathetic longing.

I knock on her door, and quickly compose my face into what I imagine is a warm smile. Evalinda opens the door. She's dressed only in her undies and a tank top, her skin covered with a fine sheen of sweat.

"Uh, did I come at a bad time?" Please, let me not see Rob half-dressed, like I've just interrupted them!

"Oh no, come on in. I was just dancing," she says and pulls me into the room. Loud music—which I recognize from my mother's collection: a famous band from the sixties with a lead singer who's fond of leotards and flowing scarves—booms out over a vast expanse of beige carpet, large windows, and pink roses. No Rob.

Evalinda swirls her hips and, since I'm straggling behind with my hand in hers, I follow with a slightly off-rhythm sway. "Isn't this just the greatest? Do you like them?" she shouts over the music. A large-screen TV shows the singer twisting himself into a pretzel with his scarf.

"My mother does."

"It makes me want to dance and dance," Evalinda exclaims joyously, and twirls me around. White overstuffed couches, an enormous crisp-sheeted bed, and pink roses, pink roses, and more pink roses spin around me.

Unless Rob's in the bathroom, he doesn't appear to be here yet.

The song trails off into silence, and Evalinda bounces across the room to turn the volume down just as another favorite of my mother wants to know if we think he's sexy.

"Swear to God you won't tell," she turns to me.

I have no idea what she's talking about, but I nod. "I swear."

"It's him."

"Who?"

"You know, the guy I was talking about."

"I'm sorry, I don't follow."

She points to the TV screen. "Him. My boyfriend."

I look at Rod Stewart humping his mike.

"No, not him." She giggles. "The band before. You know. Him! The lead singer."

The relief is so overwhelming I have to sit down on her bed.

"Wow."

"Yeah, right?"

"Yeah," I repeat. I'm speechless. The door to my future possibilities is yanked wide open; the force of it knocks my breath out.

She sits down next to me. "Now you understand why I can't talk about it, right? This would be like all over the place if anyone found out."

I nod understandingly. His wife is nearly as famous as he is, an American movie star years younger.

"This is killing me, you know." She sighs and falls on her back. "They are here on tour right now, so they are, like, everywhere—can't turn on the radio without hearing him, can't turn on the TV without seeing him, but I can't be with him. It's totally killing me inside!" She grabs a pillow and clutches it to her chest. "Oh God. Is he the sexiest guy in the world or what?"

I'll take the what. But I grin like a moron. No Rob and Evalinda. I'm such an idiot. After all, she was rather free-spirited last night and his was not the only lap she visited.

Her head bobs up. "You won't tell a soul, will you?"

"Of course not." I shake my head vigorously. "So, how did you meet him?"

She takes a deep breath, and tells me of bright lights, stage, the roar of an audience, music pumping, voice so sexy, backstage, friends, introductions to this one and that one, and oh my God this one, looks and smiles, drinks and gropes, windy streets, jackets lost and borrowed, tongues and lips in secret places oh my God so good. She rubs her legs against the sheets as she talks and I feel like a schoolteacher with my hands primly folded in my lap. It sure doesn't sound like Simon and me last night.

"Have you ever taken it up the ass?" she says suddenly.

"Um, no." I choke. My face burns so hot I'm in danger of catching on fire.

"Well, usually I'm not into it, you know—but with him, oh God, it's so hot. You have to try it sometime."

"I don't exactly have anyone to try it with at the moment," I mumble.

"But you must have a crush. Right?"

"No, not really," I say, and wipe my sweaty palms on my jeans.

She laughs. "You're blushing. Who is it? Anyone I know?"

I'd like to lie, but I've never been very good at it. "Um—maybe." His name pounds silently inside me like a heartbeat.

"Come on, tell me. We're friends, right? I just told you my biggest secret."

It's that "we're friends" that gets me. I look at the carpet and whisper his name. She stares at me for a beat, then jumps off the bed. "Rob? You're in love with Rob?"

I laugh and hang my head so my hair covers my face. "I'm not in love with him, I barely know him."

"But you want to fuck him, right?"

I flinch at the word choice, but yes. God, yes.

"You're in love with Ro-ob, You're in love with Ro-ob," she sings and bounces around me. I giggle like an idiot. She stops, puts her hands on her hips, and regards me with a slight frown. "Well, we'll need to fix you up, cause he'll be there later tonight, at the club."

He will? My world jounces around me like a carnival ride. I have that same sensation of an adrenaline rush, of pure joy.

Evalinda pulls me to stand. "This makeup's got to go, and what are you wearing? Don't you have something . . . slinkier?"

I shake my head.

"Never mind," she says, "I have a shitload of stuff here, let's see what'll fit." She drags me to her bathroom, which is a veritable palace of white marble, and opens two doors covered with mirrors, revealing a closet filled to bursting with neon colors that burn brightly next to the obligatory blacks.

She pulls out clothes, holds them up to my face, and discards them on the floor. "Nah, the blue is not your color; pink's okay; here, green." She holds up a sparkly green top that perfectly matches my eyes. Then she finds a black leather mini that fits me if you roll up the waistband twice, and completes my get-up with a pair of silver strappy sandals a size too big. Then she pushes me down on a chair and starts adding makeup to my already painted face. My eyes get blacker, my lips paler, and my hair bigger and messier. When I stand up to take in the finished picture, she sighs happily. "That's the shit," she says. "You'll have Rob on his knees."

If only.

She begins her own makeup, which I quickly note will look exactly like mine.

"So, what is he like?" I say, my ears burning with embarrassment. I can't even say his name.

"Great photographer, our little Rob. And sexy." She glances at me through the mirror. "Don't worry. Not my type. Besides, I would never go near a fashion photographer again."

At dinner, I sit on a red velvet couch between two swarthy old men in silk shirts. Evalinda sits at the head of the table like a queen, and Lorna, with her Persian-cat eyes and former drug problem, is wedged amid additional dark-skinned men, one of whom actually wears a turban and a black robe. The restaurant is smoky and heavy with gilt and mirrors. I can see us all reflected into infinity: Evalinda, Lorna, and I like three drops of milk in the coffee of our dinner companions who sport names like Ahmed and Mohamed.

Lorna once again didn't seem overjoyed to see me when I walked in behind Evalinda, and after my question about what magazine she was here for, she snapped she wasn't. And spoke to me no further. So it takes me by surprise when, at the end of dinner, she enters the ladies' behind me, waits for the door to close, and says, "I need to ask you something."

"Sure," I say. I run my hands under the faucet. I don't really have to go, I only wanted to check my face.

She leans on the sink right next to me, close enough for me to see her eyes have that strange glassy look of too much drink. I wonder if mine look the same.

"You know, Abdul, who was next to you?"

"Yeah?"

"He likes you." She pauses and waits for something.

I dry my hands with a paper towel. "That's nice. I like him too, he's very sweet," I say. This is true. Moments ago we had a pretty decent conversation about the merits of *The Red and the Black*. I'm happy I may have impressed him with my knowledge—

Lorna interrupts my musings. "Fifty thousand francs."

"Excuse me?"

"He's offering you fifty thousand."

What's she talking about? This dialogue is bizarre even for two drunk girls. "I'm sorry, I don't understand."

She rolls her eyes. "He's offering you fifty thousand francs to spend some time with him. On his yacht."

A paid vacation? Fifty thousand francs? My mouth probably hangs by my knees.

And then I understand. "Is it—does he—what does he want in return?"

"Your company, silly," she says breezily. "I'm going too."

I goggle at her. This is unreal. Someone would pay that much money for *me*? Fifty thousand francs wink at me from a distance. I could make a down payment on an apartment with that amount of money. I could get my own apartment in Paris. Fifty thousand francs is so much! And all I'd have to do is what I did with Simon last night. It's only sex.

But I know I never would. "Sorry. I can't," I say to her.

"Suit yourself." She shrugs and leaves me at the sink. I wait for her to exit the bathroom and then I stare at myself in the mirror, hoping to find what Abdul thinks is worth fifty thousand francs. All I see is a cosmetically enhanced image of what I see every day. Me. Me, who is suddenly worth more money than my parents make in a year, combined! I only wish I could tell them.

Abdul's offer puts a bounce in my step, a twist in my hips, and a sexy pout on my lips. By the time Evalinda and I leave, arm in arm, I feel almost as beautiful as she. We are magical. We are two queens of the night. Men whistle appreciatively as we pass them in the restaurant and on the street. So what if my feet are wobbly in her shoes and my skirt hangs lopsided. I am worth fifty thousand francs.

·   ·   ·

WE ENTER A DARK cavern where a disco ball throws crazy diamonds over an undulating crowd, mirrors cover every surface, including the tables, and the smoke nearly masks the dank toilet smell. I can almost hear the gasps when Evalinda and I make our way across the room to a table in the corner. Men reach for us, arms outstretched, begging for a smile. "Ciao, bella—let me buy you a drink—hello beautiful—sit with me." But I only have eyes for one. My heart beats with the music.

Celebrate good times, come on!

He's reclining on a banquette, holding a glass. He sees us and grins that pirate grin of his, which immediately throws me into palpitations. He's wearing a white shirt and faded jeans, leg casually crossed ankle over knee. He puts the glass down and stands up. The girl with the pink hair is seated next to him and throws a glance our way; the rest of the people at the table don't even bother. Evalinda grabs me by the elbow and propels me through the crowd toward them.

"Rob, this is my friend Jirina," she says.

"We've met," he says simply. "Hello again."

"Hi," I say. Nothing else comes to mind, at least, nothing verbal. His eyes are the dark, polished hue of roasted coffee beans.

I'm worth fifty thousand francs, I think, and straighten a little.

Evalinda winks at me and announces, "I'm going to say hi to a few friends, be right back," and disappears into the crowd. Rob's pink-haired assistant, Chelsea, deflates, and scoots further in on the couch.

"Please, have a seat," Rob says, and moves in slightly, making room for me next to him. The music pounds away, happy and loud. We sit.

"Can I get you a drink?" he says and hails down a girl with a tray. "What would you like?"

What sounds sophisticated? I pick Evalinda's choice of drink at dinner. "A whisky, please, no ice."

Rob's eyebrows rise a little. He's impressed, I can tell.

"So, is this your first time in Milan?" he shouts over the music.

"Yes, it is," I shout back.

"How do you fancy it?"

"Excuse me?"

"I said, how do you like it?"

"I guess it's okay." My whisky arrives and I take a deep, fortifying swig. Ugh. It tastes like something that should be used on amputated limbs. Mia's missing finger. That's right, Rob still does have a girlfriend. Mia. I dismiss her with another swig. "But not what I imagined," I shout.

Rob moves in a little closer. "How's that?"

"Sorry?"

"How did you imagine it?" he repeats, his face getting deliciously close to mine.

Thank goodness for alcohol. My tongue is suddenly loose and limber. I laugh. "Well you know, Italy." I describe my fantasies of what Italy ought to be: cobblestone streets with flower-dripping balconies and busty black-clad beauties that beat off amorous admirers as their mothers cook up pots of spaghetti, the scent of which should pervade the air along with dramatic exclamations of saints' names and "mama mia's."

"There are places like that in Italy," he says after I finish my descriptions. "The Great Lake region, Lago di Como, Lago di Garda, and they are not too far from Milan."

"I take it you've been there?" I say and dare to lean in even closer. Our faces are only a foot apart.

His eyes twinkle. "Yeh. Some of the most romantic spots in the world."

I immediately imagine him on some flower-swathed balcony, kissing an ugly redhead. I withdraw slightly.

"Another spot I'd really like to see is Rome," I add quickly. "Especially Caesar's Forum." Now is my time to shine. I can tell him all about Julius Caesar, Octavian, the fall of the Republic and the beginnings of the Empire. . . .

"Sorry, can't hear you."

I lean in closer. He smells of grapefruity soap, a scent so delectable I want to lick him. "Roman ruins. I'm interested in Roman ruins."

"Ah. Did you see the Roman columns here yet?"

He didn't see me today. My disappointment is quickly replaced by another thought: I've completely passed up an important part of history—Roman history at that! I barely even looked at the statue of Constantine.

"I was working there today," I shout.

"Really? So was I," he says. "I didn't see you."

I gulp the rest of my antiseptic and set the glass down on the table.

"Why didn't you say hi?" His nearness, his heat, the smell of him is disconcerting.

"I, um." I stumble. "You guys looked busy. And so were we."

"What magazine are you working for?"

"*Linea Italiana*, with Olivieri."

He nods, thoughtfully. "Shame."

"Sorry, didn't hear you."

He leans in closer to me. "I said, too bad!"

I can feel his breath on my hair. "Why?"

"Because—"

I turn and our lips come within kissing distance.

"I tried to book you for *Bazaar*," he says. Before I even have a chance to let this sink in, he draws back and his eyes fly up over my shoulder.

I turn—to Simon.

The air is sucked out of my lungs, as if I've put my mouth to a vacuum cleaner hose. Simon's face glows sickly in the dark, and his teeth are gloomy and sad. He's holding a drink and moves in closer to me, looming uncomfortably above us.

"Where have you been, luv?" He slurs his words and wobbles from side to side as if he can't find his balance. "I've been looking through every club in the city for you. Thought you got kidnapped by one of the Italian wankers."

"You know this bloke?" Rob says.

I want nothing more than to deny it. But I nod.

Simon bares his teeth in a semblance of a smile. "Oh, we know each other well, better than well, wouldn't you say, luv?" He leans over me, his mouth slack and loose—trying to kiss me!

"Aw, come on luv, what's the matter?" He attempts to straighten up. "What, you prefer Aussie convicts now?" He gestures at Rob, spilling his glass over Rob's legs.

"Excuse me," Rob says, and stands up. The liquid has made a rather unsightly stain on the front of his jeans. They are chest-to-chest, Simon reaching Rob's shoulders. Rob pushes him lightly to the side so he can pass by. Simon loses his balance, and falls on top of me.

I shake him off.

Rob has already disappeared into the crowd, but I see Evalinda's blond mane heading for us. "What's going on?" she says to me, frowning at Simon, who's splayed out by my side. "I just passed Rob, he looked pissed off."

I shrug, crestfallen.

Rob's assistant spots Evalinda and jumps up off the couch.

"The last cover try we did today?" she says to her. "I got the proofs back from the lab, and let me tell you, it's a stunner."

Evalinda beams at her. "Yeah?" She touches her own left cheek. "Could you see the pimple?"

"Nope. Totally blown out."

"Hi there," Simon cuts in.

"Hi," Evalinda says without looking at him. She puts an arm around the assistant. "The one with the shoulder up, how did that work?"

"I didn't see that one yet."

I fidget miserably in my seat. Evalinda looks down at me. *"So? What happened?"* she says in Swedish.

Suddenly I'm too tired to go on. My life is drained of everything good, nothing but mud remains. *"I don't feel well. I'm going back."*

"Don't be a party pooper," she says.

"What are you talking about?" Simon interjects.

"Who are you?" Evalinda scowls at him.

"Simon," he says. "Miss-Jirina-here's special friend."

Evalinda looks at me. *"Who the fuck is he?"*

"No one of importance."

"What? What language is that?" Simon slurs. I want to hit him.

"So, get rid of him and let's party on."

Pink-haired girl twitches impatiently. "The ones with the hat? Also fantastic."

"Yeah? Could you see my eyes?" Evalinda turns back to her and Simon takes the opportunity to put his arms around me, burying his face in my neck and drooling. I push him off again and stand up. *"I really have to go."*

"Whatever. See you later," Evalinda says and squeezes past me to sit in my former spot next to the assistant.

I walk away with Simon panting at my heels.

THERE ARE PLENTY of taxis outside, lined up in front of the entrance. I get in and Simon clambers in behind me before I can object. I give the driver our address, and pull away as far as I can from Simon. I lean my head on the glass, and try my hardest not to hear his breathing; the slightly clogged nasal wheeze and noisy exhales prickle me with disgust. Stop breathing, for God's sake.

In the lobby, I quickly pass the modelfuckers—who are still here, although their ranks are diminished—with Simon trailing behind me like a beaten dog. I run up the stairs before he has a chance to follow me, but get stuck fumbling with my key at the door, and he catches up.

"Good night," I say emphatically.

He leans his shoulder on the doorjamb. "Did I do something to offend you?" he says. "If I did, I'm sorry."

"No," I sigh. "It's okay."

"Can I come in?"

"I'm really tired."

"It's our last night. Please. Just a hug and a snuggle?" His face is crumpled like a little boy's, his eyes keep closing, and he can barely stand up. Then there is the loneliness of my room, gaping at me through the open door.

"All right," I say.

EVALINDA'S CLOTHES GREET ME in a wrinkled heap on the bathroom floor, a reminder of last night's dashed hopes. I will return them in Paris, after a thorough cleaning. Simon opens his eyes when I come out of the bathroom.

"My plane is leaving in three hours, so I'm going down for breakfast," I say, and pull my duffel out from beneath the bed.

He rubs his eyes. "I'll come downstairs with you."

"No, that's okay. People might see us."

"Well, then, can I come to the airport with you?"

"No, don't. I hate good-byes." It has a nice melodramatic ring to it, so I repeat it. "I detest good-byes."

He sits up and leans back against the headboard. "You have someone waiting for you, back in Paris?"

"No," I say and realize my mistake. Damn it, I should have said yes.

"I have a girlfriend in London," he says quietly, with a sad sort of a smile.

My hands, full of dirty clothes, stop in midair. What? How dare he? A jumbled mass of emotions rips through me: anger, understanding (this is why he didn't want to be seen coming out of my room!), frustration, and on the tail end, something like greed. Someone wants him—maybe I do too?

He smiles, revealing his gray teeth and white stuff gathered at the corners of his mouth. Ugh, I don't.

"I have a boyfriend in Sweden," I say unconvincingly.

He nods. "So—"

"So," I repeat.

"So—what should I say to my girlfriend?"

I can't believe this. Is he offering to break up with her? After all that's happened, after he's ruined my chance with Rob, it's a Mickey Mouse Band-Aid over my torn, shredded heart.

"Say hi," I say.

CHAPTER 10

H

ome is as chlorinated as ever. The apartment is quiet and dark but for the gurgle of the aquarium filter. When I enter my room, Britta is on the phone and we flinch in unison. Her golden locks are gone! Small, tight curls hug her head like a ski hat.

"Jirina," she exclaims, whispers a few cryptic words into the receiver, and hangs up. She stands and hugs me.

"It's awful, isn't it?" she says. As she pulls away, I get to study her. With her hair short, she looks thinner than I remember. She tugs at her hair nervously, as if the action will grow it back.

"No, no, it's really—" I can't think of a word that will be both honest and flattering.

"The clients weren't responding to my look, you know, so Jean-Pierre thought I should go more current, more modern," she jumps in.

"Yeah, it's definitely that, more modern," I agree.

She smiles gratefully. Our room is a mess, her clothes are strewn everywhere, including on my bed. I move her clothes aside to set my bag on it. "I'm sorry, let me get these out of your way," she says, scoops them up, and tosses them on her bed. "So, how was it? Did you have fun? How was the photographer?"

"It's a long story," I say. "I'm sorry I didn't have a chance to say goodbye—"

"Oh, that's okay. I'm the one who should apologize." She sits down next to me and throws me a sheepish smile. "I found the bottle of the shampoo you bought me. That was so incredibly sweet of you and especially after I was such a complete asshole. I'm really truly sorry. Now come on, tell me all about your trip."

I make a pile of "clothes in immediate need of wash" and a pile of "can still be worn" while I describe my trip. Britta seems distracted and jumpy; she keeps rearranging her legs, smoothing down her T-shirt, and tugging on the waistband of her jeans that seem a little looser.

I don't tell her everything; mostly I describe the clothes, the makeup, the locations, and Evalinda. But I do tell her about the weird incident with Lorna.

"Fifty thousand?" she says with huge eyes. "Would you—I don't mean this in any weird way, but would you, did you consider it, even for a second?"

"Well, not really," I say. But the meaning of her words dawns on me: Her question is a sort of admission that she would. Maybe for a second. Maybe more. "Well, okay, for a second."

She smiles. My bag is empty, my clothes are tucked away. I sit down next to her. "So, what's up for today? I really need to buy that makeup and find a Laundromat."

"Let's do it tomorrow," she says.

"What should we do tonight? Want to see a movie or something?"

"I, um, I have plans tonight."

I wait for her to tell me the plans, but she blushes and fidgets with her hair.

"Is it a guy?" I joke.

She turns beet red.

My mental dominoes fall into place. "What, you didn't call that guy from the fountain, did you?"

She looks at me with momentary confusion, and then her face melts into relief. "Actually, yes. I did."

"What about Lars?"

"Lars is bye-bye."

"You're kidding!"

"No." She laughs. "Lars was puppy love. He meant nothing." Her face suddenly gets very serious. "Oh God, Jirina, have you ever been in love? Like, really in love?"

I nod, but I already know this is not a question. This is Evalinda verbatim. But I must admit, their confessions warm me, make me feel included. And I've finally moved out of the toilets. "What's his name?" I say obligingly.

"Uh, Francois." She grabs my arm. "And he's so amazing, the sex, oh my God, I never knew it could be like this. Maybe because he's older—"

"How much older?" I interrupt. He didn't seem that much older to me, twenty or so, I'd thought.

"Thirty," she says quickly and lets go of my arm.

"Wow, yeah, that's old." I wonder how old Rob is. He must be about that age too. An older man. Just thinking about him is like immersing myself in a tub of hot water, painful and pleasurable at the same time. But then Simon pops up like bile before vomit. Why on earth did I sleep with him? Then again, thanks to him I'm no longer a virgin. That would be a certain turn-off for a man. An older man. I shove Simon aside. He was nothing but a tool, a wrecking ball necessary to eliminate the old so the new could rise.

"Yeah, I've kind of met someone too, someone older." I know I've instantly turned five shades brighter.

"Really?" she says. "That's so great. I'm dying to hear all about it"— she looks at her watch—"but I have to get ready." She gets up to glance at herself in the mirror. "I have to wash my hair, and shave my legs and stuff. Tomorrow though, let's make a day of it, we'll go shopping and you can tell me every single detail."

I GO OUTSIDE to buy a sandwich, and when I return, I hear the shower running. Olympe's stroller is still gone. I call Hatty.

"Why haven't you called?" she says immediately.

"It's a long story; I've been away—but guess what?" I must, *must,* tell someone. My words slip out with all the finesse of a bowel movement. "I'm not a virgin anymore!"

I instantly feel lighter. However, the silence that follows immediately indicates I've made a huge mistake.

"Oh," she says.

"You see, I was on this trip in Italy—"

"Listen, I really want to hear all about it," Hatty says, her voice cracking, "but I can't right now. I have to go. I have . . . a doctor's appointment."

We hang up. A 7:00 P.M. doctor's appointment.

The sun is dipping behind the buildings across the street. For nine years, Hatty has been my only friend and ally. I used to tell her everything, except for my trysts with Bengt. Her reaction to my kissing him in the nightclub was bad enough. She didn't speak to me for a week. It took a lot of cajoling, and admitting I must have been drunk out of my mind to kiss such a freak, before she relented and let me slide back into my spot. Only now do I realize our friendship had no room for real boyfriends. I have torn our unity. I have cheated on Hatty and left her standing on the border of childhood alone—while I got a lift to the other side.

I pick up the phone again.

Mother tells me Kristynka is on a play date and thank you for the money.

I wait in vain for her to ask me how things are going; instead she asks if I have spoken to "Satan." She always refers to Father with an epithet, mostly simple ones like "the devil," or "Mephisto," but with the occasional "Lord of Darkness," or "His Majesty, King of the Underworld," thrown in when she means to be funny. He, in turn, only calls Mother a slut when speaking to his wife.

I assure her I haven't spoken to Father yet, and she sighs. "Good."

"Mom, guess what. I just came back from Italy."

"Italy? Where in Italy?"

"Milan."

"That's the armpit of Italy," she snorts.

"I didn't know you had been to Italy," I say.

"Well—I haven't," she admits. "But remember Luciano? He was Italian."

"So—Italy came to you."

"That's funny." She laughs and I grow warm and fuzzy. Is it possible, now that we are apart, that she'll like me better?

"Can you please tell Kristynka I miss her?"

"Um, I don't know. I don't want to remind her. She didn't bring you up all last week, so she's adjusting pretty well. I don't want to mess her up again."

"So are you saying I shouldn't speak to her at all anymore, as long as I'm gone?"

"No, of course not. But until she gets used to it, why don't you send a postcard instead?"

I swallow my anger and whisper good-bye.

The outside door slams, and Olympe's wails fill the silence. I stick my head out the door. Marina glances at me from behind the stroller in which Olympe is having a meltdown.

"Hi, I'm back," I say.

Marina doesn't say a word. She walks to the front of the stroller, and bends down to pick up her child with quick, irritable moves.

Britta comes out of the bathroom, wrapped in a towel. Her wet hair is slicked back, boy-style, and completely unflattering.

"Have you seen my jeans?" she says in Swedish. *"My Gloria Vanderbilts?"* A muscle in her jaw twitches, as though she's grinding her teeth.

"No, I don't think so."

"They are missing. And I just got them."

"Britta, I swear I haven't seen them." Not another shampoo incident!

Olympe is stuck; Marina yanks at her a few times, which only makes the child cry harder.

"I'm not saying it's you."

"Well then, who?" I say at the same time as she points an accusing finger at Marina's bent back. *"Oh, come on. Why would she take your jeans? You're being paranoid."*

"I know her better than you do," she says. Her hand that holds her towel shakes. *"She's a fucking cunt."*

Although I know Marina doesn't understand us, the word sears right through me. *"Don't say that!"*

I step up to Marina who's bent over the stroller, struggling with the latches. "Can I help you?"

"Fuck, fuck, fuck," Marina says through clenched teeth.

"She's been stealing my stuff ever since we got here," Britta shouts over Olympe's wails. *"She's a stealing, jealous, stupid cunt."* Her voice slides up and out of control before she slams the door to our room shut behind her.

Has she gone completely insane? I want to run after her for an explanation but this is when Marina simply gives up and walks off into the shadows of the forbidden hallway. Olympe cries, "Maman," after her, but

Marina doesn't even turn around. Although Britta's accusations are way over the top, I must admit Marina is not easy to like.

I bend down to the poor child. I undo the harness buckles and take her in my arms. She cries and cries. I spot an empty bottle in the stroller, pick it up, and with Olympe balanced on my hip, I go to the kitchen. She keeps turning her face toward the dark hallway, whispering "maman" in tiny, heartbreaking sobs. How can mothers be so cruel?

I rinse the bottle and open the fridge. There isn't much there, a few yogurts, a couple of hunks of cheese, and some butter. In the door compartment, I spot a container with pink letters, "Bebisol," and pull it out. Olympe sits on the floor, her tear-streaked face intent on me. I open the bottle and taste its contents. It tastes like vanilla milk, and the name Bebisol sounds like bébé, or baby, so I pour it in and hand it to child. I set her in my lap and let her drink her milk, while rocking her and brushing little sweaty tendrils off her forehead. Marina is a beast. There are people in this world who shouldn't have children. Olympe quiets down, and lies on me with a sweet, warm weight. This is what I'm good at. This is what I love to do.

When Marina finally shows up in the kitchen, Olympe is asleep in my arms. Marina's pale eyes are swollen and red, as is her nose.

I can't help but to feel sorry for her.

"Is it Suong's day off?" I inquire softly so as not to wake the child.

Marina lights a cigarette off the stove and takes a deep breath of smoke. "She quit. Goddamn fucking bitch."

Adrenaline kicks in. This is my chance, my open door. I look down at the sleeping child in my arms, her half-open lips breathing a scent of innocence and milk. *She* needs me.

"Listen, I was thinking. Maybe I could help you out? Like, I could be Olympe's nanny . . ."

Marina's laughter, deep and hoarse, surprises me and nearly wakes Olympe.

"Shh, shh," I whisper, and rock her until her eyes stay closed.

"What, did you get dropped on your head as a baby, or is this stupidity recent?" Marina says, lowering her voice but still laughing. "You want to be a model slash *nanny*?"

Tears burn my eyes. "I was only trying to help," I manage and do a couple of quick sniffs like Emanuel taught me with the eyedrops.

Marina taps her cigarette ash into a coffee cup and sighs. The kitchen falls into an uncomfortable silence. "I know you were," she says unexpectedly, the merriment now entirely gone. "But certain things just don't mix, you know?" she continues. "Fashion and babies. They both require your full attention at all times. If you try to have it all, you'll end up with nothing."

I have a feeling she has revealed something to me, a personal secret. I keep rocking Olympe, although my arms are getting tired, and she's definitely asleep.

"Listen, Jirina, let me tell you something," Marina says and stabs out the cigarette in the coffee cup. "Don't sell yourself short. You're young, you're beautiful, and, more importantly, you have that certain je-ne-sais-quoi they love. You'll do well."

I am so astounded by her words that I can't think of anything to say.

"One day soon you'll thank me," she says.

"I can still help you out when I'm not working."

"Thank you." She's looking directly at me, with something almost resembling tenderness. I smile at her with all of the warmth that has risen in me.

Marina stands up and takes Olympe from my arms. She hugs her close and makes for the door. She stops at the threshold, holding the door open with her slipper-clad foot, and looks back at me. "You're a good girl," she says, almost under her breath, and the door swings closed behind them.

BRITTA IS BEFORE THE mirror when I walk in. She's dressed in her Fiorucci pants, a black tube top, and a pink-and-black headband, and holds a tiny cylinder, like a pill bottle. She snaps the lid shut.

"You okay?" I say.

"Fine."

"Headache?" I nod at the container in her hand.

"This?" She shakes it and sets it on the mantelpiece. "No, those help to suppress the appetite."

"Aren't they bad for you?"

"Gosh, no, Jean-Pierre got them for me, they are perfectly safe. And they give you a ton of energy. Here, you want one?" She grabs for the bottle.

"No, no, thanks."

She shrugs and unscrews her mascara, applying another layer.

"So, what was that all about in the hallway?" I say, and sit on my bed. "What do you mean Marina's been stealing from you?"

"She hates me," Britta says matter-of-factly. "First, there was the shampoo, then, while you were gone, other things started missing." She opens her mouth in an "O" to do her lower lashes.

"But the shampoo—"

"Never mind," she snaps. "I know who's behind this."

"Oh, come on!" I yelp in frustration. "Be reasonable. The shampoo was Olympe, I caught her pouring out mine, too. And anyway, why would Marina hate you?"

She turns to me, her eyelashes like tarantula legs. "Because I'm everything she's not."

CHAPTER 11

On a small, shady side street, a school has its red-painted doors thrown open to hordes of children. The air is fragrant with milk, shampoo, bread, and jam. I stop and watch for a moment. I spot a young girl, about twelve, who is leading her towheaded little brother across the street. Her face is very serious and she walks with such brisk steps the brother has trouble keeping up. I know exactly how she feels. For a moment, a longing overwhelms me. I edge back and lean up against a parked car. She stops at the door, adjusts her brother's white collar, and gives him a little shove up the stairs. That could be me. That was me, only a few weeks ago when my biggest problems were homework and waking up on time.

But other images snake into my thoughts: Kristel calling me a communist whore and pushing me into a bathroom where she dunked my head in the toilet because I had worn lip gloss to school. My mother slapping me across the face in a moment of fury, simply because I looked like my father. My father tearing up his birthday present from me—a short story I had written for him on the theme of fathers—which he judged sentimental slop.

No, I can't go back. I don't want to go back.

A thin woman in a red skirt interrupts my musings. She taps my shoulder and says something, looking at her watch, and points to the school. She wants me to go in? Why?

Then it hits me. I toss her a haughty smile, shake my head, and march off, insulted to the roots of my hair. She thought I was one of the students!

When I get to the agency, I'm so early the door is still locked. I sit on the step and take out my voucher booklet, where the top one is filled out and signed by Francesca. Three hundred francs for three days, fifty for each travel day. Four hundred francs.

I hear the click of heels before I see Anne tottering down the cobblestones in the yard. With her honeyed tan, a red ribbon in her shiny dark hair, and red sandals, she looks like Snow White after a beach vacation.

"Jirina, ça va?" She smiles. I wait for her to unlock the door and we walk into the dark room together. She flicks on the lights and the room takes on its habitual glare. It smells of stale smoke and paper glue. We walk to the desk, which is clean, dotted with empty ashtrays. Anne pats the chair next to her and bids me to sit. "So, how was the trip?"

I tell her it was great and hand her the voucher. She waves it away and lights a cigarette. "Non, the vouchers you save for Jean-Pierre. We don't deal with the payments. But I need to talk to you about being included in our new headsheet." She exhales smoke over her shoulder. "Sorry, does this bother you?" She holds her cigarette up.

"No, not at all, I kind of like it," I tell her truthfully.

"So, as I was saying, the headsheet. You will be in the 'New Faces' category. We have three: 'New Faces' for the beginners, 'Models' for everyone else. And the 'Extraordinaire' are our stars, Evalinda, Josephine, you know. The cost is twelve hundred francs. Also, it is time for you to have the composite printed, and that will be eighteen hundred francs."

"But, but," I stutter, "I only have four hundred from *Linea*."

"Not a problem." She waves her hand. She looks at my stricken face. "I see Jean-Pierre did not take the time to explain things to you, eh?"

I shake my head.

"Ce comme ça. Every expense you incur while with our agency will be charged to you as soon as you have the money to cover it. For example, the ticket to Paris, your room and board—ah oui, do not think Marina is taking in the girls from the goodness of her heart—the cost of the visa, and of course, your pocket money. If you get no work, well, then the agency has lost this money. If you do work, all the money you make will first go to pay your debt."

"But Jean-Pierre already gave me the money from *Les Mariages*."

"Bon, of course, you need some pocket money, non?"

I nod miserably. I would never have taken two hundred if I knew I was in debt! "Can I find out how much I owe?"

"You need to see Jean-Pierre about that. But I also have the good news, you have a booking on Wednesday for *Chic & Cheap*, it is a catalog, Tarif 6, so you will make eight hundred francs."

I instantly feel much better. Another job!

"So much money for a catalog?"

"*Oui*, that is standard rate. But if you work for the Germans, or the Japanese, you get a thousand in cash."

"Wow!"

"Did Jean-Pierre not explain this either?"

"Well he did, a little bit. He told me about editorial—"

"Hold on," she says and picks up a ringing phone. "Hallo, oui? Hold please." She puts the receiver down. "Editorial, which pays the least, will make you seen, so you can get advertising jobs that pay the big money. Tarif 9, which makes two thousand five hundred francs for eight hours is the standard rate if you're new, even more if you are established. Catalogs are the most boring job, but the one you can get the most often. There are many clients from different countries, and if they are not French, they will pay you cash. Tu comprends?"

I nod. I have a thousand more questions, but the phone keeps ringing and Anne seems flustered. I jot down my appointments for today, thank her, and take my leave.

WHEN I COME HOME from go-and-sees, Marina and Olympe are in the living room. Marina stares at the fish with her little cigarette dangling from her lips, and Olympe whines by the dark TV screen.

"Would you like me to take her for a while?" I offer. Marina turns to me with a sigh of relief.

I give Olympe a bath and play with her in my room, then I discover a bowl of cold pasta in the fridge and feed us both. Marina still sits before the aquarium, so I offer to put Olympe to sleep. This feels so much like my life back home, I think, while I lie on the floor next to Olympe's crib, holding her hand. And suddenly, I'm very grateful to Marina for having refused my offer. I've only worked four days as a model, and only one in which I approached the high, the thrill I thought every day would bring, but I have discovered I like feeling pretty.

Britta is back when I walk into our room.

"Hey, where were you?" I say. "I thought we were going to go shopping."

"Oh, sorry. I forgot."

At least she's honest.

"So, how was it? A good day?" I continue, wishing nothing more than for our earlier warmth to rekindle.

"Yeah, good." She goes to the fireplace and shakes out some pills into her hand.

"You're not taking the diet pills at night, are you?" I say. I can hear the tone of patronage in my voice; I probably sound like her mother.

"No, no, these are to calm down," she says, and swallows.

I'd like to ask her why she needs to calm down, but Britta crawls into bed and turns her light off. I follow suit. This doesn't seem a good time to mention I'm working tomorrow. We lie there, breathing in the darkness. Her breaths are short and uneven.

"Britta," I whisper. "Are you all right?"

"Uh-huh."

I decide to share some of my misery to cheer her up. "Today, I had a go-and-see where this fat lady looked at me and asked me if I was bulimic. Do you know what that means?"

"Uh-huh."

"Yeah, well, I didn't." I laugh. "Not until I asked Anne about it later. So listen to this. I—like a moron—told her 'yes, of course.' "

A faint gasp, maybe a giggle, escapes from her side of the room.

I wait. But she's quiet.

"Can you imagine?" I continue, although I know my joke has died. "I'm telling this woman that 'of course I'm bulimic.' "

"Jirina," she says softly. "I didn't even have a go-and-see today."

PAUL GISCARD GREETS ME in his bright white studio, and instantly puts me at ease with an easy smile and deep soft voice. His salt-and-pepper hair is in wild disarray, his shirt is clean but seriously wrinkled, and his glasses magnify his kind blue eyes. For a moment I think I recognize him, from a previous go-and-see maybe, but an instant later I realize I merely recognize the idea of him: This is what I thought Rob Ryan would look like. Boy, was I wrong.

He leads me to the makeup room. "Bon, you can start your makeup and hair, I will give you one hour. Is that good for you?"

Oh no. A catalog shoot. Anne did tell me! And I have no makeup, never mind hair stuff. There is another girl sitting down in the makeup chair, leaning on the counter and rubbing cream on her face. Her short red curls need no further introduction. It's Mia.

And to make things worse, I know there is absolutely no way to get around this—I will have to ask to borrow her stuff.

"Mia, this is Jirina," Paul says, pronouncing it the French way, *Zheer-reena.* "I will now leave you girls alone to work the miracles."

Mia turns around to face me. "Hi, *Zherreena*, nice to meet you."

"*Yeereenah*," I correct her.

Her skin is so mottled with freckles, she looks like she has chicken pox. Her lashes are practically white, and her features are indistinct and pale, until she flashes me a large toothy grin. Then I see the Mia of the *Elle* covers. Her face lights up and transforms her into someone I want to know. Except I don't.

"I'm sorry, *Yeereenah*." She pronounces it slowly and deliberately, as though she's memorizing it. "I hate it when people screw up my name, and there isn't much to screw up. Still, the Americans call me Maya as often as not. Come, sit," she says gaily, and with one hand pulls out the chair next to her. "You want a coffee?"

I shake my head. "No, thank you." I stare at her assortment of powders, bottles, and brushes laid out on the table before her. As much as I need her to be nice and lend me her stuff, I also almost hope she won't so I can hate her in peace.

"Hey, if you need to borrow anything, just take it," she says. Hating her is becoming harder by the second.

"If you wouldn't mind," I say. "I left all my makeup at home."

"Oh, go on, use whatever you want." Not a word of my stupidity of having arrived at a catalog shoot without makeup. Not even a questioning glance.

"Thank you so much," I say and pick up a bottle of foundation. I slather my face with it, and it turns a peculiar shade of white. Mia laughs.

"I think you need something a bit darker," she says and hands me another bottle. I glance at her hand for the missing finger, but her fingers are curled around the bottle, revealing nothing but a smattering of freckles. "Where are you from?" she asks as we both bend close to the mirror.

"Sweden."

"I'm Swedish too," she exclaims in Swedish. "What city?"

"Lund."

"Really? Then we are neighbors! I'm from Malmö. Do you by any chance know a woman named Malin?"

"She introduced me to Jean-Pierre."

"So you are with my agency," she exclaims brightly. "Malin found me, too. Is she still redheaded and wonderfully mad?"

I agree she is and we slide into small talk of our respective cities (Lund, Malmö), the foods we miss (lingonberry cordials, Marabou milk chocolate, Jarlsberg cheese–and-jam sandwiches), and gossip about ABBA ("Did you hear Frida has moved to Switzerland?").

When I get tied up with the choice of eye shadows and their applications, Mia stands up. "Here, why don't you let me do it?"

Her hands, warm and soft—unlike my own cold sweaty ones—touch my cheek. She asks me to close my eyes, but not before I've caught a glimpse of a stub where the little finger ought to be. But instead of being repulsive, it looks almost cute. Not almost. It *is* cute. She bends down close, and I inhale her scent, the scent that Rob goes to sleep with and wakes up to. Sweet. Comforting. Vanilla?

Her hands on my face are a little slower, a little more hesitant than Emanuel's, but when I look up in the mirror, the effect is pretty good, and far better than I could ever accomplish. "Thank you so much," I say. "You're really good."

"My pleasure. And anyway, there is not much I could do to ruin your face."

Hating her may be impossible.

A small woman clad in black bursts into the room, her arms filled with clothes wrapped in plastic. She drops them on the floor and then, one by one, hangs them on the empty clothing rack in the corner. "Salut, Mia," she says.

Mia stands up to kiss her cheeks and they exchange a few quick words in French.

"Germaine, did you meet Jirina yet?" she says to the woman.

Germaine waves to me. "Bonjour, Jirina."

"She's my neighbor in Sweden and she was discovered by the same lady as I. Isn't that a coincidence?" Mia says. "Germaine, what do you want for hair today?"

The woman tells Mia hers is fine the way it is; indeed, it would take a magician to transform her short crop of curls into anything else. She asks me to side-part my hair and blow it under. As if I ever owned a hair dryer. Mia gives me a quick, understanding glance. "Your hair dryer is in my bag under the table, thanks for the loan," she says to me.

Hating her *is* impossible.

The woman unwraps an outfit and hands it to Mia. "I will get a coffee, and then we can begin, yes?" I struggle under the table to retrieve the hair dryer from a brown leather bag with silver buckles. When I finally free it from a bunch of various-colored panty hose, Mia has slithered into her outfit in what must be record-breaking time.

"Come on, sit down, I have about five minutes," she says, out of breath.

I plunk down in the chair, and she takes a round brush, curling my ends under and blowing them hot. I would never have known how to do this.

"Are you living with Jean-Pierre, then?" she shouts over the noise. "What do you think about Marina?"

"At first, I really disliked her," I shout back. "But she's grown on me."

"Yeah, I know what you mean, I felt the same way when I lived with them. But once I sat down with her and talked about home, she turned out to be okay. I still think she needs to do something about her depression though."

"Yeah, I noticed she seems a bit sad."

Mia looks at me in the mirror. "She's been battling with it for years. I suggested she see a psychiatrist, and I think she would have gone if it weren't for Jean-Pierre. Unfortunately, the French views on psychiatry are pretty old-fashioned. They prefer to just drink themselves into oblivion. And that, of course, only aggravates the depression. Jean-Pierre running after young blond models doesn't help either, nor does her marijuana smoking."

Poor Marina. Depressed and lonely. I vow to double my efforts to be kind and helpful to her.

"How do you know so much about this, the depression and stuff?" I say.

Mia switches off the hair dryer. "I studied medicine and psychiatry at the university, before I came to Paris. But then I ran out of money, so I came here. As soon as my jobs start dwindling, I'll go back to do my doctorate."

If she weren't Rob's girlfriend, she'd be my hero.

"What kind of doctor?" I ask.

"I haven't decided quite yet, but I think I'd like to specialize in pediatric psychiatry. Lot of hurting children out there."

She *is* my hero.

Germaine walks in. "Come, Mia, let's get started," she says and then looks at me. "Very nice, the hair is perfect."

I grin at Mia gratefully.

"Let's get this baby on the road," she says and puts her arm through mine.

Mr. Giscard has us both step onto a mottled-gray paper background and an assistant clicks the little black box in front of our faces, which makes flashes pop from the umbrella lights.

"Bon, we are ready," Mr. Giscard says and bends behind his camera.

I stand stiff, a hand on my hip. Mia throws a casual arm around my shoulder and Mr. Giscard exclaims, "Beautiful, stay there, girls." Germaine joins us on the set and she lies down at the edge of the paper background holding a large white piece of cardboard. She brings it down in a quick snapping motion and it gusts my hair off my face. "Voilà, hair by Germaine," she jokes. Mia's hair is too short to be affected, but at least our faces stay dry, while the rest of us melts inside our coats.

When I tilt my face up in half profile and send my eyes to the camera, Mr. Giscard shouts, "Stay there, Jirina, stay there!" and clicks off the film like he is possessed, and we are done in three rolls. We go back to the makeup room to change.

It's so easy. There is no excitement here, just endless repetition, like working on an assembly line. Anything we do on the paper background is fine, especially when I tilt my head just so. Paul takes three rolls of every outfit, single or double, and all he says is "Beautiful." The hardest part is the quick changes, having to peel off soggy undergarments and woolen panty hose only to pull on another pair in a different color. By four o' clock, we've done twenty-four outfits. What a difference from *Linea*, where we did six or eight a day.

Germaine peels the plastic off a gleaming white fur, "the cover" she says. I start pulling on my jeans when she says, "Ah non, attends, this one is for you, Jirina."

I glance anxiously at Mia, who starts clearing the table of her makeup. She looks at me in the mirror and winks. "Go out there and kick butt," she says. "In this business you don't have much time before they kick yours."

MARINA IS PAINTING HER fingernails by the table and Olympe is on the kitchen floor, playing with a couple of plastic bowls.

"Hi, I'm home," I announce and bend down to Olympe.

"Regard Gigi, je fais la cuisine," she says. *I'm cooking.*

"You look nice today," I tell Marina. Her hair is swept up in a chignon, and she is wearing makeup and long, dangling earrings. It looks a little odd, though, with her dirt-speckled bathrobe.

"Have to go to a fucking wedding," she murmurs. "Jean-Pierre should be back soon."

"Oh, don't worry, I have nothing to do tonight. So, whose wedding is it?"

"Two people who shouldn't be getting married," she deadpans.

This is obviously not the right topic to cheer her up.

"But thank you for babysitting," she says. This is the only noticeable change since our conversation, but now when she looks at me, I imagine it's with kindness. She screws on the cap of her nail polish and lights up a cigarette. I do "mixy-mixy" with Olympe on the floor, when Britta enters the kitchen. She's all made up, dressed in a miniskirt and a pink top that's slightly transparent so that her nipples are clearly visible. Marina quickly turns her back to her, and gazes out the window.

"Oh, Jirina, you're home," Britta says brightly.

"Getting ready for a rendezvous with your older man?" I semi-joke.

"Um, yeah. Marina is going out, so, do you think you could take Olympe out to the park for a while?"

I understand. She wants to bring her boyfriend over, for sex probably. And I love being included in her confidence again.

"Sure, but Olympe has to be in bed by nine, and I need to give her a bath. So, I'll be back at eight?"

"Yeah, that's great," Britta says.

"I'll take Olympe to the park if that's okay with you," I say to Marina. She doesn't respond or turn, so I take it as a yes and scoop Olympe off the floor.

BOIS DE BOULOGNE is called a park, but is more like a chunk of forest and countryside plunked down on the outskirts of the Sixteenth arrondissement. All around us people are picnicking on blankets in sun-dappled shade. I find the playground, and set Olympe in the sandbox, where we jointly "borrow" a couple of buckets and shovels to dig a hole. A little girl with brown pigtails decides to help us out and, after a while, I withdraw a little to the edge of the sandbox and let the two do the work. My thoughts make a straight line for Mia. Rob and Mia. Images of his caramel skin next to her freckles, his strong arms around her pale body, are entwined with visions of white curtains fluttering in the breeze, although I have no idea what the curtains have to do with anything.

I'm so lost in thought I barely notice the afternoon sun glide behind the clouds. But within minutes the air turns dense and dark. I glance at my watch. It's only a little past seven. The playground suddenly clears of kids, strollers, and nannies. I put Olympe in a swing as the wind kicks up in gusts, making Olympe's dandelion hair stick straight up. She looks a little puzzled, as I swing her all by her lonely self, the swing creaking like rusty hinges. I check my watch again. 7:10 P.M. A heavy, hot hush descends over the park. A fat raindrop hits my nose, then another. Olympe squints up at the sky. "Regard Gigi, il pleut."

Britta can't possibly be mad at me for not staying out in the rain. I'll be as quiet as a mouse, and won't even peek into our bedroom. I bundle Olympe into her stroller. Heavy black clouds trail behind us, as if they are intentionally hunting me down out of the park and down the deserted streets.

THE SILENCE IN THE apartment is so absolute that the gurgles of the aquarium and the tapping of rain on windowpanes take on the crescendo of a symphony, punctuated by thunder like timpani in the distance. The door to our bedroom is closed and I run past it as quietly as I can. In the bathroom, I peel off Olympe's wet clothes and set her in the bath. I'm also wet and cold, but Olympe is my only concern right now. Once she is warm and clean, I take her to her room for diapers and fresh clothes. An odd noise, like someone hammering something soft, beats in the wall next to the crib. A neighbor hanging a picture?

I can't find any diapers, so I decide to peek into Marina's bedroom. Two weeks ago I wouldn't have dared. With Olympe balanced on my hip, I open the door.

At first, it's the sound that hits me. Low groans. Heavy breathing. A rhythmic *thump-thump* of the headboard against the wall.

And then I see Jean-Pierre. The flash of lightning that briefly illuminates the dark bedroom is unnecessary; I already recognize that the short blond ringlets on the pillows do not belong to Marina.

My brain liquefies and drains out my pores, leaving me deaf, blind, and dumb. I'm suspended in a vacuum, until an involuntary shiver brings on a wet lick of my clothes. Very quietly, I close the door and set Olympe down.

"Papa," she says with a smile and points to the door. "Papa dort." *Daddy is sleeping.*

And this is when I hear the front door and the click of Marina's high heels on the wooden floors. "Maman," Olympe shouts and rushes down the hallway. I lose her behind the bend. It's hard to breathe. All my movements come with a delay. Thunder rolls through the apartment. I open the bedroom door. My heart beats so fast and hard I can barely speak.

"She is home," I manage.

Britta's head flies up. "Marina!"

And I realize I'm no longer alone in the doorway.

Another flash of lightning illuminates us as if we are all being photographed: Jean-Pierre, mid-thrust, eyes wide; Britta, hand over mouth, one bare leg off the mattress; Marina clutching Olympe, frozen in a painful embrace like a Pompeii statue, and me, turned to a pillar of salt.

"You fuck!" Marina comes back to life. "Pas dans mon lit!" *Not in my bed!* Olympe, surprised and scared, pushes away from her mother. Marina drops the child. Olympe's scream is a perfectly fitting soundtrack to the horror movie in which we have suddenly found ourselves.

I bend down, pick up the child, and hug her close.

Marina's teeth are bared in a grimace of naked torment.

She is saying something to me.

A language I can't understand.

Not until she pushes me aside to lunge at Jean-Pierre does my brain translate correctly.

"I trusted you."

In Swedish.

CHAPTER 12

I walk into the kitchen holding the sobbing child. Olympe keeps crying. *"Maman—papa—"*

"Shh, it's okay, everything is going to be okay, tout va bien," I assure us both. I rock her in my arms. Marina is Swedish. That's what Mia meant when she was speaking of "home." All this time, Marina understood.

When Britta walks into the kitchen, she is fully dressed and she clutches her handbag with both hands to her chest like a shield.

"Come on," she says.

"What? Where?"

"Jean-Pierre is renting us a room in a hotel."

The only thing I can think to say is: "But—I have to pack." What about Olympe? What about Marina? Who will help them? How will they get by without me?

Britta sniffles. "You don't really."

"What?"

"Well, not here at least."

I carry Olympe to our room. The wind noise of a tunnel sucks out all other sounds. The window is wide open; the curtains beat like anxious white butterflies, and the rest of the room is empty. Drawers hang open, sheets are ripped off the beds, Britta's belongings no longer litter her nightstand or the mantel. I walk to the window with Olympe in my arms and look down. All of our possessions are strewn across the pavement, getting pounded by the rain.

"Well, we're finally getting our clothes washed," I say to no one in particular. It strikes me as quite witty, but Britta doesn't laugh.

Jean-Pierre enters the room behind us and reaches out for Olympe. "Here, give her to me."

She holds on to me. "Non. No papa. Je veux Gigi."

Gently, I pry her little fingers from my neck. "You go with papa. Allez avec papa."

Jean-Pierre takes her from my arms and carries her out.

Her voice sounds down the hallway. "No maman, je veux Gigi."

I look at Britta. My teeth start to chatter.

She begins to sob. "I'm sorry. I'm so sorry."

THE HOTEL IS ON a side street, only a block from the agency. From the way Jean-Pierre and Britta are greeted at the reception, it's obvious it's not their first time here.

How could I have been so stupid? So blind? All the signs were there. I still feel numb, but a prickle announcing the thaw shoots through me at faster intervals.

Jean-Pierre rents two rooms: one for himself, one for us. But once we drag our bags into the dark musty room, Britta wants to know if it's all right to go to Jean-Pierre's room. "I really need to be there for him right now," she says. "He needs me."

And I don't? I'm fine left here, in a red-damask-wallpapered cubicle with chipped furniture, a saggy bed, and a window that faces a brick wall? She leaves before I can voice my objections. I sit on the edge of a bed covered by a blanket in lurid purple-gold-and-red paisleys. A gold-framed mirror hangs on the *ceiling* above the bed. Great, I can see myself sleep.

Marina's last words burn in my ears. *I trusted you.* Bitterness swells in me like a hot-air balloon. I've been good. I've tried to help everyone. How is it that I'm now a traitor and alone? Why does this keep happening to me?

I shuffle my dirty and wet belongings in my equally soaked duffel bag. I pull out the address book I got from Hatty, with her name prominently written under "H." I flip to Emanuel's number and pick up the greasy handle of the phone.

A recording of his singsong lilt tells me he's away on a trip, back next Monday. I hang up.

Anna Karenina died for her adultery, as did Emma Bovary. Their illicit passion made them bad, hence, they had to die. I picture Britta in a four-poster bed, drawing her last breaths and reaching out to me for forgiveness; I stand, arms crossed. I won't forgive. Go ahead and die. Make my day.

I go to the bathroom and pee. As I reach out for the toilet paper, the room sways and my heart starts pounding. I have just enough time to wipe, button up my jeans, and roll myself into a ball on the floor before I'm overwhelmed by the waves. My heart condition is back to stay. I haven't outgrown it, and the last time wasn't a fluke. My blood pumps too fast, the veins in my neck feel as if they will burst with the pressure. I struggle with air, I fight for each breath, and sweat pours off my body. I try to focus on something, anything but my immediate misery. Crinkly hairs are stuck in the dirty grout of the floor. I count them. Five. No, six. The white tiles are a shade of neglect, yellowed around the edges like old paper. Another bathroom floor I'll get to know in great detail.

Once I'm able to stand up, I go back to the bedroom and dial Evalinda. She answers on the third ring.

"Allô, oui?" she says breathlessly.

"It's Jirina. I'm so sorry, am I calling at a bad time?"

"No, not at all. Hi, what's up?"

I try to explain my situation as succinctly as possible, but my voice keeps breaking and I gulp like a stranded fish.

"Listen," she says. "Why don't you come over and tell me in person?"

I WAKE UP WITH sunlight tickling my nose. The two large windows that face the street are ablaze with morning light. I shift my weight on the couch, a brown-leather antique, beautiful to look at but not particularly comfortable to sleep on. I straighten my legs over the armrest and survey the small room: The walls are uneven in texture, like those whitewashed in a farmhouse, and slope at a ceiling supported by heavy wooden beams, a reminder of the attic space it occupies. An American *Cosmopolitan* cover is prominently displayed on the wall opposite the couch, surrounded by three *Elle* covers and a *Madame Figaro*. Funny, I always thought Evalinda had more covers. Maybe they are in the bedroom, at the back of the apartment.

A wooden chest serves as a coffee table, and on the other side are two upholstered beige chairs. I wiggle my toes, behind which I can see the kitchen nook, with a tiny stove and a couple of cabinets painted white. Across this is the door to the bathroom. I get up, stretch, and head for it. It's small, tiled in white, with bottles and jars occupying every available shelf, the sink, the bathtub rim, the top of the toilet tank, and even the floor behind the toilet. My bottle of baby oil and shampoo won't feel lonely.

The bedroom door is still closed, so I go back to the couch and dream of refurnishing: white couch right here, no coffee table, sheer lace curtains to take the edge off the river glare, vases of fresh-blooming lilacs in the window sills, and no pictures of Evalinda. She comes out of the bedroom as I'm deciding whether I'd hang a Monet print or a Renoir. She is in her underwear and a tiny T-shirt that looks like it belonged to a baby. An internal scab from yesterday rips off at the thought of Olympe. I won't be there for her anymore. What will happen to the poor child? I quickly pinch myself so I don't start crying.

"Good morning," Evalinda says. "Want some coffee?"

"I'd love some."

She stops at the kitchen nook and unscrews the top of a jar. She looks in it and sighs. "Well, you're gonna have to go out and get some then, 'cause I'm all out."

I jump up. "Sure. Where do I go?"

She tells me how to get to the little sundries store around the corner.

"Would it be okay to use the phone before I go?" I ask, scooping up my sweater.

"Sure, but Paris only."

I'm mortified she'd think I would take advantage of her and call, what, Sweden?

"Of course. I was only going to call the agency, so they know where I am," I explain quickly.

Anne picks up on the other end. "Oh, thank God, we've been very worried. I have heard what happened last night." I'm intensely relieved at not having to make the humiliating explanation.

"I have spoken to Britta—she wants you to call her, by the way—but she didn't know where you have disappeared. Where are you?"

"I'm at Evalinda's apartment," I say, with a hint of pride.

"Ah, Evalinda," Anne says. She doesn't sound impressed. Or pleased for that matter. "Are you going to be staying with her for now?"

"Yes, I'll be house-sitting since she's going away."

"She is?" Anne's voice takes on a shrill note. "Let me speak to her, please."

I reach the receiver across to Evalinda, who takes it nonchalantly as she lights a cigarette.

"I told you I was going to the States," she says. "Okay, so maybe I didn't. So what? It's just a long weekend." She holds the phone out at an arm's length and makes a grimace of boredom while Anne's voice pours out in angry waves. When the tinny voice ceases, Evalinda puts the receiver back to her ear. "So? Honestly, I don't give a shit what you tell them, tell them I died or whatever. I'll be back on Sunday night, so you don't have to have a shit-fit about Monday."

I'm aghast and impressed at the way she speaks to Anne. Like she doesn't care. Like they work for *her*.

"Here, she wants to talk to you." She hands back the receiver. Anne's voice sounds clipped. "I canceled your go-and-sees today, but you have one, at four o'clock tomorrow—I know, I know, it is Saturday, but it's the only time Hedwig can see you, and it's an important one, a trip to Morocco for *German Vogue*." She gives me the address, which I jot down in my Sirens diary. *Vogue*: the epitome of fashion. I wish I could call Hatty and tell her.

WHEN I GET BACK to the apartment with a bag of coffee, a note is taped on the bathroom door. BRITTA CALLED, URGENT is scribbled in Evalinda's bold, sloping hand, and a telephone number to what I presume is the bordello hotel is written underneath.

Evalinda comes out of the bathroom, fully dressed in black leather jeans (in this heat?) and the same small T-shirt. "Did you see?" She nods at the note. "A friend of yours called."

"Yes, thanks."

"My plane leaves at three," she says, "so I better tell you how everything works." She shows me the three locks with their respective keys, a precaution she finds necessary "because of all my crazy old boyfriends." She also instructs me to pick up her laundry (yippee, Laundromat) and tells me when I answer the phone to tell anyone calling for her that she's away on a trip. "If it's Didier, Jean-Marie, or Claude, tell them I'm off having an affair with Prince Albert of Monaco."

She pulls out a huge brown-patterned suitcase from her bedroom and dumps it on the couch. It looks like it may have belonged to her mother, or grandmother.

"Is it an old one?" I inquire gently. Even my duffel is nicer than this. Maybe I should offer mine?

"Old one? No, it's the new model from last season. Vuitton, you know."

"Oh, of course, Vuitton." I nod as if I know.

A great amount of leather, silk, and cashmere—"of course it's soft, it's *cashmere*!"—gets swallowed by her Vuitton bag.

"You have no idea how much I appreciate this," I say as she throws on a leather jacket with fringe, silver studs, and enormous shoulders. In my humble opinion it doesn't really suit her; the shoulder pads make her head look like a pin. But what do I know. It's a *Montana*.

"Don't forget my laundry, and do not, under any circumstances, let any guys in here, no matter what they say. Got it?"

"Got it."

Once the door closes behind her, I take a closer look at the bedroom. A small window, draped with a patterned sheet, doesn't let in much light; an enormous mattress covered in sheets printed with black and gray geometrics sits beneath a large black-and-white poster of a naked Evalinda. She is in full frontal, her hair blown off her face, her arms spread up behind her head, her perfect breasts thrust out. Her bedside table groans under the weight of old magazines. Although I feel slightly guilty, I pull out the drawer. Inside are watches of heavy metals, gold, steel—platinum?—with names like Ebel, Rolex, and the already familiar Cartier. She must collect them, like stamps.

A door on the left wall opens to a walk-in closet, crammed with mostly black items that smell strongly of Evalinda: pungent florals and steak. I peek into a couple of old shoeboxes that are filled with trinkets and jewelry, where I spot the Cartier bracelet from Antoine intertwined with a plastic hoop earring.

One kitchen cabinet holds beige ceramic plates and cups, the other a package of powdered milk, a box of stale tartines, two glass jars of jam—the top of one coated with mold—and lots of dust. In the fridge I find yogurt a month past its expiration date and a carton of that nuclear milk that lasts for, like, a year without having to be refrigerated. And that's it. Somehow, I pictured Evalinda with more. Bigger. Glitzier. Although she lives on rue Bourbon, her apartment is more suited to the likes of, say, me.

My snooping session has left me with a fair amount of guilt and not much else, so I decide cleaning it would be a nice "thank you" gesture, besides being a great killer of time. My exploration revealed no cleaning products, so I head out to find a supermarket.

I find none on the island of Ile St. Louis, so I cross the bridge to the left bank, and plunge into tiny crooked streets with souvenir shops. I pass boutique after boutique, selling clothes, jewelry, candies, books, until one stops me. A toy shop. Brightly colored wooden toys share space in the windows with beautiful porcelain dolls in frilly dresses. My eyes are drawn to a baby doll in a large box: a newborn infant, complete with an umbilical stump, a real tiny diaper, and slightly pursed mouth with enough space for a pacifier. It looks so real, with its squinty blue eyes, bald head, and protruding tummy, as if the toy maker had made a cast of a real-life baby. And I already know I must buy it. For Kristynka, of course.

The doll costs eighty francs, leaving me with sixty. Once I finally find a supermarket, I spend an additional fifteen on cleaning spray and a dishwashing liquid, and lug my purchases home. It's five o'clock and I dart out again to get Evalinda's laundry, and simultaneously drop off all my clothes. A tiny Asian lady behind a wooden counter takes my ticket stub, hoists a package wrapped in brown paper before me, and demands forty-three francs. There is no question I have to pay for it; Evalinda left me no money. I'm left with two francs. My own clothes will obviously stay dirty.

Back home, I turn Evalinda's boom box to a classical station and clean like a madwoman. I will have to survive the weekend on two francs, but I already know I can manage. When I was eleven, my mother left for a two-week vacation and entrusted us to Father's care. Father showed up on the first day, gave me twenty kronas, and that's the last we saw of him. For a week, I stretched the money he gave me, using it mostly for milk for Kristynka. We ate a lot of pancakes until I exhausted the flour and eggs in the pantry. The second week, I went to the supermarket and stole a loaf of bread and a pack of cream cheese, on which we subsisted until Mother came back. She never asked about Father, so I never told her.

This time, there is no baby to feed. This thought leads me straight back to the baby I bought. The living room and the kitchen are now spotless;

I'll do the bathroom and bedroom tomorrow, I decide, and squat on the floor to study the baby in the box. Besides the doll, there is also a blanket, a white cotton shirt with ties, a pacifier, and a tiny striped cap all folded into their own small compartments in the box. The baby's face is scrunched up, its blue eyes stare at me imploringly to take it out of the box and hold it. I know I won't open it; it's a present. And I'm much too old to be playing with dolls. But now it's nine o'clock, the apartment is getting dark, and loneliness threatens. I go to sit on the windowsill, to watch flat-bottomed Bateaux Mouches glide by, dissolving the darkness with twinkly lights and puncturing the silence with bright laughter of the people on-board. Evalinda's pack of cigarettes lies on the coffee table.

What the heck, this is as good a time as any.

I pull out a long slim Dunhill and light it on the stove, for I can't find a lighter or matches. The smoke fills my mouth, pungent and acrid. I blow it out. My mouth tastes like a car engine smells. I take another mouthful and this time, force it out my nose, like I've seen Evalinda do. It stings. So far, I don't exactly understand the pleasure in this. I take the cigarette to the mirror in the hallway, where I continue to exhale, practicing the quantity, the velocity, and the quality of the smoke curling from my nostrils and lips. I accidentally inhale a few times, and that sends my stomach into an uproar. I extinguish the cigarette in the crystal ashtray on the coffee table. I'm not hungry anymore, and that's good, I can save those tartines for tomorrow. I put my jammies on and crawl into Evalinda's bed. The mattress is enormous, "California King," Evalinda proudly told me. "No one in France has one of these. I ordered it from the States."

I close my eyes, and my brain promptly goes into overdrive. I'm equally wedged between happiness and despair: For every minute I'm exalted over the fact that I now live in Ile St. Louis with Evalinda, *the* Evalinda, and have a go-and-see for *Vogue* tomorrow, images of last night interrupt my flow of well-being like boulders on a highway. What will happen to Olympe now? Is Jean-Pierre going to divorce Marina and marry Britta? What will happen to poor Marina?

The bed is too vast for comfort. I feel like a lonely little leftover: the last gherkin in a jar, the last sardine in a tin, the last lentil in the box. *The baby in the box.* I get out of bed and squat next to the box again. Why couldn't I take it out, just for a little while? The poor thing looks as lonely as I feel. No one will ever know. I carefully unpeel the tape that secures the top flap, and slide out the tray with the baby and all the accessories. The baby is held to the cardboard with wire, which I untwist from its wrist, ankles, and neck. I hold it in my arms. It even smells like a baby, but it feels cold, so I undo the blanket and swaddle it.

The bed is still vast, but now I don't feel so lonely with the baby lying next to me.

AS SOON AS I turn the shower off, I hear the phone. I wrap myself in a towel and run to the living room. If it's Britta, I'll tell her . . . I don't actually know what I'll tell her. I know what I *should* tell her—to buzz off, with friends like her I don't need enemies, blah-dee-blah—but the truth is, I'm lonely. And I'm not very good at being lonely. My plastic baby still lies in bed, an embarrassing reminder of how pathetic I am.

But when I lift the phone, it's a hesitant male voice. "Allô, Evalinda?"

"Sorry, she is not home," I say. "Who's this?"

"My name is Hugo," he says in English with a heavy French accent. "A friend of Evalinda's."

She never mentioned his name, but I'm nothing if not diligent. "She's having an affair with Prince Albert of Monaco."

He laughs. "That is a good one! When she will be back?"

"Uh, I don't know."

"Okay, that is not a problem. And if I may be so bold, who are you?" Something about the soft tone of his voice and the old-fashioned turn of his words is comforting.

"I'm a friend too. I'm apartment-sitting."

"Bon alors, friend, are you perhaps interested in coming to a party tonight?"

"Oh no, thank you."

"Why not?"

I think about it. Why not indeed? My Saturday night plans are pretty solitary. Of course, there is the money issue. "Well, maybe," I say.

"Parfait," he interrupts. "I will come and pick you up around nine." He hangs up before I can say anything further, but I'm pleased. My evening is set, and if I'm lucky, maybe there'll be some free wine at the party to take the edge off the empty apartment.

The note with Britta's number keeps hitting my eyes as I clean the bathroom. Once everything is spotlessly clean, I have another cigarette on the windowsill, get nauseous, eat a tartine, and drink some water, and it's still only noon. I make my duffel into an impromptu bed for Kristynka's baby, kiss it, and tell it to sleep before I draw the zipper. Then I go to remove the note from the door. I look at it. I crumple it up. I smooth it out. And call the hotel.

BRITTA IS ALREADY SITTING at a table in the corner of the café when I get there, her face buried in her hands. A lonely cup of coffee sits before her. She looks up when I pull out my chair. Her face is blotchy and her eyes are bloodshot and swollen, as though she hadn't slept all night.

"What's going on?" I ask, trying to keep my voice cool and uninflected.

She fumbles with her purse and pulls out a pack of cigarettes, tapping it on the table automatically, as though she's been smoking forever. "So you are staying with Evalinda?" she says and draws a cigarette out of the pack with her mouth. A smooth move I commit to memory.

"Uh-huh. What's the emergency?" I continue to emulate Evalinda's tone when she was on the phone with Anne.

Britta lights her cigarette with a pink Bic lighter and trembling hands. She takes a deep drag and, as she blows out the smoke, her face crumples. "I'm sorry. Oh God, I'm so sorry." Her eyes bubble up with tears. "Oh Jirina, I don't know what to do!" She puts her elbows on the table, and covers her face with her hands. Her previously perfect nails are bitten down to the quick.

"He—he said it's over."

"Who?"

"Jean-Pierre!"

"What?" My question is an exclamation of surprise, rather than one requiring explanation, but Britta continues. "He said I was too young. He made a mistake."

No kidding. "I'm sorry. What are you going to do?" I say.

"I don't know," she cries. "He left the hotel, he went back to *her*." I'm glad to hear that, although of course I wouldn't dream of saying it out loud. Britta sobs so hard the table shakes, causing her cup and saucer to vibrate glassy notes against each other.

"I'm all alone." She looks at me with tears dripping down her cheeks, her mouth a sad crescent with thin strands of spit hovering between her lips. "Please, please, you're my only friend."

We pick up her stuff at the hotel and she pays for a taxi back to Ile. St. Louis. "Evalinda is coming back on Monday," I tell her, "so only two nights, okay?"

"That's fine," she hiccups. "It's just that now, I can't stand to be alone, you know?"

"I have—a meeting later, at four," I tell her and hope she won't ask what it's for. She doesn't.

We climb the stairs to the apartment, and I set her bag down in the bedroom. She barely even looks around before collapsing on the sofa in fresh tears.

"I know he loves me," she sobs. "He told me he does. But I'm too young, too beautiful, he's afraid that I would leave *him*!" She laughs bitterly. "So he chooses to give me my freedom, to grow up and blah, blah, blah." She reaches for my hand and clutches it to her chest. "Oh God, I just want to die!"

I sit next to her on the couch, holding her hand while she cries and rants for what seems like hours. And at 3:40, I realize it *has* been hours and I have to run. My appointment with *Vogue*. Yesterday, I had a vision of getting ready, slowly and meticulously, washing my hair, shaving my legs, applying the little bit of makeup I own, maybe even supplementing it with a little from Evalinda. Now, I have no time to do any of it. I'd rather that Britta doesn't know I'm going for a go-and-see, so I decide to put on my mascara and lip gloss in the subway.

"I have to go now," I tell Britta. She turns to me with big, horrified eyes.

"Not now," she exclaims. "Oh Jirina, please don't leave me *now*."

"Britta, I'll only be a half hour, an hour at most."

"Where are you going?"

"I—um—"

"Not a go-and-see, is it?" The word sound nearly obscene, the way she spits it out. "It's Saturday!"

I nod, unable to look at her. "It's, uh, for a trip."

She bursts out in a fresh round of tears.

"I'll only be a half hour," I repeat pleadingly.

"Go, just go." She waves me off.

"Are you sure? I mean, if you really need me to stay—" I hesitate and pray she won't.

"Go to your go-and-see. Go!"

I leave her still sobbing on the couch. I didn't have the time or the inclination to change my clothes, so I'm stuck with my baggy jeans and a white T-shirt.

This time, the go-and-see is in a hotel, the Trémoille, on a quiet street behind the Champs-Élysées.

A dried-out broom of a woman opens the door for me. "I don't need the bed turned down," she growls at me. At first, I'm completely puzzled, than it dawns on me: She thinks I'm a maid!

I blush. "Um, I'm sorry, I'm here for a go-and-see?"

She stares at me in apparent disbelief, and then waves me in. The room is lovely, large and high ceilinged, with a blue-and-white color scheme. As usual, clothing and accessories are strewn everywhere. The woman moves aside some clothes on the couch and sits down. "You—stand there," she commands, and points to the middle of the room. I stand where I'm told, my plastic shopping bag with my portfolio slipping in my sweaty hand.

"Put the bag down."

I set it down and wait. Nothing happens. She sits on the couch, staring at me, without the slightest expression.

"Would you like to see my book?" I offer nervously.

"Nein."

I continue to stand, she continues to stare. Her hair is yolk-yellow, short, and sticks up all over her head like straw, and her skin, accentuated by the all-white pants and blouse, has the color and texture of Mia's brown leather bag.

Minutes tick by, each one heavy and laden with silence. I start to sweat. What does she want from me? What am I supposed to do?

"You have a pimple," she announces suddenly.

My hand flies up involuntarily to my chin, where, yes, as of this morning I have a zit.

She puts up a warning finger. "Quiet."

I didn't say anything! My face twitches, wanting to break into a wholly inappropriate smile. I think of Britta and my promise to be home soon. How long will this go on?

"Now, you turn from the back," the woman barks at me. I turn around and try to rid myself of the feeling that I'm standing before a firing squad. At least now I'm looking out the windows. Woolly clouds roll above gray rooftops, and in the distance, the wail of a siren cuts through the hum of traffic. My pulse speeds, fueled by my old, irrational fear that I have done something wrong, and am about to be arrested. The siren fades. Another few minutes go by in silence. My legs are going numb.

"Yah, now you do the pauses," I hear the woman say. Pauses. What in the world does that mean? I twist my head over my shoulder. "I'm sorry?"

"The pauses!" the woman snaps, and seeing I'm obviously too dense to understand, strikes a pose on the couch, hand on her hip, chin jutting out, cheeks sucked in. Oh, poses.

"From the back?" I ask.

"Nein," she sighs. "From the front."

I turn again, put one leg in front of the other, hands on hips, and give her that cocked tilt of the head that Mr. Giscard liked.

"Now, another," she says. I oblige with a sideways turn, hands still on hips, and face straight at her.

"Keep going," she says.

This is ridiculous. For the first time, I become aware of how silly all this must look to an outsider. A camera is what validates this silliness. Without a camera to capture my turns and—what I imagine to be—high-fashion looks, I feel unmoored and adrift in a sea of pointless grimaces and twitches, as though I am having convulsions. I keep posing and twisting myself, until I'm wrung dry of ideas and energy.

"Danke schön," the woman says after what seems like hours. With relief, I get ready to leave, but no. Now it's time for a few Polaroids.

I hope Britta is okay. I promised an hour at most.

The woman shoots off a roll of close-ups, waiting between each shot for it to develop. I tremble with impatience. The she decides she needs full length, and then she thinks I should try on a few dresses. I know I ought to be thankful, for she is showing interest, and this is *Vogue*. I oblige her with my friendliest smile and take a purple silk gown into the bathroom. The waist on the gown is so tight, I have trouble zipping the side up. When I come out of the bathroom, the woman commands me to suck in, and with one hand firmly tugging the dress down, the other zips it in one forceful move. Unfortunately, the zipper snags the flesh on my ribcage. I yelp in pain and start bleeding. She frowns at me as if it was my fault. Once the bleeding subsides with the help of some toilet paper, she does more Polaroids, in the dress, close, far, and middle. By the time she allows me to leave, the afternoon sun is gone. I glance at my watch. Three hours. And that's not counting the trip on the Metro.

THE LIVING ROOM is nearly dark by the time I get home. Both windows are open wide to the river breeze. The floor is strewn with papers, which shift in the wind with a ghostly rustle. Britta is asleep on the couch. I step up to her softly and switch on the lamp.

I look down on the littered floor. A chill encloses me as if I've just stepped off into an unheated swimming pool.

The papers are photographs of Britta: test shots from Sweden, Polaroids from Paris—*all with black, gouged-out faces.*

I crouch down. Every single photo has been altered with a lead pencil and a lot of manual force; some pictures have been attacked so viciously the paper has torn. The most recent ones, taken after Britta had her hair cut, have clumsily drawn long curls scratched around their missing faces. "Britta, wake up." I shake her shoulder. "What's going on?"

No response. Her body is heavy and strangely yielding. I turn the lamp so the light falls across her face. Her eyes move rapidly under the lids, her mouth is slightly open, and drool has dried on her chin. I feel as though I've swallowed a pound of gravel. My mouth is dry, my stomach churns painfully, and I'm too weighed down to move. But move I must.

"Britta, wake up!" I shake her harder. She doesn't react. I look around me in despair. The faceless pictures glare at me accusingly from the floor. It's eight o'clock on a Saturday night, the agency is closed, my two francs won't get us anywhere, and I don't even know what number to dial for an emergency. I go back to my only alternative, shaking her as hard as I can. She moans. She's alive, thank God. In *Christiane F.* there are a few nights where Christiane and her heroin-addicted boyfriend try to quit cold turkey, and spew blood all over walls. I look around again. There is no blood here, but this time I spot the orange plastic pill bottles on the floor, half hidden under the couch. They are both empty. The names on the labels mean nothing to me. I put them down and run to the sink and fill up a glass of water, run back and try to force the water into her mouth.

It just dribbles out. I throw it in her face. She murmurs something, but doesn't wake.

With my heart pounding so fast I'm afraid I'll also pass out, or get my attack, I begin to boil water for coffee. Somewhere in the recesses of my mind is a story about an overdose that is cured by lots of coffee. Or was that alcohol poisoning?

This is my fault. If only I had come home earlier. If only I had lied about the go-and-see, if only I hadn't left her alone—

While the coffee brews, I run to the bathroom and turn the shower on. My idea is to pull her into the bathtub, something much easier imagined than actually done. Britta's body is like a sack of wet sand. I manage to slide her off the couch and drag her across the floor, holding her under her arms. Once I get her to the bathroom, all my strength is gone and my arms feel like gelatin. I get the coffee and bring it to the bathroom. If this doesn't work, what will I do? Can I dial a zero, like in Sweden, to get an operator? What is the French word for "emergency"? No idea. Not even a twinkling of an idea. Don't even know how to say "urgent." Or "help."

I squat down next to Britta and support her head as I tip the coffee into her mouth. It sits there, brown and viscous, dribbling down the sides of her lips. With the last of my strength, I shove her into the bathtub, head first. I turn on the cold shower and she opens her eyes. Yes! She moans, dry heaves a few times, and then vomits all over her chest. I crouch next to the bathtub, whispering, "It's okay, everything's gonna be okay," and rub her back in small circles like I used to do to Kristynka when she was sick.

Her unfocused eyes fall on me.

"Britta, what did you do?"

She doesn't respond. She curls up under the freezing water that ricochets off the tile and drenches the floor. Her face is dangerously close to the water at the bottom of the tub, so I keep turning her head so she can breathe. Finally, I turn off the water.

There is a faint knocking somewhere and it takes me a moment to realize it's the door. I run and throw it wide open.

On the doorstep stands a man my height, with unruly brown hair and a crooked smile.

"Bonsoir, I'm Hugo," he says.

"Oh, thank God," I exclaim and throw myself into his arms.

CHAPTER 13

I pull him into the bathroom with a jumbled torrent of words. "My friend—overdose I think—found pills—doesn't wake up—coffee—please, help."

He takes off his black jacket and rolls up the sleeves of his blue shirt. "What did she take?"

"I don't know, but I found some empty jars, I think diet pills and something to calm down?"

"Bring them," he says. He seems completely at ease, as if this happened to him on a daily basis.

I get him the jars and he studies them. "This one is basically speed, yes, people take them sometimes for losing the weight, and this one—quaaludes. How many did she take?"

"I have no idea."

"She vomited, yes? And that is good, we have to make her do it again." He pulls Britta up to sitting, and pries her mouth open. "You do not have a feather by any chance?" he says. "Or a little stick, like from an ice pop?"

I shake my head. He shrugs, and sticks his finger into her mouth while holding her jaw open with his other hand. He slides the finger in deeper and Britta heaves. He does it a few more times, until Britta throws up again. Then he turns the water back on. Britta opens her eyes, and this time I think she sees me.

"Good, good," Hugo says. We are all wet now; I'm shivering so hard my teeth chatter.

"You go and change your clothes, and bring her some also," Hugo says. "She will be okay."

When I come back to the bathroom, Hugo stands up and dries his arms. "Bon," he says, "if you need me, just call, I will be outside."

Britta is sitting up in the bath, but she keeps nodding off. I remove her clothes and fill the tub with warm water, and then pour some of Evalinda's La Grande Passion body wash into a washcloth. I soap her up, mostly her back and her neck and the top of her breastbone; the rest seems too invasive; too private. I let the water out and wrap a towel around her. "Britta, can you stand so I can dress you?" I say. She nods. I help her out of the tub, and she sits on the floor while I pull on her pajamas. Once she is dressed, I call for Hugo. He makes her drink some more coffee. This time Britta swallows it.

"Good," Hugo says. "Now we walk her."

The three of us, Hugo and I supporting Britta between us, pace the living room to the windows and back to the bedroom in uneven halting steps.

"I'm sorry, I'm so sorry," Britta moans as we walk. We stop when she begins to heave and, with a terrifically well-placed gush, nails Evalinda's stack of laundered clothing in the corner.

HUGO COMES OUT of the bedroom, rumpled and squinting at the sun. "Bonjour," he says. In the morning light, his brown hair is actually not brown at all; it's a deep auburn. His skin is very pale, slightly freckled across the bridge of his rather large nose. He looks younger than I thought him last night, mid-twenties perhaps?

"Your friend, she is sleeping good now," he says. "She will be okay, but maybe not feel so wonderful when she wakes up." He plops into one of the chairs.

I clutch my coffee mug to my chest. "I don't know how to thank you—" I begin, but he waves me off.

"I will accept a coffee as a return for the services, yes?" He smiles. I get up and pour him a cup.

"Now that we have had the pleasure of sleeping together, perhaps you can tell me your name?" he says as I hand him the cup.

I tell him, correct him, and finally give in to "*Zheerreenah*."

"I'll never know how to thank you enough," I say again and sit on the couch.

"Do not worry, I am happy I could be of help." His smile is still crooked, and sort of sweet, although it shows way too much gum above small teeth.

"You must have thought I was crazy last night, when you walked in and I threw myself at you like that," I say.

"It is true, I was a little surprised to have a beautiful girl throw herself at me, it is not often that it happens." He scratches his head. "Uh, never, actually."

I sip my coffee and let the compliment warm me. "So, how do you know Evalinda?"

"I did an interview with her, a few years ago," he says. "I am a writer, a journalist."

I'm impressed, but simultaneously confused. He was so cool and collected last night. "Oh, I thought maybe you were a doctor," I say. "Or in the medical field somehow."

"That is funny," he says, and brushes his hair off his face.

"Well, you seemed so capable, like you knew what you were doing—"

"This is because I was a junkie," he says calmly. "I have much experience with people who take the drugs."

"Ah, junkie," I say, trying to seem equally calm. "Is that, like, heroin?"

"Mais oui, it is heroin," he confirms.

This is great. My friend has just overdosed, and I let a junkie in to help us. Not to mention Evalinda's explicit instructions not to let any men into the apartment.

"Does this make you not comfortable?" he says. He pronounces it *comfort-table*.

I exhale. "No actually, it doesn't." I say the words and realize I'm not lying. "It makes me think you must be very brave to quit."

He assesses me with a quick glance. "And how do you know of such things, if I may ask?"

"I read *Christiane F.*," I say.

He smiles. "You know, they are making it a film."

"I prefer to read."

His focus on me sharpens, as if he were mentally photographing me. "Then we have something else in common," he says. He stretches his arms and yawns. "And now, for the problem—what will you do with your girlfriend?"

It's a good question. It's Sunday, she has to be out of the apartment by tomorrow morning, and it dawns on me I can't simply tell her to leave; not now. But what else can I do? Move in with her to the bordello hotel? But how will I ever be able to go on a go-and-see, leaving her behind? "I have no idea. What do you think?" I ask.

He sets his cup down on the table, and gets very serious. "I think she should go home. Back to her family."

"But I don't know if she'll want to. We both just started modeling—"

"Then it is even more of a good reason to go home. Things, they will not get easier for her, you know."

"It was kind of my fault," I say. "She was really upset and I left her alone—"

"Did you buy her the pills?"

"No."

"Did you force her to take them?"

"Of course not!"

"Then, how was it your fault?"

"But—"

"You asked for my opinion," he interjects. "So, I will tell it to you. I have the experience with the things of this nature, and I can tell you if she stays in Paris, it will happen again. She needs to be where she is comfortable, and where she cannot get the pills and drugs. She needs very much the support—is that the correct word?"

I nod to all of the above.

"So we call the parents and explain. And we bring her to the airport."

"I'm not allowed to use the phone except for Paris," I say. "And I have no money."

"Do not worry. Now you go and find the number."

His pale azure eyes regard me seriously beneath straight, thick eyebrows that nearly meet above the bridge of his nose. And I'm suddenly very happy to have let this junkie into the apartment.

I wake Britta to get her mother's phone number. "Britta, listen," I say. "I'll call your mom and tell her what happened, and then Hugo and I will take you to the airport." I fully expect her to fight me on it, but she just curls up under the sheet.

"Thank you," she says. "Tell my mommy I'm sorry and I love her and I can't wait to be home."

Her mother's reaction on the phone is no less foreign to me. Instead of accusations and shouts, she cries and thanks me profusely for saving her daughter's life. In vain, I explain I didn't do much; it was all Hugo. She tells me she will immediately prepay a ticket for her daughter if we could be so kind as to get Britta to the airport as soon as possible. "Tell her," Britta's mom says, "that I love her, and anyone who doesn't see how beautiful she is inside and out can piss off."

I hang up and pack up Britta's belongings. She has just tried to commit suicide, her modeling career may be over, and she is about to leave Paris—so why is there a chip of envy in my heart?

HUGO'S CAR TURNS OUT to be a ridiculous little Jetsons' vehicle, in a glossy red that shines like nail polish. Hugo presses a button on his key chain, and the doors fly up comically like wings. Britta, although deathly pale and unsteady on her feet, eyes the car with obvious admiration. Inside, the black leather seats are broiling and there is no backseat, so Britta has to sit on my lap for the duration of the ride.

"All Lamborghinis are small; they are sports cars," Hugo says, sounding a little miffed.

We pick up the ticket at the airport counter while Britta rests in an orange bucket seat. Because she's still a little wobbly, we walk her to security, Hugo carrying her bag. She stops and turns to me.

"I'm just gonna rest for a week or two, and then I'll be back," she says.

"Of course," I say and hug her. She feels bony and frail, and smells of Evalinda's La Grande Passion.

I watch her amble down the corridor, clutching her purse. Her back and the slope of her shoulders look despondent and her head is a sad little shorn sheep under the fluorescent lights. What a difference three weeks have made.

I know she won't be back. And I don't think I'll miss her.

·   ·   ·

BY THE TIME HUGO'S Lamborghini roars through Ile St. Louis, it's nearly dark. I know I need to clean the apartment and do something about Evalinda's clothes, but the weekend's events have left me so drained, I don't know if I'll be able. I'm also starving. When Hugo states that he will now take me to dinner, his treat, I'm so grateful I could cry. Not that I would, of course.

The restaurant is within walking distance of the apartment. When we arrive, we are immediately ushered to a nice table for two by the window.

"You come here often?" I ask, after the chef himself walks out of the kitchen and shakes Hugo's hand.

"The chef is a friend of my father," Hugo says, but volunteers no further information. I open the leather-bound menu. Everything is listed in French. I decide on the Gigot d'agneau cuit a la façon de Grandmère, because it's something "cooked Grandmother-style" and that's the only thing I understand. The prices are missing, and Hugo explains it is a "prix fixe." "Everything at one price, also the dessert. You eat dessert, I hope," he adds with a glint.

"Are you kidding? That's my favorite part."

"Some models, they eat nothing, you know. It is painful to take them to dinner because all they want is le salade, even with no sauce."

"No dressing?"

"No dressing." He accepts my correction with a good-natured grin. "Especially, les Américaines, they are the most bad."

"So, you know a lot of models, then?" I say and strain my ears to recognize the piano music playing in the background.

"I know a few, yes."

"Oh, listen, Chopin." I hum along to a few bars. "Nocturne in B-flat minor."

"You like Chopin?" He seems relieved by a change of topic, and I make a note to ask him about the models at some later time.

"He's my favorite," I say. "My father insists Beethoven is God, but personally, I've always been drawn to the lingering sadness in Chopin. You know, Beethoven is all loud yelling and proclamations of greatness, but Chopin is just this sweet, perfectly contained sorrow."

Hugo listens to me intently with the slight crooked grin. "And, what would you say of Mozart?"

"Mozart? Impeccably crafted pop music." These are my father's words, and for once, they are useful.

Hugo smiles. "It is not often I meet a model with such knowledge of the classical music."

"But you meet many who don't?"

"What about Tchaikovsky?" he says quickly.

"My second favorite," I admit. "He's all unrequited love and torment in a really pretty pink box."

Hugo shakes his head with a laugh. "You are good! How do you know so much about it?"

"My father," I confess. "He's a principal, but his passion is the violin. He wanted to study at the academy in Prague and play professionally, but since he was not a member of the communist party, that wasn't ever going to happen. By the time they got to Sweden, Mother was pregnant with me, and he had to pay the bills." At least, that's the way he put it to me. My mother says his undiscovered greatness lies mostly in his own mind.

I tell Hugo about my father throwing open all the windows during thunderstorms and cranking up the volume on Beethoven, while marching up and down the floor, conducting an invisible orchestra, his hair standing on end in the wind, or perhaps because of the electrical charges in the air. I don't tell Hugo that I thought this was because my father was the devil, as my mother often called him, or that I'd be cowering behind a couch somewhere until he calmed down and resumed human form.

The waiter brings us a bottle of Jacques Dubois wine. I admire the label on the bottle while Hugo gives the waiter our order. "Do you think the people that make this wine actually live here?" I point to the silver print of a large castle on the label.

"Yes," Hugo says. "They live there and the wine comes from vineyards all around it."

"How do you know that?" I tease.

He shrugs. "Mon père, my father, he owns a little one. Dis donc, do you have the opinions about the writers also? You say you like the books."

"Bien sûr," I say.

"Bon. Hemingway."

"Sort of like Beethoven. All masculine bluster."

My "something cooked Grandmother-style" arrives and turns out to be a lamb casserole. I empty three glasses of wine before noticing Hugo has barely touched his. "Don't you like wine?" I ask.

"Uh, no, I mean, yes. But maybe I like it too much, tu comprends?"

I let his comment hover in the air like a bubble that pops quickly of its own accord. This Hugo, who is proving to be not only my savior and benefactor, but also such great company, has a troubled past, one I'd rather not delve into. His being a former junkie, and maybe an alcoholic, is so at odds with what I see here, across the table from me. His presence is as comfortable and familiar as family, the sort of family I dream of: a mom who bakes cookies instead of one who wears miniskirts and dates guys nearly my age; a dad who smokes a pipe and reads the newspaper and calls me his "princess" instead of one who has to be sued for child-support money. Hugo makes me feel safe. And safe, however unusual, feels wonderful. We go through American writers, French writers, and Russian writers, Hugo with a few comments of his own—Jane Austen is chamber music, Handel maybe, all politeness and good manners; Dickens is an over-romanticized Tchaikovsky, all weepy and sentimental. By the time we have our dessert, Ile Flottant, a meringue stranded in a plate of creamy, sweet custard, I'm doing some floating myself.

I shouldn't have had that last glass of port, I think, as we stand to leave. "I'm not sure I'll be able to walk," I tell Hugo before my knees buckle and the lights go out.

THE PHONE RINGS ME awake and brings on instant physical misery: a blinding headache, queasy stomach, and wilted limbs. And knowing it's called a hangover doesn't make me feel any better. I have a vague recollection of Hugo dragging, or carrying, me up the stairs and making me drink a glass of water before I fell asleep in my clothes. He is still sleeping on the far side of the bed, the sheets drawn up over his shoulder.

I run into the living room, where the shrill tone of the phone and the smell of vomit make me feel even worse. Evalinda is supposed to be back anytime now, and this is how I've repaid her: a stinking, filthy apartment, a man in her bed, ruined laundry, and a long distance phone call. I have a lot of work ahead.

"Allô, Jirina?" Anne's voice sounds urgent.

"Speaking."

"I have a little problem. Evalinda didn't show up for her booking this morning and the clients are very angry. Can you be at Mr. Carera's studio in thirty minutes?"

I realize this is not a question.

"I, um—" There is no way I can refuse, and there is no way I can go to work and clean the apartment at the same time.

Anne gives me the address; I hang up and run back to the bedroom.

"Hugo, I just got a job and I have to leave *now*," I say breathlessly. "Evalinda could be back any minute."

Hugo opens his eyes. "Do not worry, I will take care of things."

He is so sweet. How do I explain he can't be in the apartment when Evalinda returns? I feel a warm trickle down my leg. My stomach cramps are not from a hangover. What a time to get my period! I run to the bathroom, find no tampons or pads, so I wad up some paper and stick it in my underwear. I run to the closet and tear out some clothes from my bag. "I don't think you can be here when she returns," I shout out while I wriggle into my jeans.

"It is not a problem," Hugo shouts back.

I nearly fall out of the closet in my haste. "Hugo, she told me not to let any men in under any circumstances."

"And again, I tell you it is not a problem," Hugo says. He sits up in bed. "Trust me, I will take care of the things." He looks like a homely little boy with his hair all mussed up and his shirt wrinkled. The address is across town; it will take me a half hour on the subway alone. I will have to trust him.

I WORK UP QUITE a sweat dashing through the hot bright streets, my finger running along the map in my Plan de Paris, while my homemade paper napkin does its best to chafe and slide backward with every step. I have to suppress the urge to stop and plunge my hand into my jeans, right here on the street, to pull the damned thing forward. The studio is on the bottom floor of a squat white house with black shutters. Inside the large open space, two assistants roll out white paint onto an already white wall, which slopes to the floor in a smooth curve. A third assistant lugs enormous metal lights that look like giant paint cans to a line of six others already standing in a row angled toward the wall. A muscular man with long hair in a ponytail and a goatee introduces himself as Vlad, the hairstylist. "The makeup artist is not yet here, he's running late, and Mr. Carera doesn't usually arrive until noon," he informs me as he offers me the short director's chair. The tall one, I know by now, is reserved for makeup.

Vlad has his arsenal of hair stuff lined up on the table before us, and he proceeds to drench my hair with setting lotion. A few minutes later, an angular pale girl with short ashy hair arrives and greets Vlad with a thump on the back. I know better than to dismiss her as one of the assistants: With her freakish thinness and height she can only be a model, although she really looks like an overgrown adolescent boy. Her name is Jessie, she says, lights a cigarette, and plunks down in the tall chair. So far, of all the models I've met, only Lorna and Britta could be termed natural beauties without makeup. Even Evalinda looks a little freaky in the morning, with her tiny head on her racehorse body, and eyebrows and eyelashes so pale they are nearly invisible. How odd that it is Britta and Lorna who had to struggle, while I sit here, getting my hair done for a *Marie Claire* photo shoot. Does that mean I look a little freaky too? I study my mirror image, which confirms my eyes and my lips are rather large for the rest of my face, and my chin and cheekbones are too angular to qualify as pretty.

Vlad dries my hair and rolls it up on huge red rollers, while Jessie the adolescent boy smokes cigarette after cigarette. When he's done with me, he starts on Jessie, just as a balding marshmallow of a man in an embroidered shirt wheels his black makeup box to the table. His name is Davide, with an "E" at the end, "pronounced *Dah-veed*," he warns me as if I were likely to err. I tell him my name, which he immediately botches into good ol' *Zheerreenah*. He kisses Jessie like a long-lost friend until she drops ash on his shirt, which attempts to—but doesn't quite—hide sloping shoulders and a potbelly. Davide goes into a spastic dance to find the tiny hole where the fabric melted, brushing at it as though that will make it disappear. Once he's accusingly pointed it out to Jessie, he pulls out a pair of horn-rimmed glasses from his pocket, and begins scrutinizing my face. His own face is that of a flan: pale and gelatinous, with sharp beady eyes nestled in like currants; he's sweating although the studio is freezing cold.

"You have a hair growing on your nose," he says. "Here, see?" and hands me a small magnifying mirror.

It takes me a moment to find what he's talking about, but yes, oh God, at this extreme close-up, I find two tiny dark hairs on the tip of my nose. And the pores on my nose are as big as moon craters. And one of my eyelashes is pointing straight down. And there are a few stray hairs between my eyebrows. How come I've never realized what a beast I am up close?

Davide grabs tweezers and picks at my nose. It seems the hairs are too small, and after repeatedly jabbing at my nose with no success, he spackles it with concealer instead.

The rest of the makeup goes on with an equally heavy hand: foundation as thick as paste, intense black eyes with no smudging, stripes of fuchsia blush and matching sticky lips. "Mr. Carera will be using tungsten lights today," he says in explanation.

The stylist, a delicate man in a tweed jacket and an ascot, who looks as though he should be sipping tea with the Queen of England instead of cramming models into haute couture, brings Jessie a black suit just as Mr. Carera enters the studio to reverential murmurs. I immediately recognize him from my first day of go-and-sees; the man in the white lab coat who thought I shouldn't open my mouth. His pale blue eyes settle on me in the mirror. I quickly lock the cage on my white mice and give him a stiff, close-lipped smile. "Who is this?" he says, pressing a finger into my shoulder and looking around for an answer. The stylist rushes in to explain things in French.

"*Tsk*," Mr. Carera clicks his tongue. "This is what we get instead of Evalinda?"

While I stew in a cauldron of humiliation, Jessie comes out dressed in the black tuxedo. Vlad has spiked her hair a la David Bowie and she looks impossibly cool; a lanky, alien creature come to earth to mock us humans. Her makeup accentuates her sharp cheekbones and the androgynous planes of her face. Although she is not in the least pretty, I feel a pang of envy. With my hair set sail on my head, and the deadly makeup, I may look alien all right, but more like an illegal alien from a communist country who got her hands on free beauty products.

There is a hushed moment, like church, when the houselights are switched off and the tungstens roar awake. Their fiery blast hits Jessie full on. She puts a bored, elegant hand on her hip, and brings the other up to continue smoking. If she looked cool before, she is now the epitome of coolness, a perfect picture of ultimate hip; a poster child for what we all want to look like while holding cigarettes. Even the smoke looks cool, curling around her hand and lips like an art-nouveau poster.

"It's hot," she says. I try to gauge how hot, but it's impossible to tell by looking at Jessie; she is as glacial as an ice cube.

Mr. Carera bends behind his tripod. "Work," he says.

Jessie does nothing, merely continues to smoke, and Mr. Carera sighs, "beautiful," and shoots off a roll like a machine gun. That looks easy enough. I know how to smoke, too.

Mr. Stylist brings me a white suit, shaking it out on the hanger. The flash of white reminds me I better go to the bathroom first. I excuse myself and lock the stainless steel door of the unisex bathroom behind me.

The blood has gone through the damn paper and made a spot in my underwear. I try to dry it off best as I can, putting paper under and over the stain to blot it, and then wad up another, bigger clump and park it between my legs. When I pull on my underwear, I look as if I've suddenly sprouted testicles. This won't work. I feel perspiration bead on my upper lip, and become aware of a smell, sour and metallic, emanating from me. I sweat harder.

What if I made a tampon instead? After all, I'm no longer a virgin. I wad up tissue into a small tight cylinder, about the width of a thumb, and shove it in. I stand to check for blood flow; it holds. I wash my hands and underarms in the sink and find too late there are no towels or fans to dry off. I use more toilet paper, as a towel this time.

Mr. Stylist stands at the door when I exit, impatiently tapping his foot. "Hurry, Mr. Carera doesn't like to be kept waiting," he says, and hands me the suit. I try to hide behind the clothing rack, but there are only four or so dresses hanging on it. The stylist stands next to me, holding out the clothes. With a twinge I discover toilet paper fragments under my arms and pull on the suit jacket as fast as I can. But I'm sure he noticed. His face is pulled into a vague grimace of disgust that increases when I lift my leg to insert it into the pants. I'm sweating again. Davide repowders me and wrinkles his nose. "What is that smell?" he exclaims. Every school comment about being a dirty communist resurfaces and blankets me with shame.

Jessie is back in the makeup chair when I step up on the set. The moment the lights are switched on, my previous curiosity about how hot it actually is dies in the infernal onslaught. It's not just bright sunlight, it's a week of tropical sun squeezed in and concentrated in the paint cans. I'm blinded.

"Work," Mr. Carera says.

I put a nonchalant hand in the pocket and try for the haughty-alien, you-all-suck look, but Mr. Carera stands up. "What? Are you sick?"

I try my narrowed-gaze look; hands on hips, leg out like a kickstand. My eyes are starting to burn.

"Open your eyes," Mr. Carera shouts. I oblige and widen them. My vision is nothing but a glaring white field. It's a little easier than direct sunlight, but much hotter. It's so hot, in fact, my sweat seems to dry the moment it hits my skin.

"Expression! I want life!" Mr. Carera shouts.

He does? Jessie looked half dead.

But I try. I smile, I burn, I look down, I burn, I turn in profile, I burn. Firestorm, blaze, I shoot my hip out and burn. I bend my knee and burn. Flames eat my eyes, my hair, my skin. I gasp for air, which has turned into boiling tea. I'm an innocent burned at the stake of fashion. And this is when a cooling trickle reminds me homemade tampons are not commonly used for a good reason.

"I'm sorry," I say to the blinding whiteness, "but may I go to the bathroom for a moment?"

"Just do your goddamn job and then go to the bathroom," Mr. Carera's voice snarls back.

I pull my legs together, clamp my lower muscles as tightly as I can, and stare into the camera. *Fuck you.* There. I've thought it and I still stand. God must be attending to other problems right now. Maybe Grandma was wrong about God's constant vigilance to my every word and thought. I roll the word around, savoring it like a hard candy. *Fuck. Fuck you.* It's short and sweet, and it's got a nice meaty heft to it, like a well-aimed punch. Why couldn't I think it? For a split second, my brain takes a side road down the street of fuck, registering all its possibilities: as a noun— that fuck; as an adjective—fucking; and as a verb—to fuck. Amazing, one little word that conveys so much that I have until now completely disregarded. Well, no more. *Fuck you, fuck you, fuck you. Fucking asshole.*

"Yes, that is good, stay like that," Mr. Carera says.

THE BLOOD HAS SOAKED all the way through, my underwear is a bloody mess, but worst of all, it has left a red streak on the inside of the trouser leg. Trying to soak it up with toilet paper only smudges it wider. I hang the pants over the stall and try to retrieve the tampon. I put a finger in and locate the disintegrating wad, but getting it out is another problem. Finally, with my finger serving as a hook, I manage to scrape the mess out, roll up another cylinder, a bit wider this time, and stick it in. I wash my underwear in the sink, wring it dry, and put it back on. Now I'm dressed in the equivalent of a wet diaper. The stain on the pant leg I scrub with toilet paper, which leaves little crumbly bits on the fabric and doesn't do anything to the stain. I have no choice but pull the pants back on over my wet underwear, and stupidly hope my underwear won't wet the pants, and that no one will notice.

Mr. Stylist is tucking in his ascot by the makeup mirror when I exit. "You're done," he says.

"All right. Should I change into my next outfit?"

"There is no next outfit for you. You are *done*."

I STOP BY THE agency to borrow some money. I ask for fifty francs; Jean-Pierre laughs and gives me a hundred. Mr. Carera obviously hasn't called the agency yet, for everyone is all smiles. My stomach hurts and my eyes burn, but no less than my conscience. How long will it take for them to fire me? I stumble back home like a zombie, stopping in a drugstore to buy real tampons, so at least I can fly back to Sweden unhampered by toilet paper.

CHAPTER 14

I open the door to Evalinda sitting on the couch perusing a magazine, and Hugo smoking on the windowsill in a nice, clean apartment.

"Hey, there she is," Evalinda announces, as if they were just talking about me. But her voice is as friendly as her smile.

I'm confused. The apartment is spotless: A small scented candle burns on the coffee table, the stinking laundry is gone, the floors are swept and shiny.

"I told Evalinda about the laundry, that they didn't do such a good job, so you took the clothes back to have them done again," Hugo says and winks at me. He did take care of everything. I'd like to run into his arms and sob in gratitude. "How was the work?" he says.

I drag myself across the floor and sit down in the chair facing Evalinda. "One of the worst days in my life," I say. "Mr. Carera fired me."

Evalinda looks up sharply from her magazine. "Mr. Carera? For *Marie Claire*?"

"Yeah," I say and am about to ask how she knows, when I realize it was *her* job I took.

"What happened?" Evalinda says.

"They sent me home after one picture."

Evalinda smiles. "Yeah, he can be difficult, unless you know how to handle him." Which of course I don't. But this suddenly seems like a good thing.

Hugo stubs out his cigarette. "Ça va toi?" he says looking at me. "You look not so well."

"I'm worried," I admit. "What will the agency say when they find out?"

Evalinda laughs. "What, you think they will be mad at you?"

I shrug miserably.

"Jirina, get this. They, the agency, work for *you*, not the other way around!"

Maybe they work for her, but I doubt I'm in the same position.

"They won't fire you, if that's what you are afraid of," she continues gaily. "They can tell you they no longer want to represent you, but that's it. They represent *you*, get it?"

I still don't see the difference.

"Besides, they will certainly represent you as long as you keep getting work. And you're working tomorrow, Anne gave me the details."

"I am?"

"Yep. And guess who with?"

I wouldn't dare to presume, although a hot little flash of hope sparks in my chest. I widen my eyes at Evalinda in a silent plea to tell me.

"Okay, okay, no fair to keep you guessing. He's tall, gorgeous, and Australian—"

"Rob?"

Hugo suddenly stands up so abruptly, the ashtray next to him falls on the floor. He kneels down to pick up the ashes.

"The one and only!" Evalinda exclaims unperturbed. "Now hop into the shower and get dressed, we're going out to celebrate."

"Shouldn't I maybe stay at home and get some rest?" I say. "I'm kind of beat, and I have a stomachache." I glance at Hugo and back at Evalinda. "You know—*that* kind of stomachache . . ."

"I'll give you something for that. Now come on, we are going to a *concert*." She stresses the word concert. Her boyfriend's concert.

"Yes, you will have the pleasure of meeting the man," Hugo says from his kneeling position. He stands up and brushes himself off. "I better leave now," he says.

"Won't you come too?" I ask with a sinking heart.

"No boys allowed," Evalinda says. "This is strictly girls only."

"The man is a little jealous, maybe because he himself is married," Hugo says.

"That's enough, rehab boy," Evalinda hisses. "Leave."

Hugo smiles at me, but looks sad.

I hug him tightly. "Thank you so much for everything," I whisper and let my head rest on his shoulder. His arms grip me tighter for a moment, he kisses the top of my head, and then he's out the door.

"Hurry up, now," Evalinda says, jumping off the couch. "We have to be on time, or they won't let us in backstage."

BEFORE WE LEAVE, she hands me two yellow pills for my cramps, and lends me a leather jacket to throw over my T-shirt. By the time we reach the venue, the pills have eliminated my cramps along with most of my brain. I'm fuzzy-headed and giddy; my feet feel as though I'm treading on, say, a mattress. Throngs of concertgoers push up against the entrance doors, but we walk down a side street and knock on a shabby unmarked door. Evalinda flashes a plastic rectangle at the beefy man who opens it and waves us in. There are flights of metal stairs everywhere, leading to God-knows-where. The beefy man points up, and we clatter along until we reach a maze of hallways lit with fluorescent lights. Doors line the walls, some with signs, some without. It all looks alarmingly like school, and even smells of B.O., like the gym. People dressed in bright Lycra—including the men—mill about, smoking and drinking beer. "Isn't this great?" Evalinda says breathlessly, pulling me behind her. "You are *backstage*, baby."

She stops before a door with a plastic gold star taped to it. "He doesn't like to be interrupted before a show, so I'm just going to peek in and give him a kiss. You stay here." She taps out a series of Morse code knocks and, when the door opens, she disappears inside. I lean against the wall and wish I had a cigarette. A man with an incredibly long nose and shaggy platinum hair is in a discussion with two girls, who almost look like models, but miss the mark by being a tad too short and a tad—well, more than a tad—well-endowed. Another man, dressed in a shiny suit jacket, jeans, and high-heeled pink cowboy boots, is talking on a huge phone that's attached to something in a large black bag, which he has slung over his shoulder. He paces the hall exclaiming, "No fucking way—I'd rather you piss on my mother's grave—what's that?—yeah, fuck you too—"

A few minutes later, it's as if a silent alarm goes off. Everyone tenses, and their movements take on an urgent purpose. The door next to me flies open with a loud crash, and I get a quick peek at Evalinda's boyfriend as he strides out past me. He's draped with his ubiquitous glittery scarves in reds and pinks, and all I have time to register is that he's tiny! Teeny tiny, like a child, like my seven-year-old sister. Wait till I tell Hatty!

He vanishes into a mob of normal-size people who crowd around him, presumably to escort him to the stage. Evalinda grabs my hand and pulls me after them. Behind a metal door at the end of the hallway, we enter the darkness of an enormous room. The crowd roars. For one infinitesimal second, I am engulfed with the heat of the welcome, the greeting of thousands of people. So this is what it feels like. In the next moment, lights start flashing, crazy beams illuminate thousands of bobbing heads, and the crowd goes wild. Evalinda pulls me up a couple of makeshift wooden steps, and we are on stage. Granted, on the very side of the stage where we are safely hidden from the audience by enormous black boxes, but still, the stage, where Evalinda's boyfriend is but a few steps away. The band tears into an earsplitting riff of their new single, and when the drums kick in, the beat is so loud I feel it replace my pulse. Strobes flash, music pumps, the breath of thousands ignites the room. Evalinda dances next to me like she's possessed. I try to at least rock my hips back and forth, but I'm so tired I feel as though I've gone to sleep already and now can't wake up from a very noisy nightmare. Every time I blink, my eyelids feel like they are lined with sandpaper, so I try to blink as little as possible. About thirty minutes into the show, the lights onstage go blue, and the band starts to play a slower song, a love song. Evalinda's boyfriend is snaked around his mike stand. His hands, which grip the mike, are adorned with a billion rings and bracelets, and when he sings the chorus of the song, "*I live for your touch, baby, I love you so much,*" I can feel Evalinda's yearning for him to turn and sing it to *her* as clearly as if she pounded the stage with her fists. He doesn't. And, I think somewhat ungraciously, he'd do well to read a poetry book or two.

When it's finally all over, Evalinda again pulls me behind her on the heels of the band and their towel-and-water-bearing people, backstage. This time, however, we both enter the dressing room with the star taped to the door. It's already filled with people and the smell of cheese and salami, which wafts forth from platters set on a table by the wall. It all looks very unappealing, although I'm starving. Or was, in a previous life. The cheese is as sweaty as Evalinda's boyfriend, and someone has stubbed out a cigarette in the salami. I fish out a cold bottle of something from a cooler next to the table, and take it to a couch that has an open spot. The dressing room is roughly the size of a hotel room, but there are close to fifty people in here. Once I sit down, I notice I picked up a beer, and I have no way to open it, so I just use it to cool my eyes, which by now hurt so bad I wish I could pop them out of my head and throw them away. I feel someone leave the seat next to me, and the weight of someone else fill it.

"Would you like me to open that?"

I take the bottle away from my eyes. It's Evalinda's boyfriend. Even sitting, he comes up to my shoulder.

"Sure, thank you," I say. Evalinda's boyfriend takes the bottle and uses his lighter to undo the top. "What's your name, baby?" he says, handing me the bottle.

"Jirina." Sitting this close to him, I can't but note his face is sort of wrinkled. He must be old, like forty. He's wiped off the sweat and removed his shirt, or top, or whatever it was, and now is bare-chested, with a white towel draped around his shoulders.

"You havin' a good time?" he says and grins. His teeth are probably the biggest thing about him; they are huge, white, and shiny with quite an overbite.

"Oh yes, thank you," I say. It's not really a lie. I'm sure I would be having a good time if only my eyes didn't hurt so.

"Hey, Pete, you old cunt," Evalinda's boyfriend exclaims suddenly, and puts his hand on my leg to lean over me. "What the fuck was the solo at the end of 'Sweet Honey Pie'?"

Pete, whom I recognize as one of the bandmates, the one with an exceptionally long nose, puts his middle finger in the air and shouts, "Fuck you too." They both laugh as though this is incredibly witty. It seems their exchange is complete, for Evalinda's boyfriend leans back, satisfied, but his hand, adorned with enough metal to weigh more than the rest of him, is still on my leg. He gives it a little squeeze and puts his other arm over the backrest, so he is practically embracing me. I keep gulping my beer to hide my nerves, and to have something, anything, to do with my hands, which suddenly feel superfluous.

I see Evalinda squeeze her way through the crowd with a big smile. "There you are," she says to both of us. "I see you've met my little friend," she adds, looking at her boyfriend. She doesn't seem to mind his close proximity to me, so I decide to stop worrying.

"Your little friend is my little friend and we can all be friends 'cause my not-so-little friend will like your little friend," he sings, oddly out of tune. It could be the beer, or the pills, or my fatigue, or the glass of whisky someone hands me, but I no longer feel in possession of my body or limbs; they have ceased to listen to central command.

Sometime later, Evalinda somehow maneuvers me downstairs to a garage and into an enormous limousine, with a ceiling made of twinkly lights that change colors, where I'm handed Marina's small cigarette; it tastes odd and makes me cough; but we all laugh. Evalinda kisses her boyfriend, he says her little friend is jealous so he kisses me, too, on the lips, dry, and then Evalinda is jealous so he kisses her, and then we are all jealous so Evalinda kisses me, then I kiss her boyfriend and his tongue slips into my mouth, which makes me laugh because of course Evalinda's tongue will be jealous too so our tongues meet and play, mostly in my mouth, and the lights in the ceiling go purple, red, orange, yellow, green, blue, back to purple, and Evalinda is sitting behind me tickling me and her boyfriend is on his knees before us and sometimes he kisses me and sometimes Evalinda, and I laugh because the trip home is as long as if we lived in Sweden, and Evalinda pushes her hands under my T-shirt to tickle me better, but then she tickles my breasts because I'm not wearing a bra, and I'm getting sort of hot because of all this tickling so she pulls my T shirt up and her boyfriend is worried my nipples are jealous so he kisses them, dry, then wet and someone's hands—not mine—are undoing my jeans.

And suddenly, this is all wrong.

"Stop," I whisper, but the hands keep going. Mouths, tongues, hands all over me. "Stop," I say. "Stop." I put my hands in the belt loops to prevent my jeans from being pulled off but Evalinda's boyfriend keeps tugging. I feel nausea climbing up my throat.

"I'm going to be sick," I say.

The car stops. The door opens. Evalinda helps me out. "You can take a taxi from here," she says, "or you can walk," and climbs back into the car.

The limousine takes off. I huddle down and throw up a little bit, and after a few minutes, I manage to stand up.

Evalinda lied.

There are no taxis here.

·   ·   ·

I'M CRAWLING THROUGH red desert sand. The sky is a blazing fury of white light. It hurts my eyes. I want to close them, but my eyelids have shriveled away in the arid heat. My eyeballs are full of sand: sharp, piercing particles like ground glass. I cry out in pain.

And wake up. The desert fades into black. I feel awake, yet I can't open my eyes: They are still full of sand. Painfully and slowly, I peel my eyelids open. I'm not asleep; I'm in Evalinda's bedroom where, although it's dark, I recognize a faded sun behind the makeshift curtain. I'm alone, Evalinda must have stayed out. I stumble to the bathroom, my field of vision in slivers. When I try to manually force my eyes open with my fingers in front of the mirror, I gasp. The whites of my eyes are completely red. Not blood-shot, not little networks of broken blood vessels, but solid red. No trace of former white. My irises swim like blue marbles in pools of blood.

I run to the living room and half-blind tap out the number to the agency. Odile picks it up and as soon as she hears my name she says, "Ah, interesting. We already had a call from Elite models to see if you are okay. It seems their girl, Jessie, had to cancel her job today because of her eyes. Are you also experiencing this?"

"Yes, but, but—I'm supposed to be working with Rob Ryan today!"

"Do not worry, I will call and explain."

"But—"

"Jessie went to the doctor already, she was told to stay at home and rest her eyes, the situation will clear itself up in a few days," Odile says helpfully.

I hang up and crawl back to bed. My tears are as soothing as battery acid. Rob, Rob, Rob. I blew it again, and this time without Simon's help. I curl into a fetal position and cry. Fragments of last night insert themselves between scenes of an imaginary Rob who vows never to work with me again. What the hell *was* that, last night? Were we all just drunk and stupid, or was there something more to it? I'm not surprised they left me by the river; what a party pooper I must seem. But the memory of my jeans being tugged down burns as badly as my eyes.

It may be hours later when I hear the front door open. I brace myself for Evalinda and possible recriminations, but it's Hugo's voice I hear. "Allô? Anyone home?"

"I'm in here," I moan pathetically. I hear him enter the bedroom. The mattress on my side slants as he sits down.

"How did you get in?" I ask.

"Buh, the door, it was not locked," he says. "What is the matter? Are you not feeling so well?" He runs a gentle hand across my forehead. I squint at him and see just enough of his reaction as he jumps. "Mon Dieu! Your eyes! What happened?"

I tell him about the lights, Jessie and what the doctor told her. I wish I could tell him about last night, too, to see what I did wrong, but I don't want to risk his good opinion of me.

"Pauvre bébé," he says. "I will go and get you something to eat, yes? And I also brought you something to read, but obviously, that will have to wait."

He brings me onion soup and an omelette de fromage, and after I finish eating, he clears away the dishes. The mattress tilts as he sits down. "I found this in an old book shop, and I think to myself, you would enjoy this," he says.

I hear the rustle of pages and Hugo's voice settles into a sweet, hushed rhythm as he reads me the opening pages of *Lélia: The Life of George Sand*.

I THINK IT'S EARLY evening when I hear Evalinda return. Hugo has left, presumably to do the things his nursing of me prevented him from doing.

"You home?" I hear her yell from the hallway.

"Yes, in here."

Her footsteps come closer. "What's the matter, are you sick?"

I kick off the sheets and sit up, squinting at her out-of-focus outline in the doorway. I hear a gasp. "Wow, what the fuck happened to you?"

"Apparently, tungstens."

Evalinda sounds relieved. "Oh, yeah, tungstens. I heard they'll do that if you stand in them too long." She sits down next to me. "I mean, it never happened to me, 'cause Mr. Carera is usually so fast—"

"I couldn't go to work today."

"You're not still worried about the agency?" she asks with a laugh.

"It was with Rob," I remind her.

"Oh yeah," she says.

Last night sits between us like a person who takes up room without joining the conversation.

"So, have you looked into alternative housing options?" she says suddenly.

This is what I was afraid of. "No. But I'll move out whenever you want me to." Maybe I can ask Hugo for help? But no, he's already done so much for me. "And listen, I'm sorry about last night."

She glances at me with what seems like surprise.

"I don't think I would have gotten sick if I hadn't drunk all that stuff on an empty stomach." I won't mention her pills; I don't want her to feel as though I'm blaming her for making me sick.

"Oh, that," she says as if she expected something else. "Yeah, I was a bit worried about you."

I'm glad she says she was, although it didn't feel like it. But then, what else were they supposed to do with a drunken girl ready to spew? "I didn't want to throw up all over you guys, you know—"

She laughs. "It's okay." She stands up and stretches. "I need to take a shower. And listen; don't feel like I'm kicking you out or anything, in fact, you're welcome to stay for now."

I thank her and gratefully close my eyes.

THE BATHROOM MIRROR REVEALS my eyes are slightly better today; little white-caps float on the ocean of red. Evalinda is at work, and Hugo will come later in the afternoon. For now, I find my cheap plastic sunglasses, stick them on, and head to the agency. The limo incident was obviously just drunken silliness. It's probably just that I don't have much experience with alcohol. Back in school, Hatty and I congratulated ourselves on preserving our brain cells on the weekends, when the rest of our class was busy getting drunk on items stolen from their parents' liquor cabinets. They'd all describe the fun on Monday mornings: passing out in their own vomit, being carried home unconscious, having sex but forgetting whom with, and my personal favorite: "I had the best time, I was so fucking drunk I can't remember a thing." At least this is one particular pleasure I've not yet experienced.

At the agency, I ask for Jean-Pierre, although he's probably the next to last person I want to see.

I take a seat across the desk from him, the poster of Marina smiling away into space above his head. I don't want to speak to him, I don't want to be here, and I try my best not to let it show. Jean-Pierre pulls out a file from a drawer in his desk and lays it on the table. "D'accord. How much do you need?"

I ask for a hundred. "And I'd like to find out how much I owe, if that's all right."

He looks at the papers next to him, and starts typing down numbers on a calculator. "Bon, first the money you have made—*Les Mariages*, six hundred, *Linea Italiana*, four hundred, *Chic & Cheap*, eight hundred. And now for the expenses—"

"I also did one day for *Marie Claire*," I remind him.

"Ah, non. Mr. Carera called about that. He does not want to pay you, for you were not professional. And he complained about your teeth also."

They are working for me, I try to remind myself. They represent *me.* But still, I wince with shame.

"I know a very good dentist, he made a little plastic piece for Lauren Hutton, to insert in her teeth for the photos. I think you want to see him, soon—and the total comes to four thousand and fifty-six francs."

My smile is involuntary but real. This is a lot of money!

"Plus the hundred you are lending today," he says, punching in the numbers, "your debt is four thousand, one hundred and fifty-six francs."

I swallow a small piece of desire to correct his English and a large chunk of mortification. This is how much I *owe*?

"Here is the number of the dentist." He pushes a piece of paper across the desk.

I thank him and stand up to leave.

He leans back in his seat. "Where are you living now?"

"Um, with Evalinda."

"Ah, la belle Evalinda," he says. Although he's just called her beautiful, something about how he says it doesn't make it sound complimentary.

HUGO PICKS ME UP in his silly little car and we drive through rush hour traffic; small bright cars bottleneck the mellow stone streets like oversized, smoke-burping jellybeans.

"So, where are we going?" I say.

"La Marche au Pus."

"Is that a store?"

"Non, it is a market for, how do you say, bugs?"

"Excuse me?" I have no illusion of how far my hundred francs will go, but when I specified shopping somewhere cheap, this was not what I had in mind.

"You know, market where they have the stands, and they sell sometimes old things, or antiques."

"Oh, a flea market." Still, not exactly upscale.

"Don't worry, this one is very famous and special. You will see," he says, and steps on the accelerator so hard I'm shoved back into the leather seat.

The flea market is huge. I expected a few ratty stands with secondhand clothes; instead, there are hundreds of sunlit stands and a whole lot of actual stores, one right after another, set into cubbyholes on small dark streets. We pass furniture heaped up on itself in precarious mounds, stalls selling touristy T-shirts, counters stacked with old books and magazines, cubicles crammed with moth-eaten, dusty carpets, and tiny cafés and brasseries squeezed between them all, their smoke and food smells adding spice to the scent of dilapidation. A black motorcycle jacket that somewhat resembles Evalinda's costs two hundred francs. So much for fleas. So far, the only things in my price range are single chipped plates, moldy books in French, limp magazines from the fifties, and, if I were to really splurge, two T-shirts with "I love Paris" stenciled on them.

I'm about to give up when Hugo pulls me into a narrow room, filled with what appear to be old costumes. They are beautiful: Victorian white-lace camisoles with faded ribbons, shiny gathered silk skirts, and embroidered corsets. This will surely be completely out of my price range. A flash of silver on black catches my eye: a Napoleon-style military jacket, cut short to the waist, with silver braiding stitched on the front. The price tag says ninety francs.

"It is cool." Hugo nods approvingly.

"It's too expensive," I say with a sigh.

"Try it on. You know, here you are suppose to uggle."

I shoot him a questioning glance.

"You know, talk the price down."

"Ah, haggle." I slip the jacket off its hanger and put it on. It fits as though it were made for me. My T-shirt and jeans suddenly look a whole lot better.

"It is perfect," Hugo exclaims. He waves off my protests. "I will haggle for you," he says.

The price eventually settles on seventy francs, which is still more than I'd like to spend.

"This jacket was made for you," Hugo says. "If you do not purchase it, I will."

I pull out my wrinkled bills. After all, I know I'm not going to walk out of here without it.

On the way back home, Hugo plays me a tape of a singer named Jacques Brel, whom he claims I must know to live in France. "He is a French institution, although he is Belges," he says.

I lean my head on the neck rest and let Jacques Brel speak to me. His voice is thick and smooth, sprinkled with tiny hiccups and almost imperceptible cracks, like raw silk. Although he sounds nothing like Rob, it's Rob that fills my head as I listen, or at least a sort of craving for him.

Hugo hums along softly. I glance at his profile. He really isn't particularly good-looking. His nose juts out with an authority it doesn't possess; his chin is weak and recedes into the jawline, where already, the beginnings of a wattle are setting in. He must feel me staring, for he turns and briefly meets my eyes. "Oui?" he says.

His eyes are beautiful, though, the color of a clean swimming pool and edged with black lashes. I suddenly feel guilty about my unkind physical evaluation of him.

"Were you and Evalinda ever boyfriend/girlfriend?" I blurt.

He blushes. "Uh, not really."

"What does 'not really' mean?"

"It means—we had sex a few times, in the beginning, tu comprends?" He clears his throat. "But boyfriend/girlfriend—no. I do not think I am her type."

"Is she yours?"

"Buh," he exhales in that negative French way, "perhaps physically, yes, but the mind, no."

His attraction to her doesn't surprise me. But Evalinda sleeping with him? That's surprising.

"Then, why are you friends with her?" I press on.

He stares at the road ahead. "Sometimes, I get a little bit lonely," he finally says.

That feeling I know too well.

CHAPTER 15

By the time Evalinda gets back home from her job, I'm showered and dressed in my least dirty jeans and red T-shirt. My eyes look almost normal now, with only a trace of pink that looks as if I've been crying. The Napoleon jacket waits for me on the bed.

"Hugo will come to pick us up any minute now, so get dressed," Evalinda says as she swings the closet door open.

"I am dressed."

"You can't go like that," she shouts at me from inside the closet. "You look like a Swedish grade-schooler!"

I dismiss the slight pang of the insult. Wait till she sees my jacket! I pull it on and wait. She comes out of the closet in a gold-mesh tie-on top, white miniskirt, and long white boots up to her thighs. She musses her hair and stares at me.

"What do you think?" I say, sticking my hands in my pockets and throwing a momentary pose.

"Huh. That's not very sexy."

That stings. I go to remove the jacket, but she stops me. "No, no, go ahead and wear it, I don't have anything clean to lend you."

"But, if you don't think it looks good—"

"It's fine," she says. "It's not like people will be looking at you anyway." She says it so breezily, it takes me a moment to register the actual words.

Hugo arrives looking as rumpled as usual, in jeans and an azure shirt that matches his eyes. We all exchange the obligatory double kiss.

"You look fantastic," he says to me. There is a pause, in which Evalinda grins, obviously waiting for her compliment that never arrives.

"Thank you," I say, and hurry to smooth the lines that have settled around her mouth. "But who is to notice when I stand next to her," I sheepishly nod at Evalinda. She takes the compliment as her due. Hugo just smiles.

SHE IS UNUSUALLY QUIET in the car, rolling down the window and groaning every time Hugo cuts too sharp a turn or when I shift my position in her lap. "Would you sit still," she snaps at me. "You may be scrawny, but you aren't light."

The party is held on the top floor of a beautiful town house, to which we gain access by an intricate wrought-iron elevator that looks and sounds about two hundred years old.

Music, an uncertain Euro pop/jazz mix, booms dully behind a heavy wooden door, and intensifies to a roar when the door is opened by a man with a hairy chest and a purple silk shirt. Evalinda jumps into his arms and, after a brief nod hello, Hugo and I walk behind them into a narrow hallway. A large living room area opens on the left. It's the usual combo of chrome and leather in a high-ceilinged white room with beautiful ornate moldings that look like marzipan. Four floor-to-ceiling French doors lead out onto a terrace and the whole space is populated by black-clad people milling about like a flock of confused crows.

"What would you like to drink?" Hugo says, eyeing the far wall where a uniformed bartender dispenses drinks behind a lacquered bar.

"I'll have whatever you have."

"A ginger ale?" His eyebrows shoot up questioningly.

Evalinda catches up to us. "Get us two whiskys on the rocks."

Hugo nods and leaves us in the middle of the floor.

"Isn't this great?" Evalinda shouts as if I weren't right next to her. A woman with lips like a chicken butt sidles up to me. "What a fantastic jacket. Is that Mugler?"

"No, it's Bug Market," I say, and giggle. Evalinda doesn't smile. She grabs me by the hand and pulls me away a little too hard. "Let's go and see the view." We elbow our way through the crowd to the French doors, and it seems every person in the room exclaims something about my jacket—*hey, where is your horse—cool jacket*—and one guy in a blond ponytail even offers me a thousand francs for it. I'd like to stop and discuss the deal further, but Evalinda tugs me right out the door.

The terrace is spacious and rectangular. A few couches and small tables have been set up in the corners, and the whole of it is flushed with the glow of candles set in glass containers and scattered across the tiled floors and tabletops. It is otherwise almost empty of people, but for a small group that stands by the stone balustrade and doesn't even look at us.

I take a few steps to the railing. The rooftops of Paris greet me with their symmetrical planes, dark gray slabs sprinkled with what looks like burnt-orange ceramic pots. I wonder what they are: upside-down flowerpots? Tiny chimneys? Beyond the roofs I glimpse the Eiffel Tower lit up like a Christmas tree. To the far left, Notre Dame stands regal in purple shadow under a sky darkened to cobalt blue.

The small group dissipates and goes inside, leaving only a lone man, who leans on the balustrade with his back turned to us, smoking. He's wearing a pale blue shirt and his wavy, longish hair is ruffled by the breeze.

"Hey Rob, fancy running into you here!" Evalinda exclaims and runs to him. He turns around, drops his cigarette, grinds it out with his heel, and embraces her.

I stand, rooted to the tiles like a tree, and equally dumb.

"Jirina, look who's here," Evalinda says as if I couldn't see. I smile, lips closed, and feel the burning of my cheeks.

"Hello there," Rob says. In the mellow shadows, I can see only his teeth and the whites of his eyes.

Now that my dreams have been so unexpectedly fulfilled, I have no idea what to do. I've already kissed him and made love to him, married him and borne his children in scenarios so detailed and so frequent that they seem like memories and not dreams, albeit memories he doesn't share.

What does one say to a man who has been your lover for weeks and doesn't know it?

"Hi."

I'm fucking brilliant. I take a few steps closer to them. "Could I bum a cigarette?" Even better. My conversational skills are at a peak. I really need a drink.

He pulls a pack from his back pocket, taps one out, and offers it to me. His hands are tanned, with long tapering fingers and very short jagged nails, as if he bites them. One more detail to add to my fantasies.

"That's a great jacket," he says to me.

I'm so glad I bought it.

"Ooh, can I have one too?" Evalinda snatches at the pack. I happen to know her Kenzo handbag contains a pack of her Dunhills. Rob flicks the flame for her and she bends down, unnecessarily low, to reveal most of her cleavage. She straightens up, inhales her smoke deeply, and runs a lazy hand across her collarbone.

"God, I must look like a troll tonight." She exhales and tousles her hair. "No time to get ready, you know." I'm stunned. She is flat-out lying. Why?

Rob gives her a fleeting smile. "I don't believe that for a sec, darlin'. You look like a million bucks, as always."

Oh, that's why! I am embarrassed at my own naïveté and her blatancy. Rob shoots me a glance, as if to say *we both know what this is about,* which threatens to send me into dangerous heart flutters.

A short, square little guy sidles up to Evalinda out of nowhere and grabs her by the waist.

"Salut, Pierre, ça va?" she says.

"Evalinda, ma belle, I have been looking for you. Ondrej Dumowski is here."

"The Ondrej Dumowski?" she says breathlessly. "The director?"

"Eh, buh oui. Come. Let me introduce you."

She squeals in delight and pushes the man ahead of her like a shopping cart.

A silent beat falls over us, heavy and ripe with possibilities.

"How's life?" Rob says, tucking his cigarettes away.

"Fine, fine. And you?"

"No complaints." He plays with his lighter, flicking it on and off. "Although, there is this girl who I very much want to work with who keeps blowing me off."

I blush ferociously and hang my head so my hair covers my face while I think of something to say.

"That's very rude of her," I say finally.

"Yeh, it makes me feel as though she is avoiding me."

I look down. "I bet she would be very sorry to know you think that."

"Why so?"

The tiles are white stone, laid in a diamond pattern. I gently kick the toes of my Converse against the dark X of grout.

"Because avoiding you is the opposite of how she feels." I think that's the bravest thing I've ever said although I'm not certain it makes much sense, grammatically speaking. I hope to God we're talking about me.

"Oh?" he says. I can feel him studying me, but there is no way I can meet his eyes right now.

"I think maybe something happened that prevented her from showing up, like—burned eyeballs," I say.

"Burned eyeballs?"

"You know, burned eyeballs from tungsten lights, and that's why she couldn't come."

"Yeh, the ol' tungsten-burned-eyeball excuse." He chuckles.

I laugh. My hot cheeks have subsided and I look up, straight into his dark eyes. "Oči jak trnky," my grandma would say, which translates into "eyes like prunes." Not a very poetic image in any language but Czech, but accurate nevertheless. Eyes so rich a black they look nearly purple.

"And I bet she is very, very sorry, and hopes you won't give up on her quite yet," I add.

"Yeh?" His smile makes two creases on the side of his mouth, and I note his teeth are the teensiest bit sharp at the canines.

"Well, that's what I think, anyway," I finish weakly.

"I'm glad to hear that," he says. "Oh, there you are." It takes me a moment to realize he's no longer speaking to me.

I turn to Mia. She's wearing no makeup at all; her face is scrubbed clean, her freckles speckling her skin like constellations of stars.

"Jirina, how nice to see you!" She embraces me, forgoing the formal cheek kiss. I am pond scum. Here I am, hitting on her boyfriend. Understanding like a hot needle punctures me. In this equation, I am Britta. The thief, the fallen woman, the one deserving to die at the end of this story. Mia pulls away and holds me at arms' length. "What a fabulous jacket! Where did you find something this cool?"

"The flea market," I mumble. I want to go home and cry. Or die.

"La Marche au Pus at Clichy?"

I nod.

"You really have to have a good eye to find stuff there, it's such a mess," she says. "I see you've met Rob already," she continues with a smile, and slaps at him playfully. "I've been telling him he has to use you, or he'll miss the boat."

Quite suddenly, my thoughts are blown free of my lovesick cobwebs. Rob wanted to work with me—because Mia told him to? I'd like to double over with the pain, except that would look weird.

"Thank you so much," I say. "Well, I better go back inside and find my boyfriend before he worries that I've disappeared." I walk away with as much dignity as I can muster.

HUGO, MY ERSATZ BOYFRIEND, sits in one of the many chairs grouped around a mirrored coffee table. About ten people are gathered on the floor while a woman chops white powder with some small metal thing and divides it into thin lines. Hugo holds a half empty glass of ginger ale in one hand, and a stocky glass filled with caramel colored liquid in the other. He sips the ginger ale listlessly, gazing out over the coffee table.

"I'm sorry, I got stuck talking to some people outside," I say. He nods and hands me my glass. I gulp the entire thing in one go; Hugo's eyes widen in alarm. "Don't worry, I can handle it," I say. How do I explain I need to numb myself silly?

"What are they doing?" I nod toward the table.

"Coke," he says.

It must be some newfangled French way to mix it. "Oh, good, I want some. Let me just get a glass of water."

Hugo is standing up with a concerned frown when I come back. The whisky is working beautifully, bathing me in pleasant warmth.

"Are you sure about this?" he asks as I crouch down on the floor and wedge myself between a thin brown woman in black and a thin pale man in black.

"Sure, I *love* Coke."

The woman parts a small amount from the heap in the middle of the table with what I now recognize as an old-fashioned razor blade and efficiently lines the powder up in front of me. The pale guy hands me a green, tightly rolled-up cylinder. I stare at it. It looks like an American dollar bill so I unfold it. I was wrong; it's an American *twenty-dollar* bill. I nod a "thank you" to the guy and stick it in my pocket. If they want to pay me, that's their problem.

I sweep the line of powder into my glass, and wait for it to foam and turn color. Nothing happens, except for a few muted gasps from the people around the table. I swirl the cloudy white liquid around my glass, but it still doesn't look like Coca-Cola. All eyes are intent on me, so to hell with it—I gulp it down. Oh boy. It's worse than whisky. Bitter and strongly medicinal. I set my glass down and stand up. Hugo stares at me as if I grew a second head, and suddenly cracks up.

"What?" I say, trying to stand straight.

"You do not have any idea of what you did, non?" he says softly.

I feel everyone's eyes on me, their stares like headlights. I pull Hugo to a corner. "Okay, what did I just do?"

"You just drink the cocaine."

"What's that?"

Hugo bursts out laughing.

My mouth suddenly feels completely numb. I have a hard time getting my words out. "No, seriously, what is it?" I manage to roll out over a tongue that feels like a dead seal.

There is no place for us to sit privately, so Hugo takes my hand and leads me back out to the terrace. Mia and Rob are still there, on a couch talking to another couple. My body is going haywire. Lingering warmth in limbs, mouth full of Novocain, heart wrung with pain, and head wracked with as many fragmented thoughts as the lights of Paris before us.

Hugo sits me down in a chair on the opposite side of the terrace from Rob and Mia and gives me a brief lesson on drugs. *Marijuana is the least dangerous, followed by hashish, both of which make you silly and mellow.* I try to keep Hugo in focus, but my eyes can't help but dart off to see what Rob is doing. *Heroin and angel dust numb you to all pain, but are addictive and deadly.* It seems as though he is watching me too. *LSD makes you see things that aren't there, and could be dangerous if you suddenly think you can fly, like the model who jumped out the window and broke both of her legs.* I sit a little closer to Hugo and try to seem absolutely infatuated. See, I am not alone; I have a boyfriend too. *Coke is inhaled through the rolled-up money* (my twenty-dollar bill burns a hole in my pocket) *and makes you superman.* There are some drawbacks to it as well, but I'm no longer willing to sit still.

I'm endowed with special powers and energy to burn. I must move. I must dance! I drag Hugo to the living area inside, and declare the floor a dance floor. Do you see me Rob? I twirl, I gyrate, I rock to music that earlier had me half asleep. I spin like I'm possessed. Hugo takes a break, but not I. No, I don't need a break, I can do this forever. Evalinda dances with me, but she can't keep up either. Cocaine is my hero. My heroine. I laugh at my wordplay and feel an urgent need to share my dazzling thought process. Rob is by the fireplace, talking to a balding man. I dance over to them. I grab Rob's hand. "Come on, dance with me." Yeah, that's right. This is the same girl who couldn't talk to you in person. Baldie tries to shoo me off. Insignificant little fuck. I pull Rob. I know I'm irresistible. I've forgotten what I meant to share with him—besides my body. I undulate before him; I'm a snake, I'm a panther, a predator, I'm wild. Why does he look so uncomfortable? Why does he just stand there? I get closer, right up next to him. I slither and slink, my skin touching his. Then Mia bops in. Now we are a threesome. She dances in that awkward Swedish way, rocking from side to side. Just look at us, Rob. Who's the better dancer? Who's better looking?

"Sorry, but we have to go," Rob says.

I keep dancing.

But it doesn't feel so good anymore.

I SIT IN THE front of Hugo's car. Evalinda went home hours ago to call her boyfriend. Dawn begins to yellow the edges of night as we drive in silence. I'm not exactly tired: My heart still beats as if I were dancing, my mouth is still slightly numb, but the warmth of the whisky is all gone.

"Are you tired?" Hugo seems to read my thoughts.

"Not really." Just devastated.

"Bon alors, I want to show you something," he says, and steps on the gas.

We fly through empty wide avenues, strangely delicate in the dark like all sleeping things. The hum of the engine turns to a dull roar as the car starts to climb tiny winding streets paved with cobblestones and lined with picturesque cottages, where flowers overflow window boxes and old-fashioned bicycles lean against rusty garden gates. I roll down my window to a blast of a fresh morning breeze, redolent of diesel and chamomile.

"Where are we? Is this still Paris?"

"Oui, bien sûr, this is Montmartre."

I want to get out and walk, but Hugo tells me to wait a little. He pulls the car in under a gathering of trees and we get out. The air is mild and tinted pearly pink. He takes my hand and we walk to a large white structure, barely visible through the branches, as the birds wake, limbering their throats for another day of operatic trills.

The trees recede and we come to a clearing. "Sacré Coeur," Hugo says.

I stare up in awe at the monumental church that, with its white turrets and domed silver roofs, looks like a perfect wedding cake, squat and delicate at the same time.

And when we round the corner, the world opens up in one glorious breath. All of Paris is at our feet, blanketed in dusty rose. There are a million stairs before us, cascading down into the city that is about to wake up. Tiny twinkly lights of faraway street lamps disappear row by row like pearls falling off a necklace, and we stand, watching sunlight slowly lick away the night with a crisp, champagne-colored tongue, while Sacré Coeur watches our backs.

"**I HAVE GOOD NEWS** and good news," Evalinda says when she exits the bedroom. I slept on the couch, not wanting to disturb her.

"Which do you want first?"

"Uh, the good?"

"Good choice." She laughs. "My boyfriend is coming back to Paris for the weekend."

"Oh, great," I say, trying to sound happy for her.

"And—this is huge. You sitting down?"

"I'm *lying* down," I remind her.

"I'm pregnant."

"Oh my God, that's wonderful!" I shout and jump up to embrace her. She smiles. "Yeah, that's one way to get him to leave his wife, huh?"

"You are going to have a baby! Are you the happiest person in the world?"

"Yeah, I guess. So anyway—"

"Hello there, little one." I bend down to her perfectly toned stomach. "This is your Auntie Gigi speaking."

Evalinda laughs and pushes me away. "So, anyway, as I was trying to say, I need you to clear out for the weekend."

"Oh, of course, I understand." I have no idea where I'll go, but I don't need to burden her with this. "Oh my God," I repeat. "I'm so happy for you! And I'll do free babysitting whenever you need it!"

"Thanks," she says and goes to the kitchenette. "Hey, we're all out of coffee. Can you run out and get some?"

"Sure. Right away."

"And then you'll leave, right?"

That gives me a pause. But of course, it's Friday. That counts as the weekend. I'd better call Hugo.

SITTING IN THE CAR next to Hugo, I burn with Evalinda's news. But it's Evalinda's news, not mine, and she made me promise I wouldn't divulge her secret to a living soul. I already have daydreams of pushing a stroller to Jardin du Luxembourg, carrying the baby around while Evalinda naps, giving the baby a bottle, giving her a bath—I hope it's a little girl. It suddenly dawns on me that *I'm* not having a baby with Evalinda. She'll probably move to a bigger place with her boyfriend, and I will have to find my own.

"Why so quiet today?" Hugo says.

I shake off my fantasies. "So, where are we going?"

Hugo just smiles, steps on the gas pedal, and accelerates through narrow one-way streets that miraculously deposit us on the freeway.

"Come on, give me a hint," I beg.

"South," he says.

"To the South of France?" I ask incredulously.

"Non, not so far. That is one day of driving—too far—for now."

"South of Paris then?"

"Oui."

I still have no clue. Blond fields of wheat blur by, intersected with walls of spiky poplar trees; crimson poppies are scattered on the sides of dirt roads that lead to huddled villages.

"This countryside reminds me of Czechoslovakia," I tell Hugo. Spurred on by sentimentality I didn't know I possessed, I tell Hugo about my grandmother, the learning of Kultura in Renaissance castles and medieval forts, and then her death, which happened right before the end of my eighth grade.

No one told me she was sick. My last summer with her, when she was already dying, was spent in her garden drinking linden tea to soothe her often-upset stomach and listening to stories of her youth, of her meeting my grandfather whom I never knew and anecdotes about my father as a child. I was bored and did nothing to hide it; instead I often snapped irritably when she asked me to fetch something for her and our last good-bye was a quick "See you later" from me, relieved to go home for once.

"I never said a proper good-bye. I never told her how much I loved her, what she meant to me," I tell Hugo.

He lights a cigarette from the car lighter. "She knew," he says.

"Oh yeah, how do you know that?" I say, slightly miffed by his assumption.

"Because love is not about the words. For example, les Américaines, they say 'I love you' all the time. They say it to the people they don't even know so much. But it means nothing. Love is about the little things you do every day in the time you have together."

"Who died and made you the expert?" I grumble. I know this sounds juvenile, but I can't help myself. He's dismissive of my pain.

He exhales smoke, taps his fingers on the steering wheel as though he's coming to some sort of a decision.

"My mother died when I was eleven," he says.

My prickly words turn into pebbles forced back into my mouth. I nearly choke on them. "Oh, I'm sorry. I didn't know—"

"There are many things about me you do not know," he says.

CHAPTER 16

The afternoon sun lingers over on a small, champagne-colored château with a faded slate roof and sky-blue shutters, surrounded by moist green lawns. We pull into a graveled driveway, and Hugo parks the car in front of the entrance, where it looks as out of place as a rocket ship in Versailles. We get out of the car and I draw a deep, surprised breath. The magnificently carved wooden doors are open, affording a glimpse of a cool marble hallway. Music of crickets and birdcalls mingle with the soft tones of a distant piano playing a Chopin nocturne. "Oh my God, this is beautiful. What is this? Where are we?"

"Welcome to the Château de la Vallée Bleu." Hugo smiles.

I look to him for an explanation as he gets our bags out of the car. I forced all the belongings I thought necessary for a weekend in the country into two plastic shopping bags. Hugo pulls them out and I wince at their inappropriateness.

"This is the château of George Sand's personal physician. George's château, Nohant, is about five minutes from here, but it is now a museum. So I though we would stay here."

"Oh Hugo, you're the best!" I shout and throw myself into his arms. He holds me gingerly, as if I were likely to break. I pull away slightly. "I always dreamed of staying in a castle." I hug him again. "This is the best thing anyone has ever done for me!"

Hugo doesn't say anything, he just squeezes me back and then lets go of me in favor of picking up our bags.

We sign the guest register in the lobby, which is really the hallway with a small wooden counter under the stairs. The receptionist, who's also the owner, is a tall man with distinguished graying hair. "Mr. Dubois, welcome," he says with a friendly smile.

"That's funny, I didn't even know your last name," I say. "Is that Dubois like the wine Jacques Dubois?"

Hugo coughs. "Yes."

"You're not related," I joke.

"Jacques Dubois is my grandfather," he says.

"Oh." That's why Evalinda slept with him. Poor Hugo.

"I'm sorry," the owner says. "On such short notice, the room with the twin beds is unavailable, but I will give you our best one, it has a view on the park."

Hugo glances at me questioningly and I shrug. "I don't care," I say. "It's not as if we haven't already slept in the same bed—twice."

We follow the owner up the grand, sweeping staircase to the second floor. Glass-fronted cabinets line the walls, filled with curios. I glimpse letters, sheet music, gloves and such, and am determined to go through them all as soon as we have checked into our room.

The owner throws the door wide open to a white room, dazzling in the sunlight. Two floor-to-ceiling windows are hung with bloodred drapes and an antique bed of dark wood presides in the middle, with crisp white sheets. I look at Hugo and grin.

"Does this please you?" he says with anxious eyes.

"Are you kidding? This is paradise!"

WE EXAMINE THE WHOLE château together. He translates George's letters from various admirers. Stupidly, I keep flashing on Rob, and the other things we could do if I were here with him. This persistent daydreaming of Rob has become a bad habit, one I need to break. He's only interested in me for work, I remind myself. And only because his girlfriend told him so. This thought works nicely, like a swift kick to the gut. I look at Hugo, who's intent on decoding an old letter. His hair, unruly at the best of times, falls over his forehead, and with Chopin's twinkling piano notes underscoring his words, it isn't hard to pretend he is Alfred de Musset and I'm George.

We get dressed for dinner—jeans and T-shirts won't cut it here—so I pull on the flounced skirt I sewed myself in home economics, and pin my hair up. This makes me feel even more like George. My walk through the hallway takes on a slow dignity with the skirt elegantly waving around my legs with every step. The dining room doors are open to the park, four tables are set with old china, crystal glasses, and candles. The effect is magical and time-transporting, even with the other guests, who speak in soft tones over their tables. I sit very straight, aware of the length of my neck, which I imagine looks a bit like the painting of George on the cover of her biography. Our conversation slides effortlessly to literature again, and we end up in a mock fight about Balzac, whom Hugo considers "bourgeois."

After a game of chess in the library, we go to bed, chastely dressed in pajamas (Hugo's are blue-and-white-striped, much prettier than my own faded orange with printed sunflowers), and we pull out our respective books. Hugo goggles at my Kafka, which I pretend to read until my eyes close. Caught in that dreamy state when one is almost asleep, yet still can hear and feel, I sense Hugo lean over me, gently remove my book from my chest, and ever so softly kiss my temple.

On Saturday morning we borrow two bicycles after breakfast and set out to Nohant on a quiet dusty road. I had thought of it as a castle; it is, in fact, a minuscule village of golden sandstone with a fat little church roosting in the middle of a sandy square, surrounded by tiny cottages with lace-draped windows. George's estate is on the right, edged by a low wall, behind which we catch glimpses of her unpretentious home, two stories tall, shaded by ancient trees.

I can't help but pretend I'm George again as we walk through rooms filled with her belongings: a dining room of dove gray, where plates are set up as if for a dinner party, complete with place cards; a large wheat-colored kitchen where she made jam on a huge iron stove. I can see myself at the very stove, mixing jam fragrant with fruit and sugar as my children play nearby with their handmade dolls, and must curb my desire to invite my guests (the other tourists) to sit and make themselves comfortable. The last room we visit is her writing room with dark-blue wallpaper and delicate wooden escritoire, and a very small bed with curtains. I picture her in the arms of Chopin and realize they must have made love elsewhere, for there is no way two people would fit on the tiny mattress. Well, at least not people the size of Rob and me.

George's final resting place is in a small private plot next to the house. Her headstone stands tallest among the rest of her family's, but all are shaded in pond-green light by a canopy of oaks. I touch the cool stone of her tomb, ready for some deep, insightful thoughts on life, death, and art, but come up with "Hi, George, nice house." I am immediately ashamed of my trivial thoughts, as if George, hands clasped over her chest, were frowning at me from her casket. But she did love her house. The guide told us (and Hugo translated) about her love for this property, how she'd come back here when she was feeling depleted, sad or heartbroken. Here, at Nohant, she'd write, cook, and surround herself with friends and her children.

This was her home. I feel a sudden longing for a home. Not my home with Mother—where I feel like a guest that has long outstayed her welcome—but a home where I would be with people who loved me back, unconditionally. The clear absence of it in my life makes me want to cry. I don't know if Hugo senses my sudden switch of mood, but he takes my hand, and it makes me feel better.

WE WORK UP QUITE a sweat biking back to the château. We race each other over long stretches of road that are empty but for the two of us. Dusty and hot, we run up to our room to put on silly outfits for the pool since we both forgot our swimsuits. Hugo comes out of the bathroom with two pairs of boxer shorts on top of one another and I greet him in black cotton undies and a dark-blue T-shirt.

We swim in a pool the color of which matches Hugo's eyes. His thin body is as pale as an aspirin, and an angry red colors his arms where his T-shirt sleeves end. He entertains me by diving into the pool in the most comical manners: belly flops, unsuccessful back somersaults, and accidental slips.

We take our separate showers and get dressed for dinner; I have to wear the same thing as last night.

I order the lobster Medallions in Sauce à la Crème; Hugo has the Sole Meunière. He pours us two glasses of wine and, to my surprise, actually empties his. By the time dessert rolls around—literally, for it's on a cart—we've emptied the whole bottle and I'm definitely tipsy. The night air

drifting in through the doors smells sharply of cut grass, spicy and fresh.
We light up cigarettes and bring our port wine out to a swing that hangs
from the gnarled branch of an oak in the middle of the lawn. We sit down
on it together. The sky is dusted with stars, but there is no moon. I sigh
with pleasure. "This has been the best weekend of my life." Although
I can't help trying to conjure up Rob next to me. I summon my new
mantra, *he's only interested in me for work.* But instead of the swift brief
pain that ought to accompany the thought, there is an emptiness filled
with tiny wings of butterflies. After a moment of deliberation, I recognize
it as hope. Fuck me. What exactly am I hoping for?

We smoke in companionable silence.

"I am very happy you like it," Hugo says after a while and tucks in a
stray strand of hair behind my ear. I turn to him with a smile, and his
mouth suddenly clamps over mine. Wet and soft and all wrong. I push
him away in shock. The string that binds our friendship vibrates a sharp
note of betrayal. I quickly rewind our history to look for holes, for signs
that I might have given him to misunderstand, and find that none, or all,
are guilty.

His eyes are anxious in the light that pours out the dining room doors.

"I need another glass of wine," I say, and jump up. He follows me
back to the dining room and we order another bottle.

"Are you . . . okay?" he says.

"Never better." Fuck. This could be completely misconstrued as well.
I gulp another glass of wine, slam it on the table, and announce that I'm in
the mood for chess. His easy presence, his crooked smile, his pale untoned
body that felt so comforting minutes ago, now makes me flinch with mild
disgust. Maybe, with enough alcohol, it will just all go away.

Hugo seems to feel the same way, for he keeps emptying his glass and,
sitting by our chessboard, we make moves that would bring a chess afi-
cionado to his knees in despair. By the time I checkmate Hugo with my
king, things feel right again. We wobble up to our room, giggling like id-
iots. I get my pajamas and go to the bathroom. The door has a faulty lock,
so I merely kick it shut. Pulling my pajamas on proves harder than usual;
I keep falling over. But it's funny. It's all funny: Hugo, chess, my pajamas,
my toothbrush, and the way the toothpaste squirts out all over the sink.
Then my heart speeds up.

It's back.

My breath comes in short spastic waves. I crouch down on the floor and hug my knees. Breathe, just breathe. Every breath seems as if I'm sucking air through a very thin straw. Paisleys of reds and blues flitter behind my closed eyelids, but when I open them, they dart madly about the bathroom. My body shakes, I struggle for air, I hear nothing but the wild pumping of blood through my brain.

Hugo's voice comes far away. "Gigi, ça va? Everything is okay?"

No, it's not. My mouth will not form words. I groan.

The door opens.

"Mon Dieu, que est ce qui pas?" He bends down to me. "What is the matter?"

I suck in air. "I—am—sick. My heart—"

He puts his hand on my chest. "Did you take anything?"

Oh God, he must think I'm like Britta. I shake my head.

"Are you having trouble with the breathing?"

I nod.

"And it just happened comme ça? From the blue?"

I nod again.

"Has this happened before?"

"Yeah," I gasp.

"Many times?"

"Uh-huh."

"Listen to me now. If this is what I think, I can make it go away."

My body shudders involuntarily in waves. I try to concentrate on his words. He can make it go away?

"Each time you take one breath, think of your favorite color," he says. "When you breathe out, breathe out a bad color. Can you do this?"

I nod. I imagine blue. Blue like water. Blue like sky. Blue like Hugo's eyes. I breathe out muddy brown. I close my eyes and see the colors swirling in and out.

"Better?"

"Yeah," I say, and realize I am.

"I think you are only having an attack of the nerves," he says, smoothing my hair from my face.

"A what?"

"A panic attack. I have it all the times also."

My shakes are subsiding. I look at his concerned eyes and smile a little. My heart problem is not a heart problem at all. It has a name. He has them all the time. The weight of the world lifts off my shoulders and lightness streams through me. I am not going to die. It's not a bad heart caused by my mother. It is something casual, something people have. A panic attack. Tears of relief threaten to spill. I quickly blink them away and inhale though my nose, like Emanuel showed me.

Hugo picks me up off the floor, and carries me to the bed with only a slight wobble. He lays me down and pulls the blanket over me. "Better?"

"Much."

He lies down next to me and strokes my hair.

"I thought—I thought I was going to die."

"Non, non." He smiles. "It is only the nerves." He props himself up on an elbow, but keeps stroking my hair. "Of course, the first time when it happened to me, I was also scared. I went to a doctor, I thought I perhaps had the bad heart."

"That's what I thought!"

"But the doctor told me it is nothing, many people have this. People with the big imagination, les artistes, tu sais?"

"Does that mean I am an artist?" I manage a smile.

"Buh oui, if you have the panic attack, you must be an artiste." He looks so serious that it makes me laugh.

"So, instead of being diagnosed with a bad heart, you diagnose me an artist. Thank you, doctor. How much do I owe you?"

"You owe me precisely nothing."

He lies back down, facing me, still stroking my hair.

I look into his eyes, and suddenly I know how much I owe him. I bring up my hand and caress his cheek. When he pulls in closer to kiss me, my mouth is open and willing. I close my eyes and think of Rob. It's Rob that caresses my breasts, who parts my legs, who slides in and begins a sweet rhythm.

But it's Hugo that keeps whispering "je t'adore," over and over. I grab his hair and kiss him, violently, to shut him up. Our moves become frantic, sweaty, more resembling a wrestling match than lovemaking. I wrap my legs around his waist and grind my hips into him until he gasps and collapses on top of me.

We rest for a moment, our hearts beating madly through ribs and skin, and I wait for him to start up again. Instead, he rolls over and draws me close.

"Ca, c'était fantastique," he whispers into my hair. "Was it good for you also?"

I mumble a sleepy "Uh-huh." I'm relieved he found it fantastic and now I can sleep.

WE ARE QUIET in the car on the way back home. It's raining, and the fields and the sky sport the same leaden hue that fills my insides.

Hugo has put on Jacques Brel's "Ne Me Quitte Pas," and he stares out the windshield as if lost in his thoughts. Maybe he also regrets last night, I think with a slight punctuation of hope. When Jacques Brel sings "laisse moi devenir l'ombre de ton ombre," Hugo mouths the words. I translate them silently: *Let me become the shadow of your shadow. The shadow of your hand, the shadow of your dog*—dog? Did I hear that right? I glance at Hugo and he meets my eyes. A hot wave of understanding hits me: He doesn't regret last night. I have ruined our friendship.

We pull up to the apartment on rue Bourbon. Hugo turns down the volume.

"What are your plans tonight?"

"I don't know."

"Dinner?"

"I think I'd like to be alone tonight," I mumble. His disappointment is immediate and obvious; I quickly have to make amends. "What I mean is, I'm tired and I have a headache. I just need to have some alone time, you know?" I've just repeated, almost verbatim, the words of my mother when she is sick of an Uncle. It's making *me* sick.

"I understand," Hugo says. "À demain?"

"Definitely. Tomorrow."

"I had a wonderful time." He smiles his crooked smile and traces his fingers along my cheek. I curb my wish to draw away.

"Yes, so did I."

He leans in and kisses me. It's soft. Wet. Still all wrong.

.   .   .

THE APARTMENT IS A MESS. Cigarette butts, empty liquor bottles, remains of unidentifiable foods, and dirty clothes are strewn about everywhere. But the living room is otherwise empty. "Evalinda?" I try.

There is no answer.

I peek into the bedroom. It's also empty, but the sheets are pulled off the bed and lie in a heap on the floor.

Slowly, I set about cleaning the place up. I empty the overfilled ashtrays, throw away the food and bottles, and wash the dishes, while my brain runs in circles around Hugo.

Evalinda comes back as I am trying to decide whether to make the bed with the soiled sheets, or just fold them up neatly and look for fresh ones.

She stands in the bedroom doorway, dressed in baggy pants and a man's shirt, an outfit so incongruous it stops me in my tracks. "Hi there!" I exclaim and run up to her. I put my hand on her stomach, bend down a little, and say, "Hi, little one."

"Don't bother," Evalinda says coolly. "It's not there anymore."

"What?"

"I just had an abortion."

I look at her face for a trace of a wicked smile, or something to prove she's joking, but now I notice she's wearing no makeup and her face is splotchy and swollen.

"What?" I repeat, quieter this time.

"The motherfucking son of a whore split up with me. Satisfied?" she hisses, pushes past me, and throws herself on the bed. My heart swells with sorrow. No baby? It's all gone, just like this?

I tiptoe to Evalinda. "Is there anything . . . anything I can do for you?"

"Yeah, get out of my face."

I close the door behind me as quietly as I can. I finish cleaning up and then I get in the shower. Under the stream of water, I cry. I cry for the poor little baby, I cry for Hugo, I cry for myself.

Two hours later, Evalinda comes out of the bedroom. I put Kafka aside, thinking she may want to talk now, but she shuts herself in the bathroom. I hear the shower, then silence. When she comes out, she's dressed in her normal stuff, skintight jeans and a sexy top, and her face is fully made up.

"Okay, so I'm off now," she says casually.

"Off to where?"

"Didn't I tell you I was leaving?" she says.

I shake my head.

"Well it must have slipped my mind."

"But *can* you go? I mean, is it okay to go after, you know—"

"Oh come off it," she snaps. "You think this was the first time? It's no big deal. You go in, they vacuum it out, and voilà. Back to normal. Nothing more than a period."

How can she say that? How can she think that? But maybe it's her way to deal with grief.

"So listen. Same rules as last time, okay?" she says. "Hugo is all right, but that's it."

"Where are you going? When will you be back?"

"In a week. I'm going to Morocco. With your friend Rob for German *Vogue*."

"Oh," I manage. German *Vogue*! Three horrible hours I spent in a hotel room trying to please that mummified broom of a woman, while Britta tried to kill herself. All for naught!

Once Evalinda leaves I allow myself another good cry. Why did I think the go-and-see went well anyway? I try to remember the exact number of go-and-sees I've been on that never paid off—which of course were most of them—and give up by thirty or so. Marina was clearly wrong about me becoming successful; she should have hired me as her nanny. The thought of Olympe makes me cry harder.

I fish out my plastic baby from my bag under the bed. No, not *my* baby. Kristynka's baby. It's lonely and cold, just like me. I change its diaper—the box came with five—and find, with the smallest pang of regret, my baby is a boy. "I love you just the same," I tell him, dress him in the tiny white shirt, and wrap him in his blanket.

I'm only a little bit embarrassed to be talking to a plastic doll.

CHAPTER 17

The sun warms the streets and morning-fresh crowds as I stroll to nearby Café Tabac, order a café au lait, and buy two postcards. *Look for me in* Linea Italiana *and* Les Mariages, I scribble across their backs and address them to Hatty and Mother. I add a postscript, telling them I now reside with Evalinda and I'll try to call them on a weekend.

How I wish I had someone to tell about Evalinda's baby. It's still difficult to comprehend the baby is gone. But I already know Hatty would have little sympathy; she finds Kristynka spoiled and noisy, and has no fondness for children in general. Whenever I cooed over a baby in a stroller, she'd roll her eyes and stand aside with her arms crossed as though this was some private, embarrassing moment like watching someone going to the bathroom. Who else is there? Britta probably understands my daily situation better than anyone, but to call her would be to revisit something I'd rather forget. And Hugo is no longer my friend. He's—what? My lover? I wince at the thought. I finish my coffee and mail the postcards. Evalinda must be in Morocco now. With Rob. The only consistent things in my life, it seems, are the disappointments.

I can't find the name of the street for my third go-and-see in the Plan de Paris, so I look for a phone to call the agency. By the time I find one, I'm out of breath. In the reflection of the dirty glass booth I can see my mascara has migrated to places it was never meant for.

"Thank God," Anne exclaims on the line, while I try to smudge away the black traces on my cheeks with a wet fingertip.

"I've been trying to call you all morning. Your plane leaves at one o'clock."

"What? What plane?"

"To Morocco. One of the girls got sick or something, so they just called for you."

"Who is it for?" I ask as nonchalantly as I can. Every nerve ending in my body screams Rob.

"You know, German *Vogue* with Rob Ryan."

Fuck the mascara. I look at my Donald Duck watch, whose hands indicate I have two hours before my plane leaves.

The Metro seems to take forever. The minute the doors open I make a mad dash for the street and run all the way back home.

My Napoleon jacket is nowhere to be found. I heap everything else I've hand-washed into my duffel. The phone rings just as I zip it.

"Ça va?" Hugo says.

Oh no. I've completely forgotten about him.

"Ah, Hugo, listen, I'm so sorry, but I'm about to leave for the airport—"

"I will drive you—" he interrupts.

It's not easy to convince him otherwise, but to soften the blow, I set a dinner date for the following Sunday.

"Is seven a good time?" he asks.

I've been granted a week of amnesty. "Perfect. See you next week."

I MAKE MY WAY to the gate through the departure terminal and an odd walkway, a sort of plastic tube suspended in the air across a courtyard. It spits me out into a cavernous room, where small stores and stands beckon travelers to spend their last francs. I'm immediately drawn to the magazine stands. Inviting smiles, flirty eyes, glossy hair, and smooth skin wink at me to come and join them in their perfect world. A world I may already inhabit, at least one-dimensionally. I scan the titles. And there they are— the August editions of *Linea Italiana* and *Les Mariages*. My breath speeds up and my heart starts pounding. On the cover of *Les Mariages* is a girl with very short brown hair, thick eyebrows, and a Mona Lisa smile. But on *Linea*, it's Lisa, with a huge grin and a purple hat, her hands in the pockets of a tweedy jacket. I don't recognize the clothes from our shoot in Milan, but still I fight with a pang of envy. Plain old silly Lisa. On the cover. How did that happen? By sleeping with Olivieri, I remind myself.

Both magazines are wrapped in thick plastic, prohibiting me from opening them right here. I lug them to the register and give up thirty precious francs, then run to my gate and tear the plastic in a frenzy.

My heart beats so fast it feels as if it will somersault out my nose. I sweat and my hands tremble. This is it. The moment of truth. I will be in here, with all the other creatures that represent the essence of female beauty. Me, Jirina Radovanovicova, former communist cow and hot chicken—mistaken for a kid only a week ago.

First I quickly flip through the pages of both magazines, then I settle down and thumb through them page by page. My trembling subsides and a heavy disappointment begins to creep in. *Where am I?* Where are my shining moments with Frederic nibbling cherries? Where is my sex siren in the leopard tunic? Where is the ugly secretary dress, the hairy lollipop?

By the time people line up in front of the gate, I have gone through both copies so many times I'm starting to memorize them. No me. Nothing. Scant relief that Britta is not in *Les Mariages* either, nor is Lorna. I leave the stupid magazines on an empty seat and board the plane. It dawns on me—as if this trip weren't already significant enough—this may be my one last chance.

MOROCCO. THE NAME CONJURES up vast red sand dunes and swarthy men in flowing robes astride wiry desert horses, smoky bars humming with ceiling fans, belly dancing women with filmy veils and "oči jak trnky" (eyes like prunes), traitorous plots brewed over tiny cups of black coffee, and desperate lovers in hazy corners leaning in for one last kiss. Or maybe I just combined the plots of *Lawrence of Arabia* and *Casablanca*.

But my first impression is of an air-conditioned airport with toothpaste ads featuring blond models, signs for duty-free shopping, and a slight bathroom smell of ammonia. Outside, an intense gust of hot air greets me along with a dark Arab man who holds a cardboard sign with my mangled name, GIRINA. Although he wears a caftan and a turban, he more resembles a camel than a pasha. I squeeze into the backseat of his rickety white Peugeot, which smells of cooked food and farts, and we drive through wide avenues of softly waving palm trees beneath which square peach-colored buildings squat in rippling heat.

Anne had clearly stated that our shoot is to be done in a place called Ouarzazate in the middle of the desert. This is just a layover for the night. Still, all my senses are pulled taut and sharp by Rob. I imagine the hotel as an oasis in the middle of this rather dirty city, with cupolas and gardens, and Rob meeting me outside swathed in something gauzy and exotic.

The hotel is a tall white block of cement and windows. I check into my room—a beige cubicle with a bed and a large window that won't open—and plop down on the bed. The silence of my room is oppressive; it makes me feel as if I've suddenly gone deaf. An evening of self-pity and loneliness looms before me. What if I get a panic attack? The mere thought makes me dizzy with anxiety. I pick up the remote and try to turn on the TV. It doesn't work. Frantically, I debate whether I should go downstairs to the lobby and read until I get tired or take a walk, when the phone rings.

"Honey, I heard we are working together again," a familiar voice with a singsong lilt breathes down the phone line.

"Emanuel!" I exclaim. "You're on the shoot? Where are you?"

"Right here in the hotel. You and I are going to Ouarzazate together tomorrow, isn't it fabulous?"

I agree wholeheartedly it is. I won't mention I was so starved for company I'd have been willing to go on a date with Charles Manson, had he called.

Emanuel asks me to meet him in the lobby in fifteen minutes and I run to the bathroom to throw on some makeup.

He is wearing more of it than I am. Glitter speckles his cheekbones and he trails a load of his sweet, musky perfume.

"We have the evening free," he says, "so let's make the best of it. Ever been to Morocco before?"

I shake my head and he laughs. "Well then honey, it's party time!"

"Is it okay to do? I mean, are we allowed to go out?" I know I'm being paid for a travel day, and so my time doesn't quite feel like it belongs to me.

"Honey, what they don't know won't hurt them," he says with a wink.

· · ·

WE HOP INTO A *petit taxi* and Emanuel decides on the fare that will take us near the central square.

"Let's go to Kissarias," he says. "That's the souk that sells clothes. You can find fantastic scarves and djellabas." He gives me a lesson on Marrakech as we hurtle from the wide avenues of the Gueliz, the new city where our hotel is located, to the old town and the medina surrounded by ramparts glowing a warm pink. Mountains surround us on all sides, tinged with all the warm colors of a setting sun. I point out a lonely tower that rises up from the cityscape like a Lego block, and Emanuel tells me that is the Koutoubia Mosque, forbidden to non-Muslims. The streets are mostly empty of pedestrians but clogged with rusty little cars that spew black smoke into the gold-tinged afternoon.

The medina is the old center of town, where souks (marketplaces) surround the famous Place Jemaa-el-Fna. The taxi drops us at the ramparts; the streets are much too narrow for motorized vehicles. Instantly, we are beset by dark-skinned people draped in formerly white tunics wishing to exchange our money, snap our picture, shine our shoes—my Converse sneakers? Emanuel's Adidas?—and take us on guided tours. Emanuel declines. He pulls me through keyhole-shaped entrances and teensy, winding passages with covered roofs that more resemble hallways than actual streets. Bright colors assault from every angle, turmeric-yellow scarves; deep-blue and magenta djellabas (a kind of tunic worn by everyone here) with exquisite gold- or silver-embroidered edges; and the traditional black-and-white or red-and-white Arab scarves with fringe, which were popular in my school, worn around the necks or hips of the more trendy girls in class. Emanuel buys himself an earthy-red scarf with tiny gold stitching and I listen to him haggle in French with the store owner. He pays a paltry sum of ten francs, and my spirits soar. Even I can afford something here.

"Oh honey, I'm so excited," Emanuel says as we weave in and out of the tiny cubicles filled with fabrics. "Remember what I said in Milan?"

I nod with a smile. "Yeah, you and me and Rob working together?" I look down when I say Rob; it's a name I have trouble saying out loud.

"Exactly."

"Evalinda is there as well," I say, and examine gold embroidery on a hem to avoid looking too eager for his thoughts.

"Oh, *her*," Emanuel sniffs. "They will do all the body work with her, but she does not have your face. All the close-ups will be yours."

I blush with pleasure. How can I not love this man?

He waves his hand in the air. "Okay, so it's German *Vogue*, not American or Italian, but it is *Vogue*."

"What's the difference? I ask. To me, *Vogue* is *Vogue*, the epitome of high fashion, the temple at which we all worship. *Vogue* photographers are the top, and the girls they use are the ones Hatty and I recognize.

Emanuel stops at a stand with snow-white djellabas. "Honey, let me tell you something," he says, fingering the fabric. "Everything has a scale, from the best to the worst. Even *Vogue*. American is the crème de la crème. They only use the top everyone. If you have made it there, you've made it everywhere." He moves on to the next store. "Italian is the most experimental, the one no normal people actually buy, but all the fashion biz look to for inspiration and new ideas. French has the best print, so it looks great in a portfolio, and the rest—English, German—all good but not as significant. Comprende?"

I nod. A beautiful emerald-green scarf with gold threading catches my eye. When I ask the seller for the price, he tells me it's 100 dirham and Emanuel shakes his head. They begin to haggle, the seller in his white djellaba throwing up his arms in the air with dramatic flair. When he hugs himself, shaking with sorrow, Emanuel grins and tells me I can get it for fifteen dirham. The equivalent is five francs, so I happily become the proud owner of an authentic Moroccan scarf.

We enter another souk, where a twisted hallway leads us through tables full of shining, polished metals, delicate silver bracelets as thin as string, large hammered brass, and copper plates, and intricate silver and gold filigree earrings. Emanuel buys thirty thin silver bracelets and we make our way out of the souks. On Place Jemaa-el-Fna, night has swallowed the intense heat of the day and left a whisper of a warm breeze. The square is not really a square; it's an irregularly shaped open space with little stands selling tea, kebabs, soups, and other foods that send curling wisps of fragrant smoke into the air and where tourists, sporting either candy-apple red or marshmallow-white complexions, bob like buoys on the ocean. Lights are strung up between the buildings and across the square, giving it a Christmasy, festive mood. Mournful sounds of flutes mingle with drums and odd wailing notes of human voices, which I eventually identify as songs.

Emanuel and I wander about, stopping to watch a snake charmer sitting cross-legged in front of an open basket, where the head of a cobra moves like a Swedish disco devotee. Belly-dancing women with heavily painted faces and dirty feet, clad in brightly colored swirling skirts decorated with silver coins, undulate their unmuscled, even fat, stomachs. We pause by a wrinkled old man in a turban, who shouts out guttural words to a small crowd of Moroccans that surround him with laughter and applause. "He's a storyteller," Emanuel explains.

"What are the stories about?"

"I have no idea," he says. "I don't speak Arabic."

An old woman, draped in black from head to toe, grabs my hand, says something, and smiles a wide toothless grin. "She wants to tell your fortune," Emanuel says. I smile at her pruny face. She takes this for my acquiescence and begins to ramble in quick, odd French. Emanuel translates. "She says you have much luck in your future. Much money. And a handsome man." He smiles. "Who can that be?"

I blush.

"That will cost you five dirham," he says. I pay the woman and Emanuel gives her his hand to read. A frown shrinks her face into a currant. She says something to Emanuel, and he laughs, but withdraws his hand quickly as if she burned him. "Silly old cow," he mumbles under his breath.

"What did she say?"

"Oh, to take better care of my teeth or I will end up like her," he says. I somehow doubt this is the correct translation.

We keep walking, holding our new treasures, until we find a café serving tourists; Emanuel decides it's time for drinks. We both order Cuba libres and watch people in the square while Emanuel tells me in great detail about the wondrous makeup he has planned for me. I listen in rapt attention. Golden skin? Silver eyes? Monochromatic metals? His excitement ignites me. I can already see myself, vastly improved with his brushes and completely irresistible to Rob. Our spinning yarns of the immediate future are bright and filled with hope. It reminds me of evenings with Hatty.

"Is it difficult to become a makeup artist?" I ask Emanuel, and set him off on a story about makeup schools, a disappointed mother, a boyfriend (at which I still wince, at least inwardly), and other things I barely understand, but know they would be hard to apply to Hatty. When he stops to gulp his drink, I tell him about Hatty and her fervent wish.

He purses his lips. "Hmm, you know, if I get booked for the shows this year, she could come and assist me," he says suddenly.

"Really? You would do that for me?"

"For you. And for her. This is a tough business to break into. I would be happy to help someone. For you know"—he breaks into a grin, and wags his finger comically in the air—"no good deed goes unpunished." I have to hug him across the table. Too bad I can't call her right now to tell her!

"So, when are the shows?" I ask.

"September."

That douses my fire. In September I'm supposed to be back in school. Economy line. For morons with bad grades. I empty my drink. But then, who knows? Maybe I won't go back to school. Maybe I will do well enough to stay on. *Linea Italiana* and *Les Mariages* be damned. I'm here for *Vogue*. *Vogue* tear sheets may be the very thing the doctor ordered for a prolonged stay in Paris.

"Have you ever been to a gay bar?" Emanuel says, gulping his second drink. I admit I haven't. "Nothing here is as excellent as Tangier," he says. "But I know of one."

LIKE A GIRLFRIEND, he runs his arm through the crook of my elbow while we walk.

"So, what are the shows?" I finally get up my nerve to ask.

"The runway, honey. Designers show off their newest collections to the biz, before print gets them."

"Are they hard to do?"

"Nothing for you to worry about. Print girls don't do runway. For the shows, there are special models who do mostly shows or fittings. They are not so pretty as print girls; some maybe have a big nose, or sticking-out ears. The French call them 'Jolie-Laid.'"

"Pretty ugly?"

"It doesn't translate so well," he laughs. "What it means is, they are 'interesting' more than beautiful."

After five minutes of winding streets jammed with tourists, we descend into the basement of an ornate building into a tiny jewel box of a room, hung with carpets and red see-through drapes. We're greeted by sweet-smelling smoke, an incongruous bass pumping out "Another One Bites the Dust" and statues of golden male torsos writhing on tables, pedestals, and walls. They are anatomically detailed, with round butts and huge erections—which momentarily knocks my breath out—but once I see a penis being used as a coat hanger, they seem more silly than scandalous. Emanuel doesn't even notice them and moves about in a carefree way that implies he's been here a few times. We take a small table by the wall so Emanuel can have the best lookout over the room and the entrance. I'm seated facing the opposite direction so as not to scare off any hot sailors who may be romantically inclined.

"So, tell me about this man, honey," Emanuel says, and smiles. "No, no. Don't try to deny it." He shakes his glass at me. "I saw you blushing when the fortune-teller mentioned him."

It may be the alcohol, but I look into his sparkly brown eyes and spill my guts. Rob this and Rob that, my constant misses and my feverish desires. And Mia. Nice fucking Mia.

"Yeah, but everyone knows they are having problems." He leans in closer to me and raises his eyebrows. "And—he did book you for this trip."

I explain that Rob is not romantically interested in me, that it's only about work, but Emanuel starts making plans—everything from sensible advice like be mysterious and gorgeous at all times (men love a good mystery) and stay away from appearing needy or desperate (men hate needy), to more flamboyant scenarios like kidnappings where Rob has to rescue me from the clutches of an Arab sheik (Emanuel in a djellaba and his fabulous new scarf) only to find me in the desert tied up and butt-naked.

We imbibe conspicuously; Emanuel with his dainty girl drinks while I knock back Cuba libres, feeling enormously grown up and sophisticated. Back home, going to a gay bar and ordering drinks would be as likely as getting eaten by African army ants. Of course, I'm not sure gay Swedish people even exist; I've never seen or heard of one. As Emanuel chatters on, I ponder homosexuality. Is it the way they are born, or a choice later on in life after some disastrous first affair with the opposite sex? I promptly realize that can't be it, or I would most certainly be pining away for women after the Bengt/Simon interludes.

"When did you know you—you like guys?" I ask, not wanting to say "gay" or "homosexual," for the words seem impolite.

"Oh honey, I think I have known my whole life," Emanuel says. With a few more probes from me, he goes on to tell me about his first sexual encounter with a blond boarding-school boy, and his first and only real love with a soap-opera actor who got him into the makeup world and for whom he moved to Paris, only to find him in their bed with their Vietnamese housecleaning boy. Emanuel's father was dead, his mother religious and in deep denial about her son's sexuality, so he decided to stay on and sleep with as many men as possible in retaliation.

"You see, I have no one," he says. "It's all sex, all fun, all the time." He smiles a sad little smile. "And all I ever wanted was someone to hold me."

A gush of understanding floods me. How alike we are, regardless. I reach out for his hand across the table, but his melancholy attitude switches abruptly. He sits up and widens his kohl-rimmed eyes. "Oh my God, I think an angel just walked in."

I throw a surreptitious glance over my shoulder.

The Angel is a tall Nordic man with cheekbones like jagged glass, pale wintry eyes, and a platinum crew cut. He stands at the entrance, looking around with a slight scowl, as if he got here by mistake.

"I bet you a million francs he is Swedish," Emanuel whispers loudly. "If you go and ask him, I promise I will pay back. With Rob, you know?" He winks at me.

My drinks have settled and left me with that warm, languorous boldness; I'm capable of anything. So I stand up and approach the Angel. His name is Sven, from Göteborg (ah, there *are* Swedish homosexuals), he's a soldier in the Swedish army (didn't even know we had one), and, aside from bitter thin lips, he's Emanuel's dream personified.

Emanuel flirts and prances like a girl, all batting eyelashes and fake pouts. Sven, although he's accepted a drink from Emanuel, proceeds to ignore him and keeps turning to me with Swedish small talk. At one point he mentions a girlfriend back in Göteborg, which I promptly tell Emanuel as soon as Sven goes to the bathroom.

"All the military men are like that." Emanuel waves his hand dismissively. "They all pretend they are straight, even in gay bars. That's why I find them so damned attractive," he adds with a chuckle under his breath, as Sven makes his way back to us.

Emanuel buys a hashish pipe, a long glass thing in which something bubbles at the bottom. He and Sven take long, content drags from the mouthpiece at the top. I decline this pleasure, for I quite suddenly have to go and throw up. Too many Cuba libres on an empty stomach. There is no ladies' bathroom, so I have to weave through a gold and mirrored one, past three men at urinals who appear to be not so much urinating as admiring one another's equipment. I fall into a stall, where I can hug the cool porcelain bowl in peace, and my heaving periodically interrupts the sighs and groans from the adjoining stalls.

When I come back out, Emanuel and Sven rise. Emanuel tries to hold Sven's hand, but Sven brushes him off. It bothers me a little, but Emanuel acts like nothing is wrong.

"Let us put you in a cab, honey," he says to me.

He sports the biggest grin this side of the equator as they walk me out beyond the ramparts, where Emanuel hails a *petit taxi*. He opens the door for me. "Are you okay to go back alone, honey? Sven and I would like to stay out a little longer."

I'm dizzy and tired enough not to mind my lonely room at the end of this ride. "Sure. I'm fine. You have a good time."

"Oh, we will. We will." Emanuel nods enthusiastically. He tells the driver the address of the hotel and closes the door. I watch his little narrow body next to Sven's behemoth bulk walk away into the night as the car speeds me off to a blank room, a blank bed, and blank sleep.

WHEN THE PHONE RINGS I have no idea where I am, or what time it is. The world outside is still dark. I pick up the receiver. "Hello?"

A male voice speaks to me in soothing tones and endlessly repeated words that slowly burrow into my foggy conscience: "an attack—your friend—I'm sorry—badly hurt—in hospital—please come."

It's four o'clock in the morning when I arrive at the hospital and try my hardest to explain to the white-uniformed, non-English speaking staff about my friend Emanuel, whose last name I don't even know.

The hospital looks like what I'd imagine a clinic in a Third-World country would be: peeling green walls, '50s-style plastic orange chairs, and mounds of cigarette butts on filthy linoleum floors. It is one of the top hospitals in the country, an English-speaking doctor proudly tells me as we walk through corridors lit with bare bulbs. Emanuel is in a ward with twenty other beds, some shielded with mustard-colored partitions, and an overall grim air of blood and pain. One single bare bulb in the middle of the ceiling casts a sick glow and heavy shadows.

Emanuel's face is so badly bruised I wouldn't recognize him, if not for his mahogany locks tangled on the pillow. His left eye is puffed shut and an evil-looking gash on his forehead still seeps blood. When he sees me, he opens his swollen lips to greet me and I see his front teeth are missing. I gasp and press my hand to my mouth. The words of the ancient fortune-teller spring up in my hungover head.

"It's okay, honey," he says, slurring the words. "They were fake anyway, no problem to replace."

I sit down on the edge of his bed. "Who did this to you?"

Emanuel turns his face to the wall.

"It was Sven, wasn't it?"

He remains silent.

"Emanuel, you have to tell me. They must arrest him, or something. I have to go to the police!"

"No, honey. No police," he mumbles through obvious pain.

"But—you can't let him go unpunished!"

He attempts a smile. "No one would think beating a fag is a crime. Especially here. They would probably give him a medal or something." He hiccups and grimaces. "Another fag bites the dust."

"But that's so not fair!" I yell out.

The English-speaking doctor sidles over. "Please, you must be more quiet," he says, indicating the other patients with a wave of his hand.

"Sorry," I say.

Then the doctor cheerily tells me my friend will momentarily be taken in for surgery; there is some unexplained internal bleeding.

Surgery? Here? I look around in despair at the grimy, peeling walls, the dirty sheets, the moaning shapes under threadbare blankets on nearby cots.

"Wouldn't it be better to send him back to France? I can take him tomorrow—"

"Oh no, not possible," the doctor says, and with his infuriating smile adds, "Tomorrow your friend could be dead."

I turn away from him and sit back on Emanuel's bed.

"Emanuel, what can I do? Who can I call for you?"

"Don't worry your pretty little head about me, honey," he struggles out. "I'll be fine."

I stroke his hair ever so gently.

"That's nice," he whispers and closes his eyes. I continue stroking his hair, and the unhurt part of his cheek. I almost suspect he's drifted off to sleep, when I notice the tears leaking out from under his thick eyelashes.

Pity wrings my insides, but excretes no fluid relief, no tears. My innards have calcified and the pressure threatens to crush them. "Oh, Emanuel, don't worry. I'll be here. I'll take care of you," I whisper. His chest shakes almost imperceptibly with suppressed sobs. I pull my legs up onto his bed and put my arms around him, embracing him as gently as I can. He cries quietly in my arms until the doctor comes to tell me they are ready and two orderlies wheel Emanuel out of the room.

CHAPTER 18

My brain is in a post-alcohol daze and my thoughts flitter about like moths in a brightly lit room, crashing against the walls. Emanuel is in surgery. We are supposed to be picked up from the hotel at 7:00 A.M. to go to Ouarzazate. I guess it's pretty unreasonable to expect Emanuel will leave on time. What am I going to do? If I blow it this time, I will surely be fired by the agency. And Rob will think the worst of me. But how can I leave Emanuel?

I add a whole bunch of cigarette stubs to the littered floor in the lobby, waiting for news. By six, the hospital picks up speed, new people come in to replace the tired ones, the smell of coffee wafts through the corridors, and Cheery Doc comes to tell me his shift is over and, unfortunately, my friend has gone into a coma.

"What?" I stand up. "But that's not possible! He was okay, I just spoke to him—well, you know, you were there—"

The doctor takes my hand gently. "Why do you not go to your hotel," he says. "Get some sleep and come back tonight, when I am back. Maybe we will know more then."

I press him for answers, but all he can tell me is that Emanuel could wake at any moment, or not at all.

Finally, I give up and follow the doctor's orders.

•   •   •

IT CAN'T BE MUCH later when the phone wakes me again.

"What the fuck are you doing?" Shoji yells. "You're supposed to be in Ouarzazate. Hedwig called and she is absolutely furious! Don't you realize how bad this looks?"

Half asleep, I stumble my excuses and attempt to explain about Emanuel. "Can you somehow contact anyone from Emanuel's family?" I ask, only to remember he has none.

"Don't know him, don't know them," Shoji says coldly. "Right now I have a hundred other calls to make, starting with an agent to find another makeup artist."

"Please," I beg. "At least call his agent, so he can find someone, a friend or someone, because I can't leave him here by himself."

"The fuck you can't," Shoji barks. "If he wants to go out and get beaten up on his own time, that's his problem. But I must remind you, you are paid by German *Vogue* to be where you are, and your time is theirs. They didn't bring you to Morocco to babysit their makeup artist, who, by the way, didn't have enough common sense not to put himself—and you—in danger. I want you to sit by the phone and not move an inch until I call you back with further instructions." He hangs up before I have a chance to object.

I'm starving, but there is nothing to eat, so I drink a glass of tap water. The clock radio shows it's one o'clock. I sit back down on the bed and stare at the phone. Emanuel *should* have known better. Even I could tell there was something wrong with Sven. Why couldn't Emanuel have gone back with me? But his face, the face of last night streaked with tears and blood, flashes in my mind. He needs me. How can I leave when he needs me?

I pull out Kafka to ward off the loneliness of my room, and after a paragraph decide Kafka is too fucking boring. I have another glass of water. I stare at the phone. I try to turn the TV on. I try to open a window. Defeated, I sit back down on the bed and the phone rings. It's the hospital. "Your friend, he wake up and ask for you," I'm told in heavily accented English. "You come now?"

I look around my suffocating cubicle. It's been an hour since Shoji called. I'm sure I can sneak out for a little, before he calls back. "Yes, I come now."

•   •   •

WHEN I ENTER the hospital, Emanuel has passed out again, but Cheery Doc has just begun his shift. He tells me Emanuel is doing much better and his waking up, even briefly, is great news.

"Listen, if I had to leave—" I say. "Do you think my friend would be okay?"

Cheery Doc frowns. "Your friend is doing better, but things are unpredictable in his condition, you understand?"

He walks me to the ward where Emanuel lies, his face a mottled palette of violent purples and blues, with plastic tubing surrounding him like a spider web. I touch his cheek. He is warm and unresponsive. Cheery Doc clears his throat. "It seems your friend is resting now, perhaps you would like something to eat?"

I'm so hungry I'll happily devour even Third-World-country hospital fare, so I nod. Cheery Doc offers me his arm. "There is a little place not too far away."

WE WALK OUTSIDE, where the sun has turned everything into delicious shades of peaches and apricots. We obviously didn't have the same thing in mind and now I'm trapped.

"Are you allowed to leave when you are on shift?" I inquire.

Cheery Doc hangs on to my elbow with a possessive hold. "Oh, it is not a problem," he says. "I am on my break." On his break when he just started his shift ten minutes ago? I glance at his shiny gray suit, complete with a white shirt and a pink tie. It strikes me he's very dressed up for a day at work. Well, whatever. If Emanuel gets better care because I dine with his doctor, then so be it. But it better be quick.

He leads me a few streets down, to a small dark restaurant filled with locals sitting on pillows around low tables. I let him order for me, and sit in mostly stony silence while we consume couscous, a tiny sort of grain flavored with chunks of strong-smelling meat that I'm told is goat. He keeps wiping sweat off his fleshy, swarthy face with a napkin as he regales me with stories of his education and his family, at which I nod and smile when obliged. I hope he won't press any further than a lunch. Kissing or—God forbid—having sex with him is beyond me, even for a cause as crucial as this one. I keep glancing at my watch, inconspicuously at first, but after an hour, with flair and sighs of "My, look at the time!" Finally, the bill arrives, which Cheery Doc insists on paying although I snatch it up first. He tugs it out of my hand.

"In my country, a man would never let a woman pick up a check," he says, his thick eyebrows drawn together in consternation.

"In my country, this is called 'sexism,' " I say. His frown deepens. I decide not to pursue it, let him pay, and we walk back to the hospital.

Emanuel hasn't woken since we left. I thank Cheery Doc for the meal, and he pulls up a chair for me next to Emanuel's bed before taking his leave with a kiss on my cheek and a wink. I suppose I should be flattered, even though he looks like a shaved boar.

I sit on the plastic chair and watch Emanuel breathe. It's been two hours since I left the hotel. Shoji must have called by now. I imagine his reaction at not finding me in my room and tiny acid drops of anxiety sizzle inside me. This is crazy, really. Here I am, sitting at the bedside of my friend, unable to do anything for him except to have dinner with his doctor, while my career is waving good-bye.

My anticipated tear sheets in *Linea* and *Les Mariages* gape like a hole where a door should have been. *Vogue,* even a lesser *Vogue,* is what I need if I want any part of the modeling world. It's a coup, a prize I'm dismissing when it can change my life. And then there is Rob. He booked me on this trip, even if it was just to replace someone else. It must have been him, I reason, since it certainly wasn't that horrible woman. I may still have a chance, a last chance, to entice him. I have nothing but a four-thousand-franc debt to show for the month of hauling butt all over Paris, and yet I sit in a plastic bucket chair watching my friend breathe, when just over the mountains is my ticket to all I ever wanted.

I stand up. Emanuel doesn't move, doesn't blink; the only sign of life is the oxygen tube hissing into his lungs and expanding his chest in regular intervals.

I stroke his arm. "Please forgive me," I whisper.

CHEERY DOC IS IN the hallway smoking a cigarette as I walk out. "You're not leaving?" he exclaims.

I try to explain my work situation, but he glowers at me, and suddenly I'm afraid. What if he does something to Emanuel in revenge? I compose my face into a smile.

"However, I'll be back in a week, and if you can promise me you will look after my friend, I will be delighted to join you for lunch. Or dinner," I add with a flirtatious look that must seem as insincere as it feels.

"I will make sure he gets the best care I can provide," he says, and pulls me in for a wholly unexpected embrace that reeks of Old Spice and goat.

Feeling like a prostitute, albeit one with a good cause, does in no way alleviate my guilt at betraying Emanuel. Slight nausea creeps up on me in the *petit taxi*, but whether from the driving or my bad conscience is unclear.

Shoji's message greets me at the front desk.

Car will pick you and Davide up at seven a.m. My relief should be instant, but instead, my stomach cramps and I break out in cold sweat. Just what I need right now, an anxiety attack. In the elevator, I breathe in blue, breathe out red. Hugo flashes before me. I wish he were here. I barely have enough time to lunge for the bathroom before a violent gush of my lunch splatters the toilet bowl. It may not be panic after all.

I stay there for the rest of the evening and night, wracked with infernal cramps, alternately hugging or sitting on the toilet. God is punishing me for my choice. Or it could be the couscous. Or a combination of the two. Every time my stomach cramps, every time burning liquid gushes out, I think, *serves you right*. The pain is a deserving reward for my selfishness and it makes me almost grateful.

When the phone rings, I crawl to it. A blinding morning sun pours in the window.

"Your car is downstairs," the receptionist says.

DAVIDE IS ALREADY in the back of the car, in another fancy embroidered shirt and black slacks, a large pair of sunglasses slightly askew on his sweaty nose. He taps his foot impatiently as I hand the driver my bag and nearly pass out from the exertion. I climb into the backseat, where the smell of Davide's aftershave and sweat bring on another wave of nausea.

"Well, well, well," Davide says. "Look who's a half hour late."

"I'm really sorry to keep you waiting," I say, "but I don't feel so well."

"Maybe a little less partying and a little more sleep would do the trick," he says, and fans his face with a dainty little paper fan.

Fuck you, I think. You have no right to make assumptions.

I rest my head on the seat and gulp air to still my stomach. Once the car gets going, the air from the open windows helps somewhat, but the driving at top speed around bends does not. This guy is worse than an Italian. After many staccato slams on the brakes, my nausea can no longer be controlled.

"Can you please stop the car for a moment?" I shout to the driver once we are outside the city.

"Why, what's the matter?" Davide asks, smirking. I open my mouth to tell him, but vomit shoots out instead, right onto his nice shirt and paper fan. That it is nothing but clear liquid doesn't make a bit of difference. Davide squeals like a piglet. "Stop the car. Arrêtez la voiture!"

The driver pulls over, but the damage has been done. We both get out of the car. Davide tosses the fan into the sand and begins to mop his shirt with paper tissues from his handbag. Once the futility of it dawns on him, he takes the shirt off, revealing his pale flesh and a smattering of unusually placed bristly hairs and pimples. I gag again and finish my business in the ditch. When I turn back, he's pouring his bottle of Evian water over the shirt, rubbing it between his hands with a face scrunched up in distaste. "This sucks," he hisses. "My luggage got lost on the flight yesterday, I can't even change clothes!"

I mutter apologies. "I can lend you a T-shirt," I offer.

"I'll send you my dry-cleaning bill," he mutters as if he didn't hear. "This is a Yamamoto!"

I eye his water with such burning want I'm surprised the bottle doesn't melt. He notices my look and holds the bottle up, as if for inspection, swishing the water around. My mouth is as parched as our surroundings. After a moment, in which I fully expect him to offer me the remains, he pours the rest out over his shirt. He wrings it dry and sniffs it, making a face, but puts it back on.

The smell of vomit is all pervasive in the car. We sit in absolute silence and watch the mountains approach. The arid pink sands give way to lush grasses and grazing goats, and small abodes of red mud where its inhabitants are dressed in colorful djellabas rather than the whites of Marrakech. The engine groans under the strain of the steep ascent but our driver doesn't seem to notice and drives like he means to win the Grand Prix. Every screeching bend, every slam on the brake turns my stomach upside down and, after a while, I simply stick my head out the window and vomit down the side of the car. Davide pulls even farther away, his lumpy body squashed into the door as if he means to become one with it. Twice I have to shout for the driver to stop so I can exit and evacuate every bit of sustenance I've ever ingested. Thank God I brought some toilet paper.

I'm half comatose from the pain and dehydration three hours later, when the driver tells us in French we have finally made it to the top, and are halfway to our destination. As a celebratory punctuation, there is a sudden, tremendously loud crack in the cabin of the car. "Oh my God, we've been shot!" Davide shrieks and throws his arms over his head. The driver swears and brakes. I sit in mute shock. My lap is covered in tiny shards of glass, and the front windshield suddenly looks a lot cleaner. I blink a few times. Indeed: the front window of the car has imploded. We roll to a stop in the middle of the road, which, fortunately, is empty of other cars, and get out. The poor driver is covered in glass and bleeding from a cut above his eye. I'm unharmed as far as I can tell, as is Davide. The temperature has plunged a good forty or so degrees and the grass that hugs the road is stiff with frost. We shiver with cold as the driver tells us that no, we have not been shot at; it's merely the vast temperature drop that made the glass break: a common enough thing around here. This is what I think he says, for he speaks French in that strange guttural accent but waves his arms around a great deal. The instant winter feels almost good at first, but once we get back into the car and get back on the road, the disadvantages of losing a windshield become sorely apparent. My teeth chatter and my hands go numb, even though I stick them between my thighs. Davide, in his damp shirt, is no better off; I notice, with no displeasure, that his lips are turning blue.

Our descent ends in a wide, sandy, red plain, flat as far as the eye can see. The biting cold is replaced by an intense wind, but without the teeth. The driver accelerates and Davide and I are thrown about the backseat like old lozenges in a tin box.

When at last we reach the Club Med hotel of our destination, I have frozen solid and ceased to feel any pain. The hotel is a perfect example of communist architecture circa 1970: a boxy cement structure haphazardly stuck into red desert sand, surrounded by a few lonely clumps of cacti. I exit the car and nearly fall over when a hand steadies me.

"Mein Gott in himmel, what have you done to yourself?" Hedwig the mummy-woman exclaims.

There is a flash of madly darting reds, my ears pop, and then, nothing.

WHEN I COME TO, Hedwig's head bobs into my vision. Her skin sags like an ancient hound dog's from this unflattering angle.

"She fainted, imagine that." She grimaces over her shoulder at Davide, whose pudding face shines with the pleasure of mutual understanding.

"Oh, please, I had to spend six hours in a car with her, imagine *that*!"

The world spins slower; I close my eyes and draw a deep breath. I've conveniently managed to pass out in the shaded entrance. At least Rob is not here to witness my humiliation, I think gratefully, and open my eyes to see him walking out of the glass doors.

He stops. His hair, more sunshine than shade now and longer than my own, blows back off his face in the draft from the door. His skin is the color of Marabou Milk Chocolate. Once again I'm reminded of a pirate captain standing at the helm of his ship.

This is just great. Last time he saw me I was high on cocaine, this time, I'm a stinky, frozen wreck.

"Bloody hell," he exclaims. "What happened?"

"She fainted," Hedwig says.

Rob goes down on his knees and helps me sit up.

"Crikey, mate, you all right?" He brushes a few glass shards off my shoulder.

"Fine, fine," I mumble, and shrink from his touch. The last thing I want now is for him to get a whiff of my intensely personal smell.

For a moment, something like disappointment flickers across his face and he stands abruptly. I want to shout "No, no, I didn't mean it like *that*," but he doesn't look at me.

"I'll get someone to show you to your room," he says, and with a hiss of the automatic doors, disappears behind the glass.

Hedwig points an accusing finger at me. "Get cleaned up and meet me in my room. We need to do a fitting."

I stand up shakily. Bright spots like shooting stars flitter before me. I feel bruised, inside and out. Of all the possible scenarios that have played though my brain, this is one I never imagined. Clearly, I have to rescue my image and Rob's opinion.

A tall lanky guy with a ponytail bursts out of the doors with a big grin. "Bonjour, welcome to Club Med, I'm Michel, your GO," he says and flings my bag over his shoulder. "Let me show you to your room."

I wobble behind him through the reception, a white space with a ceiling fan and an imposing mahogany desk, and continue out the back door, which opens into a square courtyard where a stone fountain sprays merrily into parched air. It's sort of like the interior of a Roman villa, with pillared open hallways lining the central square. Ponytail takes a left and we walk past a series of numbered dark wooden doors as he keeps a running commentary on the Family Ways of Club Med. All Club Med guests are called GMs, and all the people who work here are GOs. There is a show in the bar every night and water sports are complimentary.

A bullish man with a craggy face and thick gray hair walks past us as Ponytail sets my bag in front of a door. The man is dressed in a white, loosely tied bathrobe, from which tufts of graying chest hair do their best to escape. He smiles at me. His face is somehow familiar, but I don't know why. I smile back.

"None of the rooms have locks," Ponytail announces brightly. "Here in Club Med, we are all just one big happy family."

My room is small and white, with two single beds and a narrow window on the wall behind the headboards, and is comfortably chilled and dark. The only nod to Arabic decor is a mosaic of blue tiles around the bathroom door. Ponytail sets my bag down, tells me dinner is served between seven and nine, and closes the door.

In the shower I search for dinner topics in which I will shine and practice quick-witted repartee. I hope to God someone will be interested in the Roman Empire or dead Russian writers.

I brush my teeth and set off to find Hedwig's room across the courtyard. All rooms are identical, but Hedwig's is crammed with metal racks holding a bright assortment of clothes. The floor is littered with clear plastic bags containing metallic sandals. Her dresser top is heaped with jewelry: huge glittering earrings, necklaces, and rings intertwined with large plastic bracelets. I glance at the clothes, beautiful gowns in jewel colors and, um, bikinis.

She hands me a tiny green bottom and a bra with inordinately long straps, and I try to figure out how to tie the damn thing in her yellow bathroom, while she hacks a nasty smoker's cough outside. It doesn't seem to matter what I do with the straps, they are way too long for any human being. Finally I exit the bathroom with the straps like noodles hanging down my back. Hedwig snorts. "No, stupid girl, they go like this." She crosses them behind my back, and keeps crossing them over my ribcage and my waist. Then she pushes me away and sits on her bed, scrutinizing me like a science experiment. In her narrow, freestanding mirror, I catch a glimpse of myself. I am pasty and dark rings circle my eyes. The teeny panties of the bikini are very high cut, revealing a fair amount of pubic hair I should have gotten rid of. The bra is too big and puckers over my breasts. The damn string makes me look like a giant ballet shoe. Hedwig wrinkles her nose.

"You do not have the body for the bathing suits," she expels witheringly, along with a great deal of cigarette smoke.

I never claimed I did. But what about Valentino? I did have a body for his couture dresses, didn't I? Humiliated, I look down at my feet and notice little black lines under my toenails. I curl my toes inward so they don't show as much. Unfortunately, my action only serves to draw Hedwig's attention.

"*Tsk,*" she shakes her head. "Get a pedicure. And also, your skin is too pale. I want you to go to the pool immediately and get some color."

Funny how an afternoon in the sun takes on an ominous tone.

She makes me try on a few of the gowns, which are sticky and heavy in the heat of the room. Every time I exit the bathroom in a new dress, she sniffs, snorts, or coughs in obvious displeasure. I'm feeling faint. Each time I bend down to pull on another pair of panty hose or a sequined cocktail number, bloodred squiggles dance before my eyes. When she frees me an hour later, I'm ready to be cremated. Instead, I go to my room, climb into the shower to shave off the offensive pubes, and change into my old blue bikini. I'd like to call the hospital, but dare not miss even a second of German *Vogue* prepaid sun. I pick up Kafka and by 2:30 P.M. I'm firmly parked on a chaise by the pool with a stream of sunlit senseless words.

THE SOUND OF A CHAIR scraping makes me jump. It's the old guy from the hallway, now dressed in a tight black Speedo with his tanned stomach bulging over it. He still looks familiar. Could he be a photographer?

A client? A hairdresser? I've met so many on go-and-sees, I couldn't possibly keep track. But he doesn't act as though he knows me, so I let it slide.

"Excuse me, may I occupy this chair?" he says.

"Of course," I say and get back to K. and his dreary world. Out of the corner of my eye, I see the man spread a towel on the chaise and stretch out.

"Kafka," he exclaims suddenly. "Ooh la la!"

I should be bothered by the interruption, but instead I'm grateful. I put the book on my stomach and turn to face him. "Have you read it?"

He grins. His teeth are nicotine stained and uneven, but still, his smile is charming.

"Yes, of course." He turns his body to face me. "That is why I am so impressing to see young girl with such book."

I'm flattered. Finally someone notices. Only I wish it were Rob.

The man props himself up on an elbow. "How you are liking it?"

I freeze. If I tell the truth—that I hate it and it keeps putting me to sleep—his first impression will be seriously compromised. But how can I keep up pretense when I've reread the first twenty pages five times and still not retained much past a blurry idea of an unpleasant young man in an unpleasant village inn, surrounded by unpleasant characters?

"I've only just started reading this one," I say.

He inspects me with a sharper focus than mere curiosity. "You do reminding me of someone," he says.

"That's funny. You remind me of someone as well. Have we met?"

"No, not possible. Such beautiful woman I would remember."

I blush. No one has called me a woman before.

He sits up. "Eh, it will later come to me. Now, I would love for finding out your favorite writers, but first, I must get for myself a drink. May I also bring you?"

"Oh, no, thank you."

"Please, I insist. It would be doing me a pleasure."

I acquiesce and ask for water. His English intonation is different, softer on the consonants than French. I wonder where he's from.

He comes back shortly and hands me a tall glass with a slice of lemon. I gulp my water—maybe the best thing I've ever had—and am told, yet again, that my literary tastes are somewhat bourgeois, I need to stock up on some Polish guy named Bukowski, and Kundera, who's Czech but writes in French. When the man eventually stands up and excuses himself, "I'm sorry having to go from such a charming company, but I am afraid I must now work," I'm sort of disappointed. His words have kept me clear of thinking about Emanuel and the rest of the mess my life entails. I will try to call the hospital as soon as the sun goes down.

I must have dozed off, for the icy shock of a wet hand brings me back to my arid red-sand surroundings, where cacti stick up in lonely clumps and white plastic chaises border the small pool.

"Jirina! I thought it was you," Evalinda says. Silver droplets slide off her honey gold skin. She is wearing the teensiest bikini bottom imaginable, nothing but a sparkling turquoise triangle held up with strings, nary a pubic hair in sight. Her magnificent breasts are bare and tanned, and with her work makeup still on, she looks like a perfect goddess. *The* Evalinda. I smile up at her, realizing how good it is to see her familiar face.

"What are you doing here?" she asks, as if I fell from the moon.

I sit up. "Working. With you. Didn't anyone tell you?"

Her round eyes widen. "Oh, *you* are the girl who got fucked up in Marrakech!"

This is what Rob thinks? That I got fucked up?

"What else did they say?" I ask.

She completely ignores my question. "I knew someone else was coming," she prattles on, shoving my legs aside to sit next to me, "but Hedwig kept referring to you as the stupid girl with bad skin, so I had no idea it was you!" She laughs. "Bad skin." She shakes her head, scattering water droplets over me. "You don't have bad skin."

This is how I'm spoken about? Stupid girl with bad skin?

"Anyway, she probably meant girl with a stupid name," Evalinda says, and points to my chest. "You better turn over now, you're getting pretty red." She presses her finger into my skin, which leaves a white dot when she removes it.

"Thanks." It's pointless to pursue what Hedwig meant; in any case, it's pretty clear it's not flattering. "How do you feel?" I say instead.

"Great! Perfect!"

"No stomachache or anything?"

"Jirina," she says firmly. "Let it go. Nothing happened. I don't ever want to hear about it again."

"Sorry."

"So anyway, I'm so glad you are here, we're gonna have so much fun!" She leans in closer·to me, her breath whispering across my face. "And, oh my God, wait till you see Rob in a bathing suit." She raises her eyebrows. "He's fucking gorgeous."

I smile stiffly. I know how gorgeous he is. Evalinda's words have me twitching in alarm. "I though you'd never go near a fashion photographer," I remind her.

"Yeah, but that's before I saw him undressed!" She giggles. "Just kidding. But if you don't want him, or he doesn't want you—watch out!" She stretches her long arms above her head, causing the near drowning of an elderly man in the pool.

"Well, gotta go, we're doing cover-tries by the Kasbah." She points to what looks like a giant sand castle in the distance.

"Oh, you know who you came to replace?" Her eyes glitter with glee. "Mia! Apparently, they got into a tiff in Marrakech, so she stayed there."

Mia in Marrakech. This information settles on me with the weight of an elephant's rump. Mia and Rob have broken up? Or is this merely a lovers' squabble? Emanuel's words come to me. *A trip is like a date.* But who's been asked out, me or Evalinda?

"Conditions are favorable for a takeover," Evalinda says, and stabs me with her finger again.

As soon as she's gone I remove my book and realize it has left a nice white rectangle on my upper stomach. Fuck! I put the book aside and fry with magnanimity. Since this is the only thing I can do right now, I will do it well. I turn over and close my eyes, letting the gentle slapping of water lull me. Rob and Mia. Mia stayed in Marrakech. I'm here instead of her. Something must have happened. And my hope burns as brightly as the sun on my back.

CHAPTER 19

My skin looked pink before the shower, but once I towel myself dry, I am flamingly red, save for a lighter pink rectangle commemorating Kafka. I'm feverishly hot and cold and dazzling rings of sun pop before my eyes. I pick up my broken powder compact, and pat a layer on, hoping to somehow disguise the burn. Instead, my skin turns a peculiar crackly gray, like old cement. When I wipe it off, my face glows even brighter. So much for my great effect at dinner. I contemplate not going. It's not as if I wasn't already pretty used to going hungry. But I do have to call Emanuel. I pull on my jeans and a T-shirt and head for reception.

The only phone for guests' use is in a glass phone booth right next to the front desk. It's presently occupied by a fluffy-haired, porky woman in a pink muumuu and four others are standing in line, tapping their feet. The dining room is filling up with diners as I wait, so I turn my back in case anyone from our group passes by. The scent of food reminds me how very hungry I am.

Finally, the last person makes their call and I step into the phone booth only to find my little note with the hospital address is no longer in my pocket. I run back to my room, and search through all my belongings to no avail. I must have lost it. Well, there is always the telephone book. I run back to reception, but now it's completely empty; everyone, including the GOs, must be at dinner. I look around the desk, even sneak behind it, but can't see anything that resembles a telephone book. I hear footsteps, and when I look up from behind the desk, it's to a vision of Evalinda in a white djellaba floating in through the back door. She looks beautiful and impossibly cool, a wide leather belt cinching her waist, high strappy sandals on her feet.

"What, playing the receptionist? I was looking everywhere for you."

"I'm trying to make a phone call," I mumble and walk around the desk.

"Well, call after dinner." She grabs my hand. "Come on."

"I'm not hungry," I try to object.

"Nonsense. Of course you are. And besides, not showing up will look even worse than that sunburn."

She pulls me into the dining room, which has been dressed for dinner with white tablecloths and candles. I catch a glimpse of myself in the windows and the sight is not reassuring: a lobster attired in clothes. Our group sits by a round table in the corner. Rob is facing us, with Hedwig, Davide, Vlad, and Rob's assistant, the girl with the pink hair, spread out next to him. Evalinda switches into a hip-swinging, slow gait. I'm conscious of waddling like a duck next to her, since all of me is on fire. I imagine seeing the two of us from Rob's perspective, and with a falling heart realize the comparison is yet again seriously unfavorable to me.

"Glad you're feeling better," Rob says as we sit down.

I blush and keep my face resolutely tilted down, so as much hair as possible covers my skin. Hedwig notices immediately. "Mein Gott, what haf you done to your skin?"

This gets everyone's attention. They all *ooh* and *aah* over my sunburn.

"Nein, this is not possible," Hedwig says. "How are we supposed to photograph this?"

Rob pours us wine. "No biggie, I'm sure Davide can fix it, right?" He looks at Davide, who snorts.

"Are you kidding? I am a makeup artiste." He pronounces it *arteest*. "Not a miracle worker."

Hedwig lights a cigarette from the candle on the table. "We cannot do the shoe shots on her either, I do not think this girl has ever heard of a pedicure. She is a dirty girl."

If I ever doubted my color could go any brighter, I'd now be proven wrong. My skin burns and pulsates like a flashing police light.

Rob glances at Davide.

"I do *not* do nails!" Davide exclaims as if he were asked to muck a stable.

Hedwig sniffs. "And she is no good for the bathing suits."

"Why can't we do bathing suits on her?" Rob asks, sounding genuinely puzzled.

"She has no tits," Hedwig says.

"She's got enough," Rob says. I feel his glance on my chest.

I want to melt into the ground.

"And"—Hedwig holds her finger up in an important announcement—"she has too much bush."

Evalinda titters. The remark sits in the middle of the table with the grace of a buffalo on skates. If hell opened up before me, I'd gladly hurl myself in. Davide giggles and Rob silently caresses the edge of his wine glass. Vlad suddenly laughs out loud.

"That's easily fixed," he says. He pauses and raises an eyebrow. "Although I myself am quite partial to the large bush." The men chuckle.

I want to die. And not figuratively. I want to die. I want to slit my wrists right here with the fucking butter knife.

"What about the evening dresses?" Rob says. "We aren't shooting those until Agadir."

"Some of those may be okay," Hedwig admits grudgingly.

Davide sighs as if the weight of the world rests on his shoulders. "Look, there isn't a damned thing we can do with her until this sunburn fades, and then she'll start peeling."

"Hey, you guys," Evalinda says. "She's here and she is not deaf, dumb, and blind." My heart swells in gratitude. She is my friend. And right now I love her more than any friend I've ever had.

Everyone with the exception of Hedwig and Davide looks somewhat chastened. Rob sets his glass down. "I'm sorry," he says. "That was hugely untactful. I suppose sometimes we forget we are dealing with living, breathing people."

The table goes silent, and it's nearly as painful as the conversation. Vlad touches my shoulder. "Here, have some wine." He puts the glass into my hand.

I take a swig, but Hedwig's eyes spear me across the table. I set it back down. Rob's assistant, Chelsea, with the pink hair, nudges Evalinda. "Hey, did you know Ondrej Dumowski is here?"

Evalinda sits up a little straighter. "What, here—*here*? In the hotel?"

Chelsea nods. "He's apparently scouting locations for his new movie at Ait Benhaddou."

"I know him," Evalinda bursts out. "I met him at a party in Paris." She puts her elbows on the table and crosses her arms so it maximizes her cleavage. "He's sooo sexy," she says breathily. Rob shoots her a sharp glance, and Evalinda, noticing it, giggles. "I just can't resist a man with talent." She winks at Rob. "Like you." She sits up and looks around the dining room. "I better go and say hi. Where is he?"

Chelsea shrugs. "I didn't see him, I only heard it from Vlad who does his ex-wife's hair."

Vlad smirks. "Yeah, and you should hear the other stuff about him she's told me."

"Like?" Evalinda leans in close.

Vlad spins stories straight out of *Caligula*: very young girls, wild orgies, but I barely hear. My food goes almost untouched, and as soon as I can, I excuse myself, blaming it on travel fatigue.

THE PHONE BOOTH is empty, but so is the reception area. Loud, happy music and voices rumble from the adjoining bar. I stick my head in long enough to see a show in progress: all the GOs are on a small stage dressed in diapers, wobbling around with big silly grins and making fart noises. I cross the room to wait on the couch. As I pass the reception desk, the large mirror behind it displays a girl with skin the color of poppies, flat, dirty hair, and unflattering clothes. I sit on the couch. I thought I knew all about being ugly. But the ugly of grade school—in comparison—is a spit in the ocean. That was a homeliness that warranted invisibility, being singled out as different and therefore avoided. This new ugly is that of a carnival freak put under the spotlight for the amusement of a crowd.

Someone next to me clears his throat and I look up. It's my friend from the pool. He holds a drink and a cigarette. "Good evening. Why you are here alone and looking so sad?"

"I'm just waiting to make a phone call," I say and dip my head so my hair covers my face.

"I go to catch for you someone. Do not now disappear." He shakes his finger at me. He goes back to the bar as Evalinda and the gang, minus Rob and his assistant, exit the dining room.

"Hey, what are you doing here?" Evalinda exclaims and runs over. "I thought you went to sleep." She plops down next to me.

"I need to call and see if I can get an update on Emanuel."

She lights her Dunhill. "So, what exactly happened in Marrakech anyway?"

I quickly outline the story for her.

"Poor Emanuel," she says with a sigh, and takes a deep drag. "That'll ruin his reputation for sure."

"What?" I sit up straighter. "What do you mean?"

"Honey, he dragged you to a bar when theoretically you guys were supposed to sit in your hotel rooms ordering room service courtesy of German *Vogue*. Not that anyone actually stays in their room on a trip—but you make sure you don't get caught, you know—and then he doesn't show up on the shoot and you miss two days. That won't go over too well on the gossip network."

"I don't have to tell anyone," I say. "I haven't yet."

"Yeah, I know. 'Cause right now you are both being tainted with the same tar brush by good ol' Hedwig. What you need"—she takes another deep drag—"is a good lie." She frowns in concentration. "Maybe, like, you went out to change some money—no, too late at night for that—okay, I got it—you went out to get some ciggies and someone mugged you and Emanuel threw himself on the attacker—wait, no, that sounds like a lie."

"I'm not sure I'll be able to pull it off, anyway. I'm not that good a liar."

Evalinda looks at me sharply. "You better learn, or you'll both be fucked." She lets out a cloud of smoke and points the tip of her cigarette at me. "You can do this kinda shit once you're established; hell, for some girls it's even a plus—heightens the mystique, you know—but for a greenie like yourself"—she pauses and flicks her ash on the floor—"you'll be labeled unreliable and no one will dare book you."

Suddenly her eyes fly up over my shoulder and, just as quickly, her expression changes from stern to her signature pout. I turn to my friend from the swimming pool, holding two glasses of something white and frothy. "Voilà, mademoiselle, while you waiting."

"Ondrej. What are you doing here?" Evalinda exclaims.

Ondrej? As in Dumowski? My new friend is the director with a propensity for weird sex?

"Jirina," she scolds me, "you didn't tell me you knew Ondrej."

"I didn't know—"

"I am sorry." He glances at Evalinda. "Have we meeting?"

That gives her a moment's pause, but still she smiles as if she hadn't just been mortally wounded. "Evalinda—Michel's party?" she reminds him. "In Paris?"

"Oh yes," Dumowski says cluelessly.

"I am here for *Vogue,* modeling, you know," Evalinda says. "Covers and stuff." As an afterthought, she adds, "With my friend Jirina here."

"You did not telling me you are model," Dumowski says to me. He hands me one glass and gives Evalinda the other. "Good I getting two," he rumbles under his breath. Evalinda makes a space for him between the two of us and sits down just as Rob and his assistant walk out of the dining room.

Rob stops cold. "I thought you went to bed."

"I have to, um, make a phone call?" The drink burns in my hand.

"Really," he says and turns to walk to the bar where a chorus of drunken voices nearly drowns out the words: *hands up, baby hands up, gimme your love gimme gimme.*

The guy with the ponytail prances in with a silly grin and his neck hung with ugly plastic beads. "Someone waiting for the phone?"

I stand up.

AFTER HALF AN HOUR of perusing the local phonebook Ponytail handed me, dialing random numbers—I remembered the name of the hospital incorrectly—and speaking to people who don't speak English, I hang up in defeat. I'm so tired I can barely stand. Through the smudged glass of the phone booth, I see Evalinda and Dumowski chatting while Ponytail yawns.

I have no way to reach Emanuel. I rest my boiling head against the door and offer up a little prayer. Please God, if you make Emanuel well, I will—I will what? This is when I'm supposed to offer something in return. Something terribly important to me. Rob. *Vogue.* But I can't. Forgive me, Emanuel. I'm not willing to trade my dreams for your life.

The floor of the reception area is terra-cotta tile. If I make it to the exit without stepping on a grout line, Emanuel will be fine. "You do not going to sleep now." Dumowski's voice catches me halfway. I spin around, keeping my feet in the square.

"I'm sorry, I'm really tired," I try.

"No, no, you must finishing your drink first!"

He's right. It's impolite for me to walk away when he's bought me a drink. I make my way back to them, my feet perfectly in the center of each tile. I make it all the way. Emanuel will be fine. Dumowski hands me my drink and I gulp it so fast I get brain freeze. Rob walks out of the bar just as I finish the glass. He strolls over to us with his hands in his pockets and pointedly ignores Dumowski.

"Did you make your call?"

"Yes." I try to hide the glass behind Dumowski's back.

He waits.

"Well then, although I am reluctant to tell you ladies how to lead your lives, I must point out we have a wake-up call at four A.M. tomorrow."

"Don't worry about me, Robby-doo," Evalinda coos. "I got plenty of sleep last night. But maybe Miss Jirina here needs a helping hand to her room."

Thank you, best friend.

ROB OPENS THE COURTYARD door for me. "So, what happened in Marrakech?" he asks casually as the door falls shut behind us.

My head reels with fatigue and alcohol. Residues of Evalinda's lie jump to my lips. "I—uh—went to change my money—no, actually, to buy a pack of cigarettes—"

Rob stops. I am forced to stop as well. The hallway is lit with golden light from the sconces and the fountain glows with the same rich hue.

I look at my shoes. "And I got food poisoning from the hospital." I realize I'm off track and quickly backpedal, "But that was *after*, you see, *after* this whole thing, I mean after Emanuel fought the guy, no, the guys . . ." I sneak a peek at Rob. He looks fascinated, like he's witnessing a car wreck.

"There were two of them, you see," I continue. "And he protected me, he protected me . . ." I trail off. Dear God, this is not working. I sound inane. Or insane.

"Okay," Rob says. "Sounds like a nightmare."

"Oh, it was, it was," I agree quickly. "But Emanuel stood up for me, he protected me."

"Yeah, I got that part," Rob says.

I'm doomed. I should have shut up. Now I look like the world's biggest, and worst, liar. I walk to my room, with Rob following me. He waits until I open my door.

"Look Jirina, a fair word of warning."

Unpleasant warmth rises to the surface of my skin.

"This guy is not a good guy."

I step inside my doorway and reluctantly turn to face him. "I think that's seriously unfair. You don't know him like I do."

He leans his arm on the doorframe, his face intent. God, he's gorgeous.

"How well can you know him after such a short time?" he says softly.

"Well enough," I say, steeling myself. "Look, believe me, I can tell the difference between good and bad. I am not an idiot." Although I may sound like one.

"That wasn't implied," he says, his face so close to mine I could lean in and kiss him. "But you're playing with fire."

Tipsiness makes me bold. "And why would you care even if I was?"

He looks straight into my eyes. "Because you're here to *work*." He turns and walks away.

I wait until he's out of sight, then I quietly make my way back to the reception. Of course I'm here to work. It was stupid of me to entertain any other thoughts. If Rob and Mia are having problems, then it's Evalinda he's interested in. What was I thinking? Since when have I been desirable? *Hugo*. Hugo made me feel desirable. Damn him.

The phone rings five, six, seven times before Mia's sleepy voice says "Hello?" I was correct in my assumption that she had stayed in the same hotel as Emanuel and I.

"Jirina, hi, what's the matter? Is anything wrong?"

Yes, I want to cry. Everything. You are so nice and I was trying to steal your boyfriend and I left my friend in a coma and I'm a horrible person and I deserve to die.

"I'm so sorry to call this late," I say, and ramble on to describe the situation with Emanuel and the phone and Cheery Doc.

"I'll go to the hospital first thing in the morning," she says. "Don't worry."

I thank her profusely until I realize I'm keeping her from sleep and hang up. That's it. Rob is a fantasy that will never be anything more.

AT FOUR A.M. we board a van outside the hotel, all of us bleary-eyed and yawning. We drive through dense blackness for two hours, nodding off until at last the horizon begins to glow with the first sunlight, coloring deep, craggy canyons on both sides of the van in pomegranate and tangerine hues. The road twists and narrows as we descend into the Dades Gorge, where the crimson soil of the desert gives way to a paradise of lush greens. Ahead, an enormous waterfall cascades in foaming whiteness down red rocks into a pool of reflected skies.

The driver parks in the shade of the palm trees and we get out and stretch. The sound of the waterfall is all pervasive, a drone as if an otherworldly choir hummed discordant notes. A mist of the waters envelops us in chilly, humid air. Evalinda is wearing a pair of shorts the size of underwear and her smooth legs glint like lacquered wood. My calves are bare, but my thighs are covered in peachy fuzz, which stands up in the cold and makes me feel seriously hirsute. I should have shaved my whole leg. I try futilely to smooth it down so Hedwig doesn't notice. Vlad and Davide spread out a blanket and start setting up their beautifying equipment. Chelsea drags big silver suitcases out of the van, her arms bulging with muscles nearly as defined as Rob's. I close my eyes and take a deep breath. My entire future hangs on this day. Tear sheets from *Vogue*: important. Being seen in *Vogue*: more important. Showing Rob he didn't make a mistake in booking me: most important. I have to prove I can do this. I will muster every little bit of physical self-control learned in the mirror, I will not complain even if Hedwig sets me on fire, I will look as though I'm having the best time of my life even if I'm tottering on the edge of suicidal depression.

"Bathing suits first," Hedwig barks, and in one clear swoop eliminates me from the picture. I'm relegated to a corner of the blanket where I watch Evalinda get cosmetically enhanced while I nibble on a stale croissant from a Styrofoam box. I will not cry.

Hedwig hands Evalinda a gold one-piece suit, which she changes into right in front of everyone, affording a good view of her completely shaven nether-parts. A part of me wants to gasp in shock: I've never seen a woman with no pubes and it looks odd, like a monstrous child—but the other side is impressed. What freedom. What sophistication. Our Moroccan driver is also spellbound, although everyone else acts like this is completely normal.

Rob has set his tripod on level ground before the edge of the pool, a sort of informal beach.

"Right darlin', you ready?"

Evalinda steps up and he explains he would like her to swim across the lake to the fall. "I've got a telephoto, so I'll see you even if you don't see me."

Evalinda dips a tentative toe in the water and exclaims, "Are you crazy? Do you know how fucking cold this is?"

Rob shrugs. "Will it make you feel better if I go in first?"

"Be my guest." Evalinda laughs and pulls my lilac sweater from the car, wrapping it around her shoulders. Rob pulls his T-shirt over his head, kicks off his boots and socks, and runs right into the water, diving in head-first. Evalinda nudges me. "Now watch." She giggles as Rob comes up for air and then strides out of the water. "Fucking gorgeous, right?" His skin looks like liquid gold in the sun, and I am instantly reminded of the writhing torsos in the gay bar. I blush to the tips of my toes at the thought of the penises and my imagination of Rob's. Evalinda pokes me. "You're blushing! How sweet!"

Rob runs up to us and extends his hand to Evalinda. "Your turn, gorgeous." I'm so consumed by jealousy it's a wonder I don't bubble up and dissolve like something tossed into acid. Evalinda tosses me the sweater, and repeats Rob's performance without the headfirst dive. Rob takes his place behind the camera, but Evalinda, after a few weak strokes, swims right back to shore and gets out. "It's too fucking cold," she yells. "I started going numb. There's no fucking way I can swim out all that way."

I volunteer before anyone has a chance to open their mouth. *Please let me do this; let me show you what I can do.* Hedwig dismisses me with a quick shake of her head, but Rob grabs her and whispers something, which makes her acquiesce.

Evalinda takes off her bathing suit and tosses it to me over the van, where I change into it—sort of out of sight. The suit is wet and freezing cold, but it could be made from flesh-eating maggots for all I care. It's cut high on the sides, all the way up to my waist and low in the front, making the best of what I have. I know I don't quite fill it like Evalinda, yet I also know this does not look bad. When I round the corner of the van, Vlad whistles appreciatively. "Who said you don't have a body for bathing suits?"

Rob looks startled and then relaxes into a smile. "That looks fantastic, darlin'."

For a nanosecond, I'm filled with an unutterable lightness of well-being.

Evalinda, who's changed into a black two-piece, sidles up to me. "Did you *shave*?" she exclaims, pointing at my crotch. "You should never *shave*, always *wax*. Look at those nasty bumps." She pulls my bathing suit up my leg, nearly tugging it right into my crotch.

"Uh, yeah, thanks," I say.

Davide brushes on a few strokes of mascara, smears gloss on my lips, and Vlad runs his fingers through my hair. "You'll be wet so there is no reason to do much," he says and nudges me to the water's edge.

"Alright, ready?" Rob says. "What I'd like you to do is—"

I waste no time and submerge myself into the icy water. And it is cold. As cold as Swedish water holes in April. But I am determined. With quick strokes I swim across the lake. I can't hear anyone on shore, because the waterfall is much too loud. I see them, the size of Smurfs, gesturing wildly; it seems they want me to go *in* the waterfall. I grab hold of a rock, haul myself up, and immediately get assaulted by the weight of the water. It doesn't even feel like liquid. It's like a hundred fists pounding my body. I cling to the rock and squint at the shore to see if I'm in the right spot. Rob is behind the camera, so I guess this is my time to shine. The rock was sharp on my feet, but now I can barely feel it, or my feet for that matter. I arch my body, letting the water beat me and try to compose my expression into a smile or at least a look of enjoyment, which is hard, because every time I tilt my face up, the water slams me in the face and shoots up my nose. I twist and turn, holding on to the rock for dear life until all of me goes numb. When I peer through the curtain of water, Rob is no longer behind the camera. Instead, he's waving at me and I assume (and hope) I can come back now. I let go of the rock. And this is when I realize my body no longer obeys me.

My limbs feel as though they aren't connected to my torso. Every command to move comes with a delay. My heart pumps wildly, but simultaneously, drowsiness almost overwhelms me. Stay awake. Move arms. Move legs.

The people on shore must have recognized something is wrong, for Rob is wading out, shouting "Come on." Or maybe they just want me to hurry up so they can keep shooting. I close my eyes and turn to float on my back, kicking with my last ounce of strength.

"Well, bugger me," Rob says, his arms around me, pulling me to safety. He scoops me up as though I weigh nothing. The bathing suit has wedged itself into the crack of my butt and I stiffen like a dead spider in his arms. He carries me out with none of that awkward wobble of Hugo's.

"Sorry," I mumble and fall asleep.

I WAKE UP in the van, covered with a towel. Out the window, I see Rob bent behind the tripod and Evalinda slowly emerging from the pond in a black bikini. She wades toward him with her great big smile and water drops glimmering over that perfect, toned body. Once again I'm reminded of a racehorse, shiny with sweat, every muscle so beautifully on display. The sunlight has turned to burnished gold. It must be late afternoon. I have slept through the entire working day.

"Gorgeous!" Rob shouts. "You're makin' me hot, darlin'!"

Why did no one wake me?

Because they didn't need me, didn't want me. I will not cry. *I will not cry.*

Everyone bounds into the van and I sit up to make room for Evalinda. Her skin is still cool and fresh where it nudges against my sweaty thigh.

"Did you have a good nap?" She laughs.

Hedwig shoots me a dirty look, and Davide, pressing his bulk into the seat behind me, snorts. "You should try sleeping during the night, for a change."

Rob takes his place next to the driver.

"I'm so sorry," I begin, "the waterfall was intense, and I—"

Rob turns around to face me. "I didn't actually mean for you to go in the waterfall," he interrupts, "but you didn't give me a chance to explain."

He must note my stricken face, for he softens. "It made a hell of a picture, though. I did a double page spread. The way you arched up, you know, with your face in the light, was magic. Want to see the Polar'?"

I nod. He frees the photo from his back pocket and hands it to me.

In a small square, framed with black, the waterfall foams over red rocks. After squinting very closely, I find myself—roughly the size of a poppy seed—in the middle of all that froth.

"Nice," I say. It's a lovely shot of a waterfall. You'd need a microscope to identify me.

CHAPTER 20

Amessage from Mia waits for me at the desk: *Emanuel is doing better, out of coma, will accompany him to Paris in a few days.* I wonder if it is possible to be in love with a man *and* his girlfriend.

Evalinda barges into my room just as I fling myself on the bed to have a good cry.

"Hey, why aren't you ready?"

"I'm not going. I'm tired."

"Bullshit. I promised Ondrej we'd have drinks with him before dinner, so come on." She walks to the dresser where most of my clothes lay in a heap. "Besides, you slept all day." She picks up my tattered bra, shakes it with a frown, and puts it back. "Did you ever reach Emanuel?" she says and pulls out my new scarf. "Ooh, this is nice."

"I contacted Mia, and she left me a message saying he was okay."

"That was a good idea," she says, and walks into my bathroom. "She was on this big hospital kick anyway," she shouts, "wanting to visit them and have some old equipment flown in from Sweden or whatever, you know, her usual do-good shit." She pulls up her skirt and sits on the toilet. "Don't know what he sees in her, though," she continues over a noisy stream of pee. "I mean, the girl is *ugly*."

"I don't think so," I say miserably. "I think she's beautiful."

"Nah," Evalinda says, flushing the toilet. She washes her hands. "Even you're better looking."

"Gee, thanks."

"You are. At least when you make an effort. Come on, get dressed."

"I have nothing nice to wear and I look like shit," I say. "Especially next to you." I'm not saying it as a compliment, only stating the truth, but I can tell this pleases her.

"I can fix that," she says. "Besides, if you don't show up tonight, they're all gonna think you're in your room shooting up or something."

Shooting up sounds like a bad thing. Evalinda makes me sit on the toilet and begins to touch up my makeup. "Did you and Robbie have a nice chat last night?"

"Not exactly, he was really down on Emanuel—"

"Ondrej and I really clicked, I think," she says as she puts black liner inside my eyes. "He's doing this movie here with Isabelle Huppert in a couple of months, and he still hasn't found the second lead, this woman who's her cleaning lady that she falls in love with, and they both escape the husband's wrath in the desert mountains, where Isabelle ends up committing suicide, and her lover, the woman, burns her body. The last scene is her pouring the ashes of Isabelle into the sands and then masturbating right there with the sand all over her."

"Sounds painful," I say.

"Oh yeah, she's like crying and making love to the sand; really painful and sad."

"Is he going to give you the part, then?"

"I'm working on it, baby." She winks. "Let's get you dressed."

She convinces me to wear my new scarf as a dress, tied behind my neck. She fastens her own belt across my hips so the scarf doesn't open, and assures me that going barefoot is preferable to my Converse sneakers.

She eyes me for a moment, steps in to tousle my hair, then steps back to take me in. "Perfect," she states. "I'm a fucking genius."

I glimpse my reflection in the glass door before we enter the reception. I look suntanned and wild, with my bare feet and scant clothes: a jungle girl.

A pasty-faced hotel guest passes us in the doorway and I catch his admiring glance, which acts like a burst of caffeine on my tired ego. "See?" Evalinda whispers. "You look hot. What do you say to your fairy godmother?"

"Thank you."

"Now, be nice back and help me out with Ondrej, okay?"

I nod. "What do you want me to do?"

"Watch me for clues."

Dumowski is right there, in the reception area, sitting on the couch in conversation with two other people. He looks up with an appreciative glint in his eye. "Ah, my beautiful friends, come sit!" He introduces us to his producer, a dark man dressed in a light suit, and location manager something or other, an olive-skinned woman with silver hoop earrings. They exchange a few more words in French, then stand up and say good-bye.

Dumowski leans closer to me. "You looking fantastic tonight."

Evalinda frowns.

"Did you have at the gorge a nice time?" he says, again to me. "Not too much tired?"

I babble on about the beauty of the waterfall until I catch Evalinda's grim face. "But since we were doing bathing suits," I say, quite deftly, "Evalinda had to do most of the work and I got to nap."

"Why? What is wrong with you in bathing suit?"

"Oh, *please*." I laugh. "Everything—if I stand next to her!"

Evalinda smiles.

"It is not possible." Dumowski whistles through his teeth. "You are looking very good at the pool to me."

Evalinda's smile fades.

Damn. Now it sounds like I'm fishing for compliments. But I work hard to suppress my own smile. He finds *me* attractive. He really is a very sweet man even though he has hair growing out of his ears.

"Now, my pretty ladies, you will have the dinners with me, yes?" Dumowski says. I look to Evalinda quickly for instructions. She almost imperceptibly shakes her head.

"I'm so sorry, I really must have dinner with our group tonight."

"Why so?" He frowns.

I grimace at Evalinda and she jumps in. "Jirina has had a bit of a rough time since she came—you don't mind me telling Ondrej, do you?" She pats my hand. "She missed a few days of work, and clients are sort of angry. She needs to restore goodwill, if you will."

It's true; still, I can't help wishing she had made something up.

Tonight's dinner is buffet style. A long table is set with rectangular serving pans, cafeteria style, and elaborately displayed vegetables on platters. Our group is already at the buffet when Dumowski leads us in.

I flash a close-lipped smile at Rob, who looks over from the couscous pot at exactly the right time to see us. He frowns back. Never mind, what he thinks of me personally no longer matters.

But once we all sit down at our table—with Evalinda's chair conspicuously empty—and I have two glasses of wine, my tongue loosens and I get into a heated debate with Vlad about the merits of Russian writers. I'm perfectly aware Rob is listening to us, and that spurs me on even more. Vlad, although of Russian heritage, was born in France, and what he knows of Dostoyevsky, Tolstoy, and Pushkin would fit in a box of hairpins. He's never read any of their work with the exception of *Notes from Underground,* and claims Russian literature is as flavorless and dense as their bread, both cases with which I strongly disagree. But oh, what a wonderful opportunity for me to shine! Davide and Hedwig are in a deep discussion about Mugler versus Montana, and poor Chelsea looks bored to tears. I finally beat Vlad into submission with a perfectly standard "How can you be an authority on a subject if you haven't taken the time to study it?" and find Rob's eyes resting on me with a kind of—admiration?

"Did you study literature as a major?" he says.

I have no idea what a major is, but I'd rather not risk nodding or getting into it. I shrug. "My father had me studying the classics from an early age." Better to switch topics to familiar ground. "What sort of books do you like?" I ask. The knowledge that he is out of bounds makes me a little easier around him, or at least capable of speech.

"Ever heard of Patrick White?" he says.

"No, sorry."

"An Australian fella, excellent stuff. You should try it."

"Patrick White," I say, and commit it to memory. Will buy one as soon as I can.

Hedwig and Davide push their chairs back and announce they are going to a local bar in the village. Vlad and Chelsea decide to go with them since we don't have to get up early tomorrow as we're traveling to Agadir. That leaves Rob and me at the table in silence. I polish off the rest of my wine. "How is Mia?" I say, in part to remind myself.

"She's good. Helping Emanuel, you know."

I freeze. Of course Mia would have told him. He must know everything!

As if he heard my thoughts, he smiles. "Yeh, I know. Good effort there on your part—covering up for him. Or trying to."

I cover my face with my hands. Shit. Fuck. How could I have been so dumb?

"And it won't go any further than this table," he says. "I like Emanuel. He's a bit of a loose cannon, but he's great at what he does."

I let my hands drop. "Thank you."

He looks at me intently and I can't help but blush. "You know"—his voice suddenly sounds uncertain, hesitating—"Mia and I . . . well, we're, we're—"

"Going to the bar?" Evalinda announces gayly behind my back. "Come on guys, let's find a table together."

What was he trying to tell me? *We're what?* We're getting married? In any case, it probably doesn't matter. I don't even want to know.

Evalinda hooks her arm through mine and Dumowski's and Rob follows, somewhat reluctantly.

Once we're seated at a corner table, Dumowski offers to get us drinks. Rob is suddenly very quiet and glum. The music pounds all around us. *That's the way, uh huh uh huh, I like it*. Evalinda pulls me up to dance. We shake and bop and I keep Rob in my peripheral vision to see if he's watching. He is. When Dumowski returns, he sets the glasses down and dances his way to us. He rolls from foot to foot much like a trained bear, and Evalinda greets him with sexy pouts and shakes of her hips. But he keeps turning to me, caressing my arm, grabbing my hand to give me a twirl. Evalinda gets in between us, and does her sexy hip shakes. I see Rob watching us with a stony expression. I try to stay tucked behind Evalinda, but Dumowski is like a heat-seeking missile angled at *me*. Evalinda slips in next to me, and pushes her hip out against mine in time to the beat. We bounce hips off each other back and forth, and she's increasing the force behind her hip swings until she's practically ramming me off the dance floor. That's when I understand this is not a dance: It's a reminder.

I'm just about to return to our table, when the song changes to a slow one and Dumowski grabs hold of me. *How deep is your love.* One of my all-time favorites. For a moment, just for a few seconds, I want to dance this song in someone's arms to wipe away the memories of every school dance I've ever attended—only to sit with a glass of nonalcoholic glogg in the corner with Hatty. I set my chin on Dumowski's shoulder from the cascading *How's* in the intro to *You touch me in the pouring rain*, and then push away with the intention of going back to the table. But Evalinda precedes me.

I see her pull Rob to the dance floor. She glues herself to him and begins her sexy undulations. At least I know he won't dance. I flash on my embarrassing attempts to engage him at the party in the penthouse. But when I glance at them, my heart sinks below floor level. Rob is dancing. He didn't dance with *me*. His eyes are nearly closed, his lips are parted, his head is thrown back in abandon while Evalinda plays the predator, going down before him, her hands trailing his legs until she's at the level of his crotch, then she shimmies up again and presses her body to his.

I look at my own dance partner. Small beads of sweat hang off the tip of his nose. If they can do it, so can I. I throw my arms about Dumowski and gyrate provocatively, grinding my pelvis into his hip. He grunts with exertion or pleasure, and grabs a hold of my butt. *It's me you need to show, how deep is your love.* Dumowski mouths the words and stares at me. I do a fair imitation of Evalinda's snaking down and back up, running my hands over Dumowski's sweaty torso. Specks of light reflect off the disco ball and melt on my skin like snowflakes: They sparkle even when I close my eyes. When I open them, Rob and Evalinda are going at it as if they were trying out for a porn movie. I crush myself into Dumowski with heartfelt desperation. He breathes into my neck, squeezing my butt, and grinding into me. I feel the front of his pants bulge. This is wrong, all wrong. I push him away lightly. "I'm sorry, I need to get something to drink," I shout over the music.

Back at our table, I collapse on the couch and empty my piña colada. When I look up from my drink, I see Rob heading back to our table; Dumowski and Evalinda are dancing now. I smile at Rob, but he looks angry. He sits down on a chair opposite me. "What the hell are you playing at?" he says, picking up his own drink.

I widen my eyes and tilt my head. "What?"

"Out there, on the dance floor."

"I was dancing. Like you."

"Dammit, Jirina, I warned you about this guy," he bursts out suddenly. "This 'thing' you and Evalinda have going might be cute or sexy or whatever in certain company, but here, with *him*, it's downright bloody dangerous. If you're gonna use your sexuality as a weapon, make sure it's well sharpened." He empties his drink, pushes his chair away, and stalks off.

He scolded me as if I were a child! The knowledge that it was Dumowski he warned me about, and not Emanuel, makes me feel no better.

Evalinda is humping Dumowski on the dance floor, and I'm suddenly very drunk.

I walk out the empty reception area, out the back door, and into the courtyard. Cool air dries my skin. The halls elongate. The sconces on the walls shake up and down, as if they are nodding yes in hyper speed. Or is it my blinking?

I find my room and fling myself on the bed. I'm dizzy, drunk, and dumb. Hey, they all start with a "D." I hiccup. I turn on my stomach and try to examine Rob's words, but my bed is spinning, preventing the loose strands of thoughts from knitting themselves into a cohesive pattern.

The door slams open. I lift my head to see a couple of Dumowskis stumble in. I'm not in the least bit surprised by his haloed twin, as though he were a cutout of paper folded and unfolded.

"Why you are leaving when we having such good times?" he says. He sways back and forth like an oak tree in high wind, but that, also, could be just me.

"Too tired." My words echo. But maybe I'm repeating them. He sits next to me. I close my eyes, but the merry-go-round won't stop. I feel his hand on my back. I think I murmur in approval, it feels nice. And the hand trails lower, and before I can react it's jammed between my legs.

"Uh," I manage and turn over to face him. "I don't—" His mouth comes down on mine. A wet tongue forces through my teeth. I press my hands against his shoulders and push. Nothing happens. He's made of cement. Wet, squishy cement. It's hard to breathe. He wedges his leg into my crotch so hard it hurts, and starts tearing at my scarf, his mouth still clamped on mine, his tongue thick and persistent. I'm choking in a black boiling ocean of saliva and rank body odor. He throws his legs around mine and sits up, straddling me, pinning my arms above my head. My scarf has come undone, exposing my breasts. For a moment, I have an out-of-body flash of a girl—her scarf knotted behind her neck, the sides flung out like wings—and a panting old man freeing his cock from his pants. "No, please," I whisper.

He grunts and attacks my breasts with his mouth.

"No, please," I say, louder this time. I clutch at his hair and try to pull him away.

He grabs my arms and pins them up. His face is wet with sweat, his lips hang loose, and his eyes are mean, bloodshot little slits.

I squirm, wriggle, and kick, but nothing I do has any effect whatsoever. It's like a nightmare where you try to run away but your legs weigh a thousand pounds and your feet are in quicksand. I close my eyes and go limp. Rob warned me and I didn't listen. I deserve this. Dumowski's groping and grunts suddenly seem detached and clinical. This is an ordeal I must endure, like a doctor's examination. I've led the man on. These are the consequences.

"Hey, Jirina, what the fuck—" I hear Evalinda's voice from the doorway. I twist my head and simultaneously I feel Dumowski let go of my arms.

Evalinda's eyes are wide with shock. "You, you . . ." her voice trails off in disbelief. I quickly grab my scarf to cover myself.

"You fucking bitch!" she finishes in Swedish. *"You traitor!"*

"It's not what you think," I cry. Dumowski looks uncertain, his bloodshot eyes darting from her to me and back.

"Yeah, I'm sure there's a perfectly reasonable explanation," she sneers.

Dumowski gets off me, and sits on the edge of the bed. He runs his hands through his hair.

"He just came in here, I had nothing to do with it!"

"Oh, sure. And you weren't practically fucking him on the dance floor either," she says. *"Thanks a lot for being such a good friend,"* she says over her shoulder, walking away.

Dumowski gets off the bed. "Well, the evening is late, I must go to waking up early, so if you forgive me—"

He closes the door behind him.

I curl up on the bed. What is wrong with me? I follow Grandma's advice and don't lie, don't steal, don't speak ill of others, try to help as much as I can, and what's the result? I betray my friend and make myself look like a whore, and I don't even understand how!

I go to the bathroom to breathe in blue and breathe out brown.

I miss Hugo.

IN THE VAN I sit next to Vlad. Evalinda elected to sit way in the back with Hedwig and Davide. I am tired. I feel old. So much older than yesterday. As if I had lived a hundred years without sleep. I watch the barren sands out the window. So far, not a single thing has gone right since my arrival.

Is God trying to tell me something? "Give up, you don't belong." But where do I belong? In our project apartment in Sweden with forever rainy skies, a mother and a father who don't remember my birthday and my fat friend with whom I now have nothing in common? In a place where my future possibilities extend to graduating from moron school so I can either get a job selling clothes to old ladies, or waiting tables? Where my hopes of a love life consist of meeting another freak of nature, perhaps a one-eyed baldie as opposed to a boil-ridden flathead?

I've had a taste of a better life, and though it may not want me, I still want *it*.

Out the window, red sands give way to blue-tinged mountains, which eventually shrink in favor of volatile green gardens and parks, before the land once again gets overwhelmed by sand, this time the biscuit-colored ocean sand of Agadir. I have one more day here in Morocco to prove myself as a model. But it also strikes me—regardless of how much I want to, how patient, how willing, how dedicated I am—the only attribute of any importance is the way I look. And there isn't much I can do to change that.

Agadir looks like it was erected five minutes ago, brand spanking clean and white, with nary a trace of the charm of Marrakech or the dust-ridden wildness of Ouarzazate. We pass a line of high-rise hotels on our left, where a sandy beach winks through the gaps between buildings. The effect is not tropical, nor beautiful: The beach resembles a highway littered with towels, parasols, and specks of humanity.

Our hotel is one of many lining the beach, all uniformly square and white. In my room I find a bedspread patterned with geometric browns and cat-vomit greens, a TV on a stand of pale Formica, and, in front of the window, a small desk with a chair upholstered in the bedspread pattern. A beige bathroom off the hall nook sports a plastic shower stall.

Why do people think a model's life is glamorous?

I lie down on the bedspread with Kafka. But the silence of my room brings on my paranoia of nonexistence, and by now I know what makes it better. I head back downstairs.

THERE IS A SMOKY bar adjoining the lobby. As I make my way to a table, I spot Chelsea sitting on a stool by the bar. She's pushing a half empty glass before her, staring into the bar counter. I sit next to her. "Hi, what are you doing?"

"Having a drink," she says.

"Is it a good one?"

"Not bad."

I look at her profile bent over her drink. I haven't paid much attention to Chelsea. I suddenly feel very guilty. How easy it is to pass over someone who's around to help.

Her bright pink hair shows dark roots, and I notice she has a small mole on the side of her nose. I order a piña colada and turn to her.

"How's it going?"

"How's what going?"

"You know, work, this trip—"

"Well, you've been here, haven't you?"

"Yeah, I have—but we haven't really talked . . ."

Her face is stony, her mouth drawn down at the corners. Maybe she feels lonely as well?

"It just dawned on me you are out there doing all this work, and you're barely acknowledged for all you do," I say.

She looks at me in disbelief. I smile back.

"Listen," she says. "You think I'm doing it for *you*?"

"Well, no—"

"You guys are such brats. Everything is about *you*, isn't it? Everyone waits on you hand and foot, you're beautiful and make shitloads of money just because of a lucky accident." She pushes her stool away and stands up. "Don't you fucking dare to patronize me."

She walks away.

I couldn't feel lonelier if I were shot into space.

And just as I think things can't possibly get any worse, Evalinda and Rob get out of the elevator. She's wearing incredibly high-heeled, diamond-encrusted sandals in which she seems to have some walking issues, for she keeps leaning on him for balance. Since I've single-handedly eliminated her first choice and she doesn't have any scruples about going out with a man with a wonderful girlfriend, the situation looks pretty clear, even though they are trailed by Vlad and Chelsea.

If you don't want him or he doesn't want you—watch out.

CHAPTER 21

At 5:00 A.M. it's still dark outside as I make my way to Davide's room, which is identical to mine, except for a heavy smell of sickeningly sweet aftershave trying to mask farts.

He sets up his tools on the desk by the window, where a gray dawn begins to light up the sky. He pulls the shade off his bedside lamp and pulls it over to the desk, creating an unforgiving white light with sharp shadows, which makes him look like a zombie.

An hour later I join him in the freak carnival. I've been transformed into a dead she-man with peeling gray skin, eyelids vertically striped with fuchsia, green, and yellow, and cheeks painted with purple slashes pointing to a magenta glossy mouth. He has outlined my lips smaller, and this lends my face an air of pursed bitterness. In his room down the hall, Vlad adds huge pink rollers that bob on my head like balloons. This is when I run into Rob in front of Vlad's door.

"Crikey," he says and recoils. "A bit heavy-handed, ain't it?"

"I thought so too," I begin, but Davide's voice down the hallway interrupts. "I had to load it on," he says, walking toward us. "She's peeling."

Rob scrutinizes me. "All right, but isn't the eye shadow a bit much?"

"Had to balance the color, to draw attention from her skin," Davide says moving in on us. I feel inanimate and garish, like one of those clowns painted on velvet.

The sun hovers behind wispy clouds as though it's still tired when we walk outside.

In a ghastly brown velvet gown two sizes too big, I'm led, execution style, to a flat shaded wall of the hotel where Rob has his tripod topped with a camera. Vlad takes out the rollers and brushes my hair. I feel smooth waves, not unlike Mrs. Thatcher's. I lean up against the wall, my hands holding onto the excess fabric, and wait while Chelsea loads film. In my dreams, I've posed in front of Rob and the camera countless times, seducing him though the tunnel of the lens. Now I'm here, awkward and hideous, and the look I send the camera is an apology for my existence. I already have serious doubts this will photograph well.

There is a moment of silence in which the absence of the expected click of the shutter is as comforting as being held at knifepoint. It seems Rob is waiting for something. If it's for me to become beautiful, we may be here for a while. I stick out my tongue and roll my eyes in a desperate attempt at loosening up. A click, and Rob laughs. He pulls the Polaroid out. I scrunch up my nose, letting my white mice poke out, and cross my eyes. I hear another click.

"All right, let's have a serious one now," Rob says.

I look into the lens and am overwhelmed at the thought of all the different possibilities of facial muscles. A tiny upturn of the lips for playfulness? A slight squint of the eyes for intensity? Rob presses the shutter and catches me in a moment of utter blankness.

Chelsea pulls the Polaroid out and hands it to him. "Let's see what we have here," he says, caressing the picture between his palms. For a moment I'm jealous of my own image. He peels the paper apart with a juicy, crackly sound and holds it into the sunlight to study it. Davide, Vlad, and Hedwig gather around. I hear intakes of breath and faint exclamations, none of them particularly jubilant. "Sorry darlin'," Rob says to me, waving the Polaroid in the breeze. "It's not quite working yet. Davide will have to go and fix the makeup a bit."

I'm dying of shame, but still would love to see exactly how bad I look. But Rob tears the picture apart and discards the fragments in a small garbage bag hung on the tripod.

"Evalinda?" Hedwig asks him. He nods.

Hedwig and Davide lead me back to Davide's room just as Evalinda, resplendent in a pink satin gown, walks to us. She turns her head away as we pass.

In Davide's room I endure another hour of scrubbing and reapplying, but when I look in the mirror, I look exactly the same. Back into taffeta brown, back to the wall, back to another Polaroid.

When Davide has finished my face for the third time, everyone is coming back for lunch.

Rob looks surprised. "Hasn't Davide fixed you yet?"

"This is the fixed version," I mumble. Everything is going to shit.

Rob runs his hand over his stubbled chin. "Now we have a few hours to relax," he says. "The sun's too bright. So let's have lunch and then Davide can fix this mess."

This mess that constitutes *me*. Oh, yeah, *now* I feel beautiful.

OVER LUNCH, LAST NIGHT is discussed in private code: *How about the watering can, did you know he was going to pull that out, I was on the floor, the way she flapped her hands, I thought*—of which I understand exactly nothing. Evalinda sits next to Rob; here trailing a hand over his arm, there putting her head on his shoulder. Did anything happen between them? My kingdom for a lovely Destroying Angel mushroom, I think, preferably cooked and served to Evalinda.

"Where were you, by the way?" Rob asks when the others pause for breath. "I called your room, but there was no answer."

No, because I was in the bar getting drunk on piña coladas so I could sleep. "I, um, went downstairs to get something to eat, and then I went to sleep." This is not really a lie; I did eat some peanuts. I shoot a glance at Chelsea. She knew where I was. But she ignores me. There is a small measure of comfort in knowing I would have been invited, but this is quickly replaced by a gnawing unease at Evalinda's constant winks and smiles at Rob, along with her cryptic referrals to the much admired "third leg."

BY THE TIME the rain starts, I have had my makeup put on and taken off seven times without doing a single shot. My skin is rubbed raw and prickles under the eighth attempt, but at least now the peeling flakes on my nose have been rubbed off. Davide slathers me with foundation and brushes on a little mascara when Chelsea knocks on the door and tells him not to bother continuing my makeup, since it's raining.

We all end up sitting in Vlad's room, with Evalinda sprawled across his bed changing TV channels, while rain taps on the windows. Our sociability would be wearing thin even if Evalinda deemed to speak or even to look at me. Rob didn't seem any different with her, so perhaps my poisoned mushroom was a bit hasty. We smoke cigarette after cigarette until I'm nauseous. My magenta Valentino gown strangles my waist, and I dare not sit comfortably so I don't wrinkle it.

Finally, after what seems like hours, Chelsea pokes her head in. "Rob thinks we're gonna get a last stab at this, so Jirina, let's go."

Davide springs to attention with his brushes, but Chelsea stops him. "No time, we've got to go now."

I follow her to the elevator as fast as my strappy high heels will allow me.

The beach is almost deserted but for Rob, Hedwig in a clear rain poncho, and a few die-hards on wet towels. My shoes pinch and the sequins on the bodice of the dress jab into the flesh underneath my upper arms. Rob looks at the sky anxiously. It has turned a strange shade of magenta, as if to match my dress.

The air is sticky and hot. A ray of sunshine slices through the purple clouds, saturating the air with baroque gold; the spray from the waves turns to sparks that fall into the pounding surf. It looks like a dreamscape. Or a nightmare.

"By the waterline," he shouts. "Not *in* it!"

My shoes are filling with wet sand, my arms are extraneous and overlong, and my hair keeps catching on my sticky face like flies to a fly strip. Rob is adjusting his camera while Chelsea waves the light meter around. Hedwig stands with her arms folded in her habitual Nazi stance. I feel the pressure of time, each second a reverberating drop in too small a container. My eyes feel squinty, my jaw is set like a lumberjack's, and my lips are suddenly too thin to hide my teeth. I feel them wanting to poke out like Bugs Bunny's.

I put my hands on my hips and stare at the white block of our hotel.

"No, no, don't look so stiff," Rob shouts. "Walk!"

I muster a vision of Evalinda coming out of the water and attempt to copy her hip-swinging gait. My heel gets stuck and I nearly fall over.

"Come on, darlin', we don't have much time," Rob shouts, glancing at the sky.

I take a step and stumble, my wet toes slipping painfully through the straps of the sandals. I take another and try to simultaneously compose my face into a serene expression when a gust of wind hits me and blows my hair right over my face. I toss it back. The motion makes me slightly dizzy and I wobble as I take another step.

"You're too close to the camera. I can't focus!" Rob waves his arms frantically. "Back, back!"

The golden sunlight of moments ago has turned lead gray. I trot a few steps back and turn around. It's now or never. I throw what I imagine is an alluring peekaboo glance over my shoulder. But Rob is not even looking at me. He's in a discussion with Hedwig, who wants to replace me with Evalinda. He shakes his head angrily, turning his back at her, and brings the camera to his face. "Come on, darlin', I know you can do this!"

I take a faltering step forward with a faltering smile, when I step on the hem of my dress and the corset is jerked down, revealing my breasts. I stop and yank it back. Every hot tear I've ever suppressed is fighting its way out. I swallow, sniffle, blink, but the pressure doesn't melt. The wind nudges my back, but I just stand there, arms limply by my side. Rob drops the camera away from his face. We stare at each other across the sand. Above us, the clouds swirl ominously.

Everything inside me is breaking: each tiny bone with a clink of shattered glass, the larger ones with a sonorous crack of rotted wood, muscles rip with the sharp tear of delicate fabrics, each blood vessel pops like an old light bulb, every vein bursts with the explosive gush of an open faucet. The house that was I has fallen down. The construction was a sham. It couldn't last.

Scalding tears gush from my eyes. I kick off my shoes, hold up the front on my dress, and turn to the deserted beach. My legs sprint into action before the thought even settles.

I'll run away.

Away from him. Away from it all.

My feet fly over sand, my breath is biting and fierce. The sun has gone for good, and the rain at first seems only an extension of my own misery. But the heavens open up, streaming water down my dress, my hair, my face.

Still, I run.

I gasp, I sob. I'm a dark purple blur, spun from the shattered remains of what I was. The wet squish of footsteps behind me makes me run faster.

"Jirina, Jirina, wait!" his voice follows.

"I can't do it!" I wail to the wind. I want to disappear.

"You can!" he shouts behind me.

"I'm no good!" I howl into the rain. "I can't!"

"Come on, girl, I know you can!"

He's gaining on me, I can hear his breath. "Jirina!" His hand brushes my back. The touch spurs me to run faster. I can't face him.

"I'm worthless, I'm useless," I sob. "I'm ugly!"

And suddenly his hands come down on my shoulders. I stumble. My momentum is broken. He holds on to me and forces me to face him. Time gurgles, extends like toffee, and seemingly comes to an end.

"You—" He catches his breath. "You're maddening, that's what you are." His hands dig into my upper arms.

My feet are in the surf, the water beats my legs, and the rain keeps pouring down. Here it comes. Another lecture.

"Why do you think I booked you?" he almost shouts.

I hang my head and add tears to my already wet cheeks. Well, that's obvious. *Because you had a fight with Mia and suddenly were missing a model.*

"Look at me, damnit." He shakes me, forcing me to look up. Over his shoulder, the beach is completely deserted now. Hedwig and Chelsea have obviously thrown in the towel.

"Why do you think I booked you, and have tried to book you since I first saw you?" he shouts. His hair is plastered against his face, drops of rain slide down his cheeks like tears. "Why would I stick my neck out to get you on this job?"

Because you wanted to keep Evalinda happy by booking her friend? Because you couldn't get anyone else on such short notice?

I shrug despondently.

"Because, you're bloody gorgeous, that's why."

I know he's just being kind so that I don't run off and drown myself and he won't have to call my agency with the bad news.

"I'm sorry. I've fucked everything up, haven't I?" I snivel.

"You've come pretty close."

My tears keep pouring out along with unattractive hee-hawing sobs. I put my hand on my mouth to stop them.

His eyes soften. "Come 'ere." He steps in closer and puts his arms around me.

I let it all go. Good thing his shirt is already wet. He smells of clean laundry and citrusy shampoo. After a little, I pretend I'm crying just so he keeps holding me, but I'm cold, so the shakes are not entirely false. I press myself as close as I can without actually pushing him backward. He holds me, stroking my hair. "Better?"

I pull away a little to nod and try a smile. "Yeah." All good things must end.

He smiles back. He is still holding on to my shoulders. Unexpectedly, he leans in closer to me and his expression turns very serious. "Good," he says. "'Cause I wouldn't want to be takin' advantage."

I see his black lashes with tiny drops of water beaded in like translucent pearls, I note streamers of gold in his pupils, as if the sun is hiding behind them, before I feel his lips on mine. This kiss is so different from anything I've ever experienced, I'm tempted to find it another name. But no, maybe later. It just feels too good.

AT SOME POINT, we unlock lips and lock hands to run back to the hotel. The rain is still pouring down. We're both as wet as if we had gone swimming in our clothes, but I could swear I'm hearing Rachmaninov's second piano concerto playing in the waves; gray has never come in so many lustrous shades. My feet are barely touching the platinum sand, the waves are crested with silver and diamonds, and the hotels lining the beach glint like mother-of-pearl. We run past the lobby to the elevators. He doesn't let go of my hand. Once the elevator doors close behind us, he presses up against me, all hard angles, warmth, and wetness, and we kiss past my floor. We kiss all the way to his room. My thoughts have all been washed away and replaced by a burning desire to drink him in, to inhale him, to suck him in so he's all mine. He stops kissing me to open his door, and suddenly a hesitation creeps over his eyes. "Do you—would you like to come in?" he says. I don't bother answering, just step over the threshold.

We fall against the wall, his hands everywhere, his mouth, my mouth, I lose sense of where I stop and he begins. There are buttons to unbutton, zippers to unzip, and in a flurry of wet magenta satin and scratchy beads, he pulls my underwear aside and pushes into me.

This is what my body was made for.

He clutches my hair with both hands and pins me to the wall. He is pressed against me, in me, filling the hunger, quenching the thirst. I clutch at his back, his neck, his hair, closer, more, deeper. Suddenly he gasps, his eyelids flicker like butterfly wings, he buries his face in my neck and stops moving.

"Sorry, darlin'," he whispers.

Sorry about what? A chill washes over me. What did I do wrong? Is he sorry about this? I stand against the wall, my pulse beating wildly in my brain. This is not the right ending!

He caresses my cheek. "Now, let me get this right," he whispers.

The rain continues to beat the windows of his darkened room. We fall onto the bed, leaving our clothes behind in a trail like sodden crumbs. His mouth becomes the conductor of sweet heat, his fingers electrical conduits. Everywhere he touches, licks, and kisses ignites a flurry of high voltage sparks that bathe me in flames. He parts my legs. His tawny hair dipping down between my thighs is a jolt; at first embarrassing—then revelatory. I want it to never end. He stops. Slowly, he kisses his way up to my breasts, and up to my lips. He tastes of me, slippery. I push him down. It's my turn.

I take him in my mouth and marvel at the warm silky skin. I'm not exactly sure how to do this, what to do. Tentatively, I let my tongue circle the head. He sighs. I form my mouth around it and suck while my tongue flickers across the ridge underneath. He breathes, "stop." Before I can think I'm doing it all wrong, he says, "too good." I feel like I won a contest. I have the ability to make him feel good. What power! He pulls me up on top. I straddle him, guiding him in, sinking down, way down until I'm all filled up.

"Beautiful, beautiful girl," he says, half whisper, half exclamation. His face is taut with concentration, his teeth bared almost as though he's in pain.

Each movement is exquisite torture, until I tremble and burn, my breath speeds, my heart speeds—I am at the brink of something indescribable—and then he grabs my hips and pushes in hard. My body spasms in happiness. I moan. Oh, wow. What's this? Almost simultaneously, he shudders, his body arches, and he cries out.

For the first time in my life reality beats fantasy.

I roll off, and nestle next to him.

This is sex. Nothing like the clammy rushing with Simon. Nothing like the sweaty wrestling with Hugo. Instead, it's the satisfaction of two bodies fitting like final pieces of a jigsaw puzzle for a perfect picture. This is why Anna Karenina left her child, why Emma Bovary kept looking, why Connie Chatterley risked her position and comfortable life, why Britta wanted to die, why I betrayed Emanuel and Mia. And it's all worth it.

We lie so close I can barely make him out. I draw away to look at him, to savor every detail of his face: the way his skin shines on his high cheekbones, the slight, elegant flare of his nostrils, the thin upper lip that doesn't quite hide his teeth, the slight indent in his chin. My grandma used to say, "God drew in the blessed one," and she'd pull me to her with her fingers on my cheeks, creating dimples. "And pushed away the unwanted one," and she'd place a finger on my chin to push me away. She was wrong. There is nothing as beautiful as a cleft chin. The skin around his eyes is slightly lighter, from sunglasses I guess, and there are a few faint lines around them and at the corners of his mouth. He may be older than I thought. Thirty? I flash on all the women he must have made love to, that he made feel this good, that made *him* feel this good, and I seethe with jealousy.

"Tell me something about you I don't know," I whisper.

"Well, darlin', there's much ground to cover." He smiles.

"Tell me a secret."

"All right, how about: I've been lusting after you from the moment I met you, at that party at Jean-Pierre's. Remember?"

"Really?"

"I was about to go up to you, and you disappeared!"

I smile uncertainly. Oh God, please, let him not have heard about the bidet.

"Very Cinderella of ya'." He smiles. "But I was at a disadvantage, I didn't have your shoe. So I had to call for go-and-sees and endure a hundred ugly stepsisters."

"Really?" I say again, flushing with pleasure. "Entirely premeditated," I add after a moment. "Had to keep the mystique, you know."

"Aah, yeh, the mystique."

"What would you have done, if I hadn't disappeared?"

"I would have come up to you and said, 'Hello, lovely lady, fancy a roll in the hay'?"

"Hmm, maybe it's a good thing I left."

He laughs. "Oh, come now, I've worked on that line for years!"

Jealousy bites me again. "Tell me another secret."

"Another? Christ, you're demanding! Okay, how about"—he inhales and whispers something into my neck. It's too muffled to make out.

"What?"

"I said, I like—sometimes I listen to—ABBA." His face is contorted into a goofy expression of shame.

"You're kidding, right?" I laugh.

"I don't really listen to them all that much, only—" he backpedals.

"I love ABBA," I cut in. "I'm Swedish, remember? They are God back home."

He laughs. "Good for me. Now, your turn. Trade."

I pause. My entire life seems made out of secrets. Where would I even begin?

"I—well, when you held me on the beach? Toward the end, I wasn't really crying. I just didn't want you to let go."

He cups my cheek. "That wasn't a secret, my darlin'."

I WAKE BEFORE HIM and scurry to the bathroom to pee and assure myself of fresh breath. The mascara has smudged a bit under my eyes, and my lips are bruised, but it lends me a sort of sexy, rumpled, morning-after glow. I creep back into bed and snuggle next to my lover. My lover. I regurgitate the word for impact. Lover. Mine. I let my eyes run over him and I shiver with pleasure. Mine, all mine. The long muscular back tapering off into a slim waist, arms tucked under his pillow, the heat of him, the feel of him. The sunlight warms my back and I stretch, feeling my body like a new set of clothes. He opens his eyes and stares at me.

"You're lovely, you know that?"

I get ready to fall back into his embrace, when his look changes from the morning contentment to a sort of clinical inspection. His eyes narrow. "Put your dress back on," he says and jumps up. "I've got to get this."

We run to the beach together, him with his camera and me carrying my shoes in my stained and wrinkled ball gown.

The air is still fresh but already warm. The beach is still nearly empty; it can't be more than six in the morning.

"Over here." Rob points to a spot in the sand. "Sit down, just like you did on the bed."

I sit with my knees drawn up, feeling just a tiny bit like an obedient dog.

He gets on his knees and brings the camera to his face. No time for a tripod, or a light meter. He's only wearing his jeans, and the bareness of his torso reminds me of its feel. I smile.

"Perfect. Hold that! Don't move," he says, and starts shooting away. The lens is an open door between the two of us; all else fades into unimportant shadows. My heart, my brain, my soul flow into my eyes and pour out like laser beams. A warm breeze catches my hair and I tilt my face and part my lips like it is his breath.

"Gorgeous. Beautiful." He circles me, intent and focused: a predator eyeing its prey. And I'm delighted to be the prey. "Brilliant. Done." He stands and brushes himself off, pulls me to my feet, and kisses me.

Back in his room, we take a shower, repeating last night's lovemaking while standing up. Afterward, he orders breakfast, which we eat at the desk in front of the window. I've borrowed his shirt; he's wrapped a towel around his waist. He reaches over the table and caresses my cheek. "Did I mention how beautiful you are?"

"A couple of times." I blush. *And I still don't believe you.* I spread a croissant with butter and jam and take a huge bite. He sips his coffee and watches me with a smile. I grow uncomfortable. "Now what?" I blurt. I mean it only in the sense of getting dressed and going to the airport, but as soon as the words hit the air, they take on an all-encompassing meaning.

"Now we are done, and off to the airport," he says, intentionally misunderstanding me, I think. A tiny chip of fear lodges in my chest.

"I mean, once we are back in Paris," I whisper. "What should—" I hesitate to find the right words. "What should I—tell my boyfriend?" Oh God, I've just repeated Simon's words.

Rob put his cup down. "What should you tell your boyfriend," he reiterates. His eyes dart out the window, onto the remains of our breakfast and back at me. But he doesn't look me in the eye. "You don't have to tell him anything," he says. "I won't tattletale."

The floor opens beneath me. I'm falling into darkness. But in some twisted way I've been waiting for something like this to happen. I've been perched on the edge, deliriously happy for what—eight, ten hours? Time to take it all away, isn't it? A little push is all it takes to go from ecstasy to despair.

"Uh-huh," I squeeze out through a locked throat. I bend down to retrieve my dress and shoes from the floor along with a few shards of my dignity. "Okay, thanks." I straighten up, arms filled with fabric. He's stubbornly looking out the window.

"So, bye," I say, desperately fighting with my voice to stay level. "And don't worry about Mia, I won't tattletale either."

He turns from the window. "Mia? Why should I—" Suddenly his face clears and he jumps out of the chair. "Mia? Is this about Mia?"

I turn to the door, but have trouble opening it with my hands full. He comes up from behind, and puts his arm on the door.

"Darlin', I thought you knew. Mia hasn't been my girlfriend for a long time."

I WONDER WHETHER IT'S possible to die from happiness as I throw my belongings into my bag. My room, my pretty room that looks just like Rob's, is clear of my stuff, and I throw a last, wistful glance around. I hadn't noticed before, but the geometric patterns on the bed, the color of chocolate and olives, are positively edible. Mia. Darling Mia. Her staying behind in Marrakech had nothing to do with a lover's quarrel; rather, she got into a huge fight with Hedwig on the first night and told her to go fuck herself. Rob took this as an opportunity to bring me on the trip with Mia's blessing. They live together, but as friends only: Mia is dating a doctor from the American clinic in Paris.

I brush my teeth, throw my bag over my shoulder, and run upstairs to Rob's room for a few more precious moments alone with him. Between kisses and packing, I try to feel out how we should proceed when faced with the rest of the crew.

"Is there anything you're ashamed of?" Rob says, cramming a bulky sweater into his suitcase.

"Of course not."

"Then"— he grins—"what's the big secret?"

I laugh. We are together. No secrets. No girlfriends. No shame. Could it get any better?

Hugo pops in like an unwanted photo in a slide show. I will have to speak to him when we get back, but for now, my future plans all rest in Rob's arms.

EVERYONE IS ALREADY in the van when we exit the lobby holding hands. Rob loads my bag into the back while I climb in and take my usual seat next to Evalinda. She lifts her eyebrows at Davide in the back. I've obviously interrupted a conversation, probably about me, and I couldn't care less. She presses herself up to the window, as far away from me as possible. And that's fine with me. Except, I probably have no place to sleep tonight.

The airport at Agadir is crowded with French vacationers returning home with freshly baked tans, and new arrivals the color of raw cookie dough. I float through departures with Rob's hand sometimes caressing my back, sometimes holding my hand, and quick stolen kisses when we are a few steps away from the crew. Rob traded his first-class ticket with Evalinda, who will now have the pleasure of Hedwig's company.

Flying has never felt like flying before. I always thought of it as sitting in an empty soda can thrown through the air. But now, the roar of the engines, the screech of the wheels on cement, the acceleration that pushes you into your seat, and that first moment of weightlessness when the nose tilts up feels as exhilarating as if I myself am running down the runway, jumping up, and flying into air. For the first time in my life, I have no wish to inhabit the body of someone else. Being me is the best thing imaginable. "I can't believe you even noticed me at the party," I say. Our fingers are intertwined on my thigh.

"Came home and told Mia I was in trouble."

"Why trouble?"

" 'Cause I saw a girl I couldn't forget." He gives me a smile that melts my bones, but then releases his hand from mine and pinches my chin. "Don't look so pleased, I almost changed my mind. That party at Michel's. You were insane. And this trip—I didn't know what to make out of you. On one hand, you are sophisticated and funny, on the other, you're a bit of a wild child."

I know he doesn't mean it as a compliment, but I can't help but to take it as one. Me, Jirina, boring hot chicken—a wild child?

"And wild children aren't really my thing," he says. "I like women."

I wonder how to mature within the shortest possible time.

"Did Mia really tell Hedwig to fuck herself?" I say quickly.

"She sure did. With those exact words." He laughs. "Mia doesn't give a shit about modeling anymore. She's gotten what she wanted out of it. In Marrakech Hedwig got on her about something or other, and Mia, being Mia, told her the truth as she saw it. Plus, she figured, her ticket was already paid for, so she would take the opportunity to visit orphanages and hospitals."

"Why did you guys split up?" I ask. "From the little I know of her, she seems like the most perfect woman in the world." Please say she isn't. Please contradict me.

"Oh, she is, she is," he says, and unwittingly stabs me. "In fact, you two are somehow similar." I know this is probably the best compliment I've ever gotten, yet it stings.

"But honestly, we were more like friends from the very start. The chemistry—you know, the heat—wasn't quite there. Not like this," he says, and leans over to kiss me. We continue kissing until the stewardess interrupts us with drinks. Rob gets a Coke and so do I, although I'd rather have plain water.

"Tell me about your family," I say. "Got any siblings?"

He reclines and takes my hand again, tracing his fingers over mine while he tells me about three older sisters and his mother who reared them by herself after his father left them. "I grew up in a house filled with women," he chuckles. "And I was the baby. So you can imagine, it wasn't roughing it—for me at least."

"Are any of your sisters married?"

"Yeh. Two of 'em."

"Any kids?"

"Let's see. My oldest sister, Andie, has two boys, I think, and the middle one, Cassie, has one."

"Do you ever get to see them?"

"When I go back home. But I've got to admit, kids aren't my thing. Noisy little baaastards."

My image of Rob wrestling with his nephews takes a beating. But then, a lot of men feel this way about kids that aren't their own, don't they?

"Are they all still in Australia?"

"Yeh. Back in Sydney. It's a great life, you know. You've got the beach within ten minutes of anywhere. You wake up in the morning, throw on your wet suit, and hit the waves before breakfast."

"You swim in wetsuits?"

"Surfin', mate. The Ozzie national pastime. Besides cricket, that is."

"What's that?"

"Cricket? You're joking, right?"

I give him a sheepish smile.

"Cricket, my darlin'," he says with an exasperated shake of the head, "the best bloody sport on the planet," and goes into a complicated explanation of guys with bats and balls. I listen and nod in a most mature manner.

THE LINE FOR PASSPORT checks is as long as a communist queue for a banana. About a thousand Japanese must have just gotten off a plane right before us.

Evalinda flicks through the pages of her passport, looking bored and pissed off. "Shit," she hisses, glancing at the line, "this sucks."

Hedwig seems tired, and Davide pelts her with questions about some upcoming shoot, which she answers in monosyllables while she fans herself with her passport. Vlad stands behind Rob and me, tapping his leg. "I need a cigarette," he mumbles.

Rob puts his arms around me from behind and I lean into him. I'm perfectly content.

Suddenly, I see Evalinda smiling across Hedwig's head. This shift in her mood is so abrupt, it's almost a little frightening.

"Hey, who's got the worst-looking passport picture?" she exclaims. "Let me see yours." She snatches Hedwig's from her hands. "Oh, you look great, look at those fab earrings." Hedwig looks pleased. Evalinda hands Hedwig's passport to Davide, who admires it, and presses closer to us. "I'll show you mine if you show me yours, Robbie-doo."

Rob hands her his passport somewhat unwillingly. "It's an old picture, mate," he laughs.

"Oh my God, Jirina, look at your boyfriend here!" Evalinda squeals with glee and holds up Rob's picture page. His hair is short and dark and he sports serious sideburns. Sort of like my father.

I laugh. "It doesn't even look like you!"

I quickly scan to his birthday. *December 7, 1948*. He is—thirty-two! Oh my God. He's older than I thought. Only a year younger than my mother! Inwardly, I shiver with pleasure at the thought. A man. My man.

Meanwhile, Evalinda has pulled my passport from my handbag. "Now, here's a picture," she laughs loudly. "Look at this one everyone!"

The black and white photo of me at eleven, with two tight braids and a gap toothed smile stares back at me. Rob grabs the passport. He studies the page intently. He has gone white; his skin is ashen even with the tan.

"Jesus fuckin' Christ," he whispers. He looks sick. "You're *fifteen*."

CHAPTER 22

"**I** had no idea you were fifteen," Evalinda says in the taxi on the way back to the apartment. "I thought you were seventeen, at least."

Every muscle in my body is coiled and stiff with hatred.

"I mean, how was I to know?" She rummages through her purse and pulls out a lip gloss. "There are no other girls here, unsupervised, younger than sixteen." She dabs on the gloss while continuing to speak with her mouth stiff like a ventriloquist, and her tone is easy, convivial. "Elite has this fourteen-year-old from America, but she has her mother with her, dragging her along on every go-and-see. And this girl looks like a total baby, especially without makeup." She screws the top on and drops it back in her purse. "You don't look fifteen or act fifteen, so I don't know what Rob's big problem is. Poor ol' Robbie. He probably thinks the French give a damn about statutory rape." She giggles. *Giggles*.

At that moment, the taxi stops before her building. Good thing; another minute in that cab, and I could become a bona fide criminal.

I PACK UP MY STUFF. Fortunately there isn't much, the only thing I've bought is my Napoleon jacket, which I still can't find.

"You know, you don't have to move out today," Evalinda says casually from the couch where she's reading a magazine. "It's Sunday after all. If you wait until tomorrow, the agency will find you a room in an apartment. And anyway, you can stay here as long as you want, really."

"I've already outstayed my welcome, I'll be fine," I force through clenched teeth. I throw in my bottle of baby oil and zip up my bag. "Thanks so much for letting me stay." I hoist the bag on my shoulder and head for the door.

"Look," she says, flinging her magazine down and standing up. She walks toward me and puts her hands on my shoulders. "I know you're probably mad at me right now, but I did you a favor." Were her eyes always this small and round? Without mascara to define them, they look shiny and piglike. I stifle the urge to strike out: kick her, punch her, claw at her hair.

"I mean, not that I knew it but—listen, he would have found out sooner or later—and then what?"

Then he would have been madly, wildly in love with me and my age wouldn't have mattered! But in a tiny corner of my heart, I have to concede she may have a point.

"Thanks a lot for being such a good friend," I say.

She smiles and hugs me. "You sure you don't want to stay?"

Once again, my sarcasm flies right over her head.

I'M STRUGGLING WITH MY bag at the curb, trying to figure out whether to hail a taxi or take the Metro to the bordello hotel, the only address I know, when a helping hand settles on my bag. Hugo. I've completely forgotten our date. And I've never been more happy, or more sad, to see him.

He's dressed up in a black suit with a skinny black tie and a red shirt, which does exactly nothing for him. He looks clean and awkward.

"What is happening, where are you going?" he asks, picking up my bag.

I tell him the name of the hotel, and the street I think it's on, and we get into his car.

He stays silent during my somewhat shortened explanation of why I had to leave. "She was pissed because a guy she liked on the trip went after me," I say. Hugo shoots me a glance.

"He was *really* old," I say quickly.

Hugo nods and steps hard on the gas pedal. After a few stomach-clenching turns, he finally says, "I am sorry I cannot offer you a place to stay, but I live with my father still."

"No, don't worry, I'll be fine," I assure him. But I know I'm far from fine. Wrecked, destroyed, and bleeding is more like it.

At the hotel, I remember I have no money, and that leaves Hugo to find his wallet. "This is a loan," I reiterate. "I will pay you back tomorrow." Hugo helps me check into my room and carries my bag in. "I do not suppose you want to go to dinner anymore," he says with a dejected little shrug.

"Not really. I'm so sorry."

"Perhaps, you want to take a bath and relax for a moment, and I will bring food to the room?"

"That would be great."

I look around my new accommodations. This room looks a lot like the one I had the first time, complete with the mirror above the bed. The bathroom is well used and not often cleaned. I wipe the tub out with toilet paper, fill it, and get in. The slight stinging of the warm water between my legs is the saddest reminder, a physical mark of my love that's, once again, unrequited.

Just three hours and twenty-four minutes ago, I was holding my dream, solid and tangible in the shape of Rob. Now all I have left are sharp, piercing fragments: the way Rob looked when he said "fifteen"; the way he avoided my hand when it tried to creep back into his; the way he wouldn't meet my eyes in the line for a taxi, when he told me he'd better get back home since he had to leave Paris in the morning. "I'll call you when I get back," he said.

I know better.

I let my tears flow and allow myself a complete, undisturbed bath of self-pity. It seems I'm broken somehow, like a mechanical toy that looks fine until you wind it up, and instead of jumping or walking, or doing whatever it is supposed to do, it spins in a helpless, sputtering circle. The people drawn to me—Hatty, Britta, Evalinda, Dumowski—are the ones who sense my brokenness, because they themselves are also broken. The normal ones eventually notice the toy doesn't work and lose interest. Like my parents. Like Rob.

A gentle knock brings me back to cooling bathwater. "Gigi, are you all right?" I hear Hugo's voice behind the door.

Like Hugo. I sit up in the bath. Hugo. Hugo will be the next to find out he spent his money on a factory mistake. Damaged goods. And then what will I do?

"Yes, I'm fine, I'll be out in a sec," I shout. I towel off and get dressed. When I exit the bathroom, Hugo has set up a feast on the bed, complete with wine, fruit, and cheese. He had taken his jacket off and opened his shirt collar. "Hungry?"

I accept a plastic glass of wine and gulp it down in one go. And then I hold it out for some more.

I STILL MARVEL how easy it was; I simply called Anne and she gave me the address of an apartment that had an available room. I could have done this weeks ago and saved myself a lot of trouble, not to mention money. Why didn't anyone tell me? But then, I never asked.

I take the Metro to my new home. Giant movie posters are hung next to ads on the white-tiled walls: *Mad Max*, *Airplane!*, *The Deerhunter*, starring Robert de Niro. Robert. Rob. The letters hurt. I look away. Any words featuring those letters are agony, even ones like "robot," "robin," "robber." Every time I glimpse even the slightest shimmer of sun-bleached hair, whether on a woman or a man, my heart drops a beat. I can't shake the feeling each time the subway doors open that Rob may be one of the incoming passengers; my subsequent disappointment is completely illogical but unavoidable.

My new apartment is in the standard Parisian building: a town house of gray stone, six floors high. It sits in the middle of a tiny narrow street on the Left Bank, only a five-minute walk from the river. A glass fright of a tower—the University of Jussieu—lords over the quiet and slightly worn neighborhood. I can barely squeeze myself and my duffel into the elevator, which wheezes and trembles as if it had asthma. On the fifth floor I have the choice of two doors, one on the left and one on the right. I take my chances on the left one with a taped red heart above the peephole, and ring the bell.

After a few beats, I hear footsteps, and the door opens to a fine-boned girl with the delicate skin of a porcelain doll and slanted almond eyes. She's dressed in a bloodred silk kimono and her black hair hangs almost to her waist. Behind her is a long narrow hallway.

"Yes?" she says.

"Hi. I'm Jirina."

"Yes?"

"Anne told me there was a vacancy? For a roommate?"

"Yes." She nods but looks no friendlier. She steps aside to let me enter. I wonder if her vocabulary extends past "yes." We walk down the long hallway, past a door that leads to a bathroom, and then to three doors, all closed. The girl points to the first one. "You. Yes," she says and turns left to open the door to her room. I open mine to a small square space painted off-white, with a floor-to-ceiling window and a mattress on the floor. I set my duffel down. There is absolutely nothing else in here. No closet. No sheets on the bed. Nothing but a nice view of the street. And a phone. I sit on the mattress.

I've been in Paris for two months now, have experienced things I could have only imagined in my wildest dreams: I've lost my virginity, fallen in love, made and lost friends, tried alcohol and drugs, worked with famous photographers and magazines, earned thousands of francs . . . and all I have to show for it is a broken heart and this room with a bare mattress. I might as well have dreamed it all from the safety of my bunk bed at home. A plastic beige phone in the corner of the room reminds me I haven't called Mother or Hatty in two weeks. I pick up the receiver.

"Hatty? It's me."

"Hi." She doesn't sound happy to hear me.

"Sorry I haven't called, but things got kind of crazy."

"Hmm."

"Do you have the time to chat?"

"I guess."

I draw a deep breath and tell her about the disaster on Avenue Niel, living with Evalinda, my trip to Morocco, my affair with Rob—everything.

"Oh my," she says when I'm done.

"Yeah, right?" I laugh bitterly. But I already feel a little better. Now that she knows everything, we can pick up where we left off; we can hash and rehash the little details like we always do.

"Yeah, right," she murmurs. She pauses, and then her voice changes to her habitual chatty tone. "Oh, guess what? I met Kristel at the Hamburger Joint in Town Square the other day, and she walked right past me like she didn't even see me. The bitch. So I walked up to her and said, 'Hi, Kristel, what line did you get into?' She totally tried to avoid me, but I had her pinned against the counter, so she had to respond. And guess what she said?"

I don't know, but more importantly, I don't care! What Kristel did and did not do at the Hamburger Joint is no more relevant to me than a report of bad weather over Japan. Did Hatty hear anything I said?

"She's going to economy! So I guess you'll have the pleasure of being in class with her again," Hatty says.

It takes me a moment to register what she just said.

"Um. Hatty, the thing is, I'm not sure I'll be coming back." A heavy silence falls on the other end.

"You're serious?"

"Well, I don't want to come back."

"But it doesn't sound like—well, like you're doing that well."

This is unfortunately true.

"I just started. I'm not doing that bad for just starting out," I defend. "And guess what—I have some good news for you." I tell her about Emanuel and his offer to make her his makeup assistant for the shows.

I imagine her lack of words as happy shock.

"I see," she says finally. I hear her take a deep breath, as if in preparation for a dive.

"Well?"

She exhales. "Um, I don't think September will work for me."

"What?" Hatty didn't even apply to a line, she says she wanted to further her makeup skills, and no line could teach her that.

She clears her throat. "I've had really bad asthma attacks lately, and I can't really leave my mom all alone, the poor thing. What would she do without me?" She plunges into more reasons why she couldn't possibly come, especially not in September, but I stop listening. I understand now. She never had any intentions of coming. Our plans were no more real than our girlish dreams of marrying two brothers and all living together in a castle with pink four-poster beds.

Now it's my turn to remain silent. I don't know what to say; what *is* there to be said?

"Jirina? You there?"

"Yeah."

"Don't be mad."

"I'm not." It's true; anger doesn't describe my feelings right now. It's more of a wistful, lingering sorrow. The grief of broken dreams.

"Hatty, take care. And thanks for listening."

"Yeah. You take care too. And call again."

But we both know the gulf is too wide and there are no bridges, no boats.

HUGO COMES LOADED DOWN with two bags full of silky monogrammed sheets, two pillows and four towels. After we make my bed, he takes me to a tiny, unmarked restaurant that looks like someone's living room. On the far end, a fire burns merrily in a stone stove, where an old lady pokes at the coal under grilling meat. Two long tables and benches line the walls; a poodle snoozes on a worn carpet. We take a seat, and the old lady abandons her fire to tell us what we can eat today. Steak and frites. Hugo also orders red wine. Sweet, sweet Hugo. Last night I got dead drunk and passed out on him, only to find a clean, aired-out room and a glass of orange juice on the nightstand when I woke up.

"Gigi, I was wondering, well, in a few days I will go home to the Loire, to see my family and also for fun—I do a car race every year—and I was thinking perhaps you would do me the great pleasure of accompaniment for me."

"You would like me to go with you?"

"Yes. In not so many words." He laughs. The old lady slams our plates before us with a frown.

"She doesn't seem to like us very much," I say to Hugo.

He smiles. "Ah, non, this is the trademark of this restaurant. You come for great steak and very bad service. It is . . . like a joke."

"Hmm, funny."

"You avoid the answer."

"Hugo, I don't know. I mean, thank you so much for the invitation, but I don't know—what if a trip comes up again?" Silently, I congratulate myself for the perfect excuse.

"Then I will go alone. You do not have to promise, only consider."

"I'll think about it." I know I won't, not really. How could I meet Hugo's family? Someone is bound to see through me, see that I'm using their son, maybe even tell him. No, going is unthinkable.

After dinner, we walk out into a velvet night. Windows of small crooked cottages glow with firelight gold, casting quick elongated shadows of the two of us on cobblestones as we walk up the hill to Sacré Coeur. Tonight, the steps are filled with people lounging, sitting, kissing, and chatting in a multilingual murmur to a background of acoustic guitars and bongo drums. We walk down a few steps to find an empty spot below a young guy who strums his guitar and sings Spanish love songs in a sweet, Paul McCartney–ish voice. Paris spills out at our feet like the glittering contents of a treasure chest under a sapphire sky.

"They will like you, you know," Hugo says.

I need to buy some time. "Who?"

"My family. My father, my grandparents—my stepmother maybe not so much," he laughs. "She is jealous of beauty, but I am not so fond of her."

I quickly jump on my opportunity to veer off track. "When did your father get remarried?"

"Many years ago now, three years after my mother passed out."

This is the worst possible time to laugh. "Passed away?" I say tightly.

"Ah oui, passed away."

"Why do you not like your stepmother?"

"I do not think even my father likes her so much. She was beautiful; my father, I think, purchased her as an award."

"Trophy?"

"Yes. She likes the shopping, the money. My father has another woman, a mistress, for the love."

"That's fucked up."

"Yes, but it is his life. He likes it so. But again, you are avoiding the subject."

"No, I'm not. You've never told me about your family, but you want me to meet them. Shouldn't I know something about them before I do?"

"So you will come."

"I didn't say that."

"Mais oui, you did." He grins and throws his arm around my shoulder, pulling me close.

"Hugo," I say, exasperated and at a loss for words. He leans in and kisses me. I kiss him back with urgency. Be gone, Rob, be gone. These lips, this tongue, were familiar before Rob's. So why does it feel so awkward?

He drives me back home. He cuts the engine and we sit in silence. The decision has been brewing away inside me, and I know I have to do it. Now. Before I change my mind.

"Hugo, do you know how old I am?" My words fall out and lay in my lap, smothering me under their weight.

"Mais oui."

And they sink as easily as if my lap were water.

"Evalinda told me long time ago."

She did? The traitorous fucking bitch. I knew it! And now my trump hand is empty.

"And this doesn't scare you?" I whisper.

"Non. You are you, it doesn't matter what age."

What I wouldn't give to hear these same words from different lips. Except I have nothing to give, nothing with which to bargain.

Nothing but Hugo.

"Come on, let's try out your sheets," I say.

CHAPTER 23

I close the front door behind Hugo in the morning. On my way back to my room, I notice the door next to mine is open. A girl with very short hair the color of eggplant sits on a twin bed wearing a pair of boy's boxer briefs and nothing else. Her chest is a flat as a child's. She's painting her toenails black and looks up as I pass.

"Hey there." She nods in greeting. "You new?"

I nod.

"Come on in." She waves. Her room is a mess of clothes, food wrappers, and empty beer bottles that do double duty as ashtrays. "Sit down." She pats the bed. I sit on top of lumps created by blankets, clothing, and a bottle, which I withdraw from under my butt.

"The name's Angie. You?" she says, continuing to paint her left foot.

"Jirina."

"Russian?"

"Swedish."

"That doesn't sound very Swedish."

I sigh. "Yeah, I know."

Her eyes, light brown with speckles of green, meet mine for a second of closer inspection. "I take it you hear that a lot." Her accent is slow and lazy, as if she is chewing gum. American, I decide.

"Uh-huh." I haven't the heart to start building a new friendship.

She shrugs and goes back to painting her nails. "When'd you get here?"

"The day before yesterday. The Asian girl let me in."

"Oh, Shit-su," she says and wrinkles her nose.

"Shit-su?" Now here's a name that's even worse than mine.

"Her name is Shizuka, but I call her Shit-su to get a reaction, you know," Angie laughs. "I mean, something other than 'yes.' "

"Any luck?"

"Nah. I don't think she knows any other words in English. Who was the hot guy in the bathroom this morning? Your boyfriend?"

I blush. "A friend."

I watch her as she laboriously paints her little toe, her tongue sticking out. With a freckled stubby nose, small eyes, and large full lips, her face verges on the homely. Her ears stick out. She's not really Hugo's type.

"How long have you been in Paris?" she says.

"Two months. You?"

"Three months and counting. I started in New York, but they told me I needed tear sheets and they are much easier to get in Europe. The States is where the big money is, so all the new girls get farmed out to Europe." She considers her toenails for a moment. "So I did my time in Milan, and boy, let me tell ya, that sucked. Three months of those Italian modelfuckers and their bullshit. And I gained like ten pounds. At least here, in Paris, the food sucks so I'm not tempted." She pulls out a bottle of beer from under her pillow and uncaps it on the bed frame. "Want some?"

"Uh, it's kinda early."

"Got a wicked hangover. Hair of the beast, you know—"

I nod to show my sympathy. It must be a bad one if she feels like a beast.

ANNE GIVES ME MY addresses over the phone for today's appointments. "This last go-and-see is very important," she says. "It is for very much money, so go in looking your best. Perhaps you could wear a miniskirt, to show off your pretty legs?"

Of course, I don't have one, but Angie pulls out a red satin dress from Shit-su's closet.

"Here, borrow hers."

"Shouldn't I ask her first if it's okay?"

"Oh, please, she takes shit out of my closet all the time without asking. Plus, we don't know when she'll be back."

The dress fits perfectly. There is something to be said for sharing an apartment with girls who are all the same dress size.

THE VERY IMPORTANT GO-AND-SEE is held in a conference room with glass walls overlooking Paris. A large black oval table lords over the middle of the room, and six people sit on one side, their backs to the view, their eyes on me. It's not that I'm no longer scared, I still am. I still want them to like me—this is, after all, a very important meeting—although Anne never said whom it's for. "Very secret," she said. "Hush, hush." But the nice dress makes me feel a little less like me, Jirina, and a little more someone else. But whom exactly, I'm not sure. Maybe just new and improved. The clients pass my portfolio around, point to it, point to me. "Thank you," a woman with tightly pulled-back springy hair says. I turn to walk out the door and stop. Before me, the wall is covered with posters of Evalinda, each pose more seductive than the next. Evalinda atop a horse, hair and mane blowing. Evalinda naked, stretched out on her stomach on a sandy beach. Evalinda in a black evening gown, descending a marble staircase. Evalinda, in a see-through tunic, walking through a jungle of greens, trailed by a tiger. On top of each poster are the same words: *La Grande Passion*.

ON THE WAY BACK to the apartment, I stop and buy yogurts, milk, coffee, some cheese, and bread. I put everything into our empty fridge in the tiny, dark kitchen. *La Grande Passion*. No sense in even thinking about it. Even if they are looking for a new girl, it certainly won't be me. I go to my room and pick up the phone to call Mother. She sounds tired and cranky; I'm instantly happy to be so far away from her. Were I home, this would be one of those evenings when I'd have to duck my shadow in fear of her temper.

"Hi. Sorry I haven't called earlier but I was away, on this trip—"

"You could have found a phone," my mother says.

"I was in Morocco, you see, working for *Vogue*, and it was really hard to get to a phone."

"Will you stop hanging on the goddamn fridge door?" she shouts. I hear Kristynka whining in the background. "But I'm hungry."

"Then get something to eat," my mother snaps and turns her voice to me. "We just got back—goddamnit, Kristynka!" I hear the drop of the receiver on the table, angry footsteps, and then Kristynka howling in dismay. "The bottle was too heavy. I couldn't help it."

My mother returns to the phone, slightly out of breath.

"So, you were saying?"

"I was away. On a trip."

"So? You could have called collect, or found a post office."

"Well, it doesn't really work like that, you see, I have to work all day and then—"

"What did I say to you about hanging on the fridge doors!" she yells. Back into the receiver she says: "Don't tell me there are no phones in Morocco."

"Well, yes, there was one phone in the lobby of the hotel, but it was constantly occupied, and—" How do I explain my working day to Mother? Or anyone, for that matter?

"I'm sure if you wanted to, you could have found a phone."

I give up trying. "Yeah, whatever. But now I'm in a new apartment, so it'll be easier to call."

"How come you're in a new apartment? What about the living arrangements with that nice man, what was his name, Jean-something?"

"Yeah, well—" Another thing I can hardly explain to Mother. "That didn't work out so well, and anyway, this is a very nice apartment with two other girls."

"Who are they?"

I describe Angie and Shizuka.

"Hmm, I don't know them," she says.

I restrain myself from snapping. "Of course you don't." Can't she ask me something that makes sense? "Can I speak to Kristynka?" I say quickly.

"Okay, but hurry, it's her bedtime."

"But it's only seven. Isn't it a bit early for bed?" I say.

"Don't get started on me," Mother hisses. "I know how to take care of my child."

Yeah. *Right.*

I hear a rustle and then Kristynka's little voice. "Hello Eena, I spilled the milk and Mommy hit me."

"If I were there, I'd clean it up and nasty old Mom wouldn't even know."

"I miss you." She sighs. This is what I wanted to hear. "When are you coming back?"

Never if I can help it. "Uh, I'm not sure. But you see, I'm making money so you can go to camp."

"Will you make enough money so you can come to camp too?"

I laugh. "I'm too old for camp, Green-bean."

"No you're not," she exclaims. "It's up to 'sixteen years of age.' Uncle Oscar read the pamphlet."

I have to smile. Going to camp was one of my dreams never realized because of our lack of money. The irony isn't lost on me: Now that I have the money, going to camp seems no more desirable than keeping a full cookie jar next to my bed. "Who's Uncle Oscar?" I say to get Kristynka off the subject.

"Mom's new friend, of course," she says. "We are going to his cabin after my camp."

"Listen, have a wonderful time at camp, away from the witch, and when you come back, I'll send you a present."

"What's the present?"

"Something very nice. A surprise."

"Okay," she says. "And Eena." Her voice lowers to a whisper. "Don't call Mommy that word, she doesn't like it."

"You *told* her?"

"Yeah. And she didn't like it," she explains still in her whisper.

"Kristynka, don't tell Mom any more of the stuff, okay? Or she'll get mad at you and hit you."

"Oh, okay. Bye then." She hangs up.

I know better than to expect gratitude from a seven-year-old, but still . . . here I am, sending money so my little sister will be able to do all I wanted and never could, and she turns to Mother. I feel betrayed and, worse, unneeded.

I try Emanuel again, but his answering machine is on. I know he's back in France, but could he still be in a hospital? I assumed he'd be better by now, since I haven't heard anything to the contrary. I leave a message for him to call me. At least I didn't get the chance to tell anyone about the job and jinx it. I will put the job out of my mind entirely. It will never happen anyway. But, oh, the butterflies when I imagine—just for a second—how sweet it'd be.

Hugo calls and tells me he's on deadline. Shit-su is in her room playing weird, spacey music at top volume and Angie blasts the Sex Pistols in retaliation. The effect is that of my parents' arguments: all noise, no sense. I do what I always did then, bury my face in a book.

So it came about that while a light and frivolous bearing, a certain deliberate carelessness, was sufficient when one came in direct contact with the authorities, one needed in everything else the greatest caution, and had to look around on every side before one made a single step.

Huh?

The part when K. and Olga were making out was almost interesting, although the *clawing at each other as if they were dogs* wasn't particularly sexy. I keep trying to imagine K. as Rob, but have to admit defeat. K. is entirely too nervous and unlikable to fit. If I want to read about Rob, it seems I'll have to stock up on romance novels. I put Kafka down. Chapter 5. Technically, I have four weeks left to finish it. I run though the pages to the very end, and pick up a pen. On the last, blank page I write:

1. *Simon*
2. *Hugo*
3. *Rob*

There. Finally a good use of the damned book.

I pull out my cold plastic baby from my duffel, and try to sleep.

WHEN I WAKE UP, the apartment is heavenly quiet and Hugo's sheets feel too good to desert. The sun slants across the window, painting a shadow of a tree onto my floor and illuminating dust particles that dance like snowflakes. Will I still be here by Christmas? Or will I be home, decorating the Christmas tree by myself after Kristynka has gone to sleep? If I am not home, will Mother even bother buying a tree? Buying it, lugging it home, and dressing it was my domain, as was the baking of Grandma's Christmas cookies. The winter Kristynka was born, I waited in vain for the Jultomten to arrive. No tree. No gifts. At first, I was certain Jultomten didn't arrive because I had been bad. It was Hatty—who didn't celebrate Christmas anyway because she is Muslim—who filled me in on the parental involvement of Christmas. The following year, I took it upon myself to buy a tree with my newspaper money, determined Kristynka would get to believe in Jultomten until she was fifteen, at least.

When the phone rings, it's no less alarming than a sudden explosion. I jump and reach out for it.

"The clients loved you," Anne shouts. "You have a call back. They want you to go and meet the director for the commercial.

"Uh, what?" I say, instantly awake but confused. Who loved me?

"Jirina." Anne's voice drops in volume but heightens in intensity. "We are talking very high prestige here, not to mention money. A contract for minimum of one year. With the residuals from the commercial, it could be as much as thirty thousand francs."

I sit up like a jack-in-the-box. "Three?"

"No, *thirty*. For the year. If they decide to prolong it, it's an additional twenty."

"Oh my God. When do they want to see me again?"

"Tomorrow. At six."

JEAN-PIERRE IS SEATED at the table in his office. The familiar poster of Marina's face looms behind him; from this angle, their two heads are stacked above each other like evil cups in a cupboard. Not that cups can be evil, per se. I sit down.

"I need some money."

"Of course, how much today?"

At last count, I owed something like three thousand francs. But it's time to take the dive.

"One thousand francs," I say firmly.

"Ah." He leans back in his chair. "Would you like me to send some to Sweden again?"

"No thank you. Not until I'm out of debt. For now, I need new clothes and makeup."

He regards me quizzically.

"And I need money to go to the dentist."

I CALL THE DENTIST and set up an appointment before Angie and I head out shopping. Despite her cultivated "bad girl" looks and attitude, she really is quite sweet. But I have learned my lesson. Friendships in this world are not unlike public transportation: You can never predict who'll sit next to you and how long they'll stay.

Fiorucci is packed, music blares, but this time, I pull off the racks every bit of clothing that catches my eyes. Angie sits in my dressing room, nodding or shaking her head with a critical frown. A black miniskirt with a side zipper—yes. A blue sweater with a panther stalking the front—yes. Ditto for a pair of black, supertight pants, and a red T-shirt with a zillion zippers. In the cheap leather stores on the side streets I find a pair of black slouchy high-heeled suede boots and a motorcycle jacket that resembles one of Evalinda's, while Angie purchases a pair of red patent-leather Doc Martens. On rue St. Denis, I also get a Walkman: the small stainless steel one, and four tapes, Adam and the Ants, Jacques Brel, Chopin, and Tchaikovsky.

At Prisunic, I buy a Bourjois foundation, powder, mascara, three glittery, sweet-smelling blushes, and two eye shadows in small round containers, and a few lipsticks. We tote my purchases back home. I have nowhere to put my new clothes, so I hang them on the curtain rod. Moments later, Angie bursts into my room.

"Did you by any chance see a hundred francs on the kitchen counter?"

I flash on Britta. "No, I can't say I have. You want me to help you look?"

But Angie isn't angry with me. "That bitch. I'll fucking kill her! It's not like this is the first time either." She storms out.

I select my outfit with great care. The black mini, my new boots, and my red T-shirt. Then I scoop up my makeup and head for the bathroom.

Angie flinches when I open the door. She's kneeling by the tub, beer in one hand, and a toothbrush in the other.

"Um, Angie, I have to take a shower and get ready for a go-and-see."

"Oh, sure." She stands up and sets the toothbrush in the glass on the sink.

"You weren't cleaning the tub with that, were you?" I nod at the toothbrush.

"Nothing like a toothbrush to get in the tiny cracks," she says.

"You used your *toothbrush*?"

"What, you think I'm nuts?" She grins. "It's Shit-su's."

·   ·   ·

MY NEW WALKMAN propels me down the street. I have discovered a whole new world. As soon as I put my headphones on, my life becomes a movie. Even a simple walk takes on significance. With Jacques Brel, I am a French heroine in a drama, briskly tottering on high heels and sucking down her last cigarette through bloodred lips. Chopin and Tchaikovsky allow me to suspend time and drift through old Paris in a full-skirted dress and cloak through misty streets illuminated by gaslight. Adam and the Ants energize my steps better than a cup of black coffee; the mad percussion beat casts a spotlight on me and nearly lifts me off the ground.

The streets are breezy and warm. My slightly damp hair smells of rosemary, and Adam and the Ants tell me to Stand and Deliver. I will nail this go-and-see. I really have a good feeling about it.

I ENTER A DARK basement room lined with thirty or so empty plastic seats. I take one and wait. One small window close to the ceiling displays the footwear of passersby like an aquarium with very strange fish. After a few silent minutes, a door opens. "Anyone left?" a woman's voice rings out.

I stand up. "Yes. Me."

She waves me into a room filled with blinding light. When my vision adjusts, my bones turn to powder and leave my skin and muscle curiously empty and unsupported.

Dumowski is spread on a folding chair behind a video camera.

It's a miracle I'm still standing up instead of puddling on the floor like the invertebrate creature I've just become.

"Ah, ma belle petite fille," he says. His tone indicates that the element of surprise is on my side only.

"Hi," I say, uncertain of what to do next. Do I kiss his cheek, shake hands, or what? He solves my dilemma by pointing at a wall lit by a tungsten. "You go and stand there."

The woman closes the door, turns off the overheads, and sits in the other chair. "Slate, please."

"I'm sorry. What?"

"Look into the camera and state your name," she says.

I feel like a newly apprehended criminal. "Hi, I'm Jirina Radovanovicova." My name has never been so long and so awkward. My last name, in particular, comes out sounding as if I have a speech impediment.

"Bon. Now, turn left and give me your profile," the woman says and leads me into a series of profiles, half profiles, and hair shakes.

"We have it." She turns to Dumowski. "Anything else?"

"Non, ça va. You can leaving now."

Her eyebrows fly up in surprise, but she nods, takes her handbag off the back of her seat, and exits.

Silence falls, thick and gluey with tension.

I stand and sweat. "Anything else I can do for you?" The light concentrated on my face makes it difficult to see his expression.

"Take off the T-shirt."

Oh, here we go. Hello humiliation, old friend. I'm beginning to understand why I am here. It's payback time. But how can I refuse? Thirty thousand francs. At least. I pull my nice new T-shirt over my head.

"The brassiere also."

I undo my bra with shaking hands.

"And the skirt."

"Is this really necessary?" I mean for it to sound sophisticated, jaded almost, but my voice betrays me and shoots out like a plea.

"Do you wanting this job?"

I unzip my skirt. It falls to the floor.

He leans forward and puts his eye to the viewfinder. "Turn to me. Turn away." He makes me walk to and from the camera. "That's enough."

I stop. Relief sweeps over me.

"Now come here."

Relief is quickly elbowed aside by apprehension. I did what he wanted. Now what?

He leans back in his chair, and now I see his fly is undone, and his stubby cock is poking out. "Come on, baby." He wiggles his finger. "Come and finishing what you start."

Time hiccups. My choices blare like discordant notes of trumpets. *Do as he wants. Get this job. Take the money. Be free. Stay. Beat Evalinda.* Or *Leave. No money. No job.* I inch forward.

It's not like I haven't had sex with people I didn't love. It's not that big a deal. Sex itself has nothing to do with love; it's a bodily function like eating, or going to the bathroom. Why not do it for a really good reason?

I step a little closer.

Whore. It will make me a whore. I will have set a price. My body and soul will be worth thirty thousand francs.

I stop.

Thirty thousand francs! Or more. I will be able to stay in Paris. I will be plastered on billboards; I will be on TV, in the movie theaters, in a double-page spread of every magazine on the market, including Sweden. Like Evalinda. Like she used to be. Or, even better, instead of her! It could be me.

I take the last step.

He strokes himself with one hand and with the other grabs me by the wrist and pulls me down. Down, down I go. On my knees. Forgive me Lord, for I have sinned. Am about to sin. No, fuck that. I'm only doing what I need to do to stay in the game.

He clutches my hair and pulls my face close to his crotch. I inhale a faint sour stink, close my eyes, and open my mouth. Rob flashes before my eyes, but I chase him away. This has nothing to do with what I did with Rob. Nothing. This is business. He grabs my head with both hands, ramming his cock in and out so fast my gagging makes no difference.

And finally, he groans, and warm, bitter liquid fills my mouth. I don't know what else to do, so I swallow. I stand up.

Dumowski zips his fly and smiles his lazy lion smile. "Good girl," he says. "We understanding each other good."

BACK HOME, I brush my teeth until my gums bleed, but the taste stays with me. I'm a whore. There. I have punctuated my brokenness with a clearly physical deed, and there is no going back. Hugo is supposed to pick us up in an hour to go club hopping. I stare at myself in the mirror, half expecting a scarlet letter to appear on my forehead. But my face is the same as always. Eyes the color of pond scum. Pointy chin. Chapped lips barely covering an Alfred E. Neuman smile. A face not even a mother can love.

When Hugo arrives, I have trouble meeting his eyes. We cram ourselves into his car and hurtle through dark streets. Angie is on my lap. I'm afraid to breathe on her, in case she can smell it. Our first stop is Elysées Matignon, a club that looks like the set from *Saturday Night Fever*, intact with a lit floor, a disco ball, and patrons in tight white pants and gold chains. Hugo is treated like visiting royalty; we are quickly ushered past the velvet ropes outside, seated at a table overlooking the dance floor, and treated to a complimentary bottle of champagne in a silver bucket. Angie's glances at Hugo keep growing in length and wistfulness and, although he is a perfect gentleman, his focus is clearly on me. If he only knew what I did today he'd surely refocus.

Angie expresses a wish for a little pick-me-up, and Hugo reaches out his hand with a folded bill to the table next to us. He is rewarded with a tiny plastic pouch. This time, I know what to do. The bitter kickback in the back of my throat is unpleasant, but the burst of energy immediately following is fantastic. I guzzle champagne straight out of the bottle and pull Angie and Hugo to the dance floor. I dance until sweat drips, until I can scarcely draw breath, until my only thought is to rest.

I head back to our table for a drink and Hugo follows me. We split the remains of the champagne and he orders another bottle. Angie is still on the dance floor, twisting herself around two dark-haired guys. Hugo leans back on the couch and watches her.

I lean in close to him. "Do you find her attractive?" When he says no, I will point out all her good qualities.

"Oui. She is mignone."

"Meaning?"

"How do you say—cute?"

"Oh." This, for some reason, bothers me. "Her ears stick out," I say.

"That is also mignone."

"What about her burps, you find them mignone?"

He smiles. "Not so much."

"Hah!" I sniffle and wipe my nose.

What's the matter with me? How did I start with the best intentions and end here?

"Are you jealous?" Hugo winks at me. He pronounces it in French, *zha-loo*.

"Yeah, right, don't flatter yourself," I retort. He only smiles.

Our next stop is Le Palace, an enormous club with three floors and bartenders dressed in snazzy red-and-gold uniforms. Then we make a brief visit to the Bain Douche, a former bathhouse which now has a dance floor next to a swimming pool and, finally, we end at the Champs-Élysées drugstore. It's a sort of tiny shopping mall, serving so-so food but great ice creams. It also sells electronics, tapes, perfumes, magazines, but no medicine

I can see. We order ice cream, which we all just pick at. It's four o'clock in the morning, and our buzz is wearing off. Angie puts her feet up on the table, right here in the restaurant. Her new patent leather Doc Martens glint like they are mirrored under the lights.

"Nice boots," Hugo says.

Angie wiggles them on the tabletop. "Thanks. They're a bit stiff though," she says. She pulls them off the table, unties the laces, and slips her feet out. She is wearing neon-green socks. "My feet are killing me," she says, and rubs one.

"Here," Hugo says and pulls the other foot into his lap. Angie closes her eyes and sighs blissfully. I won't let him touch me with those hands until he's washed them.

"Have you ever heard of this English girl, Jane Birkin?" I ask.

Angie shakes her head, but Hugo nods. "Bien sure."

"Is she mignone?" I raise my brows to lend the word a little sarcasm.

"Not really," he says. That's a stinging, open-handed slap right on the cheek. "She is beautiful." He grins. I resist smiling back, although my cheeks tickle and the corners of my mouth lift involuntarily. "Have you never seen her?"

"No."

"You know, you look a lot like her."

"Yeah, so I've been told." I swirl my spoon around my melting ice cream. "If you could fuck anyone for a night, who would you pick?" I say.

"Mick Jones." Angie jumps in immediately. "You know, from the Clash."

The Clash. Simon. I shake my head. "The lead singer?"

"No! The guitar player. Way sexier than Joe Strummer. Longish face, dark hair, sad eyes. In fact"—she giggles—"he looks a bit like Hugo."

Hugo smiles his crooked smile. "Thank you. It is a compliment, I hope?"

Angie blushes. Actually blushes.

"All right. What about you?" I turn to Hugo. Angie needs to know. For her own good.

"Buh, I am not sure—a young Brigitte Bardot?"

What? I don't look anything like her!

But nor does Angie.

"Oh, please, that's so predictable." I snap. "Any guy would say that."

Hugo laughs. "Sorry. I guess I'm just like any guy. Now, what about you? It is your turn." He continues to knead Angie's foot in his lap.

Rob. I can't think of anyone else. "Andy Gibb," I finally say. He's sort of cute, and looks nothing like Hugo.

Angie makes a horrified grimace. "That Australian pretty boy? Yuck."

I had no idea he was, in fact, Australian, but the mere mention of Rob's nationality makes me blush.

"And that is not predictable?" Hugo says, with uncharacteristic disdain.

"That's why I said it. Because you're both so fucking predictable." I slam my spoon into the ice cream bowl. It flips back up like rubber, hitting me in the chest and splattering me with sticky flecks. Hugo and Angie laugh.

"That's not funny!" I snap at them as I attempt to wipe the ice cream off with a paper napkin.

They throw each other a look that doesn't escape me. *What's her problem?*

"Let's get out of here," I say.

ON THE WAY OUT, we stop in the ladies' room to inhale the remains of our white powder, and then Hugo stops at the record counter.

"Vous avez 'Je t'aime moi non plus'?"

The clerk, a tired, older woman, nods and brings out a cassette. We crowd around it and I lean in close for a better look. A black-and-white photo looks back at me. Large, wide-set eyes, a tiny upturned nose, and sensual lips under straight hair with a heavy fringe.

"Wow, Jirina, that looks just like you," Angie says. "Especially if you had bangs." I'm suddenly gripped by a deep fervent desire for bangs. I want to be someone else. I want to look exactly like her. Not just a little, I want to *be* her. No more commie cow, no more hot chicken. No more Jirina.

"Does anyone here have scissors?"

Scissors are one of the oddball things the drugstore does sell. I run out on the street waving them around and cackling like a maniac. The cool steel flashes under the streetlights. I ball my fist around it. It's a dagger, with which I will kill the old Jirina. Hugo and Angie are behind me. "Do it, do it," Angie chants. I stop and select a fat chunk of hair above my face, pulling it down and flat.

"Gigi, are you sure?" Hugo says next to me.

In response, I lift the scissors and cut. The resistance of the hair is surprising. Like it doesn't want to be cut; like it's a living thing. I almost expect it to cry "ouch." But maybe it's just that the scissors are too dull. We probably bought the wrong ones.

My head already feels lighter. I grin. "Ta-da! What do you think?"

Hugo and Angie look at each other and burst out laughing. "Interesting," Hugo says. Angie takes the scissors from me, pushes me directly under the streetlight, and begins to snip away. "Ah oui, c'est mieux." Hugo nods. "How do you know to cut the hair so good?"

"Went to beautician school in Jersey," Angie says.

Hugo drops us off at the apartment and refuses to come up. "It is almost day; if I stay here I will sleep too long and I have many things to do tomorrow. Don't forget, eleven o'clock, Gigi."

Angie and I sneak into the apartment with the finesse of moose. Or is that mooses? Meese? "What the fuck is the plural for moose?"

This has us screeching with laughter in her room. She opens two beers, and blasts the Sex Pistols. I turn it down; it's giving me a headache. My shoulders and back are excruciatingly itchy with tiny hairs that have lodged in the fabric of my ice cream–stained T-shirt, and my buzz has been replaced with a slow, spinning descent into an oddly colorless world. I sit on her bed and she plops down next to me.

"So, is he your boyfriend, or isn't he?" she asks suddenly and catches me mid-gulp.

I splutter, swallow, and cover my mouth for a discreet little burp. "In case you haven't noticed, he has a huge crush on me, okay?"

"Yeah, but what about you?"

"How much did those cost?" I say, and pick up her discarded boot. I slide my foot in. The black, humid warmth left by Angie is like an open mouth. I giggle. I'm putting my foot in her mouth. It fits perfectly.

"Ninety francs. How *do* you feel about Hugo?"

"I have an idea. Let's trade—your boots for Hugo." I laugh. "If he wants you." Which he doesn't.

"Okay." She takes a swig of her beer and belches with the timbre of a foghorn.

Mignone she's not.

CHAPTER 24

The air outside is hot, my new boots weigh a ton and pinch my toes, and there is a hole where my stomach should be. All the food I've purchased is gone, except for the coffee, though I never had any of it. Hugo sticks his head out of the car and whistles. "Hello there, Jane. Nice hair."

Nice hair, right. I had forgotten all about it until I went to the bathroom to pee. The sight in the mirror was no Jane—more of a mangy dog. It stuck up at odd angles all over my head, all the cuts clearly visible like haphazard steps going nowhere. I went back to my room to study Jane's hair on the cassette cover, and it dawned on me she wasn't that pretty after all. In fact, her face struck me as kind of horsey. Is this what people think I look like? And here I was, making all those comparisons to Evalinda's racehorse body, when it's me with a horse face.

I roll down the window of Hugo's car, for his driving, at the best of times, makes me carsick.

"So, what, another museum?" I grumble.

He looks crestfallen. "I thought that you liked the museums."

"I do. At a civilized hour. Can you slow down a bit?"

"Ça va, on est arrivée," he says and slams on the brakes.

The streets are airless and blinding. We walk to rue de Varenne, where a white mansion spreads in the middle of the block, enclosed by lush lawns and a black iron fence. My head hurts and my feet in Angie's boots are as comfortable as if I had dipped them into a pond alive with hungry piranhas.

"Do you know the artist, Auguste Rodin?" Hugo says and pulls me merrily behind him.

"*The Thinker*, Camille Claudel, *The Lovers*? Yeah, I think I know him," I say. "If you are looking to educate someone, maybe you should have brought Angie."

He stops. "Why Angie?"

"Well, you think she's cute. Mignonne."

He searches my face; I cast my eyes down.

"She is. Elle est drôle. Funny. She makes me laugh. Now come, we only have one hour. The manager is a friend of my father, he will let us have a private visit until the museum opens to the public."

Somehow, my irritation only increases. "My shoes hurt."

"Dis donc, they are just like Angie's, non?"

I shrug. If he only knew.

"Take them off, I will carry them."

I ignore him, and limp along.

The mansion is high ceilinged and airy. Windows are open to a large park in the back, where a rectangle of violently green grass stretches to a fountain and continues to a thick line of trees that isolate us from the street. We walk in and out of white-paneled rooms where bronze statues stand like pieces of twisted, petrified tar. I never thought of bronze as being black. Hugo points and carries on like a tour guide. My head and my feet are hot and achy, and the scent of freshly cut grass is as cloying as those air-freshening trees hung in cars.

Hugo stops in the largest room, where the walls reflect the hue of rotting peaches and the sculptures are cut from white marble. Some are coarse, unpolished stone, with smooth pieces of life jutting out: a pair of monstrously large male hands clasped in hopeless prayer; a delicate female head trapped in a rectangular block; a slender-fingered hand crushing a tiny body in its palm. The only one that draws me in is a bare female back, curved into sharp rock. The delicate white marble has a tinge of pink, and gleams like waxed skin under the spotlight. There is something touching and very sad about this back. A young woman, curled up in the mass of stone from which she was made, incomplete. I touch her. She makes me want to cry.

"This is the *Naiad*. Beautiful, non?" Hugo says next to me. "Her back is so—tendre—how do you say—"

"Tender. Vulnerable. Yeah."

"She reminds me of you."

I shoot him a nasty look. "You are wrong. I am not vulnerable or tender."

"*Hmph*," Hugo snorts. "Sometimes, it is more easy to see from the outside."

"The only thing you see from the outside, Hugo, is the fucking outside."

He smiles his annoying crooked grin. I run my hand over the jagged rock the girl nestles in. I have a sudden flash of inspiration. "See this stone?" I say. "That's me. Sharp. Unfinished." I savor the words. "If you touch it, it may hurt you."

"I believe I can tell the difference and know which part to touch."

"And if your hand slips?"

"Then my hand will appreciate the smooth part more."

"The smoothness is an illusion. It's made so you will slip to the rough part without even noticing."

He turns to face me. "Gigi, what are you trying to say?"

"You should stay away from me, Hugo. Go out with Angie."

A shadow passes over his face. "Are you are trying to talk me away from loving you?"

Yes, Hugo. For your own good. No, because I need you so I'm not alone. I don't know what the fuck I'm doing.

"Hugo, you don't know me. I'm not a nice person." This is as close as I dare to get to the truth.

He shakes his head. "Ah, but you are wrong." He smiles and reaches out for my hand.

I flinch away. "No. This time, *you* are wrong, Hugo. You're judging me by my looks alone."

"Do you believe I am so, how do you say, undeep? Gigi, I *know* you. I know the lonely little girl inside."

"The word is 'shallow,' Hugo. And shallow is a pretty kind word to use for someone who likes to hang out with lonely little girls. I could think of more fitting ones."

"I only meant, a lonely little girl like I am a lonely little boy inside. We are the same, you and me."

"You and *I* are absolutely not alike." A sudden calm is come over me; I'm cold and smooth like the new scissors. "When's the last time you fucked somebody to get a job?"

"You are joking." He's smiling, but his eyes are uncertain.

"Oh, am I? Since you know me so well, you should know that yesterday, before we went out, I was on my knees blowing an old guy for a contract."

"I do not believe you."

"Jesus Christ, Hugo! What can I tell you to make you back off? Okay, how about this? Last night, I traded you for these boots that don't even fit!" I stomp my feet like a child having a tantrum.

But he smiles, a serious, almost pained, smile, steps closer to me, and takes both of my clammy hands in his.

"You should perhaps ask yourself why you are trying to make me 'back off.' Is it because you are scared? Because you are starting to love me and that is the most frightening thing that can happen?"

"Love you? Love *you*?" I laugh. My faulty toy mechanism is wound so tight, my skin vibrates. Words explode from my lips like metal coils. "The first time I fucked you, Hugo, was out of gratitude."

"Gigi—" he says, but then runs out of words. He holds his hands up, as if to physically stop me.

But I am on a roll. "Oh yeah, and the second time was to get someone else out of my mind."

I think I'm finally getting to him. His face has visibly blanched. And I'm not done yet.

"And all the rest were pity fucks," I shout at his back. "You call that *love*?"

ANNE ACTUALLY SCREAMS at the sight of me. "Tes cheveux! Your hair! Mon Dieu! What happened?" She jumps out of her chair.

"I got drunk."

She sprints across the room, grabs me by the shoulders, and shakes me. "You never, ever, do anything with your hair without the permission of the agency! Are you crazy? It could ruin your career completement!"

"It's not like I have one."

"T'es folles? Dumowski loved you, they confirmed you for the commercial!" She stops shaking me and wrings her hands. "And *now* what do we do? This is a disaster!"

"It's not bad, it actually suits her," Shoji says from his spot at the desk.

"Pas mal? What does it matter if it suits her? The clients booked her with her old hair!" Anne shouts at him.

"True." Shoji shrugs.

Only now the severity of what I've done dawns on me. I may have sold myself for nothing!

"I must call the clients and tell them, right now. And you," she says as she turns to me, "will have to go and see them again to show it."

Great. I wonder if Dumowski is still horny.

Anne gets on the phone, and after a few minutes, she nods at me and hangs up. "They will see you now."

Obediently I approach the desk and take the piece of paper with the address Anne has scrawled on it. "C'est vrai c'est pas mal, I must admit. Did you do this yourself?" she says.

"Mostly Angie did it—"

"Then she may have a career in the fashion biz after all," Shoji says dryly from the desk.

"No more such things, you understand?" Anne says. "A model can only cut her hair or dye it if she is told by the agency or if it is requested by the client. You are lucky Angie is better at hair cutting than modeling."

I CALL HUGO FROM a pay phone. I'm not sure what I'll say when he answers; I only know that somehow I must take my words back. I'll grovel, I'll beg, I'll even cry if I must. He doesn't answer.

I take the elevator back to the boardroom, where the six clients sit at the table. But no Dumowski. They take one look, nod, say they like it, and I'm done. Have I overestimated Dumowski's power in all this?

Back home I'm greeted with a half-drunk Angie on my bed. She's sniveling, and wiping her eyes with my sheets.

"What's the matter?" I say, and throw my portfolio on the floor.

She looks up. "Oh my God, your hair! It looks amazing."

"I almost lost a huge job because of it."

"Well, did you?" Her tone is unsettlingly hopeful.

"No, I had to go and see them again and they liked it."

"Good for you," she says, and bursts out crying.

"What's the matter?" I sit next to her.

"Got a ciggie?"

I take one from my bag and hand it to her.

"They want to send me to Japan." She takes the cigarette and stares at it.

"Wow, that's great!"

"Are you fucking kidding?"

"No. What's wrong with Japan?"

"Got a lighter?"

I find matches next to my bed. "Here."

She lights up and draws in the smoke. "What's wrong with Japan? You mean besides Japanese men with tiny dicks and their raw fucking fish and their god-awful English?" She exhales with relish. "Well, baby, let me tell you what else is fucking wrong with fucking Japan. It's the burial ground for models. That's where you get sent when you can't get work anywhere else. You understand? They want to send me to Japan to get rid of me."

"I'm sorry." Inwardly, I'm relieved. Off to Japan with her. The sooner the better.

"I'll fight them. They can't send me if I don't want to go. I'd rather fuck an Arab than go to fucking Japan," she says.

I go to my room and dial Hugo again. No answer. I keep dialing and hanging up after twenty rings. Angie sticks her head in at some point. "You're not calling Hugo, are you?"

"Why?"

" 'Cause he's out of town. Went to see his family. Didn't he tell you?"

"Oh yeah, he did. I just forgot."

My devastation is complete. I won't even get to apologize. I will have to live with this for a whole week.

AT EIGHT A.M. SHARP, I'm showered, scrubbed, and depilated. I walk through an empty hallway lined with doors without the faintest clue where to go. A peek through a random doorway reveals a modern, blond-wood bedroom with a cream-colored carpet and three bone-colored walls, stranded on a podium in the middle of a vast room like an islet in the middle of an ocean. The surrounding space is filled with skeletal metal stands and huge black canisters that look like tungstens.

Finally, at the end of the hallway, I find a door marked MAKEUP. I push it open. Large mirrors with globe lights cast a warm light over white counters groaning under the weight of beauty products, and two women, one who's sitting in the makeup chair and one who's bending over her. The platinum shine of Evalinda's hair is unmistakable. What the fuck is she doing here?

I step in and slam the door behind me. Evalinda's eyes meet mine in the mirror.

"Jirina? What the fuck are you doing here?" she echoes my reaction.

The makeup artist steps away so Evalinda can swivel around to face me.

"I'm not sure. I thought I was working," I say, color pouring into my face.

Evalinda looks to the makeup woman for explanation.

"Oui, oui, I was told two girls," she says, and turns to me. "You must be Jirina?" She pronounces it *Yeereenah* unhesitatingly, although she is clearly French.

"I am Natalie, I will be doing your makeup today. Come and sit, Vlad will be here any moment."

"Working? They booked someone else for this job?" Evalinda's eyes are bulging dangerously. "What the fuck?" She jumps out of the chair and attacks the phone. I sit on the short chair and listen to Evalinda scream at Odile on the phone. "Since when am I sharing—what do you mean you told me—the fuck you did—yes, I knew they were looking but—it's what? You're kidding, right?" She slams the phone down.

Natalie looks unconcerned, and resumes her sponges and foundations. Evalinda stomps back to her chair. "I don't fucking believe it. The assholes. Did you know we were working together?" She looks at me accusingly.

I shake my head.

"Bastards!" she says with venom. "Did they tell you *what* we're doing?"

I shake my head again.

"Me either." She stews. "A new concept. They can kiss my ass."

But her ass stays planted in the makeup chair until Dumowski and the dark-haired woman enter the room. Then Evalinda jumps up and throws herself at him like a drowning woman. "Ondrej, baby!"

"Ça va, ma belle?" He pats her and moves to me. "Your hairs is good. I liking it better even."

I grow hot and uncomfortable. What if he says something, or kisses me on the mouth? I already feel like they all know. Like they can tell just from watching us. But the dark-haired woman says, "Alors, on y va?"

The four of us walk to the vast room with the bedroom set, which is now filled with guys in dirty T-shirts, climbing all over walls, fastening things and yelling at one another. We walk up wooden steps on the side. The bedroom is a stage, it now occurs to me. Dumowski and the woman sit on the mattress. "Les yeux. Laissez-moi les voire."

Let's see the eyes, I understand.

"Hm—," he says, staring at Evalinda. "Trop petits, non? Trop ronde, je pense," he mutters. *Too small, too round.* He turns his focus on mine. "Elle a les yeux parfaits. We use her eyes."

I'm happy that my eyes are considered perfect and better than Evalinda's, but what is going on here? Why the comparisons? Is this a competition? Are they going to send the loser home?

They move to our hands; Evalinda wins with her nicely manicured ones, ditto her feet. Oh God, please don't let me have done this in vain, I pray, only to remember God is probably not on speaking terms with me anyway.

"Now, show me the breast," Dumowski says. Evalinda immediately pulls up her tank top and flashes her flawless breasts. I follow her example, although my heart beats a little too fast. Free. Naked. Nothing wrong with this.

"Elle a des seins magnifiques," the woman exclaims and touches Evalinda's breast. She weighs it in one hand like a piece of fruit. Evalinda grins.

"I like the small breast," Dumowski says. "More 'moderne.'"

Evalinda's smile fades.

"No, no, our woman has the breast. She is a woman, not a little girl," the woman says. I blush with shame and Evalinda's triumphant grin is back. So far, she's outnumbering me three to one. If this is elimination, it seems I'm out.

But there is more. They ask us to remove our jeans, and move on to the legs, which I win instantly. Then we are asked to turn around and draw our underwear up our butts. The guys in the dirty T-shirts slow their work to watch.

This one also goes to me. It's a draw. So now what?

"We will use her lips and teeth." The woman points at Evalinda. My heart drops. Evalinda will win after all.

Dumowski frowns. "Non, I think Jirina's lips are more nice. Sexy."

Evalinda shoots a glance at me, at Dumowski, back at me, and her grin fades. A slight flush spreads over the bridge of her nose and cheeks. Almost imperceptibly, she shakes her head and mumbles, "Putain." "Putain" can be used as an exclamation, like fuck, but it really means whore. She can't possibly know!

"Mai, les dents—," the woman objects. Oh yes, my teeth. My little white mice. They will finally be my undoing.

"I like the teeth," Dumowski says. "Ça fait on peu original, comme La Birkin, tu crois pas?" My teeth are original, like Jane's? I'm almost willing to give him another blow job.

Evalinda nods to herself, her mouth a stiff line.

On the way back to the makeup room, it's just the two of us in the long empty hallway. Halfway, she grabs my arm. "Did you fuck him?"

Oh God, she knows. Is it that obvious? All of me is instantly on fire. But she continues. "That night in Morocco? After I walked in on you?"

"Of course not," I say. She squints at me. I stand unflinching, victoriously honest. "He left right after you did."

She lets go of my arm. "Don't underestimate me, Jirina," she says. "I'm not stupid."

"That wasn't implied," I say. Rob's words that night in Ouarzazate. Will I never stop thinking of him?

ONCE WE START SHOOTING, all becomes clear. Evalinda and I are one woman. One woman with my eyes, nose, mouth, ass, and legs, but with Evalinda's breasts, hands, and feet.

I have to sit in her lap, while she brushes mascara onto my lashes. Of course she misses a few times and rams the mascara into my eyeball, and then we use my other eye. The camera is a beast of a whole different breed; large and whirring during the shots, it requires three sweaty guys to manage it. One sits on a little stool on a cart and actually shoots the film, one keeps pulling out a long string all the way to my eyelashes for focus, and one pushes the cart around. Doing a commercial is much faster than a photo shoot. We rehearse a move with the camera, then Dumowski shouts "action," we repeat the moves, Dumowski yells "cut," and the guy looking through the camera tells Dumowski whether or not he was happy with the shot. If not, we do it again. There is very little actual action, but a lot of waiting around for people to fix the lights, reload the camera, and touch up hair and makeup. We do a shot of Evalinda applying my lipstick, another of her smoothing lotion onto my leg, and all the while the two of us are in such close physical proximity we could be Siamese twins. Her smell wears on me and makes me slightly nauseous, and the touch of her skin makes my own crawl. While we wait for the next shot to be set up, we smoke in silence, the tension between us thick enough to suspend objects in the air.

Angie is not home when I get back to the apartment, but Shit-su knocks hesitantly on my door and hands me a note. "Telephone, you, yes?"

I try not to be disappointed when I see Emanuel's name instead of Hugo's.

HE OPENS THE DOOR in a shiny purple robe. He looks thinner than I remember, and when I hug him, his usual scent of Opium and the smoothness of silk don't adequately distract from the bones I feel underneath.

His apartment is one room, divided with a gold curtain for the bed nook and a Chinese screen that hides the kitchenette in the corner. His Queen tape plays in the background. We walk onto a small terrace, where we sit at a round table with a flickering candle; the view before us is of three adjacent building walls. He pours me some wine while he fills me in on his hospital stay in Morocco, and the subsequent care at the American Hospital here in Paris. It seems Cheery Doc did take good care of him. Cheery Doc also invited Mia to dinner. She gladly accepted, thinking she'd get all kinds of interesting details on the care of Morocco's ailing, but had to fend off his advances instead. We toast to Mia.

"So honey, now you tell me all I missed. I already know you had a good thing going with Rob. Mia told me."

I need no further invitation to break down. I tell him about the beach, the sex, the airport. Evalinda's betrayal.

"Have you talked to him since?" Emanuel asks.

"No."

"Why not?"

"Emanuel," I burst out, "you should have seen his face when he said 'fifteen.' It was as if he found out he had slept with a leper!"

Emanuel just shrugs. "Maybe he is over it now."

"He hasn't called me."

Emanuel takes a sip of his wine. "Maybe you should call him?"

"You serious? It wasn't me who pushed him away!"

"Ah, pride. Sometimes it's good, but mostly it only keeps you from what you want."

This is too painful. I change the subject. "So, how's work?"

"Could be better, could be worse. I've only been back for three days, but I have a shoot with Mr. Carera next week.

"That asshole."

"You have worked with him, I see."

I try to tell him about that day, but when I get to the period part, Emanuel puts his hand to his ears. "That's way too much information for this girl, honey."

I've emptied my glass, Emanuel pours out another one. It's nearly ten; I will have to leave soon. I put my knees up and hug them. The candle on the table flickers and goes out. Emanuel leans over to relight it.

"Emanuel, how do they do it?"

"Who, what? Ouch—" he says and shakes his hand. "Burned my finger."

"The girls. Models. How do they stand this job without killing themselves?"

"Oh, honey." He sighs and puts the lighter away in his pocket. "Most of them don't think about it like you do. The best are either the ambitious girls who will walk over dead bodies, or the stupid ones. It does get more easy, you know. Once you get a little more well known, people treat you better and you learn how not to hear the rest."

"So the key to survival is being deaf?"

"Yes. Or stupid." He grins. "The dumb ones are the best to work with—they don't question anything."

"What about girls like Mia?"

"Aah, now, you see, Mia is a lady. She came, saw what the deal is, and decided to use instead of being used. But Mia is also a little older." He narrows his eyes in thought. "If this business used women instead of girls—which of course would never happen, because, you know, older skin just doesn't bounce light like young skin does—but anyway." He shakes his head. "Where was I?"

"If they used women instead of girls."

"Right. If they did, this biz would be completely different."

"How so?"

"Well, you can't push a woman around like you can a teenager. A woman would call their bullshit."

Yeah, a woman wouldn't do what I've done.

"I did something bad," I whisper.

"What?"

"No, nothing. Never mind."

He smiles. "I hear you. Listen, so have I. So many times I couldn't even count them."

"Have you ever fucked someone for a job?" The words jump out on their own. I cast an anxious glance at his meticulously kohl-lined eyes for his reaction.

He laughs. "Oh honey, I sure wish I could! I'd be the worlds' biggest slut with no regrets and lots of money."

I have to laugh, too. This is the attitude I want. This is how I want to see it. So why do I keep feeling so dirty?

"Have you ever spread evil rumors to eliminate a rival?" he says.

"Not yet." I grin.

"Atta girl!"

"What does *that* mean?"

"It's an American expression and it means"—he frowns and then laughs. "I actually have no idea what it means." We both laugh.

"Okay, how about—since we're on the subject of being bad—have you ever intentionally hurt someone who loved you?" I say.

"Of course." Emanuel smiles. "Isn't that what love is all about?" His voice slips from easy banter to a bitter bite. "You love them, they hurt you, you hurt them back."

No, that's not it, I want to say. He loves me, but I don't—I glance at my watch. It's ten thirty.

"Emanuel, are you tired yet?"

"Not at all."

"There is this guy, Hugo . . ."

Emanuel listens in silence with an occasional nod or murmur of understanding. When I describe Hugo's constant little kindnesses, my stomach knots up and I feel as though I'm on the verge of discovering something important, something that has until now eluded me. But whatever spark of wisdom that's on the tip of my consciousness dissolves into a puddle of guilt when I describe the scene at Rodin's museum.

Emanuel lets me finish before he sighs, "Honey, I'm afraid you have confused love for love of the hunt."

"Huh?"

He leans back in his chair and sets his wineglass down. "What I mean is, Rob. You thought you couldn't have him, right? He was like winning a prize, a conquest? Is that the word?"

I nod.

"And girlfriend, I know, nothing is more exciting. Then you have this boy, Hugo. You knew from the beginning he loved you. Maybe it is being young, or poor judgment, or in my case"—he throws his arms up theatrically and points both hands at his chest—"deep insecurity; you know, I think I'm not deserving of love, so if someone-who-can-have-anyone wants me, it makes me more worth having." He laughs a little and shrugs. "But the good ones, you let slip away and don't know what you have lost until it's too late."

He's right. It took Hugo's absence from my life to realize how much I care. "Oh God, Emanuel. What do I do now?"

"If Hugo is any kind of a man, he will not forgive you. And if he does, you will never respect him. It's over, girlfriend. The best you can do is move on."

CHAPTER 25

When Evalinda walks into the makeup room this morning, her demeanor is completely changed. She runs up to me and bends down to give me a hug. "Sorry," she whispers, "for being such an asshole yesterday."

She must have believed me about not having had sex with Dumowski that night in Morocco. Which wasn't a lie. And besides, I didn't have sex with him. A blow job isn't fucking.

On set, she does a shot of putting on her bra, and then she is done. The rest of the shots are all me: my legs, my butt, and a full nude from the back. When I next see her, she is dressed in her street clothes, while I'm waiting for the camera.

"Poor baby," she says and puts an arm around me.

What is she talking about? "Who?"

She squeezes my shoulder. "Never mind. I don't want to ruin your day."

"Jesus Christ, Evalinda, what is it?" I say, shrugging her arm off. "If you have something to say, then say it!"

I can tell she is momentarily taken aback. I've never spoken to her like this before. In a way it makes me feel good, but her sudden change of mood—I now know—can be dangerous.

"It's nothing. I have to run or I'll be late for—oh, never mind. You have to work now, so don't worry your pretty little head about anything.

Just remember, I'm doing you a favor." And with that, she turns on her heels and walks away, leaving me with a nagging low-grade anxiety. The last time she did me a favor, she ruined my life. What in the world is she talking about now?

As the day drags on, Emanuel's words keep resurfacing to torture me. Doubtless, he was right about many things yesterday, but not about Hugo. I know Hugo will forgive. He's Hugo!

As a distraction, I make plans with my new money. I've made eight thousand francs in two days. Once I do the photo shoot, I will get another four, and the rest is supposed to trickle in within a year. I will send half to Mother and Kristynka. Six thousand each. That's three months of my mother's salary. I will look into the prices of apartments on Ile St. Louis, and with the remainder I'll buy a bed and whatever else I can afford. I'm busy decorating a simile of Evalinda's apartment, when I remember I also owe the agency. The apartment will have to wait. As much as I would love to decorate it—at least in my mind—once I move in I will be alone. Unless—unless I ask Hugo to be my roommate? Maybe that will be the sort of apology needed to get him back.

When the day finally ends, I run out without saying good-bye to anyone.

I turn up the volume on Tchaikovsky's piano concerto in B-flat minor and float down the street. Every person walking seems to be heading for a passionate reunion in a lover's arms. I stop by a newsstand with a vague hope of seeing myself in print, although I know this to be impossible. The fashion magazines are lined up vertically in hanging racks; my fingers brush over glossy faces: a wide-lipped French actress on *Elle*, Josephine's crystal blue eyes on French *Vogue*, Melissa, a cute-as-a-button model who's with my agency, on the cover of *L'Officiel*. I pick up *L'Officiel* and flitter through the pages. Here again is Melissa, in a six-page spread on a beach. In one picture, she wears a blue bikini and a matching headband, and she sits in the surf, her cherry-red mouth open in a wild laugh at the shock of a crashing wave. Upon a closer look, I see the little hairs on her arm stick up; the wave was probably freezing and in all likelihood swept her away in the next frame, depositing a load of sand into those high-cut briefs. On the next page, she reclines on one elbow on a terra-cotta tile floor in a beaded, stiff cocktail dress, peeking out coyly from behind an enormous bow on her shoulder. Her smile belies the fact she's probably been leaning on that one elbow for some time and is by now in considerable pain; the slight sheen on her face is a dead giveaway to how hot she must be and that the makeup artist will jump in shortly to repowder her.

I shove the magazine back in its slot and my eyes fall onto the coarse colorless print of a newspaper.

My heart stops.

A pair of black eyes stares out at me, eyes so familiar and yet so wrong when the color has been sucked out of them.

L'HERETIER TUÉ DANS UN ACCIDENT TRAGIQUE.

My blood coagulates into cement. Tragic accident, I understand. *Tué.* What does that mean? Tu means you. *Tué.* I struggle with the word, as if the exact translation would change the meaning of what I already know. *Tuer* is a verb meaning to kill.

It can't be. My world turns black on the edges and tilts. I look at the tiny text for an explanation of this horrible joke.

Course de voiture—something car—*pneu creve*—something broken— *lac*—lake—*la ceinture a enfonce*—the belt did something? stuck?— *noye*—drowned.

My heart is suddenly exploding in my chest. I look around wildly; I need someone to translate this because I'm reading it all wrong. That's what it is, it's the language. I'm misunderstanding it all.

"Please, what does this say?" I turn to the newsstand owner. He looks at me as if I'm crazy. Of course, he doesn't speak English.

"Ça fait trois francs," he says. I fish out the coins and throw them on the counter.

I look back at the words I hold in shaking hands, trying to avoid Hugo's eyes. The words are growing blurry, as if I'm reading them through a wet windshield with no wipers. Someone stops beside me and reaches for a paper.

"Please." I turn to him. "What does this say?" I think I may be shouting. He turns quickly and walks away.

My every breath breaks my chest. "Please, someone, can't you tell me what this says?" I hold up the paper before me. "Please?" People walk past me with frowns or smiles: *Elle est folle*—*bue comme un pompier*— They aren't making any sense. I'm not drunk like a fireman.

I walk in circles. "Please?" The blackness on the edges of my vision threatens to overwhelm me. *Il a manqué du temps.* My knees buckle. He ran out of time. I go down on the pavement. He ran out of time we ran out of time no more time.

ANGIE IS CURLED UP in a ball on my bed, with the same paper. Her eyes are red. "Did you—have you heard?"

I nod and sink down on the floor with my back against the wall. I read it all again after I finished throwing up on the curb. From what I now understand, Hugo entered a car race like he did every year. But this time he got a flat tire at a critical point, his car swerved into a lake, his seat belt got stuck, and he couldn't get out in time. He drowned.

"Do you know anything about the funeral? When it is? Where?" Angie says.

"No."

"We have to go! You have to find out!"

"How?"

"I don't know, call his parents, his friends, somebody."

"I don't know any of them."

"How come you don't know any of them?" Angie exclaims angrily as if this were my fault.

"There's much about Hugo I don't know." His own words back in the car, back in time.

Angie's fixation with the funeral doesn't dissipate. She makes me dial Hugo's number where, predictably, there is no answer. She runs out to get every paper on the newsstand to see if there is any mention of a funeral, while I sit on the floor in darkness. Evalinda. She's the only one who I could call who'd know.

She *did* know! Her words flash through me like lightning. *Poor baby— don't want to ruin your day*—she knew! And she let me walk around naked for the whole day in front of a crew of sweaty guys. My hatred rises like fever. But how could I have kept working if she had told me? I would have lost my head, like I did later on. She *did* do me a favor. I pick up the phone and dial her number. I have no idea what to say. But I'm saved from the effort by an endlessly ringing line. Angie comes back, and together we comb through every single word. No luck. Only endless descriptions of the accident, over and over, along with theories of why it happened, and how bad his father must feel losing his only son. We finish Angie's supply of beer. In drunken sorrow we lie on my bed, smoking and bursting into intermittent sobs.

"It was all my fault," I whisper.

"What?"

"The day he left—I said some awful things to him."

"So?"

"I hurt him. I hurt him really bad."

Angie gets up on an elbow. "Wait, are you telling me Hugo died because you had an argument? His car got a flat tire because you were mean to him?" Her voice climbs dangerously. "His seat belt thingy malfunctioned because of *you*?" Her eyes are crowded with tears. She blinks and they slide smoothly down her cheeks.

"Well, no . . ."

"Or maybe he chose to not struggle with it because of something you said? Is that it? He gave up because *you* rejected him?"

Yes. That is the image that keeps knocking at my brain, trying to get in to take up residence and live with me for the rest of my life. Hugo in the car, small, airless black space, foamy water rushing in, climbing like his panic, his fingers, his gentle pale fingers stabbing at the red release button of a seat-belt buckle, my words swirling like debris, chilling his skin, invading his mouth and nose and ears and eyes and then, the last moment when he lets go, lets it happen, lets go of me.

I can't breathe. I'm going to be sick.

Angie has turned a bright, furious red. "That's taking a lot of fucking credit!" she shouts in my face, spraying me with tears and saliva. "You fucking traded him for a pair of fucking shoes and now that he's dead, you have the nerve to assume it was all about you? How dare you! You selfish fucking bitch! Since when does the fucking universe revolve around *you*?"

I don't answer. I can't. I have to go and throw up.

SHE WAKES ME WITH a fresh beer and a newspaper. "I'm sorry about what I said last night," she says. "But I'm hurting too, you know." Her eyes are bloodshot and her nose is swollen. The sight of her pain is soothing—she understands mine—but simultaneously infuriating. How dare she feel what I feel. She can't possibly compete!

But the one who can, and does, is splattered on every front page this morning. Evalinda. Her face is partially obscured by large black sunglasses and the blaring headlines: *La fiancée inconsolable*. The inconsolable fiancée. She looks beautiful and dramatic: My Napoleon jacket suits her perfectly.

Now I understand why she was in such a rush yesterday. *She was going to the funeral.* She left me out intentionally so she could bathe in the attention. I should have known; her so-called favors are missiles designed to annihilate.

"Fiancée?" Angie's eyes are round with disbelief. "What the fuck did I miss?"

Hatred, so intense I'm not sure if my blood is boiling or turning to ice, pumps through me, making me sweat and my teeth chatter. "She fucked him once or twice," I say through clenched teeth. "I suppose that qualifies her for fiancée-dom."

"That publicity-hogging cunt!" Angie shouts.

She tapes up every picture of Evalinda in the hallway, and we take turns hurling Angie's Swiss army knife at them while we continue to drink beer. Shit-su climbs out of her room just as Angie holds the knife up, steadying it for a throw. She squeals and runs back in, slamming the door behind her. That sets me up on a wave of laughter that carries me effortlessly into tears. How many times have I imagined Rob's death in my arms, to masochistically feel the pain of my love? The death of my little sister? My own? Hugo is one I never thought of. And the reality hurts so much more than anything I could have dreamed up.

I cry until there is no more water left in my body, the skies outside darken, and the streetlights ignite.

I BUY NEW SHEETS and ball up Hugo's and toss them into a plastic bag, which I tie and set in the corner underneath my dirty laundry. I want to throw them away, but find I can't.

And then I get the Sex Pistols and the Clash albums, as per Angie's recommendation, a package of coke, and a room full of beer because Angie is all out of money. I even get a new handbag to replace my plastic supermarket sack, and a new watch, a black-and-white Swatch. The shopping is temporarily distracting, but ultimately no more productive than pouring water into a cracked glass. Once I have my purchases back home, they cease to interest me and my glass is empty again. Emanuel is away on his trip with Mr. Carera, so Angie and I become joined at the hip. We spend an inordinate amount of time thinking up revenge for Evalinda: We lure her into dark street corners where we throw boiling oil into her face; we spread rumors she has gonorrhea, syphilis, and crabs; we invite her to our apartment where we offer her rat poison in a beer; we call up every photographer and tell them she's on drugs. It seems somehow more productive to do this, rather then talk about *him*. Although I wish we would; it's not as if a minute goes by without Hugo in my thoughts. My last words to him are permanently and painfully imbedded in my mind, where they rise and bare their fangs every so often to take a bite out of my guilt-ravaged heart.

I HAVE FEWER GO-AND-SEES now, but apparently for more important clients. I'm not sure if it's my new clothes or haircut, but their reactions seem different. They smile, take one of my newly printed composites, and thank me for coming. At one go-and-see for *L'Officiel*, I'm even offered a cup of coffee while I wait for the beauty editor. She greets me by name, *Yeereena*, without a single comment about the difficulty of the pronunciation, or my heritage, and parades me through the offices, introducing me to secretaries and assistants.

"Regardez, comme elle est belle," she tells everyone. "Regardez, ces jambes, extraordinaire, non?" Although she is speaking of me in third person, what she says is radically different from what I am accustomed to. "Look, isn't she beautiful? Aren't her legs magnificent?"

WHEN ANGIE AND I go out to the clubs, we both—as though by an unspoken agreement—avoid Elysées Matignon, Le Palace, and Bain Douche. That leaves us Regine, with its wild, red-haired proprietress after which the club is named, filled with Arab royalty. Angie does her best to seduce Prince Abdul of such-and-such, and King Farouk of so-and-so, but they seem interested only in girls with boobs and long hair. I flirt with a bartender, who, when the spotlight hits him just right, has azure eyes. And that's suddenly enough to go home with him and let him fuck me on his mother's Persian rug.

I never even ask his name. When I come back to the apartment, I open Kafka and write: *4. Unknown*. But Hugo's name slaps me with fresh misery. I attack it with a pen and scratch it out. Now it's a very obvious black stain that looks like a coffin.

I take my lighter, put the book in the fireplace, and set fire to it.

IN THE MORNING, I find Angie sobbing into her suitcase.

"What's the matter?"

"Japan."

"What, they want you to leave now? Today?" I sink down on her bed. Now that Hugo is out of my life, I have no idea what I'll do without Angie. So much for learning my lesson.

"My ticket." Angie slaps the paper rectangle angrily against her suitcase.

"So, you are going—"

"What else can I do?" she yells and tosses a balled up jean jacket into her suitcase. "Of course I'm gonna go. What did you think?"

I guess I thought that Angie, through sheer willpower, would somehow stave it off. If big-mouthed, assertive Angie couldn't, then who could?

"I'm sorry. I will miss you."

"Yeah. Thanks. Me too."

I help her pack, and in return, or maybe as a parting gift, she gives me the name and telephone number of her dealer.

"His name is Bruno," she says. "Don't call him before six."

"WE SHOULD CALL BRUNO today," I say to the huddled shape in bed. "I'm out, and it's your turn to pay." I open the fridge. "Any beers left?"

Emanuel stretches and yawns. "Isn't it a bit early, honey?"

"Nah. It's one. And anyway, I have a wicked hangover." I find a bottle of beer hidden behind the milk. I uncap it and take a long swig. "Hair of the beast, you know."

Emanuel laughs, sits up, and promptly grabs his head. "Ouch. Give me one too."

"Sorry, last one. We must share."

He kicks off the covers and goes to the bathroom, where he noisily pees. We have settled into an easy rhythm in the three weeks since Angie left and he came back from his trip. We get wasted at night, crash at his place, wake, have a line or two to wake us up, and later another few lines to get us through the nights. In Emanuel, I have finally found the perfect partner. No jealousy, no backstabbing, no competition.

"So, what's your tally for the weekend?" I shout at the bathroom.

"Five," he shouts back. "But three of them were just blow jobs at the baths."

"Giving or getting?"

"Both, honey, what kind of a slut do you take me for?" he says, coming out of the bathroom. "You know, sometimes I think you're a gay man trapped in a woman's body."

I take it for the compliment it is.

"Of course," he laughs, "you get all the straight boys I fancy."

At last night's party, I ended up in a bathroom with a guy whose name I can't remember, but whose teeth reminded me of Rob. He fucked me on the sink. Afterward, when he asked for my number, came my moment of satisfaction. I smiled at him and said, "What for?"

"Well, you know, to see you again."

"And why do you assume I want to see you?"

That left him mute and open-mouthed.

I wrote him in as *Unknown No. 2* on my little secret list in the back of my modeling diary, which starts with *Unknown No. 1*. Then there is James, an English student whose hair was sunshine striping shade, and Bertrand, who asked me if I was comfortable and had a receding chin.

Emanuel slips his pajamas off—he wears them as a courtesy to me, since he normally sleeps naked—and I catch a sight of those odd bruises on his legs.

"You know, you really should see a doctor about that," I say, and light up a cigarette, which promptly make me even more nauseous.

"Actually, I have an appointment today," he says with forced casualness and pulls on a pair of red harem pants.

"What time? I can go with you," I offer. "I only have one go-and-see today and I'll be done by two." I don't mention it's not only the bruises that worry me. He has also lost so much weight, he can't wear his jeans anymore.

"It's at four. But you don't have to—"

I cut him off. "Hey, that's what friends are for."

. . .

THESE HANGOVERS ARE a bitch. I've gotta cut down on the alcohol. Emanuel and I sit in a taxi, wedged in traffic in the middle of the Champs-Élysées. I roll down my window to get a little breeze, but get rewarded with hot air and diesel fumes instead. Emanuel sits quietly slumped in the corner. His eyes are on the crowded street, but they're unfocused, as though he is looking inward. I know how scared he is of doctors; I look around for a distraction, maybe some outlandishly dressed American tourists, or some cute boys, when I see the billboard. The very same billboard where, when I first arrived in Paris, the girl was stripping off her clothes on a weekly basis. She was naked by the end of July. Now, the billboard is occupied by a different photo. The type says: *MARIE CLAIRE*, in large red letters and a smaller type says: *VOUS VOIR LE MOIS PROCHAIN, see you next month*. But it is the girl in the picture who makes me feel as if I'm free-falling off a cliff. A girl dressed in a white tuxedo, her hands in her pockets, her glossy brown hair sleekly outlining a sculpted face, and an icy green cat stare. The girl is me. But it's impossible! This is the shoot from the Mr. Carera job that went so disastrously wrong. Maybe I'm hallucinating, since I haven't eaten all day and had a beer on an empty stomach.

"Emanuel," I croak. "Look!"

He scoots closer and leans over my lap. "Oh, honey, look at *you*!"

I have a sudden urge to get out of the car and dance beneath my likeness; I want everyone to see this! I want them all to know it's me! I want to call everyone I've ever known, including fucking Evalinda, and brag. Mother, Father, did you know your unwanted daughter is twenty feet tall on the most popular street in Paris, and she is beautiful? Yes: Staring at myself across a jam-packed street, I see for the first time how others might see me. My inner Narcissus shouts with joy: Look at these carved cheekbones; look at that perfect little nose; look at those huge almond-shaped, water-green eyes. I want to press myself against myself, kiss myself, lick myself; I want to somehow process this picture internally, I want it to roll into my mouth and photocopy it onto my insides, to meld that beautiful her with the sweaty me stuck in a taxi in a traffic jam.

The motor kicks into gear, our driver steps on the gas, and I watch myself disappear into a haze of exhaust smoke.

.   .   .

THE DOCTOR'S OFFICE looks more like an apartment, with its leather couches and curtains. Emanuel signs himself in, and we sit.

"You okay, honey?" he says to me. "You look a little green."

"Shouldn't have mixed my liquor last night," I say. I am, in fact, feeling worse and worse. Maybe it's a panic attack? I focus on breathing in pure white like snow, like my billboard, and breathing out greenish brown. My eyes cloud with tears. I sniff hard.

"Maybe you should have the doctor take a look at you too, while we are here," Emanuel says.

"Oh, please, there is nothing wrong with me a good stiff drink can't fix," I say and my world turns black and gets sucked into a glowing rectangle which gets smaller and smaller like a just-shut-off old-fashioned TV screen.

WHEN I COME TO, I'm lying on an examination table, with an IV in my arm. Emanuel is next to me, holding my hand. He gives me a sheepish smile.

"You were dehydrated," he says. "But you'll be fine."

"Oh shit, Emanuel. I'm sorry. Did you do your checkup yet?"

"Don't worry about me, honey. The doctor said he couldn't find anything wrong with me. A little low on the white blood cell count; probably fighting off a virus or something."

"Yeah, and you probably gave it to me," I say and smile to show it's a joke. I sit up slowly. My head still spins a little.

A knock sounds on the door, and the doctor walks in holding papers. "Ah, vous vous sentez mieux, je voir," he says. He takes my arm, feels my pulse, and nods. "Tout va bien," he says. "C'est normal dans votre condition."

I look to Emanuel. "What is he talking about?"

"He says you're doing fine, and this is normal in your condition."

"What condition?"

Emanuel turns bright red. "Um, it seems you are not only dehydrated, but also a little bit pregnant."

CHAPTER 26

My first reaction, after the initial shock, is wonder. How did this happen? It's not like I slept through sex ed. I know what the deal is when a sperm meets an egg. I just didn't think it would happen to me. Not like this. I thought—this seems ridiculous in retrospect—that you had to be married, or in a relationship, although I have no idea where this notion came from. And then . . . my wonder is replaced by joy. A baby! A warm little baby to hold and hug in bed. I will never be lonely again. I grin at the doctor, I grin at Emanuel, who pats my hand as if I had just received terrible news. A tiny little human being is taking shape inside me right now. It's growing little legs and arms, its tiny heart is already beating. This much I know from a book Hatty's mom gave me right before Kristynka was born, a book full of beautiful pictures of babies in utero, where I could study the progress my little sister was making every week or month while still in Mother's stomach.

It's only in the taxi that the full picture unfolds before me, like a rolled-up map that little by little reveals country after country, continent after continent as it's pulled down. What about money, apartments, and work? And then there is the question of fatherhood. The doctor said I am about eight weeks pregnant, so this child was conceived roughly six weeks ago. Six weeks ago, I was in Morocco. But I was also in the château of George Sand's personal physician.

．　　．　　．

I SIT ON THE TERRACE as Emanuel sets up the food in the kitchenette and I try to count how much money I have left from the commercial. Unfortunately, I think it's all gone; I may even be in the minuses again. But I still have the photo shoot coming up, not to mention the residuals. And two jobs next week, one for a catalog, and one for *Elle*. My career is finally looking up.

"So, do we know who the 'guilty fella' is?" Emanuel says, using one of his Americanisms. He sets my plate down.

"Small problem," I admit. "It could be either Rob or Hugo."

Emanuel pulls out his chair and sits down. "Hmm, one is dead and the other is not interested in having *or* sleeping with—children."

"That's low, you asshole." But of course he's right. I will have to be a single parent, like my mother. I shudder. Absolutely not like my mother!

He sits down. "But what difference does it make besides whom to ask for the money for the abortion?"

"I'd rather not talk about it right now, if you don't mind." An abortion? That's fine for the Evalindas of the world. To me it's as unthinkable as drowning a puppy.

He doesn't bring it up again.

ON TUESDAY MORNING I go to the agency to find out exactly what my money situation is.

Jean-Pierre opens my file. "As of today, you are owing the agency three hundred francs."

That's not too bad. But it is frightening to see the speed with which my eight thousand disappeared. I can economize. I can learn to be better with numbers. And I certainly don't have to keep sending half to Mother. I very much doubt she will love me any better anyway.

I thank him and walk out to the bigger room. I sit on top of the desk next to Anne.

"You know, the booking for *La Grande Passion* is on Friday," she says and spins the bin around to my chart. "It will be with Evalinda again, but the photo shoot is different. They will take individual pictures, but use only one of you."

"Will only one of us get paid, then?"

"No, of course not. You will both be paid, but the money from the usage of the photo will only go to one."

"How much is that?"

"Usage for one year—about ten thousand francs."

Great. Another day of competition with Evalinda. And too much money is on the line for me to be cavalier about this. Not until now do I remember the dentist and my plastic piece. It should be done by now.

"Yes. And also good news; *L'Officiel* wants you for a trip to the Bahamas next week. And after that, you have an option for *La Redoute*, a catalog shoot in Tunisia. The fall and the spring, they are always full with trips."

No spring trips for me. By then, I'll be a house on legs. The thought is not at all pleasant.

"And *Linea Italiana* and *Les Mariages* will be out next week. Come here if you want to see. It will not be in the newsstands for two more weeks."

"What do you mean? I already bought them and my pictures weren't there."

"You bought the August issue; of course they were not there. The magazines shoot three months in advance, sometimes longer. Did you not know?"

I shake my head. Once again, I've made an assumption that made me miserable, for no good reason. The pictures *were* used. Happiness shoots up my spine. I'll finally have tear sheets in my portfolio, like a real model.

The front door opens and two skinny girls stumble in, a brunette with too much makeup and a fine-boned blonde on her heels. They look terrified, clutching their big bags and suitcases.

"Jean-Pierre, the new girls are here," Anne shouts and slams his door with the back of her hand. Jean-Pierre walks out of his office with a big smile. "Ah, mes belles petite Americaines. Bienvenue! Welcome."

I watch him kiss their cheeks, and show them around the room. "This is Jirina." He introduces me. They look at me with huge eyes and shy smiles. I see their anxious desire to please rising off them like steam. I smile back. Give them one, maybe two months for those fresh smiles to be forever changed to cynical smirks. I wish I could issue a warning, let them know what's in store, prepare them somehow for the high winds ahead, but I know it'd be useless. Would I have listened to a girl so casually and comfortably sitting on the desk if she tried to warn me when I first arrived? Of course not. I'd have been much too much in awe of the speaker to even pay attention. Her ease here in this scary new world would have been so at odds with her words, she might have been speaking Mandarin and I would have nodded, smiled, agreed, and not taken in a single word.

"And now I will bring you to my apartment and you will meet my wife," Jean-Pierre says and helps the blond one with her bag.

"Good luck," I say, and wave.

MY OLD APARTMENT reeks of marijuana. The doors to all rooms but mine are closed. I enter it and pick up the phone. Mother and Kristynka should be back by now.

It's Kristynka who picks up on the other side.

"Eena, hi, it's me, Kristynka," her squeaky little voice announces importantly.

"Like I would think you were anyone else," I laugh. "How was your vacation?"

"Good." Her voice trails off.

"What did you do?"

"Um, I don't really remember."

I have forgotten how to talk to seven-year-olds. "What was your favorite part?" I try.

"I don't know."

"Did you go swimming?"

"Yeah. Oh, guess what, Mommy said maybe she would buy me a guinea pig. And I will name him Silly Smurf."

"Well, I sent Mom some money, so now she can."

"Uh-huh. You want to talk to her?"

"Yeah, all right."

Mother's hello sounds happy and relaxed. The new boyfriend must be working out well.

"Jirinka, I'm so glad you called."

She rarely calls me the sweet diminutive of my name. Grandma never called me anything else. "Did you get the money?" I say.

"Yes, we did, thank you so much. You really didn't have to."

"I was thinking maybe you guys could get a color TV."

"Are you sure you wouldn't mind? I feel a bit guilty about spending your hard-earned money on such trivial stuff."

"Mom, I made it in two days."

I hear her inhale. Yes, Mother. Two months of your salary in two days.

"And I think it's time Kristynka finds out that Smurfs are blue," I add.

She laughs. "I was also going to use some to redo your room, buy a new desk for your homework and all. What do you think?"

"Uh, Mom, I wanted to talk to you about that." It's my turn to inhale. "I'm doing really well now, I have these trips coming up in September and all, and I was, well, I was thinking, maybe I could take a year off and stay in Paris."

There is a quiet pause. "But what about your school?"

"Actually, if I stay a year, I will get extra points and then I could apply to the humanities instead. You know economy was my last choice."

"A year?" She sounds dismayed. "Lucifer will have a shit-fit."

"But it's not about his life, is it?"

"Yeah, but guess who's going to get gutted? The wicked uncaring mother who lets her little girl parade half naked before uneducated smelly Frenchmen." She sighs.

"So?"

"So, this is a lot to process. And he will try to finagle out of child support again."

"I will keep sending money."

"Listen, Jirina, this is not about the money, really. On one hand I know I should make you come back and attend school. What if this modeling thing doesn't work out after all—and from what I understand, it's not a long-lived career. But on the other hand . . ." Her voice trails off.

"On the other hand?" I nudge.

"Well, I'm well aware this is an opportunity not everyone gets. When I was younger, I wished—oh, never mind . . ."

"What, Mom? What did you wish for?"

She makes a little embarrassed sound, half giggle, half apologetic cough. "Did you know I wanted to be a singer when I was your age?"

"Really?"

"Yeah. That's how I met your father. He played the violin in a band and I sang."

"And what happened?"

"You mean besides getting married to your father and having two kids?"

"Yes. What happened with your singing? Why didn't you?"

"Your grandpa and grandma wouldn't hear of it."

"Why?"

"Not a proper job."

"Kind of like modeling, huh?"

I hear her breath catch. "Yeah."

"So they wouldn't let you?"

"They wouldn't let me do anything!" Her voice is suddenly filled with its habitual bitterness. "I wasn't even allowed out of the house until I was good and married. And how was I supposed to accomplish that when I wasn't allowed to go out?" She spits the words out as if they taste bad. "So of course, I slept with the first man I met, and got pregnant. I was eighteen, Jirina. Eighteen. Not ready to be a mom. Not ready to be married!"

This information is not shocking for its content, but for the way it's dispensed. My mother is telling me this as though I'm a friend. As though we are equals. My throat gets clogged with emotion, and all that comes out are faint murmurs of sympathy.

"I've often wondered how my life would be different if they hadn't held me back," she continues. "Not, mind you, that I would ever trade you or Kristynka for a life in the spotlight, but still. You have the chance I wished for."

We're silent for a moment. I savor her words, silently rolling them around before swallowing them and letting them warm my innards. She wouldn't have traded me. I was more important than whatever a glamorous life could have provided for her. I want to reach my hand through the phone line and touch her; smooth her hair away from her face, pat her back, or some such small, unobtrusive gesture that would allow me to feel the reality of her. Instead, I say the only thing I can think of. "Does that mean yes?"

She sighs. "I may not always have been the greatest mom—I started too young and for all the wrong reasons, and if you're resentful of that, I understand—but I will not commit the greatest parental sin and stand in the way of your dreams."

We are hundreds of miles apart, connected through a crackly line, and yet I have never felt this close to her. "Thank you, Mom."

We talk a little about a possible visit, sometime later in the year when I've found an apartment. After we hang up, I find the plastic baby and all its accessories in my duffel and laboriously stick it all back in the box. It's time to send it away to its rightful owner.

ON THE WAY BACK to Emanuel's apartment, I stop at the Champs-Élysées under my billboard. The grand thrill of the first sighting may have subsided a bit, but still, I stand there, stupidly hoping for someone to realize it's me. The girl on the billboard looks so self-assured, so confident. I have to smile when I remember what I was actually thinking when this very image was snapped.

A picture is supposed to be worth a thousand words. And like all clichés, it turns out to be true.

After my last go-and-see, I buy some spicy Vietnamese food to bring home. I've been craving spicy foods and I can't eat anything else. A little box with my plastic tooth insert sits in my bag. I can't wait to show it to Emanuel.

Emanuel lies on the bed, watching his newfangled purchase, movies on cassettes.

"Anne called for you. She left addresses for tomorrow's go-and-sees and the details for Friday's job."

"Oh, thanks. Who's the photographer on Friday?"

"Have a guess."

"Not—not Rob?"

"Yes, Rob. How's that for coincidence."

I sit down on the bed next to him. "What are you watching?"

"*Valley of The Dolls*. Excellent stuff. Are you okay, honey?"

"Yeah. I think so. I'm over him, you know."

"Uh-huh." He looks at me with a raised eyebrow.

"Anyway, I have something to show you." I jump off the bed.

"Okay, tell me what you think," I say from the bathroom. I take the piece out and snap it onto my front teeth. I had thought it would be just a little sliver that went in the space between my teeth, but it's actually fully shaped plastic teeth that cover my own. I smile at myself in the mirror, amazed by the straight line of teeth. When I tried this with chewing gum, it never looked this real. I step out. "Well?"

Emanuel looks at me, his eyes wide, and bursts into laughter.

"What?" I say, a bit hurt.

He just keeps laughing.

"Oh, come on, this was expensive!" As soon as I speak, the teeth want to pop out. I push them back in with my tongue.

"Oh honey, I'm sorry, but it's—appalling! Have you looked at yourself?"

"Yeah."

"You look like a donkey!"

I turn around and face the mirror. Emanuel is right. The teeth are enormous and bright yellow. I do look like a donkey! How come I couldn't see it? I spit them out into the sink.

I didn't see it because I didn't want to see it. Like so many things and people in my life. My mother. Hugo. Probably Rob, too. And me? I'm at the top of the list. Staring at my image in the mirror, I realize I have a lot to rethink.

I WALK BACK HOME from my go-and-sees. My Walkman has run out of batteries, so I stick it into my bag. I haven't walked the streets of Paris without my movie fantasies for a while, but I find that without the music, my head stays wonderfully clear and free from melodramatic images. Jardin du Luxembourg spreads out on my right, and the voices and laughter of children echo through trees that cast dappled shade over pale gravel. I've resumed my thoughts from last night, like a book that I have to keep rereading to understand. Angie was right. I've been operating under the illusion that it's all about me, that people's reactions to me are a direct consequence of my actions, that they had no lives, no motives without me. Bad things happened because I was bad. But all along, it's been the year of Christmas without Jultomten. It's simultaneously devastating and elevating to find the world is so much bigger.

I find an open gate and continue down the park path lined with horse chestnuts and linden trees. Spots of sun play peekaboo over my T-shirt and spill over to the gravel. Children's voices draw me to a fenced playground, already in shade, where a miniature Eiffel Tower strung up from ropes sits in a sandbox, and little adventurers hang off it like monkeys. I peek in through the metal bars. Brightly colored seesaws squeak, a tiny yellow merry-go-round spills its laughing passengers, and a green-and-red jungle gym creaks under the weight of excited feet. A little boy, maybe four, is methodically filling his bucket with sand and then walks over to a little girl and pours the sand over her dandelion hair. She swats her hands about her head and screams. She turns her incredulous face on the boy, and I jump. It's Olympe. She rubs her eyes and starts crying in loud, helpless sobs. No one seems to notice. Quickly I scan the playground for Marina, but no one there looks even remotely similar. Olympe keeps crying. Sand is sticking to her face and dribbling into her mouth. And the little boy has filled up yet another bucket, and is making his way toward her. The new Jirina should walk away. It's none of her business any longer. She knows she can't fix everyone's problems; she is not responsible for them. She has her own problems to attend to. But I barge through the gate, quickly tossing my five francs at the lady in the booth entrance, and run to Olympe.

I bend down to her and wipe sand off her cheeks. "Olympe, c'est moi, Gigi."

She squints at me. Sand is stuck to her lashes. I take a corner of my T-shirt and gently wipe them. The little boy stands behind her, his bucket too heavy for him in his indecision. "Et toi, arrete." I flash him a frown. He drops the bucket. I reach behind Olympe and grab it. "Viens." I gesture to the little boy. He hesitates. I take the bucket, refill it with sand, and quickly turn it upside down. I pull it off, and stand to stomp on the resulting excuse for a sand castle. "Voilà!" I shout. And I refill the bucket, repeat the action, and invite the little boy to stomp on it too. He kicks it with one foot. Olympe stands and kicks it too. This is when a stern, grayhaired woman approaches us: Olympe's new nanny. I introduce myself and haltingly explain I used to live with Olympe. The nanny nods, and retires back to a bench where she resumes her conversation with two other middle-age battle-axes.

I can scarcely keep up with making sand towers for Olympe and the little boy to tear down. We all laugh, get sand everywhere, and it doesn't matter. I remove my new boots and jump in with them. This is where I feel the best. This is what I love to do. This is where the world shrinks down to a manageable size and I become important.

EMANUEL GREETS ME with a home-cooked meal, ropa vieja, his mother's special recipe. After dinner, he fishes out a packet of coke. "There's a party at Claude's house tonight." He winks at me and lays out the powder on the coffee table. "Straight from Bruno's best."

"Emanuel, first of all, I have to work tomorrow, and secondly, I'm not doing any more drugs."

"Why?" he exclaims, and an instant later his face drops. "You are not thinking about keeping it?"

"What?" I say incredulously. "Did you think I'd just kill it?"

"Honey, you're fifteen!"

"So?"

"So, are you in a position to have a child? What about your career?"

"I don't know, I haven't thought that far yet," I admit.

"Then, let me spell it out for you. If you have a baby, you will have no career. You cannot have both."

"Why not?" I say stubbornly.

"Honey," he sighs with exasperation, "you couldn't work while you ballooned out, and that's what—five, six months? I don't know much about this stuff, but I do know that if you leave for more than three months, no one will remember your name."

"But my billboard, my commercial, my pages in the magazines—"

"Are a good start. That's all." He cuts me off.

"But aren't there any models with kids?" Evalinda was going to have hers. For a millisecond. But then, she was going to have hers as long as she thought the baby would have a father. No father, no baby.

"Frankly, my dear, no. Haven't you learned enough of this business to see one can't even keep a dog? Never mind a child."

Tears tickle my eyes, and I look down at the white lines decorating the table. As much as I want to make this work, Emanuel may be right. So far, if I want my baby, it means going back home or finding a rich man real soon—one who will marry a fifteen-year-old. *That's* gonna happen.

"Listen honey, I'm here for you no matter what you decide." He snorts two lines. "But I hear abortions are no big deal these days."

I already know that.

I WAKE UP EARLY. Emanuel is still asleep, his arm slung over his eyes. I get up and take a shower as quietly as I can, get dressed, and go downstairs to the café Tabac for my morning coffee. My booking starts at nine, at the Ritz Hotel. I have an hour and a half, so I decide to walk.

Instead of the familiar path by the riverbank, I slowly weave my way through the shady backstreets of the sixth arrondissement. Already, they are filled with people purchasing their baguettes, pain au raisins, and croissants. On rue de Seine, I pass an open-air market. At first, it's the smell that hits me. Fish. Cheese. Two unwashed body smells that would be repulsive in any other context, but here, with the slinky silver of fish scales and the creamy yellow of ripened cheese wheels, it's not only appropriate, but lovely. Little old ladies with net bags touch, sniff, and weigh the wares as they haggle in loud unmusical voices. Breads. Pastries. Chocolate browns, milky whites, raspberry reds. Meats. Chickens hung by their saffron-colored feet, their bald staring heads dangling. At the suckling pigs I have to avert my eyes. They look too much like babies.

I narrow my thoughts down to the small spot in my abdomen, right below my belly button, where my tiny baby lies. I picture her fully formed, only the size of a grain of rice. I know Emanuel is right. I can't keep my baby and stay. Where in this world of foreign countries and airplanes and trains and cars, unwieldy woolen clothing and runny makeup, grim-faced black-clad people tapping their watches, the uneven clicks of the camera shutter, booming music, tornado-speed fans, melting lights—where here is room for a child?

A longing for Hugo slices through me. He would have understood. He would have helped me to decide what is right. Even if the child weren't his, he would have taken care of me. He *did* know me. He knew me best.

I make a left onto Boulevard St. Germain, past the little boutiques and cafés, where tourists sit on small wicker chairs turned to the street, imagining themselves Parisians—if only for the duration of their Coca Cola's—which of course, no self-respecting French person would drink. I try to conjure up Rob, but aside from hair of sunshine and shade, and a faint memory of grapefruit-scented shampoo, I can't picture him very clearly. What I do remember is how he made me feel.

I pass a couple, who, with their sneakers, blond Timotei hair, and sensible baggy jeans and money belts, are clearly foreigners. The man turns to the woman, and I overhear him say in Swedish, *"Now, here's a beautiful French girl, and you said there weren't any."*

My first instinct—to respond with a Swedish "thank you"—gets washed away by a wave of gratitude. They think I'm French.

With a smile, I keep walking down the avenue, heading for the river. I don't even need my Plan de Paris; the streets and avenues are copied inside my mind. Straight up St. Germain and across the bridge, past Place de la Concorde, with its phallic obelisk, down a few steps on rue de Rivoli, left on a side street to the Place Vendome, with its eighteenth-century manors and Kenzo and Mugler stores tucked in discreetly next to the Ritz.

The dusty little cars spewing smoke, the blue-and-white street signs posted high on corners of sandstone walls, the dog poop and cigarette butts underfoot, the tall old trees filtering sunlight into gold coins and scattering them into a diesel-and-coffee-scented breeze, the facades of buildings with tall windows, carved friezes of leaves and garlands, and heavy wooden doors are all welcoming in their familiarity. Even the people that bump into me and flinch with a sour frown, as if it were my fault, are endowed with the feel-good coziness of home. My home.

THOSE BLACK EYES still have the power to make my heart speed.

"Hello darlin'," he says. He's wearing his faded jeans and a washed-out T-shirt that may once have been blue or gray, and his hair is a little shorter. Somehow—although he's clearly broad-shouldered and obviously taller then me—he strikes me as a little less substantial than I remember. He opens the door wider so I can walk in.

The woman with the tightly pulled-back hair from the commercial is here, leaning back on a cream sofa. Her name, I now know, is Rashmi. All through the commercial I thought Dumowski kept saying don't rush me, when in fact he was calling her by name. Natalie is getting her brushes ready on a delicate table by the window, which stands open to the breeze and a perfect view of Place Vendome; Hank, the hairdresser with no hair, is putting hot rollers on Evalinda's head. I kiss everyone hello, and when I get to Evalinda I bend down to kiss her as well. She flinches as if I were about to bite her.

"So sorry for the loss of your fiancée," I say softly into her ear.

"Oh, come on, you know what the papers are like," she says with her wide-eyed innocent look.

I sit on my heels. "And thanks for not telling me about it."

"Oh, you're welcome. I knew it would have been impossible to work—knowing."

"You were absolutely right. Dumowski came up with all these other shots he wanted to do that they hadn't planned, and I could never have done it if it wasn't for you." This unplanned lie slips out effortlessly.

"He did?" she says and turns her head, which causes Hank to burn her with a roller. She screams and makes a fuss about his clumsiness, while I take a seat next to Rashmi.

"Coffee?" she offers and I accept a cup and a croissant.

I keep Rob in my peripheral vision at all times, but a strange calm has descended over me. It's not that I don't care, far from it, but the usual anxiety is gone. This room contains two people who have hurt me beyond words, and now they can't do any worse. Rob and Chelsea are checking equipment: pulling out film, loading the cameras, blowing the lenses clean, but his moves are nervous and forced. Finally he lights a cigarette and sits down in the chair next to me.

"Great haircut," he says.

"Thank you."

"So, how are ye'?"

"Very well. And you?"

"Good, good," he mumbles, looking at my croissant. "Actually"—he stands up suddenly—"would you mind . . . could you come with me for a sec?"

We walk to the far corner of the suite, where no one can hear us.

"Look. I know I was a complete wanker. Back at the airport," he says.

I nod in agreement. This seems to embarrass him further. He runs his hand through his hair in an achingly familiar way.

"Robbie, I'm ready!" Evalinda shouts.

He acknowledges her with an impatient nod, rushing his next words. "Listen, this suite has been rented overnight. Would you—could you stay for a bit, after the shoot? I really need to talk to you."

"Come on, Robbie, these shoes are killing me!" Evalinda shouts again.

"Okay." I assume he will apologize further, and then what? A little spark of excitement nudges in.

"Thank you," he says, and flashes that grin that used to make me weak. "And, oh, wait, I've got something to show you now," he says, and takes my hand. The feel of his hand is as electric as ever. He pulls me back to the coffee table.

"Robbie?"

"Just give me a sec, darlin'," he shouts back. He rummages through his black canvas bag and pulls out a photo, an eight-by-ten, and puts in on the table. It's me, on the beach, that morning in Agadir. My hair is tousled; my slightly open lips look bruised with kisses. But my teeth, my white mice, are peeking out! Is this a joke? A kind of reminder of how I should keep my mouth closed at all times? I look up at Rob. But he's smiling; his eyes are gentle and shiny with—what? Pride? Affection? I glance back at the photo. And this time I see it. I look fine. More than fine. I am beautiful. No less so for the type on top, in an eye-catching hue matching my dress: *Vogue*.

"What do you think?" Rob says. "It's just a mock-up, but you made the cover, darlin'."

I will be on the cover of *Vogue*. I feel around for a sense of victory, arrival, inclusion, and find it's there, only miniaturized next to the importance of the other thing inside me.

I hear a sharp intake of breath behind me; Evalinda has hobbled over to us and now stares at my picture with the expression of someone who found skydiving is no fun without a parachute.

"When—what—when did you do this?" she says.

I smile at Rob. A little shiver runs across my skin when our eyes meet and he smiles back.

"Oh, you guys—" she says as if just struck with a thought, "it was after you fucked, right? How great, to have a picture of that." Her voice sinks into wistfulness right before she exposes her fangs. "Especially since it didn't last too long."

I can't help but admire her gift for reversing situations to her benefit. I look back at the picture. I sit with my legs curled under, and my arms casually rest on my knees, one slightly more bent than the other, the hand elegantly half-open, like a flower. The space around me is filled with the soft hue of sugar cookies, in which the purple of the dress draws the eye to the center: my face. Vulnerable, glowing, expectant. A girl in love. This is what people will see and they will become a part of that morning, and, though they may not understand, they will see me at my most naked. This is what Evalinda understands. Vulnerability. The perfect little sore spot she can stick her finger in.

So I laugh. "Yes, it's nice to be on the cover of *Vogue*. You should try it sometime."

She flinches, her smile replaced by an uncertain smirk. "So, are we gonna work today?" she snaps at Rob.

He puts on music she requests, something by the Rolling Stones. She takes her place in front of the open window and Rob bends over his camera. He does a Polaroid and waits for it to develop in his hands while I sit on the couch and watch Evalinda struggle with the folds of her dress, pieces of hair that keep blowing into her face, and shoes that don't fit. She's rattled, and the more she tries, the further she'll sink. Modeling is a lot like quicksand that way.

Rob doesn't seem happy either. He takes Polaroid after Polaroid, makes her change dresses, puts her on a chair, stands her back up, moves in closer, and backs away.

By the time we break for lunch, my hair and makeup are done, and so is Evalinda. She is full of apologies: "Not a good day for me, I'm simply not myself," and with an anxious glance my way: "Maybe you've seen it in the papers, my fiancée just died, you know, a tragedy—"

And then she is off. I'd be lying to say I wish her well.

Rashmi hands me a red dress. My boobs have gotten bigger, but my waist is still the same. Hank whistles. "Damn girl, this is how this dress is meant to be worn."

"What would you like for music?" Rob asks. "I'm afraid I don't have any, you know, Swedish bands." He smiles and my pulse quickens.

"Do you have 'Je t'aime moi non plus?'"

"Uh, I'm not sure." He flips though his cassettes. "Who's the artist?"

I'm slightly disappointed. Besides the odd ABBA, what other music does he listen to?

Hank laughs. "I know this is unexpected for an old fairy like me, but it so happens I have it on a comp tape."

"Right, darlin'," Rob says. "Let's try the bed." He says it in an offhand, flirtatious manner, one he probably uses with all the girls. For a moment, jealousy bites. What is it like to know your boyfriend's job is to make beautiful girls feel even more beautiful?

The cassette is slipped in, the bass kicks in the ethereal organ, and Jane sighs: "Je t'aime. Oui, je t'aime."

I sit down on the bed, place my hands on the white sheets, and lean toward the camera. I know this has the best effect on my breasts; they're full and nearly bursting from the corset. With the images of myself on the billboard and the mock-up *Vogue* cover tucked into a mental back pocket, I can see myself as others see me: beautiful. I let the music flood me. Tu va et tu viens. You come and you go. I bring a leg though the slit of the dress. Entre mes reins. Inside me. Between my kidneys, actually, is the correct translation. Hugo laughed when I asked about it, and told me poetry can't be translated. Nor can this, I think, this feeling of being beautiful and desirable, this power that radiates from my toes all the way to the ends of my curled, mascara-ed lashes.

"Oh, bloody perfect. Stay there. Don't move!" Rob's actions are frantic, like a starved man at a buffet. Slowly I remove a shoe. He rips the camera off the tripod and circles me, like that morning on the beach. I remove my other shoe. I'm in control; this is all about me. Screw the clothes. I scoot further in on the bed and begin to unpin my meticulously styled hair. Little by little. The last pin comes out and my hair tumbles free. Hank makes a move to come and fix it, but Rob stops him with one hand. Everything I do needs to be captured on film.

"Yeh, darlin', don't stop."

I shake my head and let my hair fall into tousled waves. And I slip off one shoulder strap.

"Aah, yeh."

But the lens is no longer a tunnel between just Rob and me. Somehow—maybe because of the music—Rob and my memory of Hugo merge together into one ideal man, and he in turn expands into an embodiment of all men. All the men in the world who will see this picture. And women. I want to seduce them all.

I let the other strap slip. Then, quickly, I pull the sheet to my shoulders and wriggle out of the dress. I kick it to the floor. I remove my underwear, get up on my knees, and hold the sheet for strategic coverage. Rashmi gasps in surprise, but doesn't stop me. One hip out. Her face turns attentive, almost hungry. Hank smiles like a proud daddy. I let the sheet down a little. Natalie has put a hand on her chest and stands absolutely still. We all feel the magic that crackles all around us. Eyes in the camera. Viens. Viens mon amour. Come my love.

"Bloody hell," Rob sighs. Chelsea barely has time to reload. The music has stopped long ago, but I can still hear it. No. Come. Now.

And then, as if sunlight withdrew, the magic is gone and Rob drops his arms. They shake ever so slightly; it must have been heavy to hold the camera all that time. He hands it to Chelsea and kneels before the bed.

"Thank you, darlin'," he says. "That was magical." A slight sheen of sweat gleams on his upper lip.

I nod. I know.

I pull on my clothes and remove my makeup very slowly, so by the time I'm done, Natalie and Hank are leaving. Chelsea packs up the film, gets her instructions, and runs out.

"Don't worry," Rob says to Rashmi. "I'll take care of the room."

She nods at him and smiles at me. "Thank you. That was perfect."

The door closes behind her and it's just the two of us. My knowledge of the hidden third gives me the upper hand. I sit on the couch and pull out a cigarette, although it really doesn't taste good anymore. Rob kneels on the floor, stuffing away the last bits of equipment into his camera bag. His hair is falling over his eyes.

"*Right.* I behaved like a real wally," he says not looking up. "And of course you had no reason to call me back."

The little word attached to the rest of the sentence sticks. "What do you mean, call you *back*?"

"I left so many messages with Evalinda. You could have at least picked up the phone and had a go at me."

The effect of what he just said sweeps over me with the magnitude of a tidal wave. I stub out my half-smoked cigarette. He didn't know I moved out. Evalinda never told him. Of course. And because of stupid, misbegotten pride and my inability to see past my nose, I'd lost the momentum.

He stands up and brushes his hair away. I stand up as well. "I moved out. I didn't know you called." The space between us is slowly eaten by my footsteps.

"Ah, fuck. Didn't Evalinda tell you?"

"No. But what difference would it have made if I knew? What would you have said if I had called you back?"

"I would have said I'm sorry."

I stop. We face each other. "That's it?"

His face is suddenly still and drawn, almost sad. "No. I would have also told you, you are an incredibly special girl."

"Girl?"

"Yes. Girl. A girl with the potential to become the most incredible woman." He tilts his head ever so slightly. "A woman worth waiting for."

I look at him. Really look at him. Funny, I never realized his eyes were a bit close set. This is the man who has been the object of all my feverish wants and dreams since my arrival. But how well do I know him? Have I confused wanting him with loving him? Or is it the same thing? I wonder whether I can learn to surf and love cricket. He says I'm worth waiting for. Is he worth catching up with?

He opens his arms. I hesitate.

They say that when you die, your whole life flashes before you. I'm certainly not about to die, at least not as far as I know, but my life in Paris, my three months, wash over me in a massive surge. I've learned much, most of which consists of the knowledge that the more I learn, the less I know. The only thing of which I'm absolutely certain is that I've left childhood behind for good. There is no going back.

I am standing, at the edge of a precipice. With one step I will either learn I can fly, or find out the hard way that I'm no bird. But I already know hot chicks don't fly. Chickens, however—well, at least they have wings.

Acknowledgments

Although writing itself is a solitary task, no author can exist without readers. I'd like to thank all those who have read and reread this work, given me invaluable input, comments, critiques, and even the occasional praise.

Thank you:

My partner in crime and sister of my heart, Joanne Batty, for endless brainstorming and rereading, and for letting me scrounge.

My teacher, colleague, and friend Jessie Sholl, and the rest of my workshop, Lorna Graham, Shizuka Otake, Melissa Johnson, David Simonetti, Chelsea Ferrett, Angie Mangiano, Rashmi Dalai, for helping me to excavate the story.

The amazing Casey Fuetch, for cutting it into shape.

My editor at Hyperion, Zareen Jaffery, for finding it and polishing it to a shine. (And providing me with a quote.)

My dear friends Tracy Rapp, Jacqui Mahan, Emilia Lopinska, and Alexandra Wentworth for reading and making sure I didn't bore them.

Anna Crean, my right hand and left side of the brain, for reading, debating, cheering me on, and otherwise spoiling me.

My "little sisters" Kamila Zmrzla and Ilona Hmelnicka, not only for reading, but also for making my life easier.

My brother Kym, for last minute assistance.

My friend Mark Lamprell, for vital "Aussie" info.

My manager, Heather Reynolds, and my lawyer, Peter Thall, for all their sound advice and friendship.

My fantastic agent, Marly Rusoff, for pushing me harder.

I'd also like to thank Anne Ricard and Anne Veltri, my two "Annies," for guiding me through the fashion jungle.

And, of course, Ric, my love and lover, and Jonathan and Oliver, my two boys, for making every day a beautiful one.